At The Broken Places

**A fictionalized story of adventure and love,
based on a young man's real-life journey into
World War II**

**By
John A. Reed
and
Clark C. Brown**

At The Broken Places

·BIG BROWN·
Publishing

Published in the United States of America through:

·BIG BROWN·
Publishing

Scottsdale, AZ

Library of Congress Control Number: 2015911519

ISBN: 978-0-578-15047-5 (paperback)

Editor: Ann N. Videan, Book Shepherd at
Videan Unlimited, LLC, http://ANVidean.com

"Clark Brown took the two most significant experiences of the 20th Century, the Great Depression and World War II, and wove a fantastic, edge of your seat, informative, and fun read. I'm impressed with this great adventure and would recommend *At The Broken Places* to anyone."
—Mike Venezia, author and illustrator of Scholastic's *Getting To Know The World's Greatest...* series'

"Inspired by the wanderlust of the ghosts of Hemingway, Shaw, and Wells, *At The Broken Places* unfolds the compelling, gritty tale of a young man's coming of age in the social, political, and cultural world of the 1930s and 1940s. I found Mike Kane's personal journey, through the black days of depression and broken dreams to accepting the uniqueness of his own manhood, thoroughly engaging."
—Roy Davis Varner, author of *A Matter of Risk: The Incredible Inside Story of the CIA's Hughes Glomar Explorer Mission to Raise a Russian Submarine*

"It takes a soldier to tell a soldier's story. Clark Brown is a decorated Army officer who molds John Reed's draft of a novel into a compelling read. Imagine being sixteen in 1934. Mike Kane, the fictional hero, decides to become a writer. He drops out of school and into the gritty rough and tumble of Philadelphia. Failing at earning a living, he enlists in the Army. Everything that follows is not what you expect. Hang on for the bumpy ride of a young man with a dream. He's on a collision course with history. Compelling story. Spot-on period detail. Superbly crafted into a novel for our time. Read this book!"
—Dixie Swanson, author of the *Accidental President Trilogy*

Acknowledgments

When I started to work on John's manuscript, I felt I was entering John's personal sphere as perhaps an unwelcome guest. I also experienced a heavy responsibility to hold in my hands the result of thousands of hours of his work; the product of his thoughts, memories, and tears; his choices of what stays in and what goes, to preserve his dignity and others'. I needed to remain accountable for his choices, as he held dear those friends—alive or dead—who might be recognized for their parts of the story, no matter how cleverly he fictionalized them. He fully expected to live long enough to publish the story and receive communication from his old buddies.

I entered into this agreement at Susan's request. Susan is my wife, and John Reed's stepdaughter. I realized I could rely on only her to keep me true to John's perspective, but I also needed to reconnect with the memories of my own relationship with him. Those memories, though more than forty years old, started to come back. I would sit quietly and let those visions float through my mind (trust me, no séance stuff for me), and merely get back to those talks and Scrabble games, the discussions, and the arguments over many a word. I relearned a lot about John, especially how he stood hard on principles and values. Soon, I was sensing his guiding hand as I relived those vivid memories sitting quietly alone in my office. Finally, I was ready to start working for him and Susan on his manuscript.

I knew I needed help, and luckily I found it close by. Susan was my inspiration, my energy source, and my muse, my Greek Thalia. She provided that steady leadership, guiding me through the rough patches, and reminding me John was never so serious and I should lighten up. She was just what I needed to keep the fires lit during the process.

I discovered quickly I also needed a different kind of help to organize the nearly five hundred typed and handwritten pages into a format compatible with my iMac. Carlos Marquez, an IT genius I had worked with before, stepped up to help. He loaned me his scanner and, after two weeks, I had downloaded the draft notes of the manuscript. He didn't stop there. He continued to fix the compatibility problems—and some of my headspace problems—as only a friend could.

So, between John, Susan, and Carlos, I had what I needed to start work on this book. That work lasted nearly two years. About a year into the process, we felt we had a first draft, and needed people to read it to gain their guidance. We selected avid readers; many belonged to book clubs and some were published authors. I owe these ten fearless word warriors my undying thanks for suffering through reading the manuscript twice, the second time around July 2015. So, thank you very much.

- Larry Bloom—the call-me-out guy, who challenged my use of phrases and words no longer befitting our time.
- Astrid Franssen—the bolt of lightening across the street, who expressed what she liked, or didn't, and why, with the same energy.
- Joe Hall—the quality assurance officer of our gang, who doggedly pursued every last scrap of detail to ensure that our high standards prevailed.
- Leslie Krat—the straight talker, our no-frills, to-the-point, kick-butt, make-it-happen cheerleader.
- Marcia Perlmutter—my first volunteer, who was always kind, yet thorough, and a very deep thinker. She also became a muse to me.
- Buddy Perlmutter—for allowing Marcia to drag him in, and providing some significantly important cultural input to the story.
- Merri Rubin—a call-it-like-it-is friend, who provided both witty, and sometimes heated, feedback and everything between, which was always correct.
- Susan Stevens—for being our jack-of-all-trades, who performed everything from software fixes to sentence repairs, sometimes simultaneously. *Anything to push it forward* served as her motto.

- Dixie Swanson—my friend and former classmate in Rice University's novel writing classes, who kept me real, and reminded me of the lessons we learned.
- Roy Varner—my strident friend and colleague for nearly thirty years, who took time from running his company and writing his own book to share his wise thoughts, and even wiser questions.

I want to also thank my brother Bill Brown, who provided his name for Mike's second squadron commander. He was exactly the person I had in mind when I wrote his character. He also flew for the U.S. Air Force during more modern times.

I would be remiss if I didn't mention my friend and confidant Victor Lebo, who tirelessly listened to me during the whole grueling process. Thankfully, he gave only sparse advice, knowing I had plenty of input already from the ten above, whom I thanked already. He is a very wise man.

Without a doubt, Ann Videan, our editor, deserves enormous thanks from us for providing needed clarity and structure to the book. Without her, we would have never given birth to this important story.

Thank you all,
Clark Brown (and John)

"The world breaks every one and afterward many are strong at the broken places."

A Farewell to Arms

Ernest Hemingway

Table of Contents

To all the old soldiers I ever met,
especially those who didn't fade away,
but died in the full bloom of youth.

Preface

John A. Reed's untimely death in the late 1970s ended his pursuit of publishing his first novel. John was my wife Susan's stepfather, whom we both loved and admired very much. She found his first draft among some boxes in our garage in 2012, and carefully tucked the pages away in a safe place. A few weeks later she asked me to do the work necessary to publish it out of respect for him. I agreed, but didn't start until November 2013.

John was a retired Army master sergeant who had served in the Army Air Forces during World War II, flying as a waist gunner on B-17s and B-24s. After the war, he served in intelligence units until he retired. He read insatiably and wrote many book reviews, and some articles for the *Christian Science Monitor*, *The New York Times*, and *Mademoiselle*. His interest in writing is also reflected in the main character, Michael Kane, which makes us a little suspicious that a lot of John's real story is part of what we read about in Mike's/John's life during the Great Depression, his bumming on a train, soldiering in Hawaii, and fighting in the China-Burma-India Theater of Operations during WWII.

As we grew to know one another over the years, we discovered a lot in common, since I served twice as a combat soldier in Vietnam, only fourteen hundred miles from where he did. We often sat up late drinking whiskey and playing Scrabble, arguing over a word until we finally went to bed. Never play Scrabble with someone who starts by asking you to choose one of several dictionaries to support your play.

I finally won one game, and that was debated afterwards for years.

I love my father first, but John was a close second.

When I started this project, I reviewed nearly five hundred pages he had produced on a manual typewriter, with handwritten edits, which he worked on in his basement right up to the time of his hospitalization and subsequent passing. I wondered if I could ever match John's dedication to his writing, but I was determined to try... and just as determined to keep his "voice" as I went forward with his story. I made some changes to the manuscript and shaved it down, but I never corrected a word of spelling, as you might imagine.

So, here is John's novel, cleaned up by me, and encouraged by Susan, who approved every change. If you are a person who enjoys literature, or American history, or World War II history, or why Tom Brokaw called John's generation the "Greatest," read this book and salute John, his service, and his memory, along with those who served with him around the world.

Clark C. Brown
Lieutenant Colonel, U.S. Army, and Associate Professor
United States Military Academy, West Point (Retired)
Scottsdale, Arizona

Part I

Philadelphia

Chapter One

While war loomed in Europe, on May 29, 1934, Mike Kane was listed as Central High School's sprinter in the 440-yard dash at Philadelphia's Track and Field City Championships. His feet tensed in the holes he dug earlier in the cinders with his trowel, and he leaned forward on his fingers, waiting for the shot from the starting gun. Energized by the cloudy and chilly morning, he strained to hear the starter's shot through the crowd's loud cheering from the bleachers near the starting line. At 5'7", with a muscular 143-pound frame, Mike was known to be the top dog in this race, which required a fast start and the guts to sprint full out all the way to the finish.

"Bang!" Mike flew out in front of everyone. He had a nice lead at the first turn and settled into his stride down the straightaway. With no one close behind him yet, he focused on the final turn and his time at the finish line. His confidence let his legs stretch out and he felt a lift that was hard to explain.

The next moment, his feet churned in the air and his face and hands fell hard on the cinder track. When he got up on his knees, the race was over. He looked down and found he had stepped on one of several apples that shouldn't have been on the track. Help arrived as he struggled to stand, embarrassed, angry, confused, and disgusted. Thankfully, he saw his coach coming over. Surely, his coach would assure him the wrong he had suffered would be put right.

Instead, the coach said: "If I had no arms or legs, Kane, I would still cross that finish line."

That added "shame" to Mike's stew of emotions.

Later, everyone said it was unfair but, still, he had lost. This was his signature race, and yet he had suffered defeat. Mike asked himself: *Is this the pattern that's forming my future? If so, God help me!*

This was an important question on a big day for Mike, because it also marked his sixteenth birthday and, by law, he could quit school without his father's permission. He planned to do just that, as fast as he could. The still air of Depression-era Philadelphia suffocated him, and he needed to get the hell out while he still could.

Mike had planned to become a writer since he turned twelve years old, the year his mother died. He read Ernest Hemingway's *A Farewell to Arms*, which brought on that reckless idea, and there had been no turning back. He didn't need high school to become a writer. He only needed a vision.

After cleaning up from the race in the School's shower, he walked down a gloomy corridor toward the principal's office. Entering, he leaned against the waist-high, wooden railing, waiting for the secretary to look up. The tall, gaunt woman finally greeted him.

"Yes?"

"I just turned sixteen and I wanna quit school."

"Have you got all your books and your locker key?" she asked.

"Yeah," Mike said. "The books are in my locker."

"How many subjects did you take?"

"Five."

She opened the desk drawer and extracted some beige oblong slips of paper. Counting out five slips, she stood up and handed them to him. "Have each teacher sign one of these when you turn in your book, and bring them all back here with your locker key."

During the first two class breaks, Mike turned in his German, History, Biology and Mathematics textbooks. The first four teachers had signed his slips with perfunctory expressions of regret. At ten minutes to two, he found himself outside Goldman's English class to turn in his last book. When the bell rang and the classroom emptied, he went in.

Goldman was erasing the blackboard, but turned and saw Mike. "You were absent, Kane."

"I'm quitting school," Mike said, proffering his book.

Lester Goldman took it and sat down at his desk. He was a tall, strongly built man, in his early thirties, with close-cropped black hair, already sprinkled with gray, and an intense, intelligent face. Ten years before, he had been a good halfback at Temple University. Rumors pegged him as a Socialist, maybe even a Communist. Mike admired him tremendously.

"So, you're quitting school," Goldman said. "And what are you going to do now?"

"Get a job."

"There are fifteen million men out of work. Tell me, big shot, where are you going to get this job?"

"I'll get one," Mike said, his eyes glancing away. "You don't have to worry about that."

"Where?" Goldman demanded.

Mike stared at the blackboard behind the teacher. This was why he had saved Goldman for last... fearing he would ask hard questions and, at the same time, wishing he would. Mike hoped Goldman would heap words of praise upon him, and admit he could be a great writer.

"Sit down, Kane," Goldman said, his voice calm. "Of the hundred and twenty students I teach, you are one of maybe ten that enables me to hope I'm not in the wrong business. Stay in school. Graduate. Temple or West Chester State are not expensive. Maybe I can help you to get a scholarship."

"I can't stay in school," Mike said.

"If you don't get a job, you can't help your family, either."

"I don't mean that. I mean the only things I'm passing are English and History. I will flunk Math, Biology, and German. If I don't quit, I'll be kicked out."

"You could go to summer school."

Mike shook his head. "I'm wasting my time in school.

"If you quit school, you'll spend the rest of your life as a laborer," Goldman warned him.

Mike thought of the books he was going to write and all the money they would earn him.

"That's not so."

"No?"

"No."

"How will you avoid it without an education?"

"I'm going to be a writer, that's how."

"That requires education, too."

"Mark Twain didn't have any. Jack London and Ernest Hemingway didn't either."

"You left out Charles Dickens, and the champion, William Shakespeare. But they had genius, which is even better. And the ability to educate themselves."

"I can educate myself." Mike met his teacher's gaze levelly. "Mark Twain said, 'The secret of getting ahead is getting started.'"

"Okay, but Mark Twain also said, 'To succeed in life, you need two things: ignorance and confidence,' and you seem to have both," Goldman said. "Maybe you're right. At least you won't end up teaching school. That's one thing for which you do need formal education. Even William Shakespeare couldn't get a job teaching English in the Philadelphia school system."

He handed Mike his card. "Here's my phone number. Keep in touch once in a while."

Mike got to his feet quickly and took the card. "Gee, thanks, Mr. Goldman."

Goldman leaned back in his chair and took a hard look at Mike.

"Be careful what you wish for, Kane. Life is going to be very tough for boys your age. I hope you realize that. Given the history of capitalist economies, it'll probably take a war to bring prosperity back, and you'll be just the right age to fight it." He got to his feet. "I've got a two o'clock class and I'm late already."

Pulling two worn books out of the row on his desk, he pushed them toward Mike: *A Dictionary of Modern English Usage* by K.W. Fowler, and Funk and Wagnall's *College Standard Dictionary*. "If you're going to educate yourself, you can use these."

"Gee, thanks, Mr. Goldman." Mike turned and left, sensing he had crossed a major hurdle in his life.

He grinned as he skipped down the street, taking the first steps of his new life. He would soon leave Philadelphia, and travel to Europe, Asia, and the lush islands of the Pacific. He would write about his exciting life and wild adventures. Hemingway had nothing on him.

In fact, Mike was emulating Hemingway in many ways. It was well known that Hemingway was a fighter, so Mike trained as a fighter, too. Fighting experience was easy to come by on the streets of Philadelphia, especially in his neighborhood. After being beat up a few times, Mike took boxing lessons at the Rec Center, and found the basics came to him naturally. After that, he practiced on the streets and soon built a reputation. He earned respect, and was left alone, and he learned to be very careful about picking his fights.

Chapter Two

M ike felt his spirit suffocating. Since his mother died, he found it hard to see a bright side, and easy to feel hopeless. He couldn't help but think he carried a curse making everything he did turn bad. He knew he must leave Philly before he gave up on life entirely, like many before him.

He was poor, even among the poor. His father's house had two tiny bedrooms, and a toiletless bathroom upstairs. The downstairs consisted of a wee parlor, a dining room, and an unheated, shed-like kitchen furnished with a gas range, a cast-iron sink, and a wooden icebox. Behind the house, a minuscule yard accommodated an outdoor privy. The rent cost fourteen dollars a month.

Mike stood in the kitchen slicing cold boiled potatoes into a frying pan. When they browned, he would add three eggs, and the result would make a dish called farmer's breakfast, even when served as dinner. Mike and his father ate it two or three times a week. It was one of their favorite meals.

He looked at the beat-up alarm clock, which his father carried upstairs every night and downstairs again in the morning, except when he was drunk, then Mike performed the chore. It read a quarter to six. Working or not, out of habit, the old man came home about this time every afternoon.

Mike paused in his slicing and began to read the preface to the Fowler book: "I think of it as it should have been, with its prolixities docked, its dullness enlivened, its fads eliminated, its truths multiplied." He didn't know the word prolixities, so he opened the *Funk and Wagnall's* and found its definition. "Wearisomely long and verbose..." *Man,* he thought, *self-education is a breeze, and a lot more fun than sitting in a goddam classroom.*

Just then, the front door opened and steps sounded in the vestibule. Even before she came into the kitchen, Mike knew it was Rose Hanley, his father's long-term girlfriend.

Rose carried a covered dish and, under her arm, a package wrapped in brightly colored paper. She placed the dish on the table.

"I brought you some raspberry Jell-O for dessert. The Acme had a sale on it."

She handed him the package. "Happy birthday, Michael."

Mike knew it was a book as soon as he took it into his hands. He tore the paper off.

"*The Story of Philosophy* by Will Durant," he read aloud while leafing through the pages, wide eyed and grinning. "Thanks, Rose."

"I knew you'd like it," Rose said, beaming with pleasure. "I remember how popular it was when it first came out. I got it on sale."

"I sure do like it. This is my lucky day." He pointed to the two other books on the table. "Mr. Goldman gave me these today."

"That's nice," Rose said, patting his cheek. "I'm glad you're happy."

She sat down heavily in one of the chairs. "Lord, I'm tired. Today was the first day of our annual Founder's Day sale, and I ran my legs off waiting on customers. You'd wonder where all the money comes from with so many out of work."

A plump, dark-haired, pretty woman, in her middle thirties, Rose worked as a saleswoman at John Strawmaker's department store in the center of town. She lived just four doors up the street from the Kane's with her seventeen-year-old sister Teresa. They lived in one of the houses with the bricks thickly painted, and an indoor toilet.

"I'm sorry about your race today," Rose said. "How could apples end up on a track?"

Mike shrugged, "I guess nobody cares. Doesn't matter now. I quit school today, Rose."

"You didn't!"

"Yes, I did."

"And what are you going to do now?"

"Get a job."

"Michael, Michael…" Rose threw her hands up. "Why did you quit? A boy who likes to read the news as much as you do should know there are no jobs. Did you talk it over with your father?"

"I mentioned it to him. He doesn't care."

"You're right about that. He doesn't care much about anything except the drink." Her eyebrows knitted in sympathy. "You haven't had an easy time of it in the four years since your mother died. Thank God you take after her instead of him. The depression gives him the perfect excuse for not working."

"Why do you stick with him, Rose?"

"He's not a bad man. He's just weak. Besides, he's the handsomest devil that ever walked."

"Did you ever think of marrying him, Rose? You practically support us now as it is."

"Of course I've thought about it. I've thought about it a lot. But Teresa doesn't like your father. She says the day he moves into our house is the day she moves out. Teresa graduates from high school next month and in a couple of years she'll get married. Then we'll see."

She looked away and wiped her eyes. "I'm worried about Teresa. I think she's mixed up with Red Donovan."

"Oh, no," Mike groaned. "Not him."

"Friday, I was at Mandel's buying some aspirin, and saw Teresa and Red walk by. She was holding his arm. Of course, I can understand it. He is handsome."

"Red is handsome?" Mike scowled. Red had a turned-up nose with wide nostrils, which he often picked in public. Mike considered him repulsive.

"He certainly is," Rose said. "But I wish he'd use his attractions on somebody else."

"Look, Rose," Mike said, "You hafta talk to her. Donovan is a loser. Just keep her away from him for a few weeks and your troubles are over. There's no way Red won't be in jail."

They heard the front door open and waited until Paddy Kane came into the kitchen. Rose glanced at his flushed face and sighed. "Oh, Paddy, you've been drinking."

"Three shots and a beer is all, Rose, I swear it," Paddy said, smiling at her.

"Where did you get the money?"

"Lemme tell ya, Rose," Paddy said. "Johnny Sloan got his violin outta hock and we went out as street musicians, me singin' and him playin'. We worked Girard Avenue from 26th Street to Fairmount Park, passin' the hat. Eight dollars and seventy cents we split, four thirty-five apiece." He began to empty small change out of his pocket, "Count it, Rose," he said, his voice excited. "There should be four ten there. Tomorrow we'll work Columbia Avenue, west. I'll bet we do even better. I tell ya, Rose, things are gonna improve around here."

Rose counted the money with the quickness of a born shopkeeper. When she finished, she looked up. "Three dollars and seventy cents. You must have had some drinks you forgot about."

"Three whiskies and a beer is all I had, and it was Sweepstakes at a nickel a shot. The cheapest whiskey you can buy. I musta miscounted the take."

"How much money do you have put away in the rent book, Michael?"

"Seven dollars."

She swept the pile of change into her handbag and gave Mike three one-dollar bills. "Take ten dollars over to

Rappaport's office tomorrow. Tell him you'll bring the rest before the fifteenth." She turned to Paddy. "And you, Patrick Kane, bring home *all* the money tomorrow."

"I always do, Rose, you know that," Paddy said with a smile. "Now don't I?"

"You usually do, but by no means always." She smiled and patted his cheek.

Mike held up his recent present. "Look, Pop, Rose gave me this book for my birthday."

"Jesus, kid, I clean forgot." Paddy's face flushed darker and he extracted a quarter from Rose's purse. "Here, go to a movie, and happy birthday. Oh, and I'm sorry about the race."

✦✦✦

At supper, Mike asked his father. "Pop, have you ever thought about marrying Rose?"

His father looked up from his plate, mild surprise on his face.

"How can I marry her if I ain't got a job?"

"Would you marry her if you did have a job?"

"What's the use of talkin' about it? I haven't got one and, at forty-one, I'm not likely to."

"But suppose you were lucky enough to find a job," Mike insisted.

His father finished the food on his plate before answering.

"She's a good woman, Rose is. Your mother was a good woman, too, Mike. Good women expect too much from a man, and you're bound to disappoint them. Especially if you take a sociable drink now and then like I do."

He got up and walked away from the table. "I gotta meet Johnny Sloan and talk about tomorrow."

Mike shouted after him: "Hey, Pop, I quit school today!"

His father answered over his shoulder. "Whatever you think best, Mike. You know what you're doin'."

"I'm gonna get a good job!"

He spoke the words to a closed door.

Chapter Three

Coming home from the library Sunday night before Labor Day, Mike saw a well-dressed Negro walking down the street. The man approached Mike's friend, George Hubbell. Without warning, Hubbell attacked the man. Mike acted on impulse and pushed Hubbell down, allowing the Negro to get away safely. Hubbell was bigger and angry, though—knowing Mike's skills—he backed up and went on his way.

Why the man had crossed into Hubbell's all-white neighborhood was a mystery. The event left Mike feeling sick with disgust. He was on a new course in his life, and this clash made him pause. The question, "Who am I?" was valuable to ponder, but now he found he needed to know, "What am I?"

Am I an American, or just a white American? If this brutality is part of America, well, that's not for me. Where is the spirit of brotherly love that Philadelphia was so proud of?

He thought the answer must be that his friends felt just like him, but somehow excused their behavior due to the bad times. Mike couldn't live like that any more.

He needed to take action and change things. He would bring America back to its core values through his writing. He couldn't write about Philadelphia, he was too close to that story to be objective. No, he needed to visit exotic places and write about interesting experiences. That took money, so he needed to find work fast. Either that, or stow away.

In the meantime, Paddy Kane's career as a street singer lasted only three weeks. Things moved along very well until

Johnny Sloan went on a bender. He not only hocked his violin, but sold the pawn ticket to Tommy Gallagher, the cop on the beat, who wanted his son to take violin lessons. So, Paddy went back to the life that suited his temperament best: an occasional day's work cleaning Rafferty's saloon, or the bar in the American Legion post after a weekend's celebration.

Once in a while, he picked up a few dollars singing for tips in one or the other of the two places. His voice was mediocre, a light baritone, which he could force up into a quavery falsetto. His repertoire was sure-fire with a half-drunken audience. At Rafferty's he sang *Danny Boy*, *Did Your Mother Come from Ireland*, *Mother Machree*, and *Galway Bay*. At the Legion, he added *My Buddy*, *Over There*, and *Mademoiselle from Armentieres*, with some mildly risqué verses. At both places his biggest hit was *A Shanty in Old Shantytown*.

Mike looked for work diligently but, at summer's end, still remained unemployed. He tried the hosiery mills, but they were all on short time. When they looked for help, somebody's son got the job—like Willie, whose old man was a knitter at Eberle's.

He tried Exide Battery, where his dad had worked, and Budd's, and SKF, and Stetson, and Railway Express, and Western Union. All were laying off people instead of hiring.

He tried all the department stores, and countless offices in the center of town. His typing skills clocked at thirty words a minute, but many grown women could type seventy-five, and take shorthand as well, so they snapped up the few available positions.

One hot day in early August, he walked the six miles to the corner of C Street and Allegheny to try for a job at Pennsco Radio. Word had gotten around that Pennsco was hiring, so when Mike arrived shortly before eight o'clock, hundreds of men milled around outside the factory gate. Promptly at eight o'clock, a big man with sharply creased trousers, a white shirt, and flowered tie, came out into the yard with a bullhorn. A hush fell over the waiting men as he spoke.

"Most of you men might as well go home. We only have twenty-five job openings."

He waited a few moments for the crowd to thin out, but only a few people left. He raised the horn to his mouth again.

"How many men will work for forty cents an hour?"

A roar sounded, and a forest of arms went up.

"How many will work for thirty-five?"

Another roar went up and almost as many arms were held aloft.

"How about thirty cents?"

Standing on the outskirts of the crowd, Mike had abandoned any notion he might get one of the jobs, but he waited around, curious to see the outcome.

"Twenty-five?" the man with the bullhorn roared, and angry noises began to rise from the crowd.

"What does he think we are, a bunch of monkeys?" a man near Mike growled.

"Twenty cents?" the man with the bull horn cried, oblivious to the rising anger.

One stentorian voice, contorted with rage, bellowed: "Whadda ya think you're runnin', you sonofabitch, a slave auction?"

Some of the men up front began prying at the iron bars of the front gate, but its massive strength held them back. Then somebody lofted a large stone over the gate. The auctioneer, suddenly frightened, ran across the yard, the horn held over his head for protection.

The crowd roared epithets even after the retreating figure disappeared into the building. It was Mike's first experience seeing an angry mob. A strong and quick-tempered leader could have made them do anything: break all the windows or even burn the building down. If they had gotten their hands on that bastard with the bullhorn... Mike shuddered at the thought.

✦✦✦

When not looking for work, Mike spent a lot of time in the library reading books, especially by Mark Twain and Ernest Hemingway. He also relaxed by hanging around the corner of Etting and Master near Mrs. Williams' candy store. The neighborhood hangout served not only Mike's gang, but also other young men in their late teens and early twenties, and a sprinkling of older men.

Mrs. Sarah Williams—a fat, gray-haired woman in her late fifties—was all about business, but also enjoyed visiting with the neighborhood patrons. She made people feel welcome and comfortable around the store, so people always liked gathering there. One of the regulars, Doc Greene, spent two years at the University of Pennsylvania, therein earning the moniker 'Doc,' which his friends bestowed on him out of respect. Also a World War combat veteran in his mid-thirties, and an ex-bootlegger who had seen a bit of the world, his opinions on all subjects were widely regarded.

One night in early September when Mike walked into the store, he found it empty except for Mrs. Williams behind the counter, and Albie Haney sitting on the big, insulated, wooden box holding bottles of cold soft drinks. Albie's face lit up when he saw Mike.

"Hey, Mike," he said, grinning, "I been waitin' for ya." He held out his right hand showing two pennies nestling in the palm. "I wanted to buy us two cigarettes."

Cigarettes sold for fifteen cents for a pack of twenty, but Mrs. Williams also sold them singly for a cent apiece.

Albie struggled off the soft drink box and limped over to the counter. "Two Chesterfields, Mrs. Williams," he said in his high-pitched, nervous voice. How could Albie be only twenty-two? His wizened face looked more like forty.

The store door opened and Tom Dooley walked in. Dooley served as the Republican ward leader—a red-faced, distinguished-looking man about sixty, with a job at City Hall. Doc Greene said the only work he did at City Hall involved reporting there once a week to collect his pay. Dooley bought five-for-a-nickel Phillies, and lit one of them.

15

"How's your mother, Albie?" he asked. "How does she like her new job?" Dooley had gotten her a job cleaning an office building on Fairmount Avenue: five nights and Saturday afternoon for six dollars a week. Doc Greene said she'd be better off on relief. In Philadelphia, a family of four got five dollars and fifty cents a week, and she wouldn't have to spend carfare.

"She's pretty good, Mr. Dooley," Albie said. "But her rheumatism bothers her pretty bad sometimes. She didn't make it to work tonight."

Dooley blew out some smoke and rotated his right shoulder like a pitcher warming up.

"I know how she must suffer, kid," he said. "I got a pretty bad case myself. Tell you what you do." He reached into his inside pocket for a small piece of paper, wrote something on it, and tendered it to Albie. "You take this note down to Mandel's and ask for a big bottle of Sloan's liniment, compliments of the 26th Ward Republican Club. It works wonders for me."

"Gee, thanks, Mr. Dooley. I'll take it down to Mandel's right now."

"Could you get me a job, Mr. Dooley?" Mike asked after Albie left.

"Times are tough, kid, and lots a grown men are outta work. Any jobs I come across I gotta hand out to heads of families."

"Then how about my father?"

Dooley chewed on his cigar and frowned.

"You know how many jobs I got your old man over the years?"

Mike shook his head.

"Neither do I 'cause I lost track of them. Besides, I hear your old man is a Franklin Roosevelt supporter these days. Tell him to try the New Deal's Public Works Administration."

Dooley went quickly out the door, and a moment later Doc Greene came in. He wore a disgusted look on his long, hollow-cheeked face when he spoke to Mrs. Williams.

"I hope you kept your eye on the merchandise while Dooley was in here, Sarah."

"Doc, you shouldn't talk that way about Mr. Dooley," she protested with a smile. Doc was one of her best customers and she didn't want to antagonize him. "He does good things for lots a people in this neighborhood. He certainly helped me out the time the city tried to make me fix the pavement after the city sanitation truck damaged it."

Doc leaned his long, thin frame on the candy counter and shook his head solemnly.

"Sarah, you'll never learn. Don't you know Dooley sent those city inspectors to harass you, just so he could call them off and earn your gratitude. There're two votes in your house."

He turned around and addressed his harangue to Mike, his voice surprisingly deep and resonant coming from so narrow a chest cavity.

"The Republicans have been robbing this city since the Civil War, and one holdover is good old Tom Dooley. Dooley is Robin Hood in reverse. He helps the rich to rob the poor."

Sarah huffed a small laugh. "You're a fine one to talk after the way you earned a living during Prohibition."

"You're right, Sarah, and I paid off every thief between here and City Hall. I know them."

Doc turned as Dutch Koenig and Stash Nowicki came in. "Aha, the president and vice-president of the Loafer's League. How long is it since you two bums had a job?"

"Two years and four months for me," Stash answered with a smile on his big, square, face.

"It's three years for me. That's why I'm president," Dutch said. He slicked back his thick blond hair. "And, if I had Stash's oversized hat full a nickels, I could retire permanently."

Stash's first name was Stanley, so the nickname was inevitable. He didn't get angry at Dutch's gibe. He rarely got angry at anybody, and never at Dutch, his closest friend.

Willie Bruno walked through the door, and Mike grinned at him. Along with Sam Schwarz, Willie was his best friend since childhood, partly because their back yards connected. Willie had quit school a week before Mike.

Almost on Willie's heels, Father August came into the store. The pastor of Saint Ludwig's was a tall, thin man, with close-cropped, gray hair, and a severe expression on his face. Nobody went to his Confession except old people because, in that iron presence, no young person could work up the nerve to confess the sin of having impure thoughts. He also gave out the stiffest penances anybody had ever heard of, like fifty "Our Fathers," and fifty "Hail Marys," or a couple of "Stations of the Cross." Dutch said, with the man's personality, his name should be Father January instead of Father August. Doc once said the Father lived as if he was straight out of the Middle Ages, and bet he wore a hair shirt and iron undies.

Most of the people in the store—good Catholics— murmured: "Good evening, Father." The priest looked around disapprovingly.

Mike always felt uncomfortable in Father August's presence. He hadn't been to Mass or Confession since last year, after reading George Bernard Shaw and H.G. Wells, two writers the Archdiocesan newspaper attacked as enemies of the Catholic Church.

Mrs. Williams shouted, "Okay, outside, boys! The store is too crowded for my fire insurance."

Mike's tensions dispensed with a tight exhale, and everyone followed Doc outside and wandered up the street to the next corner. They settled on the wide steps of the Department of Sanitation district office. In their spoken shorthand, they called it "the corner," as they called Mrs. Williams' shop "the store," and the Athletic Recreation Center "the Rec."

A few married couples sat on the steps of their houses up the street, enjoying the beautiful evening. Across the street, at the Rec, Georgie Hubbell was hitting fungoes to some of the younger kids. Georgie could really hit a ball, and they watched until he hit one over the wall of the enclosed swimming pool in deep right field. That ended the game, and the kids shouted with disappointment, but Georgie grinned as he picked up his jacket and sauntered over to the corner. He knew everybody had been watching him.

"Doc, if I could of hit a curve ball I'd of been playin' in the outfield alongside Al Simmons when the Athletics won all them pennants."

"He was a Polack, Simmons was," Stash said.

"Yeah," Willie added, "his real name was Simmonski."

"It was Szymanski, Willie," Stash corrected him.

"Do you know what Connie Mack paid Simmons a year?" Georgie asked, and answered his own question. "Thirty-three grand, and that's not countin' the World Series money." He shook his head in wonderment, "Just think, I could have been makin' that kind of dough."

Georgie was the best ball player Brewerytown had ever produced. When the season started and the pitchers discovered he couldn't hit a curve ball, they curved him right out of the league, and out of big-time baseball. After that, he made seven bucks a game playing in the semi-pro Suburban League, enough money to get drunk every weekend.

Mike saw Georgie's future stretched out in front of him as straight as the Pilgrim's Progress, except Georgie's path led to perdition. At forty, he'd be a member of the bottle gang, cadging money for drinks and sleeping in Sol Rudnick's junkyard. At fifty, he'd be in the morgue at Municipal Hospital, waiting to be planted in Potter's Field. He wondered if his father might suffer the same fate, but he shook his head. Not as long as good old Rose hung around to look after him.

Red approached, sporting a gray, sharkskin suit and a pearl gray, snap-brim hat.

"Jesus Christ, look at Red!" Dutch snorted. "He musta robbed a bank."

"No," Georgie Hubbell said, laughing. "He's got a new racket. He hangs around them joints on Market Street pickin' up queers, and when they take him back to their apartments, Red works them over and rolls them. The last queer he picked up is loaded with dough, and he buys Red clothes and gives him money. So, Red is hangin' on to him."

When he neared the corner, Red took his new hat off and held it behind him. He knew Georgie might take a notion to bash it in, or even jerk it off his head and stamp on it. Once, he had done the same thing to a new hat his own brother wore.

Georgie held out an open palm. "Hey, Red, lemme try on your new skimmer. I'm thinkin' of takin' up pimpin', and I wanna see how I look."

Red put the hat farther behind him. "Nothin doin'. I paid good money for this hat."

Georgie laughed raucously. "You mean one of your fag friends paid good money for it."

"Hey, Red," Willie said. "Why don't you open a whore house? You could run it by hand until you make enough money to hire some girls."

"Don't be a wiseass, kid, or I may hafta open up your stupid Dago head," Red said.

On the other side of the street, Mike saw Teresa Hanley passing. Walking fast, she cast quick glances in their direction. Red saw her, too, and left shortly after. Mike ambled off the steps to watch them. When Teresa arrived at the next corner, she crossed over and waited for Red. They disappeared around the corner.

Mike shook his head. So she is mixed up with him. Well, I'll have to talk to her. I'll tell her what kind of a guy he is.

Marie Drean and Ruth Wilson came out of the store eating ice cream, and Dutch waved at them. They waved back. Dutch turned back to his friend. "Come on, Stash, let's go up and sit with them."

Mike had attended Saint Ludwig's with both girls, and remembered the crush he once had on Marie. Pretty girls always went for older guys, though, and he had never had a chance, particularly when a good-looking bastard like Dutch made a play for Marie. Poor homely Ruth had been willing to settle for him, or almost anybody else, but even with Stash,

Ruth struck out. Everybody knew Stash had been in love with Teresa for years.

Doc stood up and stretched his long frame. "What do you say, Georgie, want to go up to Rafferty's and have a couple of beers?"

"You buyin'?" Georgie asked.

"Who else?"

Willie stared at their backs as they walked up the street. "I wonder how much dough Doc Greene is worth?"

"Plenty," Mike answered.

"What's plenty?"

"He once told my old man that when the bootlegging business went well, he supplied as many as ten speakeasies a week. At every one of them, he dropped off two to three hundred dollars worth of booze. Just count it up. That's two to three thousand dollars."

"A week?"

"That's right."

"Jesus Christ! He must be worth a bundle."

"Well, he had lots of expenses. He had to pay off the station house, the vice squad, and the politicians. Not to mention the judges he had to fix when he got locked up."

"I'll bet he's worth at least fifty grand."

"At least, even though he spends plenty. A lot of people wouldn't have coal in their houses in the winter if it weren't for old Doc. Last winter he put four tons in our house, and when my father tried to thank him, he pretended he didn't know what the old man was talkin' about."

The clock in Saint Ludwig's boomed nine times. Willie looked up at it. "Man, I'm hungry. Old man Schwarz will be shutting the store soon. Maybe Sam can slip some fruit out to us."

He started walking down 27th Street, and Mike followed him. "I sure wish I could make some dough. We're still four bucks short on the rent money."

"Me, too," Willie said. "It's all right for Dutch and Stash to brag about the Loafer's League, both their fathers are master butchers at Vogt's. Besides, Caz Nowicki is a strong-arm man with the hosiery union, and my old man says them guys make thirty-five bucks a week." He shook his head. "Man, Caz is a rugged sonofabitch, ain't he? Is he ruggeder than Stash?"

Mike shrugged. "They are brothers, but two different kinds of people. Stash never loses his temper, and Caz loses his at the drop of a hat. But nobody's stronger than Stash."

Willie laughed. "Jesus, you're right there."

"Maybe we oughta go junkin' tomorrow," Mike suggested. "I could use the money from the rent book to bankroll us."

"Okay, I'll go," Willie said.

"We'll need a pair of scales."

"I got a pair. Mr. Drean gave them to me when he got the job at the post office."

"Can you drive the horse and wagon?"

Willie began cracking an imaginary whip. "I was born to drive horses."

When they got to Max Schwartz's store, they saw Sam sweeping the floor, and old Max counting the day's receipts. Willie waved to attract Sam's attention. He nodded his head and motioned them away from the window, but Max turned and saw them.

"Your goy friends are here again looking for a handout," he growled, loud enough for the boys outside to hear. "Okay, okay, I'll feed you!" he shouted at the window. He grabbed a bag, threw in some speckled apples, a small bunch of brown bananas, and a bunch of bruised grapes, and thrust the bag at Sam. "Tell them to remember where it came from the next time they start talkin' about the dirty Jews."

Sam went outside with the bag, and they walked across the street to the Methodist-Episcopal church to sit on the steps. When Sam opened the bag, Willie leaned over it to peer in.

"Man, we hit the jackpot." He patted Sam's shoulder. "Your dad's a good head."

"He is good hearted, but he gets grouchy sometimes, and I get the brunt of it," Sam said. He began parceling out the fruit, keeping a banana and an apple for himself.

"Sam, your old man ain't even in it with my old man when it comes to being grouchy," Willie said. "Shit, I can't even remember the last time I heard a pleasant word outta him."

Mike chewed a grape and swallowed. "I hafta say my old man won't work, but he's easy to get along with."

"Mike, you don't know how lucky you are," Willie said.

The lights in the Schwarz store went out, and a moment later Max came out, locked the door, and shouted across the street to his son. "You be home by ten. And stay out of trouble."

He started down Girard Avenue and they watched him until he turned left at Bailey Street, toward the house on Master where he lived with his wife, four kids, and his wife's mother. It was one of the good houses in the neighborhood, made of gray stone, with a gray stone porch attached. Mandel, the druggist, lived next door.

"None of you guys know how good you got it," Sam mumbled between bites of his apple. "You don't have to work all summer and after school."

"Cheer up, Sam," Willie said. "Some day you'll inherit the store and you can hire somebody with a strong back and a weak mind to do the brute work. Like Mike, here."

"No, I won't. My father wants me to go to pharmacy school."

"Is that what you're gonna be, a pharmacist?" Willie asked.

"It looks like it, but I sure ain't lookin' forward to it. Two more years of high school, then four more years at the Philadelphia College of Pharmacy." He shook his head.

"Why don't you tell your old man you won't do it?" Willie demanded.

"You don't know my old man. You just can't talk to him. You know the Mandels live next door to us, and they got five daughters. I'm sure Mr. Mandel and my father have got some scheme cooked up for me to marry one of the Mandel girls and take over the drug store."

"Which one is it?" Willie asked eagerly. "Is it the oldest one? Man, she's got a pair of knockers you could hang your hat on.

"No, it can't be Rachel. She's eighteen and she already has a boyfriend."

"What's the next one's name?"

"The next one is Sylvia. She's sixteen."

"You better hope it ain't her, Sam," Willie said. "She is really homely."

"Next is Natalie. She's the prettiest one, but she's only thirteen. The others are just kids."

"She's the one," Willie said. "She won't always be thirteen. Hold out for Natalie."

"My father acts like he's still in the old country," Sam said. "And he's been here since he was six years old."

"Where was your father born?" Mike asked.

"In Germany, in a city called Darmstadt."

"Oh, yeah, I heard of it," Mike said. "You still got any people livin' there, Sam?"

He glanced away. "Not that I know of."

"Good, things are not very good for the Jews in Germany since Hitler took over."

"I saw him in the newsreel," Willie said. "He looked like Charlie Chaplin havin' a fit."

"There was a long article about Hitler in the Sunday paper a couple of weeks ago," Mike said. "He was born in Austria and they say his real name is Schicklgruber."

"Schicklgruber?" Willie laughed. "Jesus, no wonder the poor bastard's crazy."

Sam looked at his watch. "It's goin' on ten. I gotta start home."

They all stood up, and Mike put a hand on his buddy's shoulder. "We'll walk with you."

24

Outside Mandel's, a parked car caught their attention. The new, fire-engine-red, Essex convertible with a rumble seat, justified their admiration.

Willie stopped and rolled his eyes. "That's what I call a real pussy wagon."

"I wonder who owns it?" Sam asked.

"Nobody in this neighborhood." Mike looked through Mandel's window and saw two young men and two girls sitting at a booth. The two young men rose and walked over to the counter to pay the check. Both taller than Mike, they wore Saint Joseph's Prep athletic sweaters.

They're probably football players, Mike thought. He looked at the two girls still sitting in the booth. The one facing him, a chesty blonde, slid out of the booth and stood up. The other one followed her and turned around. He recognized Patricia Galvan, who graduated high school a couple of years before.

She was dressed in a long, light-blue dress, and she combed her thick, dark-brown hair smoothly in a pageboy cut that reached almost to her shoulders. Her smile showed nice white teeth and the tip of a pink tongue. She was an entrancing sight, and Mike's heart began to pound. He backed into the shadows when she came out and he watched as one of the young men helped her into the front seat. The other girl and her friend got into the rumble seat.

"Nice wagon you got there, buddy," Willie said to Patricia's escort as he walked by.

"Thanks, sport," the youth muttered. He closed his door, started the engine and, gunning it, made a screeching turn onto Girard Avenue.

"Snotty bastard!" Willie shouted after him.

Sam stared down the street where the car had turned. "Patricia Galvan sure is a pretty girl."

"She sure is that, and then some." Mike whistled under his breath.

Willie leered at him. "The blonde wasn't bad, either. When she climbed into the rumble seat I almost saw me some hair pie."

"Let's go," Mike said. He was afraid if they started talking dirty about the blonde, they might get around to including Patricia. "We don't want to make Sam late."

"Yeah," Sam said. "My father's already on the porch looking down the damn street."

When they got to the corner, they parted company with Sam and wandered down to Mrs. William's store. It stood deserted with the lights out.

"What are we gonna do now?" Willie asked.

"I'm going home. I wanna do some readin'. What time do we meet?"

"How about seven o'clock. Here on the corner?"

"Okay, I'll meet you here."

◆ ◆ ◆

At home, Mike stumbled through the dark kitchen and found a match for the Welsbach mantle light in the dining room. Almost all of the houses in the neighborhood, even on Etting Street, already had electric lights, but the Kane household remained in the gas age. Rappaport, the landlord, said he would put electric lights in, but he'd have to raise the rent to twenty bucks a month. So, the old man would have to get a job and pay the rent regularly.

Christ knows there isn't much chance of that, Mike thought, as he climbed up on a chair to reach the mantle. He remembered once, when he was about ten, climbing up on the table to light the lamp, and putting his foot in a bowl of cranberry sauce his mother placed there to cool. His father still talked about it, and it always made him laugh.

It brought back happier times when the old man still worked at Exide Battery and there was money for turkey at Thanksgiving, and pot roast on Sundays with onions and potatoes cooked brown in the gravy. The old man hadn't cared much for work even then, and he had developed an ailment called "lead belly." It came, he said, from working around batteries. So, he had quit the job.

In those days, though, when his Uncle Frank was still alive and making good money as a hosiery knitter at Thomas E. Brown's, he always made sure the rent was paid. He also slipped his sister a few dollars for groceries.

Once, when Mike was in the eighth grade and had run track for Saint Ludwig's at the Perm Relays, Uncle Mike had even bought him a pair of track shoes. Christ, he was the only kid in the neighborhood who had ever owned a pair. With those spikes digging into the cinders, he had run an anchor lap that brought the crowd to its feet. His mother and his Uncle Mike both died from tuberculosis, the curse of his mother's family. Both her parents and a younger brother had died from it before Mike was born.

His mother had been a tall, thin, and pretty women with brown hair and eyes. She was strong willed, but gentle with everyone she knew, always doing for others, and always smiling. She had never asked for anything for herself, but always gave to others from what she had. When she suffered, no one knew it; when someone else suffered, she sensed it and tuned in. She was beyond the level of anyone he knew or ever heard of. To Mike she was *it*.

His eyes grew moist thinking of his mother as he rummaged through her sideboard drawers for some writing paper and an envelope. He had told Willie he was going home early to read, but he really planned to write Patricia a letter. He had made up his mind to do it while walking back from Girard Avenue. If he couldn't fight those rich goofs from Saint Joe's on their own grounds, he'd fight them on his.

He'd win Patricia by the power of his pen. He was a writer, by God. Not that he couldn't have played football at Saint Joe's, if he had been lucky enough to go there. Maybe he wasn't as big as that clod Patricia hung out with earlier, but he was big enough: five-foot seven and a hundred and forty-three pounds on the Rec scales. Albie Booth wasn't any bigger, and he played as an All-American at Yale. Mike had scored thirty points against Kingsessing in the Recreation Touch Football League last winter, and Doc Greene had called him the shiftiest broken-field runner he had ever seen. He smiled at the memory of Doc's compliment.

He found a writing tablet and sat down at the dining room table to plan the letter. He'd write the letter first in pencil, then copy it in ink. Maybe he could even type it on the typewriter in the Rec office. That would be really neat. Moistening the tip of the pencil, he drew the tablet toward him and began the first draft.

At midnight, while still working on the third draft, his father came home. He could hear the old man fumbling with the front door, so he put the writing tablet under the chair and pretended to read. His father stayed as good-natured drunk as he did sober and, after telling Mike not to stay up too late, he staggered upstairs. Ten minutes later, snoring wafted down the corridor.

At one o'clock, he read the letter over. It's good, he whispered to himself. It's damn good.

Chapter Four

It's damn good passed through his mind only once more before the alarm clock bonged. Mike sat bolt upright and peered at it through bleary eyes. It read six-thirty. Christ, I'm tired. Then he remembered his vow to earn the rent money. He ran into the bathroom to wash up.

The bathroom was as tiny as every other room in the house, with no sink, only a small bathtub, gray-white with age, and a wooden medicine cabinet with a spotted mirror. Thank God he could use the showers at the Rec, because the tub served as a toilet.

Pulling off his undershirt, he leaned over the tub and vigorously washed his face and upper body. He wet his hair and rubbed soap into it so it would stay after he combed it.

He walked over to the mirror, parted his hair on the side, and slicked it back like his favorite movie star William Haines. *What a great job he did in that movie* Brown At Harvard, he thought.

Peering at himself critically, he wondered if he was good-looking to girls. His teeth looked pretty good, his hair was straight and light brown, and tended to fall over his forehead when it dried out. Well, maybe he wasn't handsome, but he was better looking than a lot of guys.

He decided he didn't need to shave, and turned back to the tub to urinate.

Downstairs on the kitchen table, he found a box of puffed rice and a note from Rose. "If you look in the icebox you'll find a quart of milk. Also, the damp wash goes out tomorrow, so gather up your dirty laundry and, Michael, you bring it over tonight."

Reading the note, he wondered how in Christ's name they would ever make it without Rose. Well, she wouldn't regret it. When he struck it rich, she was the first one he was going to take care of. He poured the puffed rice into a bowl, added milk and sugar, and spooned it down rapidly. He'd better get his ass out of here. It was almost seven and he didn't want to keep Willie waiting. He finished off the cereal by drinking it, and hurried out the door. When he got to the corner, Willie stood waiting.

"Late again, Mike," he kidded. "Beautiful fall day to be doin' this. Look, I got the scales." He held up a contraption with a handle on top, a hook at the bottom and, in between, a long, narrow dial that registered weight. "And lemme tell ya, these scales weigh light. Ya can bust your hump tryin' to lift a bundle of newspapers and the scale says maybe twenty pounds."

When they got to the junkyard on Cabot Street, two wagons were already harnessed up, and a colored man was backing a horse into the shafts of a third.

"Jesus, I hope we're not too late," Mike said.

Willie reassured him. "Not a chance. Old Sol's got ten, maybe fifteen teams."

Sol Rudnick's office lay just inside the yard. The cluttered cubbyhole held an old, roll-top desk, a scarred chair, and an ancient safe. Sol sat in the chair, his bulk filling it to overflowing. He turned around when he heard the door open.

"We wanna rent a team, Mr. Rudnick," Mike said. "You know, a horse and wagon."

Sol grunted. "I know what a team is, boy. You got a buck and a half?"

Mike took out the slim sheaf of bills he had taken from the rent book. "We have, Mr. Rudnick, but we'd like to use it to buy stuff with. Can't we pay you when we get back, outta what we make?"

"Suppose you don't pick up a buck and a half's worth?"

"You know me, Sol," Willie said. "I've been out here before with Georgie Hubbell and Mr. Drean, our next door neighbor. We always done good."

Sol put on a pair of smeared glasses and peered at Willie. "You're Joe Bruno's boy. Okay, tell Walker to give you a mare."

"How much is paper goin' for?" Willie asked.

"Twenty cents a hundred. Don't you pay more than eight cents."

"What about rags?"

"Nine cents a pound, maybe twelve if they're white. Stay away from metal. You don't know enough to make good buys."

At Willie's suggestion, Mike asked for three dollars worth of change, and they went outside into the huge yard. Mike had walked past it a thousand times, but he had never gone inside. Willie pointed to a big stack of bundled paper and rags. Perched on top sat two huge rats.

"That's where the bottle gang sleeps," Willie said.

Mike remembered a joke an aspiring comedian had told at a Fairmount Theater Amateur Night. "Did ya hear about the big fire that left twenty people homeless last night?" Pause. "Sol Rudnick's junk yard burned down."

Everybody had laughed uproariously, including him. Now he shuddered.

"Jesus, it must be cold in winter."

"It must be," Willie said, "when they ain't fulla Sneaky Pete whiskey."

Walker, the colored man who ran Rudnick's stable, led out a mare he called Emma and hitched her up to one of the wagons. "Now don' yoo boys run this hea howse! And git back hea by fou, iffin yoo wanna git weighed and paid, and have a little jingle lef to git yo'self laid."

He laughed and handed them a feedbag with some oats in it. "And don't feed her nuttin' but this hea oats."

He patted Emma on the rump and turned to take care of another customer.

◆◆◆

They had decided to work the Kensington area where Willie had worked once before.

"We made thirteen bucks that day, and Mr. Drean gimme three. He knows how to tell pewter, and block tin, and copper, all that good stuff you can make money on."

They turned east on Columbia, and Willie pointed to a dingy corner grocery. "That's Aunt Sadie's joint, where all the older guys go to get their ashes hauled."

"You mean the grocery store?"

"Yeah, Sadie's joint's on the second floor."

"You ever gone in there?" Mike asked.

"Naw. Dutch showed me where it was and talked about it."

When they got to Eighth Street they saw a row of porch houses. "Let's try these," Willie said. "You knock on the doors, and when you get a customer, I'll park and bring the scales."

"You know I never did this before," Mike said. "What should I say?"

"Just ask them if they got any old newspapers or rags. Some of them may give them to you just to get rid of them. If they don't, tell them you'll pay a good price, then call me over."

They were almost at the end of the block when they got their first bite. A short, thin, woman about fifty, opened the door.

"We don't want to buy anything," the woman said.

"We're not selling anything, ma'am," Mike said. "We're lookin' for old newspapers and rags. We can haul them away for you or, if you have enough, we might be able to pay you for them."

The woman looked at him doubtfully. "How much will you pay for newspapers?"

Willie climbed down from the wagon, the scales in his hand, in time to hear Mike's reply "Ten cents a hundred."

"Is that a good price?" she asked skeptically.

"Is that a good price?" Willie broke in. "Missus, my partner's gonna bankrupt us. Eight cents is all we can pay."

The woman had a mouth that closed like a steel trap. When she opened it she pointed at Mike: "He says ten cents," She started to close the door.

"Okay, Missus, ten cents it is," Willie said. "How much paper you got?"

"Quite a bit. It's in the cellar."

She opened the door wider and they followed her through the house and into the kitchen where a door led downstairs. Against the cellar wall, bundles of newspapers sat tied and stacked.

"There's forty bundles there, and they weigh at least forty pounds apiece."

Willie frowned. "I'd say your husband estimated a little heavy."

He hooked the scales into one of the bundles and heaved it off the ground. The needle registered twenty-six pounds. He looked at Mike, "I'd say these scales weigh a little light. Let's say the bundles weigh thirty pound apiece."

"Forty," the woman said.

"Okay, Missus," Willie said smiling. "Let's split the difference. Thirty-five."

The woman shook her head. "Forty," she insisted.

"Look, lady, what do you want?" Willie asked. "We added ten pound to the scale."

"I want every bundle figured at forty pounds," the woman was adamant. "Thirty times forty is sixteen hundred. That's a dollar and sixty cents if you want to buy the paper."

Willie spread his hands. "Jeez, you drive a hard bargain, ma'am."

Mike paid her and took the bundles from Willie through the basement window.

As they drove away, Willie grinned. "Everybody's happy. That woman thinks she dicked us, and I know we got the better of her. Them |bundles weigh fifty pound apiece if they weigh an ounce. That's at least four bucks we'll get for paper we paid a buck-sixty for, so we already got the team money back and maybe enough to buy lunch. If you had just said eight cents a hundred, we would of done even better."

They continued up Allegheny Avenue, stopping at house after house without finding another customer. By the time they got to Fifth Street, it was after twelve o'clock and they stopped in a taproom across from the Westmoreland Rec for lunch. For thirty-five cents, a young German girl with blonde pigtails and a rosy-cheeked plain face served them hot roast beef sandwiches and a mound of mashed potatoes. When she came back with a slab of apple cake, and a mug of root beer, Willie complimented the waitress on her cooking and asked her to marry him.

"My mother does the cooking," the girl said and smiled.

"Then ask your mother if she'll marry me," Willie smiled back.

Mike sat mute, envying Willie's ability to banter with girls.

"You want my autograph?" Willie asked. "I'm Frankie Darro, the actor."

She giggled and left. Mike calculated that, after paying, they would still be ahead twenty cents. He slipped a ten-cent tip under his plate. At least she would know he wasn't a cheapskate.

They walked outside, belching loudly, and Willie gestured across the street at the recreation center. "Remember when we played that soccer game here last year?"

"Sure do. They beat us seven to three, but I got a goal on a penalty kick."

"All I got was the shit kicked outa my shins," Willie said. "And Georgie Hubbell got in a fight with their manager and we had to run for our lives."

An elderly man came out and pointed up the street. "Hey, boys, look at the parade."

They looked up the street and saw a column of people marching, some of them carrying hand-lettered signs. When they got closer, Mike could see they were all old people, their signs read "GOD BLESS DR. TOWNSEND." They turned into the recreation center and marched in.

"It's them Share-the-Wealth people," the elderly man said. "You know, the thing started by that fella in California. I can't think of his name."

"Share-the-Wealth was started by Senator Huey Long from Louisiana," Mike said with a smile. "The man in California is named Dr. Townsend."

"You got it, son," the man agreed. "Townsend's his name. He wants to give all the old people two hundred dollars a month, and they gotta spend it before the next month starts." He shook his head. "It won't happen. The Jew bankers won't allow it."

Mike wanted to ask him if he meant Jew bankers like J. P. Morgan, but he kept his mouth shut, and the man walked away. By now he understood that prejudice never listens.

"Let's go listen to them for awhile, Willie."

Willie walked over to Emma, still hitched to a traffic sign. He took the empty feedbag from around her neck and put it under the wagon seat.

"Okay, but we can't stay long. We still ain't made any money."

✦✦✦

About a hundred people gathered in a rough semi-circle around the steps of the administration building, and on the top step stood a man dressed in a clean, faded brown shirt and a pair of corduroy trousers. He sported a shock of gray hair, bristling above a pair of heavy eyebrows, which made him look fierce. A pair of five-and-ten-cent store reading glasses kept slipping down his nose, which he pushed back impatiently. He raised his eyes to the crowd.

"First off, I want to read this letter from our so-called representative in Washington. It's an answer to the letter you instructed me to write at our last meeting." He adjusted his glasses and began to read in a deep, booming voice.

"Dear Mr. Arnold:

It was with a great deal of interest and pleasure that I read the letter from you..." It droned on and on in meaningless political language: "I have heard from all sides... As you know, experts have estimated that... I close with the hope that I may be able to meet with you personally when I return after the congressional session."

"It's all words!" the man shouted, his voice shaking with rage. "He's trying to bamboozle us with words! Let's remember his words the next time he comes around looking for our votes!"

Jesus, what a powerful old man, Mike thought. He looks like H. G. Well's description of Gladstone: "He had a gaze like an eagle and the finest baritone voice in all of Europe."

"There are ten million of us!" the old man roared. "Let all the politicians feel our anger!"

A man at the front began speaking loudly, and Mike instantly recognized the voice.

"Hey, Willie," Mike blurted, elbowing his friend. "Listen. It's Mr. Goldman."

"Dr. Townsend can't solve your problems," Goldman said. "I hate to say this, Mr. Arnold, but I have to agree with your congressman. It's the only thing I ever heard him say that was true. The only way Townsend can put money in your pockets is to extract it from people as poor as yourselves. What we need is an entirely new system. One based on people's needs. The sooner you learn the present system is corrupt, and only Socialism can provide a decent life for everybody, the sooner you'll avoid the tragedy of raised hopes, followed by cruel disappointment from every quack who comes along with a magic formula to make capitalism work."

Boos issued from the crowd, and Mr. Arnold shouted, "Just what are you, mister?"

"I'm a Democratic Socialist!" he yelled. "Like Eugene Debs and Norman Thomas!"

"Debs was a traitor!" somebody in the crowd shouted. "He wouldn't fight the Germans!"

"Debs was a pacifist!" he retorted. "And a Socialist who wouldn't fight capitalist wars!"

Mike saw a tall, thin, old man, in a Spanish-American War uniform, approach to confront Goldman. Two medals on his faded, blue jacket clanked when he shook his finger at his rival.

"Was you at San Juan Hill like I was?" the old man asked.

"I wasn't even born then," Goldman said.

"Was you at Belleau Woods like my boy, Jimmy?"

"I was too young," Goldman answered patiently. "I was born in 1903."

"Fellas like you always got some excuse," the old man sneered.

Goldman shrugged his shoulders. "I don't want to argue with you, sir. I'm on your side." He brushed past the man and walked toward the exit. Mike and Willie ran after him. They caught up with him near the gate, and Mike touched his arm. "Hey, Mr. Goldman."

The teacher turned around, a pleased smile on his face. "Kane, what are you doing here?"

Mike pointed to Willie. "We were out junkin' and we saw all those old people marchin' into the Rec, so we decided to watch. I never expected to see you there."

"I live just six blocks from here and heard about the meeting. How are you making out?"

"We're doin' good. We have a team and we're buyin' old newspapers and rags."

"We're makin' out good, all right," Willie said. "If we're lucky we'll break even."

"Where do you live on Erie Avenue, Mr. Goldman?" Mike asked.

"Between Seventh and Eighth."

"You want a ride? We could be goin' up that way. Hey, Willie, let's work Erie Avenue."

Willie shrugged. "Anything you say as long as we do it soon. We gotta be back by four."

They walked back to where Emma was tied up, and Mike climbed into the wagon to sit on the stacked bundles. Goldman got up on the seat next to Willie.

"I really liked what you had to say, Mr. Goldman," Mike said.

The teacher smiled at him. "I'm glad you liked it, Kane. Nobody else did." He shook his head. "It was a waste of time, and a shame, too, in a way. Townsend's a decent old man. He woke up one morning and saw some old women pawing through garbage cans looking for food and he decided he had to do something about it."

"What do you think of Huey Long?" Mike asked.

"Huey's a real threat. Not like poor old Dr. Townsend. Somebody told me that Roosevelt called him one of the two most dangerous men in America."

"Who was the other one?"

"General Douglas MacArthur."

"Oh, yeah, the guy who chased the bonus army out of Washington."

"Townsend attracts people who, even in their hopelessness, don't forget their essential humanity. He attracts the kind of people who support harmless crackpot movements like Free Silver, or Prohibition, or the Second Coming of Christ. Huey attracts a more violent element: yahoos who will burn down your house, or hang Negroes, or Jews, or Catholics."

Willie asked, "Did you say you lived between Seventh and Eighth streets?"

"Yes," Goldman answered, "just down the block... the house with green shutters."

They stopped in front, and Goldman climbed down from the wagon.

"You're a little too young to join the Socialist Party, Kane, but maybe you'd find it interesting to come down to a meeting some night and listen to us argue. We meet on the first and third Tuesdays of every month at the Eugene Debs Hall on South Street between Eleventh and Twelfth. We're on the second floor."

"I sure would like to, Mr. Goldman. Thanks for the invitation."

They drove away and Mike repeated the information to fix it in his mind. He'd also look up the Socialist Party when he made his usual evening visit to the library.

They worked hard, but picked up only two more bundles of paper at one house—a big, brick house with a verandah stretching along two sides, surrounded by a hedge. Still, the woman who sold them the paper took the five cents Mike tendered in payment.

"That's how the rich get richer," Willie said as they carried the two heavy bundles across the wide porch and hefted them into the wagon. "They don't give anything away. Well, we screwed her outa a good fifty pounds, anyhow." He climbed into the driver's seat and slapped the reins against Emma's rump. "Okay, Emma, it's time to head for the stable."

When they got back, Walker weighed them in at 2,217 pounds. He wrote the figure on a slip of paper and they took it into Rudnick's office. Sol made an instant calculation.

"That's four thirty-four, but we'll make it four thirty-five. Minus a buck-fifty is two eighty-five. "He peeled three dollars from a roll of bills. "You got fifteen cents?"

Mike handed him fifteen cents and took the three dollars.

They walked outside and he counted all the money he had in his pocket. It came to five dollars and forty cents. He turned to Willie.

"I took five ones outa the rent book, so we made forty cents profit for a day's work. I'm really doing great after quitting school four months ago... and I haven't written a thing."

"Welcome to real life, Mike. Don't worry, we all get over the disappointment sometime."

Mike handed Willie twenty cents and laughed. "Don't spend it all in one place."

At Mrs. William's store, they bought a pack of Chesterfields and a cream soda apiece. They sat on the wooden soda box, taking deep slugs of the soda and cigarette smoke.

"My old man isn't ever gonna believe we came out even," Willie said.

"I could stop by your house and back up your story," Mike offered.

"No, I'll tell him we weighed in at a thousand nine hundred pounds and you lost money. That he'll believe."

✦✦✦

When Mike got home, he washed up at the kitchen sink, and went upstairs to read for a while before peeling the potatoes for supper. Lying on the bed, he thumbed through a dictionary and read the entry on euphemism.

"A mild or vague expression as a substitute for blunt disagreeable truth: e.g. the dead were the departed, pregnant women were in an interesting condition."

He thought about Patricia's letter, and he pulled it out of its hiding place and read it over. A wave of doubt passed over him. It didn't sound as good as it had before. In fact, it sounded goofy. *Maybe I'll add a few more quotations.* He vowed to look through Bartlett's at the library.

He folded the letter, and found the tear in the fabric under the chair to carefully replace it. He was confident he needn't worry about his father finding the letter.

He then ran his hand fondly over the backs of the books on their shelf. He owned a total of twenty-nine, and it was a pretty good collection if he did say so himself.

Chapter Five

Mike dressed in his father's suit—the only one he owned, paid for at a dollar a month, especially for Mike's mother's funeral. He wanted to look his best on his first visit to Eugene Debs Hall. The chill of October also prompted him to wear the topcoat.

Mr. Goldman had said the meetings began at eight o'clock, and it was a good hour's walk, so he left the dishes in the sink.

When he came out of the house, he saw Teresa Hanley walking down Etting Street just ahead of him. He still hadn't talked to her about Red Donovan.

"Hey, Teresa!" he shouted. She stopped and waited until he caught up with her.

"I don't see much of you anymore since you started work at Strawmaker's," he said. "How are you and old John Strawmaker gettin' along?"

Teresa shrugged. "It's a job. It's better than no job, I guess."

Taller and slimmer than Rose, and not as pretty, she had a knack for wearing clothes and always looked nice.

"You're really dolled up," he said. "Have you got a heavy date?"

She shook her head. "If you call going to the movies with some girls a heavy date."

"You wouldn't be on your way to meet Red, would you, Treese?" he blurted out.

He could see her stiffen. She turned to him. "So, you've been talking to my sister Rose. Well, don't you start on me. I hear enough about it from her."

She started to walk faster. He increased his pace to keep up. She had always been a high-strung girl, and Rose had spoiled her rotten since their parents died. Still, he had always gotten along well with her. When his mother was alive, she had spent as much time in his house as in her own. He tried to keep his voice low and quiet.

"I gotta talk to you, Teresa, even if you don't like it. It's for your own good."

"You don't like Francis," she said. "None of you do. You don't even know him."

He had forgotten Red's name was Francis, and for a moment he thought she was talking about somebody else. "I know Francis all right," he said. "I know things about him you don't know. Like where he got those new clothes he's wearin'."

"You see! You see!" Her voice rose. "You think he stole them. Or stole the money to buy them. He told me where he got the money."

"Where?"

"He hit the numbers, that's where. He had a quarter on the winning number and he got a hundred and twenty-five dollars back."

"Is that right?"

"That's right. He gave his mother fifty dollars and spent the rest on clothes.

"He's lyin'."

"He is not!"

"Yes, he is." Mike insisted, trying to keep his voice calm. "He gets his money playin' the queers. Some rich fag he picked up bought him those new clothes."

She stopped short and stared at him, a stunned look on her face. Then she slapped him, a full-handed swing that stung his right cheek. "You're a dirty rotten liar!" she screeched, and ran up the street.

He let her go, and continued on his way.

He certainly loused that up. Now, Treese would never speak to him again. What the hell was he supposed to do, though? Somebody had to talk to her, and she wouldn't listen to Rose. He knew Red wouldn't go with any girl who didn't put out. If she liked him, it would only be a matter of time until he talked her into having sex, if he hadn't done it already.

Why the hell couldn't she find somebody nice, like Stash? He was crazy about her, and wouldn't lay a hand on her, unless she begged him. But she ignored him, not knowing Stash had a crush on her. Nobody could know Stash without liking him. He was so much better than Red, there was just no comparison.

Goddamn, that's what he'd do! Get her involved with Stash. How he would manage that he didn't know. Nevertheless, he'd do it somehow. He already began to feel better.

His thoughts moved along to what he might run into at the meeting. Though nervous, he knew it wouldn't be so bad as long as Goldman was there. Maybe he could even take part in some of the discussions. After all, he knew something about Fabian Socialism, thanks to Shaw and Wells. Plus, he'd spent hours in the library looking up other kinds of Socialism.

In one of the encyclopedia entries, he found the name of Morris Hillquit mentioned as *a* dominant force in the early period of the Socialist Party in the United States. The party had started out as the Socialist Labor Party, but Hillquit led a revolt against the radical wing, headed by *"a doctrinaire Marxist"* Daniel De Leon. Hillquit had helped form the Social Democratic Party, which evolved into the Socialist Party, now led by Norman Thomas.

De Leon, along with Eugene Debs and William D. Haywood, also started an organization called the Industrial Workers of the World. The IWW wanted to set up a state run by industrial unions, and led a number of violent strikes, especially in the west.

The mention of anarchism and syndicalism in his readings led him to look up the Haymarket Square Riot of 1886, a woman named Emma Goldman, the Russians Bakunin and Kropotkin, and a Frenchman named Proudhon who wrote a pamphlet entitled *What is Property?* The answer to that question, Proudhon said, is "theft." He looked up several other French names: Saint-Simon Fourier; Cabet; Louis Blanc, who was mixed up in the Revolution of 1848; and Georges Sorel.

Mike tried to organize all the information he had gathered into some semblance of order during the long walk downtown. The names jumbled together in his head and he couldn't remember whether Cabet preceded Blanc, or Bebel came before Bernstein. *At least I remember all the names,* he told himself smugly. There wasn't another swinging dick from one end of Brewerytown to the other who had heard of any of them. Or anyone who knew Bolshevism and Menshevism came from the words bolshoi and menshoi, and meant majority and minority.

He imagined himself accidentally meeting Patricia and the goof from Saint Joe's Prep at Mandel's soda fountain counter and casually introducing the topic of Fourier's phalanxes into the conversation. "As you know, they were utopian-socialist communities," he'd say, looking straight at the poor goof. "Some of them were tried here in the USA; at Brook Farm in Massachusetts, for example. The most successful U.S. Fourierist community was started at Red Bank, New Jersey."

He could see the poor slob start to stammer and get red in the face. Maybe he'd try to squirm off the hook by switching the conversation to football. Jesus, would he be in for a shock when he found out Mike Kane had read every book on football history in the library—the books of Percy Haughton, Walter Camp, and Amos Alonzo Stagg to name just a few.

El Goofo would have to throw in the sponge at this point, and he could see him giving some tongue-tied excuse to leave, and old Mike Kane would have to walk Patricia home.

Therein lies the strength of words and knowledge. Man, he'd have to rewrite that letter and send it to Patricia. What the hell was he waiting for, when she was probably his for the taking? He'd do it tomorrow.

✦✦✦

Mike was impressed by Eugene Debs Hall. The three-story building, made of some kind of clean, light-brown stone, stood out like a sore thumb between the two dingy buildings flanking it. He found the front door unlocked, and entered and climbed the stairway to the second floor. The stairway led to a dimly lit corridor where he saw a light shining through the frosted glass window of a door. The inscription below the glass read "SOCIALIST PARTY" and he raised his fist to knock, but dropped it. Maybe he was too early. It wasn't eight o'clock yet. He'd just wait here in the corridor until Goldman came by to go in with him. Suppose he was already inside, though. Before he could make up his mind, he saw a shadow approaching, and a girl about his own age opened the door.

"Yes?" the girl asked, giving him a questioning look. She wasn't really pretty, but she had a mass of dark hair, and big brown eyes shining behind a pair of thick glasses.

"I'm looking for Mr. Goldman," Mike said. "Mr. Lester Goldman, that is."

"Lester's not here," the girl answered. She was shorter than he, and a little on the plump side, but nicely built. She was nicely dressed, too, in a bright-green wool dress.

"Isn't tonight the night you usually have your meetings?" Mike asked. He was glad he had worn his father's topcoat and suit.

"Yes, but Lester won't be here tonight. He had to go to a school meeting."

"Who is it, Naomi?" he heard another female voice say.

"It's a young man. He's looking for your boyfriend."

An older woman appeared in the doorway and smiled at Mike. She looked a lot like the girl, only thinner and more attractive. "I'm Sylvia Weiss and this is my daughter, Naomi. Can we help you?"

"My name is Michael Kane, and I used to be one of Mr. Goldman's students." He was feeling less nervous now that the older woman was there. She reminded him of Rose Hanley. Still, he knew he wasn't going into any meeting unless Goldman attended.

"So, you're Michael Kane," Sylvia Weiss said, smiling broadly. Naomi, too, gave him a tentative grin. They both had spaces between their front teeth. "Lester has told us about you."

She opened the door wide. "Come in. Lester will be sorry he missed you."

"I better not," he said. "I'll wait until Mr. Goldman's here."

He turned and walked quickly away. Sylvia Weiss called after him, "I'll tell Lester."

He walked home knowing he had looked like a real fool. It would be different next time, though, he promised himself. Goldman would be there and he wouldn't feel so strange. If he had stayed tonight he would have looked stupid, afraid to be himself, or even to say anything.

Mrs. Weiss was sure pretty. He should have known Goldman would have a stunning girlfriend. Naomi was not bad looking, but not in the same class with Patricia. She did have a nice build, and a pair of knockers you could hang your hat on, as Willie always said.

When he got near home it was almost nine o'clock, and he decided to wait until Schwarz' store closed and Sam came out. He saw Father August coming down the street and ducked behind the steps of the Methodist-Episcopal Church until the coast was clear. He didn't want to be asked why he didn't go to Mass anymore.

He could have told him all right. He would have said because the church made him feel guilty about perfectly natural things, like sex and beer. Because the church said he couldn't read certain books. Because most Catholics he knew weren't a damned bit more moral than anybody else; in fact, most weren't nearly as moral as atheists like Goldman, or Shaw and Wells. What did Hemingway say? "All thinking men are atheists."

Red Donovan stood as an example of a Catholic who didn't think straight. He'd steal anything not nailed down. Even nice guys like Willie and Stash went astray. He, himself, had done some cheating, and what made him stop a year ago was a book about honor and integrity. Not the church.

The book was *Beau Geste*, by Percival Christopher Wren, and "Beau" had taught Mike that an honorable man neither lied, nor cheated, nor stole. An honorable man was also brave, and gentle with women. *Beau Geste would have protected that Negro on the street more violently than I had*, Mike thought. *That's okay, though, because I'm still learning. I'll get there.*

He had not told anybody about the spiritual effect the book had on him. Once he had casually asked Goldman what he thought of the book, and he called it junk that reflected the real world about as accurately as a fairy tale. It was the only time he could remember disagreeing with Goldman. He told himself from then on he would make those fairy tales come true in his life.

The lights in Schwarz' store went out and old Max started down Girard Avenue toward home. Sam walked across the street and joined Mike on the church steps.

"I was hopin' I'd see you," Sam said. "I think I know where you can find a job."

"What kind of a job?"

"Deliverin' prescriptions at Mandel's. He wants somebody to work from four to nine, Mondays to Fridays, and from twelve to nine on Saturdays. What do you think?"

"Gee, I don't know, Sam. How much will he pay?"

"Five bucks a week, plus you'll get tips. Mandel has two pay telephones, too, and you can run the telephone calls. You oughta make six, seven bucks a week."

Jesus, seven bucks would pay the rent, and buy some new duds. He usually dressed like a bum these days, except when he had on his old man's one good suit and topcoat.

"Do you think Mandel will give me the job?" he asked eagerly.

"I think he will if my father talks to him. I'll tell him to put in a good word."

"Thanks, Sam, I appreciate it."

Sam waved Mike's thanks away with a hand gesture. "Willie won't be coming by tonight. Him and Albie Haney went past the store about a half an hour ago and, if I know Willie, he was on his way to sneak into the Fairmount's second show. There's a good movie playin'."

"I know. *Flirtation Walk*. It's about West Point. Boy, I'd like to see that."

"Me, too."

Mike raised his eyes skyward. "You know who I'd like to see make a movie like that? Joan Crawford and William Haines. Or Joan Crawford and Johnny Mack Brown."

"Yeah, or Paul Muni and Sylvia Sidney."

"What about Mary Brian? She is one beautiful girl. Anita Page is, too."

"So are Joan Bennett and Fay Wray."

"And Shirley Temple."

"What? Shirley Temple is only six years old. She's a kid. She can't be beautiful."

"That's true, but twelve years from now she'll be a rich movie star, and I'll be famous. I'll bet she'll be a looker, too."

"I'm worried about you, Mike. There's something wacky about your thinking."

"Just joking. Hey, I met a girl named Naomi Weiss today. Would you say she's Jewish?"

"The name Weiss could be anything, but a Naomi Weiss has to be Jewish."

"That's what I figured. It doesn't matter, but I was just curious. She's nice."

"Where'd you meet her?"

"At a place called Eugene Debs Hall. It's on South Street between Eleventh and Twelfth."

"What the hell were you doin' there? Looking for a job?"

"No, Goldman invited me there. To a Socialist Party meeting."

Sam gave him a sober look. "I'd be careful about gettin' mixed up with any group Goldman's got anything to do with. I had him for freshman English and I never did like the guy."

Mike looked surprised. "You gotta be kidding, Sam. What could you have against him?"

"He's the kind that's always makin' trouble for other Jews, that's what! Why don't he leave things alone? The Jews ain't got enough trouble, that schmuck's gotta make more for us!"

"Gee, Sam, I didn't know you felt like that about him."

"That's because you're not a Jew."

"One thing you gotta admit. He's a damn good teacher."

"Then let him teach and quit stirrin' up trouble," Sam said with a scowl.

Mike had thought of going to the library for an hour or two but, after the Goldman comment, decided he'd stay with Sam a little longer. He might have something more to get off his chest. They walked silently to the corner, where they found the usual gang on the steps.

"Willie and Albie went down to sneak into the Fairmount," Vince Anderson said as Mike and Sam approached.

"They musta made it," Jake Hoyt added. "They ain't come back."

Paul Ennis started laughing. "Remember the time that big usher hit Willie right in the mouth the minute he stuck his head in the side door?"

"Do I," Nat Brennan said. "I was right behind Willie and the punch turned him around so his blood got all over my new sweater. Christ, the blood was pourin' outa his nose."

"You know they fired the big sonofabitch," Vince said. "The manager caught him lettin' his friends in the side door at half price."

"I heard he joined the Navy," Paul Ennis said.

"Good," Jake Hoyt snorted. "I hope he gets seasick."

"Where's Dutch and Stash?" Mike asked Dominic Angelo.

Dom took a dark, crooked de Nobili cigar out of his mouth and pointed up Twenty-Seventh Street.

"Take a guess," he said.

"You heard of a German dachshund?" Jack Lynch asked Mike.

Mike nodded his head.

"Well, Dutch is a German pussyhound," Lynch snickered.

"You mean they went to Aunt Sadie's?"

"No, dummy, they're up on Drean's steps talkin' to Marie and Ruth again."

Dominic was nineteen, and a sharp dresser who wore dark suits and snap-brim hats like his idol, actor Jack La Rue. Dom could afford to dress well. His brother Pat owned a fuel oil service, with three trucks delivering heating oil to rich people's houses in the suburbs. Dom drove one of the trucks, and Jack Lynch was his helper. Jack bought his suits from the same tailor Dom patronized, but somehow they didn't look as good on Lynch. Tonight, Mike noticed, Lynch wore the Episcopal Academy jacket he had stolen from one of the houses on their route.

"I hear the hosiery local plans to strike Eberle's," Fred Yancey announced gravely. "Joe Bruno was in the store tonight talkin' about it."

"No surprise," Dom said. "Eberle's been askin' for it the way they been cuttin' wages."

Fred nodded his head. "Joe says the knitters are gettin' half of what they were per dozen five years ago. They had a meetin' last night and Emil Schmidt, the vice-president of the Federation of Hosiery Workers, was there. Emil heard Eberle's may get a big order from a California department store chain and, if they do, that's when they're gonna call a strike."

"That's the time to hit the bastards, when you got them over a barrel," Dom said.

"How many people in the neighborhood work at Eberle's, Fred?" Lynch asked.

Fred stroked his tobacco-stained, gray moustache. "There must be twenty or thirty."

Chapter Six

Mike wore his father's suit to Mandel's for the job interview, and Mr. Mandel hired him.

"I like a boy who's neat," Mr. Mandel told him. "That shows self-respect."

He should see me when I'm not wearing my old man's suit, Mike thought to himself.

"A suit you don't need," Mandel added. "A nice pair of pants, a sweater, that's fine."

Jacob Mandel was a short, thin, long-nosed man, in his early fifties, with sparse, gray-black hair, and a sallow complexion. He suffered from stomach trouble and, to ease his distress, sucked endlessly on peppermint throat lozenges with a lip-pursing motion. Because of this, his mouth was always puckered, giving him a grave, purposeful air.

"You'll make deliveries, you'll help Esther with the soda fountain, you'll unpack and stock the shelves, you'll sweep the floor. But deliveries always come first. You got a bicycle?"

"No, sir" Mike answered.

"So you can walk. A young fellow like you can walk all day."

The next day, Mike met Rose at Strawmaker's during her lunch break, and she bought him three pairs of pants, three sweaters, two pairs of shoes, four shirts, and a warm jacket. The bill came to $28.95, and Rose said he could pay it off at a dollar a week.

Mike was excited when he got home and tried the clothes on again. He never had so many new clothes. The jacket alone had cost $5.95. It was dark green, and had a lighter-green circular patch on the left breast, into which the figure of a white knight had been woven. Lots of people would mistake him for a prep-school student, an athlete, working part-time after school. Now he wouldn't have to feel ashamed if Patricia came into the store while he was working.

Mike quickly fell into the routine of the job. Deliveries waited for him when he arrived at four o'clock, and they came first. Some well-off families living within five blocks west of the store relied heavily on medicine, both over-the-counter and prescription. Women from this group, particularly, seemed to suffer from every minor ill to which the flesh is heir, and relief was no farther away than a telephone call to Mandel's.

Mr. Mandel wrote the amount to be collected on the outside of the bag for each of the morning's orders. During one glorious, three-week, pre-Christmas period that also encompassed Hanukkah, Mike made a total of fifteen dollars in tips alone.

Poor people, on the other hand, only bought aspirin, laxatives, and liniment, which they came to the store to buy. His only source of income from the poor came from running telephone calls. The charge for summoning somebody to one of Mandel's public phones was five cents, and Mike frequently went unpaid because the people called to the store often didn't have a nickel to give him at the moment. However, they always promised to pay later, and most times they did.

Mike's second major chore was helping Esther Brodsky. He washed dishes at the soda fountain, cleared the tables in the store's three booths and, when Esther needed a break, he waited on customers.

Esther was the homeliest woman Mike had ever seen. Her black hair fell lankly around a thin face pitted with acne. The only protuberances on her chest were the collarbones that stuck up like two horns above the top of her green uniform. She wore thick, black-rimmed glasses and seldom smiled, but when she did, her lips uncovered more gum than teeth. Mike found it hard to believe any man could lust after Esther. Yet, she had a husband.

Abe and Esther lived in the flat above the drug store. Esther was distantly related to Mandel's wife, as their cousins had come from the same shtetl in Russian Poland, and Mandel—who owned the entire building—let them live in the apartment rent-free.

Abe was as boisterous as Esther was quiet... a tall, heavy-set man, blue-jowled, and already balding at twenty-nine. He worked in door-to-door sales of neckties, socks, handkerchiefs, cheap jewelry, and other sundries, which included condoms and French pictures. "Luftmensch," Mandel called him: someone scheming to get rich without working hard.

Sam couldn't stand the sight of him. "My father calls him the goniff," he told Mike.

"What's a goniff?"

"A crook," Sam said. "He's another one of them Jews who makes trouble for the rest of us. His parents should have stayed in Poland. We came from Germany, so did the Mandels."

"Is there a difference?" Mike asked.

"Of course there's a difference," Sam answered. "All the rich respectable Jews came from Germany. People like the Guggenheims and Bernard Gimbels."

"You surprise me sometimes, Sam, the way you talk."

"You're the only non-Jew I'd say things like that to," Sam said. "You know that."

"Sure, I know. And I'm honored. There's lots of Irish Catholics I'm not too proud of, either."

◆◆◆

In early February, Mike made his second visit to Eugene Debs Hall. He had called Goldman to explain his schedule and the teacher had seemed genuinely glad to hear from him.

"We were wondering what happened to you, Kane. We thought we had scared you off."

"I'm sure I can make it down sooner or later," Mike told him. "I mean, after I've had this job for a while, I can probably take off early some Tuesday night."

In the meantime, he made his first visit to Aunt Sadie's. It happened so fast he didn't know he was going there himself until he practically stepped in the front door.

One night, just about six o'clock, he was returning from a delivery when a pretty, light-skinned, colored girl came by and smiled at him. The girl continued a short distance and stopped in front of a store, looked in the window, then glanced back and beckoned to him.

She wore a tan coat and a bandanna wrapped around her hair, but he could see she was very pretty. He also knew he had three dollars and some change in his pocket, and a pack of rubbers Abe Brodsky had sold him. The excitement began to rise in him and when the girl motioned again, he walked slowly down the street and stood alongside her, staring unseeingly at the window display.

"You wanna go with me?" the girl said.

Mike could hardly get the words out. "Where to?"

"Just to the next corner. To the apartment above the grocery store."

She means Aunt Sadie's, he thought. She's one of the pretty girls Dutch and Doc are always talking about. Emboldened, he turned toward her and nodded dumbly.

"I'll walk on down and you follow me," the girl whispered. "I'll wait just inside the door."

He watched her and, when she turned into a door next to the grocery store, he followed. The door stood ajar and, when he entered, the girl closed it quickly and took his hand.

"What's your name, honey?"

"Mike," he croaked.

"My name's Louise."

At the top of the stairs she tapped lightly on another door.

"It's Louise, Miz Wilson. I have a friend with me."

The door opened and a dark-skinned, gray-haired woman stood in the doorway. She looked Mike up and down, and smiled warmly.

"Come in, young man."

Mike followed Louise in, and she went immediately into an adjoining room.

Mrs. Wilson invited him to sit down on one of the chairs surrounding a round, dining-room table. A lace cloth covered the table, and against one wall sat a large sofa with flowered, blue slipcovers, flanked by an Atwater Kent console radio. Against another wall, a china closet brimmed with dishes and shiny knick-knacks. Aunt Sadie—wearing an apron over a clean, blue housedress—fit perfectly into the bright, warm-looking room. She didn't resemble any brothel keeper Mike had ever imagined. He began to lose some of his nervousness.

"Louise won't be long," Aunt Sadie said. "She's just gone to put on her working clothes."

She pointed to a half-empty beer bottle on the table. "I was just having a glass of beer when you knocked. Would you like something to drink while you're waiting?"

"I sure could use a beer," Mike said and, Aunt Sadie went into the kitchen and returned with a bottle of Schmidt's and a glass. He poured the glass full and drank it down in two gulps.

"That will be two-fifty," Aunt Sadie said. "Two for Louise, and fifty cents for the beer."

Mike handed her the money and refilled his glass. Aunt Sadie sat down next to him.

"You were lucky to run into Louise on her way to work. Louise is the nicest girl I got."

Mike drank the rest of his beer in a gulp. He was feeling light-headed and he smiled.

The door opened and Louise stood in the doorway wearing a pink wrapper and a pair of pink slippers. She looked at Aunt Sadie and the older woman nodded and smiled.

"I'm ready, honey," Louise said.

Mike went in and found her standing by the bed in the middle of the small room. Then she let her pink wrapper drop.

Mike stared at her wide-eyed, drinking in the sight of his first naked female body, the vision he had fantasized through a hundred solitary sessions. He fumbled his clothes to the floor and Louise took the rubber he had clenched in his hand, and expertly slipped it on him.

"Always use a rubber, honey," she said while she laid his clothes neatly on a chair. "That way you don't have to worry about disease, or the girl gettin' pregnant."

Louise led him to the bed and lay down, and he settled himself between her outstretched legs. Louise guided him into her and he thrust once, and then tensed his muscles, trying desperately to hold back. But it was no use and he quickly huddled against her, spending himself.

"You sure were excited, honey," Louise said. She rubbed her hands along his back. "It'll be better next time. Everybody's always in a hurry the first time."

He rolled over and stood up, and she took a tissue, slid the soggy rubber off and dropped it daintily into a wastebasket. His penis was shriveled-up, looking ashamed of its shrunken proportions. He turned away from her to dress. So what if she knew it was his first time, he told himself defensively. He knew now what he'd do next time to make it last longer. He'd take on a load of beer before he paid his next visit, like some of the guys said they did.

Louise said, "You come back, Mike. I'm here almost every night from six o'clock on."

"I sure will, Louise," he said, forcing enthusiasm into his voice.

Aunt Sadie was reading when he came out, and she looked up and smiled at him.

"What's your name?"

"Mike," he said.

"Well, Mike, you're a well-behaved young man, and we'd be glad to see you any time you want to pay us a visit."

He took the jacket he had draped over a chair, while she walked over and unlatched the apartment door, and held it open for him.

"Thanks, Mrs. Wilson. I sure will come back now that I know you and Louise."

He went quickly out of the door and down the short hallway, and she called after him, "You can call me Aunt Sadie."

Outside, he took his Ingersoll watch out of his pocket and saw it was quarter past six. He had been at Aunt Sadie's just ten minutes. He started down Columbia Avenue, walking fast and grinning like a cat. *Well, Mike, you finally did it*, he told himself. You finally know what the inside of a girl feels like. His chest swelled and he sucked in his gut as he walked along. *Man, wait until I tell Willie about it*, he thought excitedly.

Old Willie would tear out his hair when he described Louise to him. Her pretty tits standing straight out with their big, purple-red nipples; her soft, round belly; and that beautiful ass. He should have played with her more, and the next time he damned well would. Next time he'd have her climbing the wall before he got started.

He checked how much money he had left. Seventy-three cents was all that remained of the Christmas-Hanukkah bonus. Jesus, he couldn't afford to go to Aunt Sadie's very often.

As he walked past the weathered, gray bulk of Saint Ludwig's looming in front of him, a familiar feeling of uneasiness settled over him. Christ, he hoped he didn't run into Father August or any of the nuns. The nuns would be shocked speechless if they knew what he had just done. But Old Augie knew the world was full of sinners, and he would stick a bony finger in your chest and spout off about fornicators and adulterers. Mike hurried past the front doors of the church, picturing Old Augie, bent over the altar, harshly intoning Latin prayers: *Agnus Dei qui tollis peccata mundi, misère nobis.* A lot of mercy he had for the sins of the world. All he ever talked about was hellfire and eternal damnation.

Mike Kane wasn't about to buy the church's superstitions anymore. He would never intentionally act cruelly or unjustly toward anybody, especially old people and little kids. If that

59

wasn't good enough... well, they could piss up a stump for all he cared.

Latin was a wonderful language, though, and he was glad his mother had made him serve as an altar boy. He began to recite another part of the Mass he particularly liked: *Et introibo ad altare Dei. Ad Deum qui laetificat juventutem meam.* Those last words meant the joy of your youth. What a laugh that was. If you partook of the joys of your youth, like doing it with a girl as pretty as Louise, Augie would have you burning in hell forever and ever.

✦✦✦

Well past the church, Mike finally began to breathe more easily. When he got back to the store, Abe Brodsky sat at the soda counter eating a tuna fish sandwich, and he climbed up on the stool next to him. The small blobs of mayonnaise sticking out of the corners of Abe's mouth made Mike queasy.

"How they hangin', kid?" Abe asked.

"Hiya, Abe," he said. He could really have made Abe's eyes pop if he told him where he had just come from. He had too much respect for Esther, though, to even pretend to understand Abe's inquiry about the pendency of his testicles, let alone talk about Aunt Sadie's in front of her.

"Would you like a tuna fish, Michael?" Esther asked him in her quiet, serious voice. Free sandwiches were one of the fringe benefits that went with the job, and Mike had gained five pounds since starting to work.

"I sure would, Esther. I ate supper before I came to work, but I'm getting hungry again."

She placed the sandwich in front of him and he ate it with deliberate daintiness—trying, by example, to teach Abe some table manners. Abe was incorrigible, though. He finished off his glass of seltzer water and belched loudly.

"Did you hear about Eberle's?" Abe asked. "They're goin' on strike."

"No," Mike said. "When?"

"Next Monday. Unless the company gives in. Charlie Hubbell was telling me about it."

Mr. Mandel came from behind the prescription counter, a concerned look on his face.

"The company won't give in," he said. "They'll do like Essex did two years ago—close up and move south. In the South they don't have labor unions."

"That shows how much you know," Abe said. "The union's usin' tactics. Eberle's got a big order, and they gotta fill it now, or lose it."

"So, they'll get non-union labor, fill the big order, and then they'll move south."

Abe raised an eyebrow and shook his head. "It's no use talkin' to him. He still thinks he's back in the old country."

"Abe!" Esther admonished.

"Mr. Mandel may be right," Mike said.

"You hear, Meschugenah?" Mr. Mandel pointed a finger at Abe. "Even the boy knows more than you do."

He looked at Mike and tapped his temple, then turned and walked back to the prescription department. Mike followed him.

"Mr. Mandel, could I come in at twelve-thirty tomorrow and leave at five thirty? I got some personal business I need to take care of."

Mandel popped a fresh peppermint lozenge and shrugged. "So, you'll come in at twelve-thirty."

◆◆◆

The meeting was already in progress when Mike arrived the next evening, and Goldman himself answered Mike's timid knock at the door. With an effusive greeting, Goldman pulled him into the room. A number of people sat around a large, square table—among them Sylvia Weiss and Naomi. Mrs. Weiss stood up.

"It's nice to see you again," she said, smiling warmly. "We thought we scared you off."

Mike smiled at her and looked around uncomfortably as everyone stared at him.

"I wasn't scared," he mumbled. "I work nights and couldn't come."

"Well, we're glad you could come tonight." She turned to Goldman.

"Lester, Mr. Kane can sit next to Naomi."

Two empty chairs remained on Naomi's right, and Mr. Goldman led him to the one next to her, and sat down in the other.

"Folks," he said, "this is Michael Kane, a former student of mine." He pointed around the table rapidly calling out names. "Okay," he said when he finished, "where were we?"

"Talking about the Yankees' chances of winning the pennant," a short, fat man called out.

"They haven't got a chance," another man said. "Detroit's a shoo-in again."

Mr. Goldman held up his hand. "What's our visitor going to think? He's here to listen to us save the world, and he finds us arguing about baseball."

"Ask him what he thinks of the Yankees' chances," the fat man said.

"Kane may be the only genuine proletarian present at this middle-class gathering," Goldman continued.

"Don't knock the middle-class, Lester," the fat man said. "It's provided us with every revolutionary leader from Jefferson to Lenin. Trotsky was the only exception. He was born in a mud hut. He was also the only Jew in the bunch."

Amidst a burst of laughter, Mr. Goldman turned to Mike. "Aaronson, the fat proletarian, fancies himself as the local Bernard Shaw, but don't let him fool you. If Trotsky was born in a clay hut, it had five rooms. And his father could have afforded better. He was a kulak who squeezed his kopecks. Besides, Trotsky wasn't the only Jew in the bunch."

Aaronson addressed Mike. "I'll make two points, Kane. First, clay is a substance made of mud. Point two, a kulak is a prosperous peasant and, by definition, not a member of the middle class." He turned to Goldman and held up his hand. "And spare me the litany, Lester. I know Martov, Axelrod, Kamenev and Zinoviev were Jews. But I was talking about *leaders*."

"You're right, Harry, and I apologize," Goldman said. "Marx was neither Jewish nor a revolutionary leader."

"Marx was a theoretician," Aaronson insisted. "*The* theoretician. But he didn't get physically involved in any revolutions, not in 1848, or in the Paris Commune in 1871."

Goldman started to answer, but Sylvia Weiss interrupted him. "Please, Lester, let's get on with the meeting." She turned and addressed a tall man in a clerical collar.

"Andy, will you read the membership report?" The Reverend Andrew Lane adjusted his spectacles and began to read from a paper in front of him.

Mike was sorry to see the exchange of views end. He had enjoyed it tremendously, but Naomi, slumped in the chair next to him, seemed bored. She leaned over and whispered, "Harry Aaronson's a fat bore. Always showing off. Lester can't stand him and neither can I."

Sylvia Weiss whispered, "Naomi, you know that's not true. Harry and Lester are good friends." She looked at Mike. "Mr. Kane, Naomi's at an age where she can't stand any man who doesn't look like actor Nils Asther in *The Bitter Tea*. And she's a great exaggerator."

Mike responded impulsively. "Please don't call me Mr. Kane, Mrs. Weiss."

"Okay, Michael, I won't, if you'll call me Sylvia."

The Reverend Lane droned on and was succeeded by Harry Aaronson, who read a financial report. Listening with half an ear, Mike gathered that the Philadelphia branch of the Socialist Party had few members and little money.

In the chair next to him, Naomi stirred restlessly. She reached over to his coat, hanging on the back of his chair, and stroked the white knight emblem. "I like this," she whispered. "Is it a school jacket?"

He shook his head. "It's just a coat."

Discarding propriety, she abruptly stood up. "Would you like a soda?" Without waiting for an answer, she took his hand, pulled him to his feet, and led him through a swinging door of a small kitchen. She opened a refrigerator door. "Do you want grape or cream?"

"Cream. Cream soda is my favorite."

"Mine, too."

They stood leaning against the refrigerator door taking deep slugs of cream soda.

"How old are you?" Naomi asked. "I'm seventeen."

"Me, too." Well, he would be in three months, so it wasn't much of a lie.

Naomi prattled on, her big, brown eyes fastened on his face. "My mother was already married at seventeen and I was born nine months later, so I guess my parents didn't have to get married. She was a freshman in college, and my father was a senior and getting ready to enter law school. Now he's a lawyer and works for the Labor Department in Washington. They got divorced when I was eleven. Incompatibility they called it, and you know what that means."

Mike took a long drink of his soda to hide his shock. Jesus, this girl could talk, and the things she talked about—like her own mother and father. Either she was half an idiot, or one of God's holy innocents who knew not what she spoke.

"After my father graduated from law school, my mother went back to Temple University to finish. Now she teaches at Simon Gratz, and I'm a senior there. I'm going to graduate in June, and in September I'm going to college. I'll go to Temple, probably. I don't think we can afford to send me to Bryn Mawr where my mother would really like me to go. I'm glad I'm not going to Bryn Mawr. I wouldn't want to go to a school that's just for girls."

"That's one of the things I didn't like about Central," Mike heard himself saying airily. "They only had boys there."

"Yes, but it's easy for boys to meet girls. Boys only have to ask them for a date."

"You're right," he agreed. "Meeting girls is certainly no problem."

"Have you got a girlfriend?"

"Well, there's a couple of girls I go out with sometimes, but I don't have a steady girl," Mike said, the words flowing effortlessly. *You lying bastard, you never had a date in your life*, he thought. This girl was so easy to hand a line, though. He was turning into a regular Willie Bruno.

"I had a steady boyfriend for a while, but two years ago he left for college and we lost track of each other. His name was Marvin Steinberg. He went to Yale."

"Yale," Mike said the word reverently. "That's where Albie Booth went." When Naomi looked at him nonplussed, he added, "He was a football player."

"Lester was a football player."

"He sure was, and a good one, too."

"Lester says you like to read."

"I sure do."

"Who are your favorite authors?"

"Ernest Hemingway, Mark Twain, George Bernard Shaw, H. G. Wells, Jack London, Sinclair Lewis, Upton Sinclair, and Lincoln Steffens."

"I like Sinclair Lewis, too. Have you read *Elmer Gantry*?"

"Sure I read it, and I own a copy of the book."

"I hope it didn't shock you. Some of the language is pretty raw."

Mike snorted. "Shock me? You must be kidding. Have you read Balzac's *Droll Tales*? Or, how about Boccaccio's *Decameron*? What about *Candide*?"

Naomi giggled and shook her head. "No, I haven't. But, I bet you haven't read *Lady Chatterley's Lover*. My mother hid a copy, and doesn't know I found it."

Mike couldn't top that. He had heard about the Lawrence book, but had never read it.

"Would you like to come back to our apartment after the meeting? We mostly sit around and talk, and listen to music."

"Sure, but do you think your mother will mind?"

"I know she won't. She likes you. I can tell. You don't talk too much, like I do."

"She's nice, your mother."

Naomi shrugged. "I guess so."

The door opened and Mr. Goldman looked around the door to see them. "The meeting's over, kids."

They went back out into the meeting room. Everyone had left except the Reverend Lane and his wife Harriet, and Sylvia Weiss, who circled the room emptying ashtrays and straightening out chairs. Harriet Lane—a tall, slender, plain-looking blonde in her early thirties—presented a nice smile and small breasts that jounced attractively as she moved around the room.

Naomi came over and stood alongside Mike. "We live on Pine Street, between Ninth and Tenth. It's only three blocks from here."

She opened the door, and they walked together in uncomfortable silence along the dimly lit corridor, down the stairway, and through the front door. On their heels came the others, and they all started east on South Street, the three women walking together in front.

Lester Goldman stepped beside him. "Well, Kane, did you enjoy yourself? Did Harry Aaronson enlighten you with his exposition of the middle-class roots of the Socialist movement?"

"He sure did. I really enjoyed the argument between you and him."

"You know as well as I that Harry's right, Lester," the Reverend Lane said. "Every militant radical leader I can think of, from the Gracchi to the Adams family, was middle class."

"Of course, he's right."

"Then why do you argue with him?"

"Because I'm a Jew and he's a Jew. It's the nature of Jews to argue with each other. They say factionalism is the curse of all radical movements, but the real curse is their Jewishness. Thank God Norman Thomas is a nice, non-abrasive Presbyterian." He smiled at Lane. "And that you're a nice, non-abrasive Unitarian."

He turned to Mike. "Don't get the idea that all we do is read reports and argue, Kane. We do that only ninety-nine percent of the time."

"And the other one percent?"

"We write letters to the editors of the *Bulletin,* the *Inquirer*, the *Ledger*, the *Daily News*, and even, sometimes, to the *New York Times*, protesting against social inequities."

"Almost none of which ever get printed," Goldman added.

"We support strikes and demonstrations for racial justice. Andy was in Peekskill, New York, not long ago, marching in a protest parade with Paul Robeson—"

"And got myself arrested."

"At election time we support political candidates—"

"None of whom ever win, except on occasion in places like Reading and Milwaukee."

"But we're not quite as ineffectual as Andy makes us sound. As Norman Thomas said, without political agitation, Roosevelt's New Deal reforms would never have happened."

"If you're looking for a strike to support, Mr. Goldman," Mike said, "a lot of men in my neighborhood are getting ready to go on one."

"Is that so. When?"

"Next Monday. They're going to strike Eberle's Hosiery mill."

"Oh, the American Federation of Hosiery workers, Local One." He looked at Lane, grimacing.

"What do you think, Andy?"

Andy looked down and shook his head. "I'll call Emil Schmidt tomorrow and see what we can do to help."

"We can always walk the picket line and sing *Solidarity Forever.*"

"And maybe restrain the violent impulses of our Communist friends."

"They'll be there all right, breaking windows and taunting the police."

They caught up to the three women waiting for them under the canopy of the apartment building, and walked into the lobby as a group.

"I love our apartment," Naomi whispered in Mike's ear. "It's on the fourth floor."

When the elevator ascended, she took his hand and pulled him to the rear of the car.

"Do you like to dance?"

"I don't know how."

She clapped her hands. "Good, I'll teach you. We have lots of dance records. But we'll have to get to the Victrola first, before Lester puts on the Paul Robeson records."

"I like Paul Robeson," Mike said. "I saw him act in *Emperor Jones*."

Naomi shrugged. "He's all right. But it's hard to dance to *The Ballad of Joe Hill*."

The elevator stopped and they walked down a carpeted hallway. Goldman unlocked the door and stepped aside to let the others enter. It was the nicest apartment Mike had ever seen. A number of prints depicting Paris street scenes hung on the wall. A long, low sofa, and some comfortable chairs were placed around two low tables. A crammed bookcase caught his eye, next to a desk holding a typewriter, a radio, and a Victrola. An adjacent magazine rack brimmed with magazines including *The Nation, New Republic, New Yorker, Esquire, Vanity Fair*, and *New York Times Book Reviews*.

"Naomi, you take the coats into the bedroom," her mother said, "and Harriet and I will get some snacks and drinks. Let's see, Andy and Lester like beer, and Harriet red wine. Michael, what would you like to drink?"

"If you don't mind, I'd like a beer."

She looked at Goldman. "What do you think, Lester? Is he allowed to have a beer?"

"Do you drink much beer, Kane?" Mr. Goldman asked.

Mike grinned. "As much as I can afford."

"Then I guess one beer won't hurt him."

When Sylvia came back with a tray of beer and glasses. Mike took his and walked over to the bookcase. He knew it would be full of great authors, and wasn't disappointed. When the two older women returned to the living room with trays of food, Naomi followed them out of the kitchen. She walked toward him with a tall glass in her hand.

"Wait till you taste my drink," she whispered. "My mother thinks it's grape soda. Let's go into the kitchen."

From the kitchen door, she turned toward the sofa where her mother sat. "Mother, Michael and I are going into the kitchen. I'm going to teach him how to dance."

"Why don't you dance in here, dear, so we can all watch?"

"Because Michael will be embarrassed if he has to learn in front of a bunch of people," Naomi said with a frown. She turned to Mike. "Won't you?"

He nodded his head.

"All right, dear, but he may be hungry and want some pumpernickel and cheese."

Naomi made a petulant face. "We won't want to dance smelling like cheese."

Mike followed her into the kitchen and she handed him her glass. Her eyes shone with excitement. "Taste it. It's dago red. My mother gets it from a man on the first floor."

Mike swallowed a mouthful and made a face. "It's strong."

"Drink some more," she urged. "You drink half and I'll drink half."

He half-emptied the glass and handed it back to her. While she drained it, he took a swallow of beer and felt the warmth spreading through his body. Naomi looked at him, her face flushed. "I'll get some dance music on the radio."

She moved to a radio on the kitchen counter and turned it on. The music came faintly through the sound of static and she fiddled with the knobs until it came through more clearly.

"You hear that? It's Wayne King from the Aragon Ballroom in Chicago."

She began to sway back and forth, as a tinny voice said, "You're listening to Wayne King and his orchestra from the Aragon Ballroom in downtown Chicago. Now get ready to shake a leg as Wayne and the boys play another set of danceable tunes, leading off with 'Love is Just Around the Corner.'"

Naomi stretched out her arms invitingly, and Mike grinned at her. "You'll have to show me how first. I don't even know how to begin."

She smiled back at him, her cheeks even rosier from the wine. "Stand alongside me and watch my feet, I'll show you the box step. It's easy."

He stood at her side and watched as she danced around the kitchen, demonstrating the step, and singing the words of the song.

"See? You can use the box step for any song, fast or slow. Just follow the tempo."

She stopped dancing and pointed at his feet. "Now, you try it!"

He began haltingly, and shuffled clumsily around the kitchen. After a while, though, he began to move in time to the music. When the band began "All I Do is Dream of You," he stopped, helpless.

"Keep going!" she ordered. "Just follow the new tempo."

He began again awkwardly, then suddenly found his feet adjusting to the slower beat. Naomi slid into his arms, and he began to stumble again. "What do I do now?"

"Boys have to lead, Michael," she cooed. She adjusted his hand to the small of her back. "Hold me tightly enough so I can feel you guiding me wherever you want me to go."

They started again and immediately, magically, moved together to the rhythmic pattern of the music. The next song was "Have a Little Dream On Me," and he made the transposition to the new tempo faultlessly. By the time the band began the slow, dreamy music of "Moonglow," he and Naomi were dancing cheek to cheek.

"You're going to be a wonderful dancer," she murmured in his ear.

"That's because you're a great teacher," he whispered.

She lifted her face to him and he leaned down and kissed her open mouth. He felt their tongues meet, and the smooth shapes of her breasts and pelvis straining against him. The erection that began as soon as they started dancing, bulged against the front of his pants. He knew she must feel it and he pulled away, ashamed.

They looked at each other. "You've got lipstick all over you," Naomi said, laughing.

"You, too."

He handed her his handkerchief and she wiped her lips clean. Then she wiped his, wetting the handkerchief with the tip of her tongue to rub out the more stubborn stains. She stepped back and examined him.

"Do I look all right?"

She nodded her head. "And, how about me?"

"Your hair's mussed up."

A mirror hung on the wall over the sink and, while she patted her hair into place and straightened out her dress, he turned his back to her and wrestled the erection up under his belt and cinched it down.

Girls were lucky they didn't have to worry about the old dong rising up suddenly and poking out the front of their pants for the world to see. It happened all the time, on crowded streetcars, subways, and elevators—whenever a guy happened to rub up against some girl's body.

Naomi finished her primping and turned. "Are you coming to the next meeting?"

"I don't think I can get off work that often. About once a month is probably more like it."

She looked disappointed, and he smiled. "But, I will if I can."

"If you can't come, you could call me on the phone. I'm home from school every day by three, and my mother never gets home before four."

"I'll, for sure, call you then, Naomi," he said.

She took his hand and smiled happily. "Let's go into the living room and show them how well you can dance. I'll put on some Guy Lombardo records. He's easy to dance to."

He pulled away. "Please, Naomi, let's wait until I have a few more lessons before I put on a public exhibition."

"Okay, Michael." She leaned forward and kissed him quickly. "Don't you just love to French kiss?" she whispered.

He bobbed his head. "Do I ever."

Chapter Seven

At first, the union strike was exciting but, by the end, a wretched thing to watch. After it ended, what impressed Mike most was the total incompatibility of the two sets of humans engaged in the struggle. Both sides might have originated on different planets, speaking strange languages, so complete was their inability to reach out to one another. Sadly, what started with a lot of rhetoric and no comprehension on either side, soon ended in bloodshed and arrests.

Benevolence oozed from every managerial pore when mill leaders announced the glad tidings of a sizable new order secured, allowing workers to go back on fulltime work immediately, with the prospects of overtime a likely possibility. They might have foretold the coming of the plague, judging from the glum faces of the union workers who received the news.

We need more money, the workers responded. A dime a dozen more for the knitters, eight cents for the boarders and toppers, and a nickel for the hourly rate workers. We also need a union contract, mandating a closed shop, a check-off system for the collection of union dues, and time-and-a-half for overtime.

Impossible, the bosses said with genuine shock in their voices. To underbid our competitors, we shaved the profit margin to nearly nothing. And, on the matter of a union contract, they responded with voices rising as if entering a spiritual realm, there is a sacred right involved, the inalienable right to freely dispose of lawfully acquired property.

"Property hath no rights!" a man shouted. "The Earth is the Lord's and the fruits thereof." He was a Communist who believed religion served as the opiate of the people.

There's work for men who want it, the bosses said.

Some men were persuaded. John Powers, the shop foreman, and all of his clan, who lived on George and Cambridge Streets, said they'd work. They had kids to feed.

"You dirty scabs!" other Irishmen shouted at their fellow refugees from potato famines, as the police escorted them past the picket lines.

At the outset, Mike enjoyed the excitement engendered by the strike. The neighborhood was solid in its support of the union workers. Rappaport and other landlords told workers to pay what they could from the strike benefits, and there were no threats of eviction. Merchants extended credit and donated food. Dominic Angelo provided a panel truck, and Georgie Hubbell volunteered to drive it. Every morning, Mike and Willie, with Fred Yancey in charge, made the rounds picking up bags of day-old bread and cakes from the German bakery, sacks of bruised fruit from Max Schwarz, and cold cuts and cheese from the local deli. Mandel sent a first-aid kit and aspirins, and Mrs. Williams provided bottles of soda, candy, and a few cigarettes.

Abe Brodsky showed up for an hour or two every day, always with a new dirty joke. "You know how Marlene Dietrich likes to wear mannish clothes, so she can use the men's toilets in restaurants. Well, one day she was tellin' Mae West how comical it was to watch men takin' a piss, each one holding his cock in a different way."

At that point, Abe demonstrated a variety of grips: the dainty, two-finger purchase, the back-hand grasp, and so on.

"Well, Marlene," Mae told her, "if you ever see a man holdin' it like this..." Abe pantomimed a man holding his penis with both hands like a baseball bat. "Tell him to come up to see me sometime."

Lester Goldman and the Reverend Lane showed up often and walked the picket line. Mostly, though, they organized rallies and raised money for the strike fund. One day, Sylvia Weiss came with them, stunning in a wide-brimmed hat and brightly painted lips and fingernails. She came over to talk to Mike, and Willie stared at her, impressed. He was even more impressed when they engaged in animated conversation, calling each other "Michael" and "Sylvia."

"Who the hell was that?" Willie asked after she left.

"Mr. Goldman's girlfriend. You know, our English teacher. We gave him a ride from the Rec when we were junkin'."

"Oh, him! Well, one thing I'll say, he sure has got himself a good lookin' girlfriend."

Delegations from other unions came up to show their solidarity with fellow workers. Some of them were Communists, efficient and dedicated men, and talented hecklers of the police. When the scabs got off the streetcar and walked to Eberle's mill, the police herded the strikers to the other side of the street to avoid confrontation. Some of the houses on that side had porch fronts, and from the safety of the porches the hecklers screamed insults at the police.

"Lackeys! Ass kissers! Cossacks!"

The red-faced police on the lunging horses, who had never been closer to Russia's Don River than the banks of the Liffey, glared angrily and shouted back, "You Communist sonsabitches!"

Red Donovan got himself an old mayonnaise jar, cut a slot in the lid, and covered it neatly with adhesive tape— shoplifted from the five-and-ten—on which he wrote in neat, red letters, "Hosiery Local Strike Fund. Please Help!"

He worked the prosperous parts of Girard Avenue, collecting donations, which he stuck in his pocket. Somebody saw him, though, and told Caz Nowicki. Caz caught Red coming out of Rafferty's and slapped him around. He made him turn his pockets inside out, and told him if he did it again, he'd make a girl out of him by kicking his testicles up into his chest.

They sat around at night and Doc Greene told stories of famous strikes of the past. For instance, the strike against the Pittsburgh Iron and Steel Works at Homestead, Pennsylvania, back in the 1890s, when Andrew Carnegie hired armed Pinkerton detectives who fought bloody battles to put those strikes down. Also, he described how a young anarchist named Alexander Berkman shot Henry Frick, Carnegie's strike field commander, thus fixing in the public mind an image of the unions allied with anarchy.

One old-timer, born in Scranton, Pennsylvania's, anthracite region shortly after the Civil War, told them about the Molly Maguires: Irish miners, driven mad by conditions worse than slavery, who fought the mine owners with the weapons of terror and murder.

"The companies owned the coal towns," he said, "so everybody bought in the company stores and never got out of debt. However, the Pinkertons broke the Molly Maguires. They planted spies among them who testified against the companies in court, and twenty Mollies were hung."

Doc Greene said, "You know where the Pinkertons got their training and experience from? They ran the Union spy service during the Civil War."

Mike could hardly wait to see what excitement each new day might bring but, strangely, it never entered his mind to write about it. He thought about that after the strike, and decided it was because he was only a spectator of the event, and not a participant. That rationalized his inaction. Excusing his curious writer's block was becoming a habit for him.

He called Naomi one afternoon from Mandel's to tell her about his activities.

"My mother said she talked to you, and that you're right in the middle of things," Naomi sounded thrilled. "She says you're a young John L. Lewis."

"You're mother's just being nice," Mike said. "I'm not doing anything big."

The weather got colder and the violence started; not romanticized violence out of movies, but close-in, nasty stuff, accompanied by the sounds of broken bones, smashed teeth, and groaning.

Caz Nowicki sparked the violence one Sunday night. Mike and his father were eating supper when a knock sounded on the door. Paddy went to answer it, and came back to the kitchen with Caz, Dominic Angelo, and Jack.

Mike was embarrassed by their meager supper of hot dogs and cold, boiled, potatoes eaten right out of the pot. He still smiled at the visitors. "You guys want some hot tea?"

"We ain't got time," Caz said. "We're collectin' old paint, whitewash, dirty engine oil—anything that splatters and makes a mess when you throw it through somebody's window."

"I think we got part of a can of whitewash," Paddy said. "But it's probably dried up."

Caz looked at Mike. "Go get it, kid." When Mike brought it from the cellar, they discovered it was rock hard. "Thanks anyhow," Caz said. "We'll try Joe Bruno next."

Mike followed them out. "What are you gonna do with the stuff?"

"Pay a visit to Mr. John Powers and his friends," Caz said as he drove away.

"Pop, did you hear what those crazy guys are gonna do?"

Paddy took a potato out of the pot and shook some salt on it. "Sure, I heard."

"But it's not right!"

"Maybe not, but Powers ain't right to scab it, either. Workin' men gotta stick together."

"But Powers has six kids!" Mike protested.

He could see the paint cans crashing through the window, fouling the rugs and furniture, paid for at a dollar a week, and hear the crying of the frightened children.

"Why don't they drive out to the Main Line and throw paint cans at Eberle's windows?"

"Mike, they'd never get near that house. Eberle's got guard dogs, and police protection."

"So the rich get off, and the poor beat up the poor. That's not right, is it?"

Paddy stuffed the potato into his mouth and mumbled around it. "They got ya comin' and goin'."

That night they hit twelve houses, with Dominic driving, and Caz and Lynch throwing from one side of the car or the other. They worked quickly, starting at one o'clock in the morning. Fifteen minutes later, they said they drove away grinning like wolves.

The next day, only half the scabs showed up and John Powers was not among them. The talk was maybe the fink bastard had learned a lesson, and maybe Eberle would, too.

Instead, Eberle hired a security unit, led by Johnny Brannigan, an ex-New York City detective who often got his name in Walter Winchell's column. Winchell called him "the scourge of the New York underworld," and told how he had once slapped Legs Diamond around.

No one doubted Brannigan's toughness. One morning, someone from the porches on Allegheny yelled at him. "Hey, Brannigan, you'd eat shit if they paid you!" Brannigan charged the porch so suddenly that he reached the heckler, broke the man's jaw, and bulled his way back to the pavement, untouched.

The strike dragged on in the cold November weather, and the bitterness on the picket line increased. Especially after the strike breakers from Reading and Lancaster showed up and the strikers' confidence in ultimate victory gave way to angry desperation and violence. Before the strike ended, most of the militants found themselves in jail. Willie's father Joe Bruno, Jake Hoyt's Uncle Joey, and Georgie Hubbell's brother Charlie, all did thirty days in Holmesburg for resisting arrest. Caz Nowicki got six months for aggravated assault after he wrestled a nightstick away from a policeman and threw it onto a roof.

Paradoxically, the strike was almost broken by Franklin D. Roosevelt when he introduced the Work Projects Administration (WPA). As the strike fund dwindled, so did the strike benefits, and men who had walked the picket line religiously began to disappear to look for real jobs. The WPA touted three and a half million jobs for the asking... or almost for the asking. In most localities, the politicians got their hands on the program and, in the 26th Ward, you couldn't get on the WPA rolls unless Harry Dooley gave his okay. Dooley only okayed registered Republicans. Even Joe Bruno changed his party when he got out of jail, and Joe considered Roosevelt, along with Garibaldi, the two greatest men who ever lived.

Puzzled, Mike asked Doc Greene how Democrats expected to benefit from the WPA if Republicans ran it?

Doc laughed. "You must be kiddin', Mike. Harry Dooley can pull his shenanigans, but Roosevelt knows how they'll vote when those curtains are pulled shut."

Still, the strike went on, with the picket line staffed by hardliners who swore they would keep walking if they had to do it barefoot. They were still walking when Eberle made good on Mr. Mandel's prediction by closing down the mill and moving to Jackson, Mississippi. It happened over the long Memorial Day weekend, which fell on a Thursday that year, and when the pickets saw the closed mill they broke in, busted up the knitting machines, and shattered the windows.

Mike was glad Eberle took Powers and his relatives to Jackson with him. Besides that, he could point to nothing positive that came of it. To Mike, the situation represented a disgusting example of human waste and stupidity, and he hoped he would never witness it again.

✦✦✦

At Sylvia Weiss' apartment after the strike, the socialists conducted a post-mortem. The Reverend Lane, late of Yale and the Union Theological Seminary, summed up his take on it. "The guy that caused the attitude of men like Eberle is William Graham Sumner."

"He was a professor at Yale," Harry Aaronson explained to Mike. "He wrote a book called *Folkways* which says people are so set in their ways it's a waste of time trying to reform them."

"There's more," Lane continued. "He was a Social Darwinist, a disciple of Herbert Spencer. He believed natural selection operates as inexorably in the social sphere as it does among plants and animals. And, since he taught at Yale for forty years, he filled generations of future tycoons with the notion that they were successful because they were inherently more capable than other men, and that the less capable fell by the wayside as a result of competition."

"You know there's a guy in my neighborhood named Doc Greene—Doc is only a nickname—and he talks a lot like Sumner, yet he would enjoy our conversation. He doesn't believe Socialism can work," Mike said.

Goldman grinned. "Bring him down here and we'll sic Aaronson on him."

"He wouldn't come, but he has strong views on things. He went to the University of Pennsylvania for two years, then fought in the war, and later became rich, as a bootlegger."

"So what does he say?"

"He says only two things really interest most men. One is money, and the other is..." Mike hesitated before blurting out the word, "sex."

Harriet Lane giggled. "Anybody who thinks that highly of sex can't be all bad."

"Tell him we plan to have sex under socialism," Harry Aaronson said.

"So you're friend's a cynic, Kane," Lester Goldman said. "So what else is new?"

"Give Michael a chance," Sylvia protested. "Go on, what else does your friend say?"

"He says people are not good enough to be socialists, any more than they're good enough to be Christians. You know the Sermon on the Mount and all that stuff."

"Has your friend got something against Jews?" Aaronson asked. "Why doesn't he knock the Ten Commandments? They don't work either."

"Harry!" Sylvia scolded.

"He says if people were decent and unselfish enough to be socialists, then any system would work. Even capitalism. He says a benign form of capitalism is a lot easier for him to imagine than socialism because it conforms more closely to man's true nature."

Aaronson grunted. "Benign capitalism is a contradiction in terms."

"I may not agree with him," Mike added, "but that's what he says."

"Are you finished, Mike?" Andy Lane asked.

"Yeah, that's it."

"He's right about sex," Lane said. "But your friend is denying that man has a spiritual nature. He's saying the possibility of salvation doesn't exist."

"Man doesn't live by bread alone," Aaronson said, "not even Jewish rye."

Goldman got to his feet. "Be quiet, Harry. It's my turn at bat." He turned to Mike. "You're friend's putting the cart before the horse, Kane. He says people are not good enough to be socialists, meaning they are motivated by self-interest. But he doesn't say it's the present system that makes selfishness inevitable. Defenders of capitalism say a man acting solely in his own interest is somehow guided by Adam Smith's 'invisible hand' to advance the social good. Well, we say that's crap, and we've got the whole sorry history of the nineteenth and twentieth centuries as proof."

Naomi, obviously bored, decided to excuse herself. "I'm going to play some music on the kitchen radio." She beckoned to Mike, and he followed her.

"Try that argument on your friend," Goldman called out after him.

"I will," Mike promised, but he knew it would be a waste of time. He would never tell Mr. Goldman, but Doc had called both him and Norman Thomas "arrested adolescents."

In the kitchen, Naomi looked at him archly. "I hope you noticed I'm not wearing any lipstick." She leaned over and kissed him. "I'll get you a beer."

She handed him a beer just as Harry Aaronson came in, a broad smile on his face. "I got two tickets to the ballgame. You want them, Mike?"

He held out the tickets and Mike took them. "Gee, thanks, Mr. Aaronson."

"Don't thank me. I did a guy on the sports desk a favor and he gave them to me. But they're bleacher seats, the cheapskate."

"I hate baseball," Naomi said.

Aaronson laughed. "So he'll take somebody else." He turned and left.

Mike took a long slug of his beer. "By the time I'm his age, I'll be rich, and I'll have done everything I want to do. After that, I'll just give a speech once in a while and take up painting."

Naomi burst out laughing. "You are quite the wit, Mike."

Chapter Eight

Mike walked into Rose's house. He had a key, and brought his family's weekly dirty laundry stuffed into a pillowcase. He walked to the kitchen. "Anybody home?"

He received no answer, so he put the laundry on a kitchen chair. When he opened the door to leave, he heard the toilet flush. He shouted, "Is that you, Rose?"

"No, it's me," Teresa's voice answered, and a moment later she came down the stairs.

"I dropped off our laundry. The damp wash goes out tomorrow."

He pulled out his Ingersoll and looked at it. It was only three o'clock.

"How come you're home so early?"

"I took off early," Teresa mumbled. "I don't feel well."

They hadn't talked since the night he had told her about Red hustling queers, and he smiled at her. She sure didn't look well. The pale of her face emphasized red, puffy eyes.

"What's the matter with you?"

She turned away and walked into the kitchen. Mike followed her.

"What's the matter?" he repeated.

"I've got a splitting headache," she answered.

"Make yourself a cup of tea and take some aspirin, then go lie down."

The teapot was on the stove. Mike carried it to the sink and began to fill it with water.

"Here, I'll make it for you. I'll even have one with you."

She looked at him, shook her head, then put her face in her hands and started to cry.

He patted her on the shoulder. "You've got more than a headache, Treese. Talk to me." When she shook her head, he pleaded, "Please stop crying and tell me what's wrong."

"You can't help me," she said between sobs. "It's too late." She raised her head and gave him a stricken look. "I think I'm pregnant." Her voice had risen to a wail. "What am I gonna do?"

"Is it Red Donovan?"

She nodded.

He furrowed his brow. "Does he know?"

Teresa spoke through clenched teeth, her eyes narrow, and her hands in the air. "He said it was my problem! He said how did he know it was his!"

"The sonofabitch," Mike muttered. He began to improvise a plan to help.

"Look, Treese, here's what we'll do. We'll find one of those homes where girls go to have babies, somewhere a long way from here, in another state. You go there before you begin to show, and stay awhile after the baby's born, finding good parents for adoption. We'll make up some kind of a story to tell people. Maybe say you're going away to study nursing. Then, after it's all over, you come back and say you didn't like nursing. Nobody will be the wiser."

She stared at him. "Do you think we can find a home like that?'

"Sure we can. All the different religions have them, and they run adoption agencies, too." Reverend Andy Lane and the Unitarians came to mind. *All those New Englanders have loads of money. They must have dozens of homes like that,* Mike thought.

He raced on, his voice brimming with confidence. "In fact, I know just the man can help us. He's a Protestant minister. He's a great guy, and a good friend of mine. And I mean a really good friend. You don't even have to meet him. I'll take care of everything."

Teresa threw her arms around him. "Do you really think you can do it?"

"I know I can do it. You just quit worrying and leave everything to me. God knows I owe you and Rose a few favors after everything you two have done for me."

Teresa moved away and stared into space. "How can I ever tell Rose?"

"Easy. You just tell her. She has to know."

"I can't do it. She'll go on and on about how she told me so... and how could I do such a thing... and what will the neighbors say." She shook her head. "No, I just can't do it!"

She's right, Mike thought. *Rose worries about keeping up appearances.*

"Okay, okay," he said. "We'll do it like this. You don't tell her now. We wait until we have everything arranged, and then we tell her. In other words, we present her with the problem and the solution at the same time. That way all she can do is feel grateful."

Teresa raised her eyebrows and took a deep breath. "One thing you gotta do, Treese, is act like nothing's wrong. Go to work every day. Start goin' out with other guys."

She shrugged her shoulders. "But I don't know any other guys."

Mike thought of the tickets Aaronson gave him and another plan popped in his mind.

"Do you like baseball?"

She shook her head.

"Well, you'll have to pretend to like it. A friend of mine gave me two tickets to Shibe Park, and I'll ask Stash Nowicki to take you. I'll tell him I promised to take you, but I can't make it. That much at least is true. The tickets are for a Saturday doubleheader and I gotta work."

"Why would Stash want to take me?" she said. "We hardly know each other."

"He'll want to take you all right. He's had a case on you for years."

Teresa smiled. "He has? I didn't know that."

"Then you'll go?"

Teresa looked away and patted her hair. "If he asks me."

✦✦✦

After work that night, Mike met up with Sam, and they walked to the corner.

"I hope Stash will be here," Mike said. "Somebody gave him two tickets to the ball game and he wants to take Teresa Hanley. He's afraid she'll say no, so he asked me to pave the way."

"Is she gonna go?"

"Yeah."

"I thought she was goin' with Red Donovan."

"No, they went out once or twice till she found out what a creep he is."

Sam snorted. "She shoulda asked me. I coulda told her."

"Me, too."

When they got to the corner, Stash had just arrived. Mike took him aside, and showed him the tickets. He told him the rehearsed story. "And, after I told Teresa I couldn't take her she got mad, and said I'd have to find somebody else. She asked about you."

Stash's face lit up. "Did she really say that?"

"Sure she said it. So, will you take her?"

"Yeah, I'll take her," Stash said.

"Okay, I'll tell her you'll pick her up at her house an hour before the game."

✦✦✦

The next day Mike found Reverend Lane's number and, when he dialed it, Mrs. Lane answered.

When he identified himself, she said: "Oh, Michael, how are you?"

"Fine. And yourself?"

"I'm fine, too. What can I do for you?"

"Is Reverend Lane there?"

"Yes, he is. Hold on and I'll get him." When Lane came to the phone, Mike cleared his throat. "I've got a problem I'd like to talk to you about."

Lane's voice sounded cheerful, but touched with concern, the voice of a professional problem solver. "A problem, Mike? Well, fire away."

"It's kinda complicated. I'd rather not talk about it on the phone."

"How about if we talk here. Can you come to the house?"

"Sure. Whenever you say."

"I'm busy today. How about tomorrow?"

They set a time for one o'clock the following afternoon.

✦✦✦

The Reverend lived near the University of Pennsylvania in a house next to his church, where Harriet Lane was working with a pair of pruning shears in a side garden filled with rosebushes. She spied Mike standing on the sidewalk and shouted gaily, "Hiya, Michael! Come in. The gate's open."

He unlatched the gate as she called out, "Andy, Michael Kane's here."

A moment later the Reverend Lane appeared in the doorway and led Mike down a short hallway to a tiny room, crowded by a desk and chair, sofa, and a bookcase.

"This is what we refer to, euphemistically, as my study."

Waving Mike to a seat on the sofa, he sat behind the desk and grinned.

"I usually try to put my guests at ease with chit chat about the weather and other earth-shaking topics, but this time I'll dispense with the preliminaries. What's the problem?"

"It's a girl in my neighborhood," Mike began. "She's in trouble."

He stopped and Lane prompted him. "What kind of trouble? Is she pregnant?"

Mike nodded. "Not only that, but the guy who got her in trouble is the neighborhood creep. He won't marry her and, even if he would, it's the worst thing that could happen to her." He shook his head. "What she ever saw in the creep, I'll never understand."

Mr. Lane smiled. "There's no explaining the mysteries of physical attraction. Look at me, a blond, balding Slim Summerville, while Harriet was the prettiest girl in her class at Bryn Mawr."

He's right, Mike thought, *he does look like old Slim.* The dominant nose in a thin face, and that same slow, shit-eating grin... but he shook his head in polite disagreement.

"How old is the girl?"

"Let's see, she's a year older than I am, so that makes her eighteen."

"Tell me, Mike, how did you get involved? Is she a relation?"

"No, but I've known her since I was born and our families were always very close."

He told Lane about Rose and all the things she had done for his father and him.

"Teresa really hasn't got anybody else to talk to, and I just happened to walk in on her when she needed to talk it out."

"Doesn't she get along with her sister?"

"Oh, they get along all right. But Rose is much older than Teresa, and she treats her more like a daughter than a sister."

"But she'll have to tell Rose eventually."

"She knows that. But I told her we'd arrange everything first, then tell Rose. You know, find a home she can go into to have the baby. I told her all the religious groups run homes like that. Then I told her about you and that I was sure you could help."

Andy raised his eyebrows over a slight smile. "I'm glad you came to me, and I'll do what I can to help. First, you should know the Unitarians don't have the kind of resources the major denominations have. We just don't have any homes of the sort you describe."

Mike's face fell. "But weren't the Unitarians founded by a bunch of rich New Englanders like Ralph Waldo Emerson?"

"Emerson was one of the early members," Lane replied. "So was William Channing. But they weren't really rich, just famous. And the religion never managed to attract many people."

"Then you can't help?"

Mr. Lane smiled at him. "I didn't say that. I think I can help. I have some friends in the Episcopal ministry, and I'll start with them. How much time do we have?"

"I don't know what you mean."

"I mean how long will it be before Teresa's obviously pregnant?"

Mike shook his head. "I didn't ask her that. But I'll find out and let you know."

"You do that. And tell Teresa not to worry. I'm almost certain I can arrange something."

Mike walked straight to the subway stop. He was not feeling quite as chipper as he was on the trip out. And not nearly as optimistic as when he pitched poor Teresa that line of bullshit about the influential Protestant minister who is a very good friend. Still, Andy Lane had tried to sound optimistic, and so would he. He'd just ask her how long before she started to show.

The trouble with you, Mike Kane, is you're always handing somebody, including yourself, a big line of crap about all the great things you're gonna do. Like, you're gonna read *The Outline of History,* and *Modern English Usage* from cover-to-cover. Shit, you still haven't finished them, and you probably never will. In your own way, you're just as big a phony as Red. He suddenly felt tired, and he slumped over, feeling the full weight of despair closing in on him.

At the corner of 35th Street he stopped in front of an apple seller with a sign on his box proclaiming himself a World War soldier fallen on evil times. "Give an unemployed veteran a break. Buy a juicy apple—5 cents," the handwritten sign said. Fishing in his pocket for a nickel, Mike took an apple from the pile and bit into it. It was soft and pulpy, but he managed to swallow the bite down without making a face.

"How's business?" he asked.

"Rotten," the man growled.

Just like his apples, Mike thought. What a life for a man who fought for his country. Selling rotten apples that nobody wanted to buy. He threw his into a trash container.

Still, however miserable he was now, the man had experienced the ultimate adventure, and nobody could take that away from him. That was the one thing that kind of ashamed him about his father. The old man had joined the Army three months before the war ended and never got out of Camp Dix, New Jersey. Well, at least he had tried to take part. He even left Mom alone with me as a baby, when he marched off to join the colors.

He wondered if he'd have to fight in war, and the thought of it made his blood race. He didn't hope for war, but if one happened, he'd sure have to find out what it was like. Moralists said war was man surrendering to his basest instincts, but he had never read a book about the greatest of all wars that hadn't left him feeling somehow uplifted. Even *All Quiet on the Western Front* conveyed as much about the nobility of friendship as it did about the horrors of war. When he read stories about flying aces like Richthofen, Rickenbacker, and Frank Luke—with their knightly notions of gallantry and honor—the romantic aura surrounding battle became irresistible.

He enjoyed nothing more than hearing Doc Greene talk about his experiences with I Company, 315th Infantry Regiment. Unless it was hearing him talk about women and sex. Sometimes, too—since women and war seemed to go together—his stories contained all the spicy ingredients. He remembered the story Doc once told about the time he got wounded.

Doc had been hit in the leg at Chateau Thierry during the second battle of the Marne, and ended up in a hospital in a town called Bar-le-Duc. His wound wasn't too serious and he spent only a month in the hospital before being discharged as fit for duty.

"I was in the depot at Bar-le-Duc waiting for a train back to the front," Doc told him, "and I had three months' pay in my pocket. So, I decided to have a little fling before going back."

Bar-le-Duc was lousy with Military Police, but Doc managed to find a bar on the outskirts of town where he decided to hole up, drink some wine, and maybe find a girl. The owner of the joint said he didn't have any place for Doc to sleep, so he just sat there drinking. Late in the afternoon, a girl came in and bought some wine and, when she left, Doc got up and followed her.

"She musta thought I was crazy," Doc said. "She was carrying a basket, and I just walked up to her and took it, and began babbling in make-believe French. 'Vous avez place to dormir?'"

Doc said she did not speak, just walked ahead of him, and led him a mile out of town to an old stone house. She lived with an old woman about eighty whom, he later found out, was some distant relative. Her father and three brothers all died in 1916 in the fighting around Verdun.

"She worked in a factory making jams, and I gave her francs every morning when she went to work, to buy wine, cognac, and food on her way home."

Doc stayed there a week, and they slept together in a feather bed, bathed in a large wooden tub in the kitchen, and ate wonderful meals cooked on a wood-burning stove.

"Her name was Nicole Bouchere. She was nineteen, and the prettiest little thing you ever saw," Doc said. He held his hand just under his chin. "She came up to about here."

"What happened to her?" Mike had asked Doc. "Did you ever see her again?"

"No, I never did. The war ended, and they shipped us down to Marseilles, and home."

"Didn't you ever even write to her?"

"No, I started to a couple of times, but then I thought she might be married and I didn't want to cause her any trouble."

He had thought about the story often and it always made him a little sad and disappointed in Doc. Man, if it had been him, nothing could have kept him from going back after the war to find Nicole. Every time he saw her in his mind's eye, she looked like Simone Simon on the big screen as the femme fatale in *The Unknown Singer*.

+ + +

On Sunday morning, Mike went outside and sat on the front steps to wait for Rose and Teresa to come back from ten o'clock Mass. He was looking for a chance to talk to Teresa, but when they turned the corner at Etting Street, Mrs. McDevitt stopped them.

Mary McDevitt was a good soul, but Mike avoided her because she didn't bathe very often, and she could talk your leg off. Her topics always covered Holy Mother Church, and the blessed apostles. She was a fat, shapeless, toothless woman, with eight kids who went to six o'clock Mass every morning. She never left her house without her rosary beads, a house abounding with crucifixes. Doc Greene once said her penitential prayers had earned so many indulgences that nobody associated with her would ever spend time in Purgatory.

Mike didn't wait long for Teresa. After a few minutes she came up the street by herself, leaving poor Rose alone with Mary McDevitt. Mike stood up and greeted her.

"How was the ball game yesterday?"

"Oh, Michael, it was so much fun," Teresa gushed. She looked positively radiant. "Stanley is so nice."

"Treese," he said, "I talked to my minister friend on Friday, and he said it would take a while to arrange things." He lowered his voice. "He also asked me to find out how long it will be before you begin to... you know... show."

Teresa leaned toward him and whispered excitedly. "I'm not pregnant, Michael. I came around. Yesterday morning!"

"Gee, Treese, that's great news!"

She reached over and squeezed his hand. "So you can tell your friend I don't need his help. But thanks for everything. I won't forget how sweet you were."

She walked up the street, and Mike watched her with a vague feeling of disappointment.

Chapter Nine

With time off for good behavior, Caz Nowicki got out of jail in May 1935, and his friends threw him a party at Rafferty's saloon. Doc Greene and Dominic Angelo brought in most of the refreshments, along with Caz's father, Casimir, Senior.

Mike didn't get to the party until after nine, and he could hear the sounds of merriment from a hundred yards away. He also saw Jumbo Case and Walleye Joyce, two members of the neighborhood bottle gang, standing at the saloon door. He approached them with caution because three years ago, when he was fourteen, he wrote a scurrilous poem about an imaginary baseball game the pair had played. Doc got it printed in a weekly newspaper, *The Brewerytown Chronicle*. It made Mike a neighborhood celebrity, but Jumbo and Walleye had been pissed off when they read it, and he sure couldn't blame them. So, he avoided them. Especially Jumbo, who was a big, mean-looking bastard who always reminded him of Abel Magwitch, the escaped prisoner in *Great Expectations*.

Jumbo sported a huge pair of feet and, due to a nervous disorder, his right foot slapped the ground resoundingly when he walked. He slapped his way toward Mike.

"Hey, kid," he croaked, "we need a quarter for a jug. Could you help us out?"

Mike had thirty cents in his pocket and he reached in and extracted a dime.

"I'm sorry, Mr. Case, that's all the money I have," he said, proffering the dime carefully. Jumbo had an uncertain temper, but snatched the coin silently.

Walleye Joyce sidled over to Mike and peered at him with his one good eye.

"Do us a favor, kid," he wheedled, "tell Doc Greene we need a quarter."

"I sure will, Mr. Joyce," Mike said. "Knowing Doc, I should be right back with it."

He made his way through the crush in the crowded bar, toward the backroom where he knew Doc would sit with the guest of honor. He saw his father at a table with Rose, and Mary McDevitt and her husband John, and Willie's mother and father.

Rose shouted at him as he went by. "Michael, we saved you a seat!"

"I'll be right back, Rose!" he yelled. "I wanna say hello to Caz first."

He saw Willie coming toward him, a glass of dark liquid in his hand, and a glum look on his face. Willie thrust the glass toward him.

"Look what my old man's got me drinking." He frowned.

Mike took the glass and sipped. Root beer.

"I'll drink it if you don't want it. I'm thirsty. Later on we'll slip out to the bar and have a few. First, I must say hello. Where's Caz sittin'?"

Willie pointed to a table at the back of the room. Mike looked and saw the man of the hour with Doc, Stash and Teresa, Dominic, and Caz's parents. A blonde he had never seen before sat next to Caz.

He let out a faint whistle. "Who's the blonde, Willie?"

"She's Caz' girl," Willie whispered. "Sophie somethin' her name is. She's Polish, from West Philly. Come on. I'll innerduce ya."

He led him straight to the girl. "Sophie, this is another of Caz's good friends, Mike Kane."

Sophie flashed a dazzling smile, causing a hitch in his breath. "Nice meeting you," he managed.

Caz pointed to some bottles of whiskey on the table. "You want a drink while your old man and Rose ain't lookin'? Willie's old man's already got him flagged."

Mike didn't like the taste of straight whiskey, so he held out the half-filled glass of root beer. Caz poured in a generous splash of the joy juice. Mike took a sip and raised the glass to Caz.

"Welcome home, Caz. Long overdue."

Caz smiled. "Thanks, Mike. It's good to be out of the pokey." He reached over and patted Sophie's hand. "Especially when you've got somebody like Sophie waitin' for you."

Mike glanced at Doc. "Jumbo and Walleye, are outside. They need a quarter for a jug."

Doc reached in his pocket and handed Mike a fifty-cent piece.

"Give them this. Tonight's everybody's night to howl."

When Mike got back, Nat Brennan sat at the piano, and the back room was crowded with dancers. He saw that his father and Rose made a nice-looking couple. Everybody watched Caz and Sophie, though. Caz, big and dark-haired, his muscles rippling, and Sophie, red-lipped, white-skinned, and golden haired. They resembled a couple from a fairytale.

Mike felt melancholy as he watched them. He'd sure never look like Caz, even if he lifted every barbell in York, Pennsylvania. He'd sure never have a girl who looked like Sophie, either. The Sophies and the Patricia Galvans of the world were reserved for guys like Caz, and the football-playing stud from Saint Joe's. The best the Mike Kanes could hope for were plain girls like Naomi Weiss. He must have been crazy to think Patricia would even look twice at a guy like him. He'd tear that stupid letter up as soon as he got home tonight.

He gulped down the whiskey-laced root beer, grateful for the rush of warmth it brought. *C'est la guerre*, as Doc always said. Loosely translated, it meant if that's the way the cards were dealt, that's the hand he'd have to play. He wasn't ugly and Naomi wasn't all that bad looking. She had called him at Mandel's a couple of hours ago to tell him her mother and Goldman planned to go the zoo on Sunday, but she did not. So, if he'd come over around eleven o'clock, they'd have the apartment to themselves, she told him, giggling. She'd make lunch for him, she said. He took another gulp and grinned.

He finished his drink and walked over to the McDevitts, sitting alone.

"Not dancing, Mrs. McDevitt? Mr. McDevitt?" he asked, sitting down.

Mary McDevitt laughed. "Lord of Mercy, no. We're not much for dancing, me with dropsy, and John with the swollen legs from work. But we do enjoy watching, don't we, John?"

John McDevitt took a gulp of beer. He was a thin, and haggard-looking man who worked as a streetcar motorman. "I haven't danced since me weddin' day. And not much before that."

"Don't they make a lovely pair, Casimir and his blonde lady friend?" Mrs. McDevitt rattled on. "And a good Catholic girl she is, too, I'll bet. The Polish have always been pillars of Holy Mother Church. Just like the Irish and the Italians."

"I've got something for you, Michael," she said, rummaging through her purse. "Last week I made a novena in honor of Saint Teresa, the Little Flower, at the Pink Sisters Convent on Green Street. They're Carmelites, you know—the order founded by Saint Teresa of Avila. They went barefoot to humble themselves in the sight of Almighty God. But they don't follow the custom anymore. The Holy Father dispensed them from making that sacrifice. I offered up a novena to your sainted mother and other dear friends who are now among the faithful departed."

She handed Mike a small picture of the Little Flower in a pose with an armful of roses.

"You carry that picture with you, Michael, and your dear mother in heaven will always know that God will grant you the grace of a death free from the stain of mortal sin."

Mike took the picture with a smile and put it into his shirt pocket. He kept a drawerful of holy pictures Mary McDevitt had given him over the years. Fat chance he had of dying in the odour of sanctity. He hadn't been to Confession or Communion for a year and a half, and that meant he was already ex-communicated. But he'd never tell Mary McDevitt how he felt, or ridicule her beliefs. Anybody who looked like her needed the consolations of religion.

Willie came over to the table, a glass in his hand. His face looked flushed, and he winked at Mike as he handed him the glass. "Watch my root beer for me. I gotta see a man about a dog."

Mike took a sip of the drink and almost gagged. It was half whiskey. Jesus, Willie was really asking for it. If his old man found out, he'd kick his ass.

Mr. and Mrs. Bruno came back to the table, followed by his father and Rose. She smiled at him. "I see you're drinking root beer, too, Michael. That's nice."

"It's not mine, it's Willie's. Me, I'm gonna have a beer."

There was a pitcher of beer on the table. He poured himself a glass while Rose frowned.

"It's only beer, Rose. How can one beer hurt anybody?"

"It can start with just one beer," Rose sniffed. "Paddy, aren't you going to say anything?"

Paddy tried to look stern. "Rose is right, son. When you take that first drink you never know whether you're gonna end up a social drinker, or end up a rummy."

"Drink is the curse of the Irish," Mary McDevitt said, and smiled at her husband.

Mike pushed the beer away. Did she think he didn't drink when she wasn't around? Well, if it would hurt her feelings, he could wait till he got out to a bar where she couldn't see him.

"Okay," he said. "I wouldn't want to turn into an instant member of the bottle gang."

Joe Bruno scowled at him. "When you're twenty-one you can do what you want, kid. That's what I tell Willie. But as long as he's under my roof, he'll do as I say.

Marie Bruno looked at her husband. "Willie's a good boy. You're too hard on him."

"Father Flanagan says there's no such thing as a bad boy," Mary McDevitt said.

Joe grunted. "Father Flanagan never had any kids of his own."

Doc came over to the table and put his hand on Paddy's shoulder. "How about singing a couple of songs, Pat?"

Paddy started to rise, but Doc held him down and winked at Mike. "Lemme make an announcement first."

He went back to the piano and shouted for attention, and when the murmur died down, he continued in a loud voice: "Arthur Tracy couldn't make it tonight, but our own neighborhood street singer Paddy Kane has consented to favor us with a couple of songs."

Amidst a burst of applause, Paddy smiled and stood up, but Doc held up his hand and shouted for quiet again.

"First, however, and this may come as a surprise to him, our own poet laureate will recite the poem that made him famous from Girard Avenue to Columbia, and 25th Street to Fairmount Park. Ladies and gentlemen, Michael Kane in a rendition of *The Ballad of Jumbo Case.*"

The crowd burst into applause again, and Mike grabbed the glass of beer he had pushed away, and gulped half of it down.

"Sorry, Rose," he mumbled. "I'm gonna need some courage."

He drank the rest of the beer and walked over to where Doc led the applause.

"Damn you, Doc," he said with an embarrassed grin.

Nat Brennan began to play *Take Me Out to the Ball Game* in a soft, tinkling style. Mike cleared his throat nervously and began to recite.

"The score was tied at eight to eight
When Walleye Joyce stepped to the plate.
He took three cuts at the ball, and then
Walked back to the bench and sat down again.
The crowd sat down, too stunned to stand.
Why even the peerless Eye had fanned.
It looked like the game would end in a tie
When once again their hopes rose high,
For at the plate with his mighty post
Was the man all pitchers feared the most.
"Jumbo! Jumbo!" they shouted his name.
If any one can, he'll save the game.
The pitcher wound up and let a fastball go.
It was met on the nose by old Jumbo.
It was a high ball, and on the outside
And Jumbo gave it a nice, long ride.
Around the bases he did streak.
He reached home plate inside a week.
He was out of breath, and drenched with sweat,
His tongue hanging, his eyes were wet.
But he managed to gasp, though white as a sheet.
I owe it all to Sneaky Pete."

Roars of laughter rose from the room when he finished. He snuck a glance at Sophie, who was laughing as hard as the rest, and he felt a surge of pleasure go through him. Grinning foolishly, he headed for the men's room. Hunched over the urinal, he shook his head. That last line about cheap liquor always got a big laugh. No matter how often he recited it, the reaction was always the same.

He turned away from the urinal and began to button his fly. The door opened and Willie came in. Mike smiled tentatively, expecting some comment about the recitation of his poem, but Willie walked straight over to the washbasin and splashed water on his face.

Mike went over to him. "What happened, Willie?"

Willie continued to splash water on his face and Mike repeated the question. "You look like somebody just belted you one," he added.

"Somebody just did," Willie blubbered. "My fuckin' old man."

Scrubbing his wet face with his handkerchief, he choked back tears. "He tasted my root beer, and reached over the table and slapped me. Right in the face. In front of everybody!"

His eyes began to fill again. He wiped them dry. "Let's get out of here."

Mike followed him through the bar and outside, hurrying to keep up with his angry pace. They walked down 27th Street till they got to Willie's house, and sat on the steps.

"He'll never do that again," Willie said. "I'm leavin' this fuckin' place forever."

"Where you gonna go? You wanna stay with us for awhile?"

Willie shook his head. "I'm blowin' this fuckin' town. Right now. Tonight."

"But where will you go?"

"To California, that's where."

"How the hell are you gonna go to California?"

Willie jerked his thumb dramatically over his shoulder. "Right down there on 33rd Street the freights leave for Buffalo and keep goin' west. They chug all the way to California."

He stopped and looked at Mike. "Will you go with me?"

"Jesus, Willie, I can't leave tonight. Just like that."

"Tomorrow, then. First thing in the morning."

Mike shook his head. "I can't go tomorrow, either."

"Then when can you go? Or don't you want to?"

"Sure, I'll go. Palm trees and the blue Pacific. Man, I dreamed about goin' to California."

"Then what are we waiting for?" Willie demanded.

"You know I bought clothes on Rose's charge account. I can't leave till it's all paid."

"How long will that take?"

Mike shrugged. "Maybe four months, and then I'll go. It's a promise."

Willie's eyes shone with excitement. "There are movie studios there, Mike. We could start out sweeping studio floors and maybe work our way up to become actors."

Mike laughed. "We'd never make it as actors. Leading men are big, six feet or more."

"Who you tryin' to kid. How big ya think Richard Barthelmess, or James Cagney is?"

"Barthelmess and Cagney must be five-eight, five-nine."

"Five-four is more like it. Man, I could eat soup off their heads."

Chapter Ten

Sunday morning, Mike got up early and, after breakfast, shaved, scrubbed his teeth until his gums bled, and plastered his hair down with soap. He dressed carefully, and made sure to take the rubbers he had bought from Abe Brodsky. It was almost ten o'clock when he left the house, and he met a crowd of worshipers coming up the street from the nine o'clock Mass. He spotted Willie among them with his little sister and brother, and he waited for them at the corner.

"You kids go on home and tell Mom I'll be along in a coupla minutes," Willie told them.

The kids kept walking and Mike glanced at his friend. "How'd you make out with your old man?"

Willie shrugged. "He did a lot of hollerin' when he got home, but he didn't slap me around anymore. Not that I give a shit what he does now that I know we're goin' to the coast."

He looked at Mike anxiously. "You're still goin', ain't ya?"

"I promised, didn't I?"

"I know ya did," Willie said. "Sorry, I'm just anxious. I hope you kept quiet about it," Willie blurted. "There's no tellin' what my dad might do."

"Don't worry, Willie. I'm not tellin' anyone. We'll just leave notes the day we leave."

Willie grinned. "Man, we'll have a ball out there. Ya can pick oranges right offta trees."

Mike grinned back. "And sleep on the beach, or under a palm tree if we have to."

"And just think of the girls. Wow." He lifted his eyebrows and grinned. "Oh, didja hear what happened at Rafferty's?"

"No. What happened?"

"Caz worked Red Donovan over. Nat Brennan just told me about it."

"What did Red do this time?"

"Well, he looked in the back room and saw Sophie dancin' with Dom Angelo, and he says, 'Who's the blonde floozy dancin' with Angelo?' Caz overheard him 'cause he came outta the john just as Red opened his big trap. So, Caz came up behind him, ripped the back of his coat right up the middle, wrapped it around Red's neck, and began to strangle him."

"Jesus! Where is Red now? In the hospital?"

"No. Doc Greene and Stash managed to pull Caz loose, and Red ran out the door. But not before Caz told him to leave town because he was gonna punch him every time he saw him."

"Whadda ya think Red will do?"

"I don't know, but if I was Red, I'd move someplace far away, Hawaii maybe."

"You can say that again."

"Hey, Mike... I gotta go. I haven't had breakfast yet and everybody's waitin'."

After Willie left, Mike walked to the building on Pine Street where Naomi lived. He purposely dawdled on the walk to make sure he wouldn't get there early, and when he turned the corner at Tenth Street, Naomi peered out a window at him. She waved that the coast was clear.

He took the stairway steps two at a time and, when he arrived at the fourth floor landing, the apartment door stood open slightly with Naomi peeking out. She opened the door wide and he went in quickly. She closed the door and bolted it. She seemed upset.

"You're late. I guess you weren't exactly excited about coming here."

He grinned at her. "Sure, I was excited. I just didn't want to get here early and take a chance on running into your mother or Mr. Goldman."

She leaned against the door in a provocative pose, her red sweater straining against her large breasts. He advanced toward her. When he got close, her hands pushed him away.

"Were you really excited?" she asked, her brown eyes enlarged by her thick glasses.

He walked away to the bookcase and perused the books. How, he asked himself, would Caz handle a situation like this? With wit, he was sure, but with a certain amount of firmness, too. Caz was a great kidder, and he had laid more pipe than a plumber.

He walked back to her and, with a sudden movement, pulled off her glasses.

"I know how to handle you. Without your glasses you'll be completely at my mercy, ha."

She giggled and groped her way toward him as he backed away.

He continued back until he collapsed onto the sofa, Naomi on top of him. She grasped for the glasses and, afraid they would break, he surrendered them. She sat up at the end of the sofa and put them on.

"Whatever it is you're going to do to me, I'd at least like to see it," she said between deep breaths. "Without my glasses, I'm as blind as a bat." She looked at him with her oversized brown eyes. "Just what is it you have in mind?"

He moved over until she was pinned against the arm of the sofa. Pulling her close, he kissed her. Her mouth opened and he slid his tongue over her lips and teeth, tasting the flavor of her mouthwash. He began to fondle her breasts and, when he felt the nipples grow hard, moved his hand stealthily under her skirt, pausing to see if she would resist. She didn't, so he began stroking her gently. Soon she was squirming, her breathing quickened, and she began to make thrusting movements against his hand.

Mike knew he had to make some adjustments before he could continue. He was twisted up in his jacket, and his testicles were tangled up in his underwear and beginning to hurt. He stood up suddenly to take off his clothes and Naomi opened her eyes in alarm.

"Don't stop now," she gasped, "please don't stop."

"I won't, Naomi. This won't take a second."

He wrestled his jacket off and flung it aside, then pushed his pants and shorts to the floor.

"I was about to make a mess in my pants if I didn't do something fast," he explained.

He sat down and draped his handkerchief over his erection. "Would you hold this in place in case I have an accident?"

She reached over and gripped him tightly, moving her hand up and down, and he put his hand under her skirt and resumed his gentle stroking. She came just before he did. They pulled together, and hugged each other, and kissed.

After a while, Naomi struggled free and they stood up and looked at each other.

"I must look a mess," she said.

"Me, too." He looked down at his shriveled penis. When Naomi saw it she giggled. Mike blushed as he quickly pulled up his shorts and pants and buttoned up his fly.

"I'm hungry," she said. "Would you like something to eat?"

"Yes, great idea. And a bottle of beer if you have any."

"I have better than that. I have a bottle of red wine from the Italian man on the first floor. My mother doesn't know I have it, so we can drink the whole bottle."

She went into the kitchen and came back with the wine and two glasses.

"Have some of the wine while you're waiting. Do you like corned beef sandwiches?"

"Yes, that would be great."

Walking back to the kitchen, she paused at the door and said. "If you look behind the books on the bottom shelf of the bookcase you'll find a good book to read while you're waiting."

Mike guessed the name of the book was *Lady Chatterley's Lover*, and he found a paperback edition published in Paris. Looking for the dirty parts, he found one on page 196. By the time Naomi came back with the sandwiches, he was reading avidly.

She sat down beside him. "You must have found one of the juicy parts."

He grinned at her wickedly. "He calls his thing John Thomas, and hers Lady Jane."

"I know. I think it's cute." She poured the glasses full of wine, took a sip, and raised her glass, "Here's to John Thomas, a thing of great promise."

Mike gulped half a glass and toasted. "And here's to Lady Jane, long may she reign."

"Let's eat. I'm starving." She gave him a damp washcloth to clean his hands, and shoved the plate of sandwiches between them.

Mike ate his two sandwiches quickly. When he finished, he lay back and watched her nibbling daintily, wiping her mouth with a napkin after each bite.

"You know, I've tickled Lady Jane, but I haven't seen her yet. You will let me see her?"

She put the last of the sandwich into her mouth and stood up, wiping her fingers.

"I'll think about it." She pointed to a door. "Go into my bedroom and wait for me."

He filled his glass again and gulped it. He was really getting loaded, but that was good. Between the hand job and the wine, he would take a long time to come when they did it.

He went into the bedroom and began taking off his clothes. It was really a nice place, bright and cheerful with drapes on the windows, and cream-colored furniture.

He draped his clothes neatly over the desk chair, and was standing in his shorts admiring himself in the mirror, when the door opened. Naomi stepped into the bedroom, wrapped in a large bath towel. Her eyes shone when she dropped the bath towel and stood in front of him, her legs slightly spread and her arms held high, lifting up her big breasts.

He stared at her, his mouth agape. Her breasts were really big... bigger than he imagined, and she had a patch of black pubic hair between her well-shaped legs. She was stunning.

"You weren't behind the door when they passed out the female goodies, were you?"

"You're not going to make love with your shorts on, are you?"

He pulled off his shorts, and Naomi lay down on the bed, spreading her legs wide.

"Lady Jane is at John Thomas' command," she cooed.

He climbed onto the bed and crouched over her, gazing between her parted legs, drinking in the sight of true naked womanhood, trying to imprint it in his mind. He began to kiss the pink, tumid flesh, but Naomi pulled him on top of her.

"Let's do it," she commanded. "You don't need a rubber," she said through clenched teeth.

"Do you want to get pregnant?"

"I'm safe. I just had my period. Didn't you ever hear of the rhythm method?"

"Of course, I heard of it. We Catholics invented it."

Reassured, he eased into her. They began to thrust against each other urgently. Naomi moaned loudly, but Mike remained silent and determined with his face buried into the pillow above her hair.

Afterwards, they rolled apart to catch their breath. Panting, Mike stared dreamily at the ceiling. "Wow," was all he could think of to say.

Naomi turned toward him. "I guess you noticed I'm not a virgin."

"No, I didn't notice."

"Well, I'm not."

"So what. Neither am I."

"Don't you want to know who did it to me?"

"If you want to tell me."

"It was Marvin Steinberg, the boy who went away to Yale two years ago. We did it in the back seat of his father's car."

"Well, at least you picked a Yale man."

"It was a mess. I didn't enjoy it at all."

"The way I heard it, no one does the first time."

"But I enjoyed it with you, Michael."

He took her face in his hands and kissed her lightly on the lips.

"Me too, Naomi. And I didn't enjoy it the first time, either."

He rolled onto his shoulder and looked at her. Naomi looked back. "Do you know what Sigmund Freud said about John Thomas and Lady Jane?"

He snorted with laughter. "No, but I'm sure you're about to tell me."

"He said something like 'John Thomas and Lady Jane are the least beautiful parts of the human body. Yet no other sight gives human beings more pleasure than they do.'"

"You know, he's right. This big, old, purple-tipped thing is sure no thing of beauty."

"I like it better the way Lawrence describes them. And the way Lady Chatterley and her lover twine flowers in each other's pubic hair."

His finger touched her cheek softly. "You know, Naomi, you really are something."

Her large, brown eyes gazed up at him. "Do you really think so?"

"Yes. It's how we talk together. I've read a lot of books, but I never read Freud."

"He was a dirty old man. But I've got some things to show you, if you're up to it."

Chapter Eleven

Mike paid off his clothes, but the weather that January of 1936 was too cold to bum on trains.

"A man could freeze to death in cold like this," Willie said. "Let's wait till it's warmer."

Mike was more than happy to agree. It put off for at least two months the unhappy chore of telling Willie he didn't want to go at all. In the meantime, maybe Willie would meet a girl who would let him have a little, and he'd get hooked, and not want to run off to be a bum.

Doc Greene had been right, as usual, when he said that the promise of pussy has turned more men onto the paths of righteousness than the promise of salvation ever did. Look at Stash. His old man had gotten him a job as an apprentice butcher at Vogt's, and he and Teresa were engaged. Things had sure turned out all right for them. To top it off, Red Donovan left the neighborhood and, rumor had it, he was living with a rich queer in Ardmore.

He wished Willie would change his mind, because he sure didn't want to leave. He knew he was hooked on Naomi. He knew it, since he never even thought about Patricia anymore. One night she had come into Mandel's with the rich goof from Saint Joe's and looked right past him like she had never seen him before. It hadn't even bothered him.

Things were really going good for him. He had finished *The Outline of History* and was reading Shaw's *An Intelligent Woman's Guide to Socialism and Capitalism*. Old Shaw was really something. "Landlords," he said, "inflict upon society an injury of precisely the same nature as does a burglar when he places a gun to your head." Man, this was the way to learn about economic systems.

Also, his old man started working Fridays and Saturdays as a bartender at Rafferty's, and brought home eight to ten bucks a week.

Yep, things were going good. Except for one, small cloud on the horizon. The last two times he had attended the Socialist Party meetings, a young guy showed up at Naomi's invitation. He was a guy she knew from Temple... a twenty-year-old junior named Bernard Gottbaum. Naomi said she felt sorry for him because he was shy and didn't have many friends. The tall, gawky-looking joker, with teeth like a horse, also smoked a pipe. He really looked goofy when he laughed with the pipe clenched between his horsy teeth.

Mike didn't know how shy Gottbaum really was, because the guy often sounded off at the meetings with quotations from R. H. Tawney and Max Weber, two writers Mike had never even heard of. Bernie also had a car: a 1934 Ford V-8 roadster. It was a real pussy-wagon, and if that hadn't cured him of his shyness, he must really be hopeless.

Well, old Mike Kane didn't have to worry about Bernie Gottbaum. By this time, Mike sometimes popped off at the meetings with quotations from Shaw, and Shaw was a hell of a lot wittier than Tawney or Weber. Besides, he was still the man in the saddle. On Thursdays, Naomi only had classes until eleven o'clock, and every Thursday, promptly at eleven thirty, old Mike would show up and, right after lunch, they'd hit the sack for a little matinee performance.

He had already made up his mind to ask Naomi to marry him as soon as he found a job that provided even the hope of supporting them. She could finish college if she wanted. In four or five years, he'd be ready to write the novel that would make him rich and famous. After all, Scott Fitzgerald wrote *This Side of Paradise* when he was twenty-three, and

Hemingway wasn't much older when he wrote *The Sun Also Rises*. No, the future didn't hold any terrors for Mike Kane.

One night at the end of February, he went to a meeting at Eugene Debs Hall, and not only was Bernie Gottbaum present, but Naomi invited him back to the Weiss apartment after the meeting. So, for the first time, the couple shared no quick kisses or stolen feels in the kitchen.

Still, Mike enjoyed himself. For the first time, he got a chance to put Bernie down. Somebody brought up the topic of Hitler, and Bernie—pipe clenched between his horse teeth—said, "His real name is Schicklgruber, you know."

Mike responded eagerly. "No, it isn't. His father Alois was born out of wedlock to a woman named Maria Anna Schicklgruber. But, Alois' father eventually married Maria and, long before Adolph was born, Alois' birth certificate was changed to Hitler. The whole story is in John Gunther's *Inside Europe*."

Bernie looked at him sourly. "Well, whatever the jerk's real name is, he's no laughing matter, especially for Jews."

He turned to Goldman. "Do you have any relatives in Germany, Lester?"

Goldman shook his head. "Not that I know of. Maybe some distant cousins."

Bernie said, "Well, we do. My father's two sisters and their families are there."

"I know it's easy for me to be optimistic, Bernie," Andy Lane broke in, "but I don't think anything very drastic will happen to your family. Harriet and I have been talking to some good friends at Bryn Mawr with important connections in Germany, and they tell us there's a lot of internal opposition to Hitler. Not only in the universities, but in the Army, and among the working class—most of who, don't forget, are Social Democrats. Our friends say the generals will let Hitler go so far, but when he oversteps his bounds, the Army will kick him out and take over."

"Will they kick him out before or after the war starts?" Harry Aaronson asked.

Andy Lane smiled. "There won't be any war, Harry. My friends tell me the workers would refuse to fight, maybe even start shooting in the wrong direction."

"Do any of your friends happen to be Jews?" Aaronson asked with a doubtful grin.

"As a matter of fact, I don't think so."

Before he left that night, Naomi got Mike alone in a corner and whispered to him not to come to the apartment on Thursday. She said she had a special class to go to in the middle of the afternoon. The next week she called him at Mandel's on Wednesday and told him she had another special class to attend the following afternoon. The next day he walked down to her apartment house, arriving about twelve o'clock, and parked right in front of the building sat Bernie's green, V-8 Ford.

Mike's heart seemed to flop over in his chest, and he had to stop in the expensive saloon on the corner for a quick shot and a beer before starting the long, sorrowful walk home. That night he told Willie he was ready to head for California any time he said.

Because of the extreme cold, they didn't leave until the last Saturday in March 1936.

Part II

Escape to California

Chapter Twelve

Their leaving started badly. They intended to go earlier, but a bum who panhandled them when they arrived at the freight yard at eight o'clock in the morning explained that the Nickleplate freights to Buffalo, New York, left in the evening at nine o'clock sharp. The bum also pointed to some empty boxcars and told them to climb in one before departure, at about eight-thirty, and to close the doors and hide in a corner until the cars started moving.

They both had left notes behind, so they spent the entire day hiding and waiting for evening. Mike had written a letter to Sam, which he mailed the morning they left, but the only person he told ahead of time about leaving town was Mr. Mandel, who told him he was crazy.

"They got the same things in California we got here: unemployment and hard times."

On Friday night, when he left the store, Mr. Mandel gave him a full week's pay, plus an extra two dollars, and a small first-aid packet. Mike pinned the money inside his shirt pocket.

At five minutes before nine that evening, they eased the freight car door open and climbed in.

"Jesus, it's dark in here!" Willie shouted when they eased the door shut.

Mike gripped his arm. "For Chrissake, Willie, keep it down till this thing gets movin'."

They groped their way to a corner of the boxcar and sat on their shoulder bags.

"It's bound to be a cold night," Willie whispered.

"Have you got an extra sweater with you?"

"Yeah."

"Good. Me, too."

"I wonder how long it will take us to get to Buffalo?"

"Sometime tomorrow, the guy who panhandled us said."

"Yeah, but what time?"

Mike shrugged in the darkness. "Your guess is as good as mine."

"Ya think they got the notes we left by now?"

"Musta. I left mine on the kitchen table."

"Me, too. What did you say in yours?"

"Not much. I just told my dad not to worry, and I'd write when I got to California."

He didn't tell Willie he had also asked Rose to take care of his books, and had given *Married Love or Love in Marriage* to Nat Brennan, so its discovery wouldn't shock Rose.

"Mine was the same, but I told them we're hitchhikin' so he wouldn't look here."

"Good idea. Oh, ya know we're gonna miss Teresa and Stash's wedding next week."

"Yeah, we oughta be in L.A. then. We'll send them a postcard. An April wedding, wow."

They lapsed into silence and, after a wait that seemed interminable, the line of boxcars started with a jerk, then stopped and started jerkily again, repeating the process several times until the train gradually began rolling and picked up speed.

"Well, I guess we're on our way," Willie said.

"Yep, we are." Mike stared into the utter blackness.

Willie rummaged in his bag. "I'm gonna put me other sweater on. It's gettin' chilly."

"Me, too."

"Then maybe I'll try to get some shuteye," Willie said. "I didn't sleep at all last night."

"Me, either."

They pulled on the sweaters and stretched out, their heads on their bags, and lay silently, lulled by the rhythmic clack and rattle of the car's wheels. Mike thought he heard the faint cry of a child, but quickly discounted it, and soon fell fast asleep.

✦✦✦

Mike sat up with a start, as the car's door screeched open. With relief, he recognized Willie silhouetted by the faint light streaming through the open door.

Willie turned and buttoned his fly. "Sorry, but I had to piss so bad it woke me up."

Mike stood up and stretched himself. He felt the stiff soreness in his muscles as he walked to the door and peered out into the gray light. Dark mountains loomed in the distance as he unbuttoned his fly and carefully aimed downwind.

"Ya see the mountains?" Willie called out over the train noise.

Mike slid the door closed, lessening the incessant clacking noise of the train's wheels.

"Yeah. They must be the Catskills or maybe the Adirondacks."

"How close ya think we are to Buffalo?"

"Not very. I think we start west around Albany and leave the mountains behind."

"I'm hungry. Ya wanna eat the candy bars?"

Willie dug into his bag and pulled out two *Oh Henry!* bars. He handed one to Mike, and they washed them down with water from Paddy Kane's old Army canteen.

Willie shivered. "I ain't been warm since yesterday afternoon."

"Move around a little. The sun will soon show itself and warm us up."

They walked around until the sound of screeching brakes added to the already deafening noise assaulting their ears. The car slowed gradually, and jerked to a halt.

They ran to the door and opened it enough to stick their heads out. "Look, Mike, there's a lot of bums in the other box cars."

Down the line of freight cars, doors opened and men jumped out. Up ahead, stood a big water tower with the words "Kinderhook, N.Y." painted on it, and beyond the tower sprawled the beginnings of a town. The engine, stopped next to the tower, was taking on water.

The door in the boxcar just ahead of theirs slid open and a man jumped out. He reached up and lifted down two children: the first, a boy about six, the second, a girl who was a little bit older. He also helped a woman climb to the ground. She took the girl by the hand and climbed up the embankment, heading for a line of trees bordering the road above.

He turned to Willie. "There's a family in the next car. A man and his wife, and two kids."

Shoving the door open wide with his shoulder, Willie jumped down and Mike jumped after him. The man and the little boy had their backs to them, and the boy was relieving himself.

When he finished, he turned around and looked at them. "I just peed," he said grinning.

"Be quiet, Georgie," his father said. He wore a coat that hung to his knees.

The boy swam in a dirty, too-large mackinaw, and a knitted cap stretched over his ears. He wiped his runny nose on his sleeve and began to cry.

"Be quiet, Georgie," the father repeated.

"I'm hungry," the boy wailed.

"We'll eat soon," the father said. He caught Mike's gaze and shook his head hopelessly. "Do you know where we are?"

Mike pointed to the water tower. "That tower says Kinderhook. The town's just ahead."

The man peered up the tracks. "I can't see that far. Kinderhook, you say? That's but about twenty-five miles from Albany. Mebbe we better git off here and start hitchhikin'. We could mebbe miss Albany if this train swings west before it gits there." He looked around uncertainly. "We're headed for her brother's farm outside Albany. At least we'll eat."

"Where'd ya come from?" Mike asked him.

The man gave him an aggrieved look. "Delaware. Down near Newark. Couldn't pay the mortgage and they run us off. Put a sheriff's sign on the place."

"We're headed for the coast," Willie said. "California."

The man didn't hear him. "Yeah, I'm gonna git off. Watch Georgie for me, will ya?"

He climbed into the boxcar and reappeared a moment later with two heavy suitcases, their handles tied together with rope. He left them in the doorway and jumped down as the woman and the girl came back out of the trees. The man shouted up to them.

"Stay up there, Martha! We're gittin' off!"

He draped the suitcases over his shoulder and took Georgie by the hand. Pulling the boy behind him, he struggled up the embankment. Mike unpinned his shirt pocket and extracted two dollars from the slim sheaf of bills. He ran up the embankment and stuffed the money into the man's overcoat pocket.

"This'll get you breakfast in Kinderhook, buddy."

"Thank you, brother," the man said.

Up ahead the locomotive began to puff, and bums started climbing back into the cars.

Mike and Willie got into the huge freight yard in Buffalo at seven-thirty in the evening and, when the train stopped, they opened the door and peered out. Men were jumping out of the boxcars and running up the tracks.

They grabbed their bags, too, jumped down and followed.

"Where the hell we runnin' to?" Willie puffed.

"Beats me. Outta this damn freight yard I guess."

In front of them, an old man about sixty hobbled along, half-running and half-walking. When they caught up with him, they slowed down and kept pace.

"How come everybody's runnin'?" Mike asked him.

"To git outta here before they git rousted, maybe with a club," the old man wheezed.

They increased their pace, following the largest group of men, who were running across a wide expanse of track toward a low, corrugated iron fence. When they got over the fence, they followed the crowd at a dead run toward a huge empty building. Circling it, they came out on a dingy city street, breathing hard, and began walking at a normal pace.

When he recovered his breath, Willie asked "Whadda we do now?"

"We gotta get some food. I'm starvin'."

"Me, too. I could eat a horse, including the oats and the oat bag."

They walked along the shabby street for a dozen blocks until they reached an area where the houses looked a little better kept and, a couple of blocks farther, they came to a wide, well-traveled street, lined with stores.

Standing on the corner, Mike asked, "Which way?"

Willie pointed up the street. "Looks like a diner on the next corner. Ed and Elsie's Home-Style Cooking, the sign says."

"Let's pay Ed and Elsie a visit."

Outside the diner, a sandwich board listed the menu and the day's special: "Home-made beef stew with all the bread you can eat, and coffee – 35 cents."

Mike licked his dry lips. "Ed and Elsie are gonna be sorry about that. Let's go!"

Inside, the welcoming smell of coffee brewing filled the room. They climbed eagerly onto a couple of decrepit stools and leaned their elbows on the scarred counter. A short, heavy-set counterman ladled the stew from a huge pot into large bowls that slopped over when set down in front of them. A wicker basket full of bread was in front of a man two stools down, and the counterman slid it in front of them. He turned back to the griddle.

The stew was mostly potatoes and carrots sprinkled thinly with small pieces of tough, fatty beef, but they spooned it down voraciously, sopping up last drops with slice after slice of day-old bread. When they finished, they sat sipping the steaming coffee.

Willie eyed the cigarette machine. "I'd give me right nut for a smoke."

"Me, too. But we better save what little money we have."

The counterman stopped scraping the griddle and turned around. "They'll cost you twenty cents a pack in the machine, but I got some loose ones I'll sell you four for a nickel."

Mike pulled a dollar out of his shirt pocket and handed it to him.

"Give us four, then, and take out the cost of the food."

The man gave Mike a quarter change and threw a nickel into a cup by the cash register. He took a pack of cigarettes out of his shirt pocket and shook four onto the counter. He took one himself, lit it, and held out the burning match for each of them.

"You boys from around here?"

"We're just passin' through. We came in on a freight from Philadelphia."

"If you're lookin' for a place to sleep, the city runs a shelter you can stay in." He looked at the clock on the wall. "You got time. It's quarter after eight. Get there before nine. After nine nobody gets in or outta the place."

"How far is it?" Mike asked.

"You can make it. It ain't far." He drew a map with his forefinger on the greasy counter. "Eight blocks down the street to the third traffic light, four blocks left, then another block right. You can't miss it. It's a three-story, red brick building. It useta be a dress factory. I worked there when I was a kid. That's before I went into the restaurant business and got rich."

He guffawed heartily, his eyes wrinkling up behind glasses clouded with a film of greasy griddle smoke. Mike gulped down his coffee and slid off the stool.

"Thanks, mister. We better be goin'."

◆◆◆

When they entered the shelter, a man seated at a folding table stopped them. He wrote down their names and where they came from, and gave each of them an Army blanket and one gray-white sheet. The building emitted an overpowering smell of disinfectant.

"Third floor dormitory," he said. "Turn the blanket and sheet in at seven o'clock. You get one night's lodging and breakfast free. Then get outta town, or we'll book you both on vagrancy. The stairway's at the other end of the hall, and there's a washroom on each floor."

He waved them away and they walked down the long hallway.

"Friendly bastard, ain't he," Willie said as they started up the stairway.

"I guess if all you see is red-ass bums, you're friendliness wears a little thin."

Willie grinned at him. "Fee, fi, fo, fum, old Mike Kane is a red-ass bum."

"Ha, ha," Mike laughed with his nose wrinkled and his eyes crossed grotesquely.

They crammed the huge dormitory with scores of cots, placed inches apart, and lined up in narrow-aisled rows. On each cot lay a bulging mattress cover stuffed with corn straw. A person occupied almost every cot, but they found two next to a dimly lit washroom.

"You wash up first," Mike said. "I'll stay here and watch your stuff."

In Willie's absence, the lights shut off but, from the weak illumination from the washroom, Mike could see enough to spread out the sheet and blanket on each bed. He took off his jacket and one sweater and put them under the head of the mattress. After he washed up, he'd put his bag and shoes under there, too, and they'd make a good enough head rest. If he slept in his clothes, he figured he'd sleep warm, even if they turned the heat off entirely.

Willie came out of the washroom and leaned down to whisper. "There ain't no towels or toilet paper. And the water's colder than a dead witch's tit."

"You shoulda said something," Mike whispered back. "I got a towel and soap."

Willie shrugged. "I used me shirt tail."

He climbed into bed, and Mike went into the washroom. When he came back, he stuffed Willie's shoes under his mattress so nobody would steal them.

Willie opened his eyes. "What is it?"

"That poem you made up comin' up the stairs, how does it go?"

Willie recited it. "Fee, fi, fo, fum, old Mike Kane is a red-ass bum."

Mike chuckled softly. "Another red-ass bum I *know* is Willie Anthony Bru-*no*."

Willie pulled the blanket over his head. "Ya silly bastard. Go ta sleep!"

Breakfast the next morning consisted of a bowl of stiff oatmeal, without milk or sugar, a big chunk of stale, dry bread, and a cup of lukewarm, watery coffee. While they choked it down, they started up a conversation with a young man sitting next to them, who looked about twenty-five.

He had been around: back and forth to California a half-dozen times, across Minnesota and the Dakotas, and the Pacific Northwest, and through most of the southern states.

"The South's a good place to stay away from," he told them. "They'll pick ya up for vagrancy and give ya thirty days on a work gang, then put ya over the county line where another sheriff will pick ya up and give ya thirty days on his work gang. It once took me six months ta get through Georgia and Alabama."

"We're goin' ta California," Willie said.

"No picnic there, neither. Maybe ya can get some work this time of year pickin' lettuce around Salinas, or down around El Centro in the Imperial Valley."

"We're gonna stay in Los Angeles," Mike said.

"That's a smart move. Ya can always make out better in the big cities. Anyhow, pickin' crops is for Mexicans and Okies."

"One thing I gotta warn ya about," the man continued. "Stick together. There's a lotta older bums on the road will corn hole a younger guy if they catch him alone. Another thing: get inta the habit of carryin' a good, big stick. Dogs can smell a homeless man, and they don't like the odor. I got the shit bit outta me once in Oklahoma City."

He looked at them reflectively to see if they were impressed by the perils of the road.

Willie blurted out. "You don't hafta worry about us, buddy, we're both good with our dukes."

"The next leg of our trip is Cleveland," Mike said. "But how do we get back on the Nickleplate freight if we can't get back in the yards."

"Easy. Ya stay outside the yards and catch it comin' out. It'll be goin' slow. Just run alongside, gaugin' the speed, and grab onto one of the iron ladders on the side. You'll ride the top until the first stop, and then maybe ya can find an empty. If not, get inta one of them gon-dola cars. At least they'll keep some of the wind and coal dust off ya."

"Ya know when the Nickleplate freight leaves for Cleveland?"

"Sure, I know. Two o'clock sharp. The Nickleplate runs a good operation and they're almost always on time. Ya can ride the Nickleplate all the way to the coast." He spit out the wooden match he was using as a toothpick, and recited the names of the states like a litany: "Ohio, Indiana, Illinois, Missouri, Kansas, Colorado, Utah, Nevada, California. When ya go through Nevada, make sure ya got a bottle of water with ya. Water's scarce out there, and in Arizona and New Mexico. They don't just give it away like they do in other places."

When they left, Mike offered him a dime, but he waved it away. "Don't take any wooden nickels," he said. He picked up Willie's half-eaten chunk of bread and began chewing on it.

In company with about fifteen other bums, they hung around the stretch of track just outside the yards, and at ten after two by Mike's Ingersoll, one of the bums shouted. "Here she comes, boys!"

Everybody jumped up and strung out along the tracks until the engine went puffing by, then began to run, keeping pace with the slow-moving train. Mike and Willie loped at the head of the line, jogging easily with their bags hanging off their shoulders and slapping against their backs.

Mike ran about ten yards in front, looking back, when some inner sense made him look ahead just in time to skip nimbly around a signal standard as it loomed up in front of him. Without breaking stride, he grabbed the next iron ladder going by, jumped onto the first rung, and hung there.

Willie banged into the signal light, rolled over, and came up running. He clutched at a ladder two cars down. Mike watched, horrified, as the moving train jerked him off his feet, but Willie managed to hang on and stab wildly with his foot until he made contact. He crawled slowly to the top of the boxcar and sat down, his legs dangling over the side.

Mike scrambled up the ladder to the top of the car and started to run and jump, two cars back, to where Willie sat. He felt something brush lightly against his shoulders and he looked up, startled, to see a row of drag-ropes in front of him.

Willie screamed, "Get down!"

Instinctively they both fell flat, and moments later the train went under a bridge. Once clear, Mike looked cautiously behind him, and sat next to Willie. He bet his own face looked as chalk white as his friend's.

"We should both be dead right now," Willie said.

Mike looked at him wordlessly, only able to sit there gripping the edge of the boxcar with taut hands.

When the fright left them, Mike took a deep breath. "How're your legs?"

"Beginnin' to hurt. It's me shins."

He stretched his legs out in front of him and gingerly pulled his trouser legs up to his knees. Both shins were black and blue, and traversed with bloody scrapes.

"I feel like I just won a soccer game with them shinbusters from Kensington," he joked.

Mike opened his shoulder bag. "I got some iodine in the first-aid kit Mandel gave me, and some bandages."

"That shit burns. Ain't ya got any mercurochrome?"

"No."

"Then I'll do without."

"Suppose they get infected?"

"I'll take me chances."

The train had picked up speed, and the engine belched out clouds of coal dust and smoke. It burned their eyes and nostrils, and made them cough.

Willie struggled to his feet. "Jesus, the smoke's killin' me. Where's a gon-dola?"

They advanced across the tops of the cars, moving cautiously in the face of the strong wind, until they found an empty coal car halfway down the long line of freights. Climbing down a short ladder, they jumped into it—narrowly missing a cluster of men huddled together—and sat down on their bags. One of the older bums grinned at them in welcome.

"I'll be ten years older when this fuckin' trip's over," Willie said. He pulled out a soiled handkerchief and wiped his eyes and face, and rubbed it over his hair. When he finished, it was smudged black with soot, and he jammed it back in his pocket. Mike glanced down at the white knight emblem on his jacket and its whiteness had turned into a dirty gray.

The bum who had grinned at them shouted. "We're gonna ride this sonofabitch all the way to Cleveland. All the boxcars are loaded and locked."

Mike wondered how he knew, but he turned out to be right. He was a bleary-eyed, unshaven, old man, about fifty, with broken veins in his face and rotten teeth. In his way though, Mike guessed, he was as knowledgeable about things like this as the prophets are about life.

The train stopped outside Ashtabula about eleven o'clock, and he and Willie climbed out on a half-hearted attempt to find an open or empty boxcar. There weren't any.

He fell asleep about midnight and slept fitfully until about two. When he woke up, he saw Willie standing a few feet away, peering over at the other side of the car. He got to his feet and stood alongside his friend.

"Can't sleep either, huh?"

Willie stared ahead into the darkness. "Ya know what just happened?"

"No. Something happen?"

Willie pointed to the cluster of bums huddled together, and his voice choked with loathing. "I woke up a little while ago and the dirty old bastard that told us we'd hafta ride this coal car all the way to Cleveland was huddled up against me and whisperin' in me ear."

Mike looked at him aghast. "What'd ya do?"

"First, I hit him a shot in the guts with me elbow. Then, I rolled over and kneed him in the nuts, and hit him a coupla more shots." He spat disgustedly. "It was like punchin' a pile a mush."

He spat again. "If me legs wasn't so sore, I'd go over there now and kick his fuckin' ribs in."

Mike put a restraining hand on his arm. "Let me handle this, Willie. None of them are gonna bother you anymore!"

Mike got up and walked slowly over to the gang of six or seven in the corner. He could see they were consoling the older bum punched by Willie. Mike stood there patiently, glaring. One of the younger bums got up to face Mike. He was heavyset and taller, but Mike struck without warning—a swift upper cut that snapped the man's head back violently. The big guy fell back onto the rest of their gang. No one else moved in the corner, but Mike could see the whites of their eyes reflecting in the dim light.

"Look away from me, now! Do it, now, or I'll kick all your fuckin' heads in. Do it! You, too, motherfucker! Good. Don't look at me. Just listen. Here it is. If any of you assholes so much as looks at me or my friend again, even a quick look at one of us, ever, I will fucking kill you all where you stand. Any questions, shit bags?" He went over and kicked three men, who simply cowered. "No? I didn't think so. And don't think I can't see your fucking eyes in the dark!"

Mike walked back and sat down with Willie, and stared at the bums in the corner.

"Thanks for covering for me, Mike. If I coulda, that's what I woulda done."

✦✦✦

The train got into the Cleveland freight yard about four o'clock in the morning. While walking up the tracks, they fell in with a bum who told them the freight would lay over until five that afternoon. The next layover would be in Fort Wayne.

"Fort Wayne," Mike said. "That'll be almost a third of the way. Looks like this trip'll take us at least two weeks. How much money you got, Willie?"

"Forty cents."

"And I got three, twenty. We'll be panhandlin' before we reach California."

They had long since eaten the candy bars bought in Buffalo, so they walked along the dark streets until they found an all-night diner. Searching the menu for the cheapest item, they ordered a stack of buckwheat cakes each, with coffee, for 25 cents. The diner was empty and the counterman was about eighteen, and friendly. Mike asked him if they had a washroom, and he pointed at the far end of the diner.

Willie slid off his stool. "Hold the hotcakes till we come back, chief, we're gonna wash up."

The tiny washroom offered a sink and hot water, so they took turns, one sitting in the toilet stall while the other stripped and washed all over. They changed their socks and underwear, and shook out their outer clothing.

Willie examined his shins. They were beginning to scab over, and showed no sign of pus. He slicked his wet hair back and studied himself in the mirror.

"I feel a hunnert per cent better and, when I eat them hotcakes, I'll feel two hunnert."

The hotcakes came with one thin pat of butter, but they drenched them with syrup and wolfed them down.

The counterman spoke with them in a soft accent, which Mike guessed hailed from West Virginia. When they finished eating, he said, "Yew fellas look plumb wore out. If yew wanna lay down in one of them booths in the back, I'll wake yew before the boss comes in at seven."

The seats in the booth were thinly padded, but Mike fell asleep almost immediately. When the counterman shook him at quarter to seven, he felt like he had only slept a few minutes.

"Yew gotta git outta here, I jest heard the boss's car drivin' in the parkin' lot."

Mike reached over and shook Willie awake. They grabbed their bags, thanked the counterman and left hurriedly. Outside, the sun was coming up and the air carried a pleasant coolness.

They walked up the street, and Willie yawned. "I could sleep for a week."

"I know where we can sleep."

"Where?"

"A library. But they probably don't open till nine. Maybe ten."

Willie asked a taxi driver where they could find the nearest library.

"It ain't far," the driver said. "Hop in."

"We're walkin', buddy," Willie said.

"Well, you got a long walk. The Carnegie West branch is a good three miles from here."

Carnegie West turned out to be closer to five miles, and it was almost nine o'clock when they found it. They sat on the steps waiting for it to open. Eventually, a woman opened the big library doors and smiled at them, and they followed her inside.

The library was about the same size as the Montgomery Avenue Branch in Philadelphia, with all the books in one big room. The woman who let them in hurried behind a desk and made them check their bags before she would let them in. At the far end of the room sat two padded chairs with their backs to the desk. Mike steered Willie toward them and they sat down.

Willie leaned back and shut his eyes. "Wake me when they close the place."

When Mike woke up, he didn't know whether the old man standing over him had shaken him, or awakened him by the force of his will.

"This is no hotel, sonny!" the old man growled. "That's my chair you're sleepin' in."

Mike jumped up. "Sorry, mister." He glanced at his watch. It read ten after twelve.

The old man pointed at Willie. "And wake you're friend, too. Lloyd Barnes will be here in a minute, and that's his chair."

He woke Willie up, and they reclaimed their bags and left.

"We'll get us a coupla hot dogs and some candy bars to take along, and then head for the freight yard," Mike said.

Willie put his hand in his pocket and fumbled with his crotch.

"I shouldn't have changed me underwear this morning. I had a wet dream. She don't know it, but I just slipped the peter to Caz' girlfriend Sophie."

Chapter Thirteen

Lady Luck joined them for the ride to Fort Wayne. Waiting outside the yard in Cleveland when the engine came chugging out, they saw a partly open boxcar, and managed to pull it open and jump in before the train gathered speed. So, they made the trip in comparative comfort, even though it seemed to take forever. The train stopped every half hour in towns named Oberlin, Bellevue, Bowling Green, Findlay, Ottawa, Columbus Grove, Delphos, and Van Wert.

They were lucky, too, when they got to Fort Wayne. Walking over a small bridge in the late afternoon sun, they overtook a woman. From the back, with the sun shining on her hair, she looked younger than she turned out to be when they caught up with her. She stood tall and slender, with traces of gray in her dark brown hair. Willie asked her if the city ran any kind of a place where they could get a free night's sleep.

"Not that I ever heard of," the woman said. She looked them up and down. "My goodness, your faces are dirty. Are you boys on the road?"

"Yes, ma'am," Willie said. "We're on our way to California."

Willie grinned at her as she studied their faces again. "I don't know where you can sleep, but you look hungry and I can feed you. I live just down the road."

She pointed to a two-story, green-shingled house, standing at the corner of a row of detached houses about three hundred yards away.

By the time they reached the house, Willie had told her their names, ages, and where they were from. The woman, as outgoing as Willie, introduced herself as Constance Lewis. She worked for a dentist, and had two grown children: one married son, living in Terre Haute, and another son who was a junior at the University of Indiana, in Bloomington.

They waited on a small, front porch while she unlocked the door and waved them inside. She handed each of them a towel and a washcloth.

"While I'm fixing supper, you can both wash up—even have a bath if you want to. The bathroom's at the top of the stairs, and right next to it is my sons' old bedroom. You can get undressed in there."

Bunk beds snugged against one wall; and a tall, maple dresser, and a table filled the opposite space. Against the back wall stood a bookcase, and Mike began looking at the books.

"She's a nice woman, Miz Lewis," Willie said.

"She sure is, takin' a coupla total strangers like us into her home."

"I guess we must remind her of her own sons."

"That must be it, and I guess she can tell we're harmless."

"I wonder what her husband will say when he comes home and finds us here."

Mike shrugged. "She must know him well enough to know he won't raise hell about it."

"How old would you say she is?"

"Beats me, maybe forty, forty-two, somewhere around there."

"She sure ain't a bad-lookin' woman for her age. I noticed she has nice legs."

Mike had noticed them, too, but he looked at Willie and shook his head.

"You're crazy, Willie. Mrs. Lewis is a decent woman, and old enough to be your mother."

Willie's face turned red. "Ya think I don't know that? Ya think I'd even *think* a tryin' anythin'?"

Mike bent down to look at the books again. "I hope not."

Willie unbuttoned his jacket. "Look, if you're gonna start readin', I'm gonna take a bath first."

"Go right ahead, but make it fast. We don't wanna be late for supper."

The bookcase was full of high school textbooks and old copies of the *National Geographic*. On the bottom shelf stood a lone book, Sabatini's *Scaramouche*. Mike pulled it out and read the familiar beginning. "He was born with the gift of laughter and the sense that the world was mad, and that was his only patrimony." He closed the book and put it back. Man, he had really enjoyed that novel.

Willie came into the bedroom draped in a towel, with his body still shiny wet.

"I took a shower!" Willie widened his eyes. "They got a shower built right inta the tub. And the tub's green. And so's the sink and the john."

Mike pulled his sweater over his head and unbuttoned his shirt. "I better get hoppin'."

When he came out of the bathroom, Mrs. Lewis stood at the bottom of the stairs.

"Are you boys almost finished?" she called up to him. "Supper's just about ready."

"We'll be down in one minute, ma'am," Mike called back.

The aroma of frying onions made his nostrils quiver, and he hurried into the bedroom.

"Let's go, Willie, supper's ready."

A big platter of hamburger steaks smothered in onions lay on the kitchen table, next to another platter of home-fried potatoes, and a bowl of peas with a lump of butter melting on top.

"I hate leftovers," Mrs. Lewis said. "And, save some room for dessert, there's tapioca."

Willie's eyes scanned the table set for three. "Is your husband workin' late tonight?"

"I'm a widow," she answered evenly, and passed Willie the platter of fried potatoes. "If you don't get enough to eat it's your own fault. There's plenty here."

When they finished, Willie went to the bathroom, and Mike offered to help with the dishes. Mrs. Lewis thanked him, and said she didn't need any help.

"While I clean up, you and Willie can write letters home. Your mothers must be worried."

"My mother's dead, ma'am, but I'll write to my father."

Mrs. Lewis looked sympathetic. "You can use the dining room table to write on."

He followed her into the dining room and she removed the lace tablecloth. Rummaging in a dark-wood sideboard, she handed him a box of writing paper and a book of two-cent stamps.

He was writing fast when he heard Willie coming downstairs.

"Whadda ya doin'?"

"Writin' a letter home. Mrs. Lewis says you gotta write one, too."

Willie sat down and Mike pushed the box of writing paper toward him.

"What am I gonna say?"

"Tell them you're in Fort Wayne, Indiana, and you just had a big meal, and you're feelin' fine, and you'll write again soon, and not to worry."

Mike finished his letter and stood up. "I gotta go, too."

While he was in the bathroom, he shaved and brushed his teeth, and when he came down Willie had finished his letter. He read it and handed it back. "It looks okay to me."

Willie smiled. "That was always my favorite subject in school."

"What? Bullshit?"

"No, Penmanship. You know, the old Palmer method."

Mrs. Lewis came into the room wiping her hands on an apron. She sat down and smiled at them across the table.

"I know you're good boys, and I've made up my mind. You can sleep here tonight. God knows, I'd want some mother to do as much for my sons if they were in the same situation."

Willie grinned gleefully. "Hey, that's great."

"We sure do appreciate it," Mike said, "but we don't want to put you to any trouble."

Mrs. Lewis stood up. "How much trouble can it be? I'll just put some sheets on the beds."

When she came back she carried two flannel bathrobes and two sets of pajamas.

"You boys don't seem to have a stitch of clean clothing left. You go on up and put these on and bring all your dirty clothes down to me. And no arguments! My Maytag will have them washed before Michael here finishes telling me how much trouble it is."

While they were undressing, Willie confided, "Ya know, Mike, I was about ready to throw in the towel. After we both nearly got killed, and that old sonofabitch wanted to corn hole me, and all the dirt, and goin' hungry, and no place to sleep... Ya know what I mean?"

"Yeah, I know. The worst part of all is the feeling of homelessness. You begin to feel like an outlaw, like every man's hand is turned against you."

"But now that she has treated us so nice, I'm beginnin' ta feel like a human be'en again." He put on his pajamas. "And pajamas, yet. I ain't slept in pajamas since I was a kid."

The large pajamas swam on their frames, but the boys folded and cinched, and went downstairs in their stocking feet, carrying bundles of dirty clothes. They sat on the sofa, looking at copies of *The Saturday Evening Post*, and listening to the churning of the washing machine in the basement. Mrs. Lewis came back and switched on the radio.

"It's time for *Amos and Andy*. I never miss them."

They listened raptly while Kingfish tried, unsuccessfully, to sell Lightning an insurance policy that would protect him from all kinds of unlikely catastrophes. Then *Rose Marie* came on, followed by *One Man's Family*, and *Town Hall Tonight* with Fred Allen and Portland Hoffa, and their guests, Charlie McCarthy and Edgar Bergen. They shouted with laughter when Fred threatened to turn Charlie into a rest home for retired termites.

At ten o'clock, *Tommy Dorsey* came on and when the orchestra went into a fast rendition of *You Oughta Be in Pictures*, Willie jumped to his feet.

"Ya wanna dance, Miz Lewis?"

He walked over to her, a big grin on his face, and held out his hand.

She looked at him, a pleased smile on her face. "I'm not sure I remember how."

"Sure you do," Willie said, pulling her to her feet.

When she stood up, she was a head taller than him, and she kicked off her shoes, cutting the height discrepancy in half. Willie, though—not self-conscious in the least—jitterbugged Mrs. Lewis around the room, twirling her away from him, and pulling her back, until the music ended and she sank breathlessly into her chair.

"My Lord, Willie, you can dance. I've never jitterbugged before in my life."

Willie smiled smugly. "I am pretty good, if I do say so myself."

The band started *All I Do Is Dream of You*, and Willie gestured toward his friend. "Okay, hot shot, it's your turn."

"I can't do anything but the box step," Mike protested. Mrs. Lewis, though, was standing up, her arms outstretched. He walked over to her, an embarrassed smile on his face.

He held her lightly, then lumbered off, but however clumsily he danced, she managed to follow him. Halfway through the song, he picked up the beat and began to enjoy himself.

When the music stopped, Mrs. Lewis smiled genuinely. "You dance nicely, too, Michael."

"Yeah, Mike," Willie said, "you dance like a right fielder playin' shortstop."

The Dorsey Band signed off with the lush sound of the leader's trombone. Mrs. Lewis made cocoa, and they sat in the kitchen, sipping the steaming liquid and munching Fig Newtons.

"I have to leave for work at eight-thirty," Mrs. Lewis said, "so I get up at six. Suppose I wake you boys at seven. Your clean clothes will be ready by then."

"That'll be fine with us," Mike said. "The freight leaves at eleven, so if we leave when you do, we'll have plenty of time."

✦✦✦

At eleven-thirty the next morning, still waiting outside the yards, a bum came by and told them the train wasn't leaving until two o'clock.

"They must have a special cargo on," he said. "The yard's crawlin' with railroad bulls."

After he left, they walked across the tracks and sat on a pile of railroad ties to eat the sandwiches Mrs. Lewis gave them. Mike looked down at the white knight emblem on his jacket, restored to its pristine whiteness by Mrs. Lewis' Maytag.

"We may be a little wrinkled," he said, "but I bet we're the cleanest bums on the road."

"We gotta do what she asked," Willie said. "Drop her a note about how we made out."

"We sure will. We'll send her a postcard at every stop, and a long letter from California."

Willie wagged his head. "Me own mother couldn't have treated me better than that woman."

Just after two o'clock the train came out of the yards, and they ran across the tracks and loped alongside it, letting half the line of box cars go by before swinging onto one of the iron ladders. They climbed to the top of the car and sat down, pulled their shoulder bags in front of them and huddled together against the wind.

"I don't see any gon-dolas!" Willie shouted in his ear.

"Me, neither!"

The train began to pick up speed when Mike saw a head appear above the end of a boxcar down near the caboose. As he watched, a man clambered onto the top of the car and began running toward them with a club.

He screamed at Willie. "It's a railroad dick! He's gonna knock us off the train!"

He could see the dick's angry face now, thirty yards away, and he scrambled to his feet, pulling Willie with him. They ran forward toward the engine. When they got to the last boxcar, the dick was still coming, so Mike eased himself onto the iron ladder and climbed down to the bottom rung. As he hung there, Willie climbed down the ladder at the other end of the boxcar. Above him, the dick glared down, shaking the upraised club. When he continued to hang there, the dick turned around and began to back down the ladder.

Mike jumped, trying desperately to land running. The uneven roadbed jerked his feet out from under him. He tucked himself like a gymnast, and rolled along the stony ground to a jolting halt. He lay there, his lungs and heart pumping like bellows until the sobbing gasps of air came more slowly. At that point, he carefully extended his arms and legs, and laid on his back. His jacket was torn along the left sleeve, but he didn't seem to be hurt. He sat up and saw Willie lying in a heap about fifty feet away.

He shouted to him. "You all right, Willie?" His friend groaned an answer he couldn't make out.

A long, red scrape ran along Willie's forehead, and the backs of his hands pooled with blood. He turned his friend gently over on his back.

"Can you move your arms and legs?"

Willie moved everything, but his left leg didn't stir. "Me left leg won't move."

Mike felt gently along the length of the leg, and above the ankle there seemed to be a lumpy swelling. He pulled off his jacket and put it under Willie's head.

"It may be broken. Don't move."

"I'll wrap it as tight as I can and carry you to the road. We gotta get you to a hospital."

Up on the road, a car appeared almost immediately and Mike flagged it down. The driver was a neatly dressed, middle-aged man and, together, they lifted Willie into the back seat.

When Mike climbed into the front seat next to him, the man said: "I'm trying to figure out which is closer, Lutheran Hospital or St. Joseph's hospital."

Willie groaned. "Take me to St. Joseph's, please."

The man let out the clutch. "No, I'll take you to Lutheran. It's closer."

Willie groaned again. "You a Protestant, Mister?"

"No," the man said. "I'm Jewish."

Mike patted Willie's arm. "Take it easy, Willie, we'll be there soon."

✦✦✦

The doctor who set Willie's leg looked young for a doctor and, after they took Willie upstairs to one of the wards, he talked to Mike.

The doctor flexed his fingers twice. "He fractured the fibula, the smaller, lower leg bone."

"How long will he be in here?"

The doctor shrugged. "Maybe a week. Then we'll put a walking cast on and he'll be fine."

Outside the hospital, Mike looked at his watch. It read ten after seven, and he began walking aimlessly toward the center of town with the vague notion of finding a bus station. There was always a bus station in the middle of town, and maybe he'd sleep there tonight. Without counting his money, he knew he had two dollars and twenty cents, and maybe as much as a week to wait around for Willie. Christ, he'd be panhandling before he got out of Fort Wayne. He thought about calling Mrs. Lewis, but imposing on her for a week would take a lot of nerve. Out of the goodness of her heart, she had given him a night's lodging, but she hadn't taken him to rear.

He passed a White Tower, and went in and ate two hamburgers with coffee. That reduced his money to a dollar ninety-five. The counterman told him about a bus station three blocks away. Mike decided to try to sleep there, if he didn't get rousted.

The bus station had a ticket counter looking out at a small waiting room, with a plastic sofa and two padded, plastic chairs. A discarded Indianapolis newspaper sat on the sofa with a headline that caught his eye. He picked it up and sat down in a chair facing away from the ticket counter so he needn't stare at the clerk. *NO MORE REPRIEVES: LINDBERGH KILLER DIES SATURDAY,* the headline said.

Thumbing through the paper, he read a McIntyre article about O. Henry, and read it with interest. He had always admired O. Henry, and *The Gift of the Magi* was one of his favorite short stories. One thing about the story that had puzzled him, though, was how the young couple could consider themselves poor when right on the first page it says the husband makes twenty bucks a week. Jesus, if he ever made twenty bucks a week, he wouldn't know what to do with all the money. Still, maybe twenty bucks bought more nowadays than it did in 1905, or whenever O. Henry wrote the story. He did remember reading somewhere that just a couple of years ago farmers were earning less for their crops than English farmers did back in the days of Queen Elizabeth.

He lay back and closed his tired eyes. Suddenly he felt a tap on his shoulder. Looking up, he saw the ticket clerk standing next to his chair, a scowl on his face.

"You wanna buy a ticket?"

Mike tried to keep his voice calm. "No, I'm waiting for somebody."

The man's scowl turned into a sneer. "Well, you got a long wait. There are no buses due in for three hours. And none going out, neither."

"Does that mean I gotta leave?"

"It sure doesn't mean you can bunk here. This ain't a hotel."

Mike made up his mind. "Can I use your phone?"

"It's a public phone. You can use it if you got a nickel."

Mike walked over to the phone booth and looked up Mrs. Lewis' number.

During the long walk to Mrs. Lewis' house, he wondered if he had done the right thing. On the phone, she had been instantly sympathetic, and almost the first words out of her mouth were an invitation to come back to her house immediately.

Maybe he could do some odd jobs in payment? Well, he'd see when he got there, and if she looked like she regretted her impulsive generosity, he'd leave quietly. When he arrived, though, her solicitude still seemed genuine.

"I haven't had time to take the sheets off your bed," she told him at the door, "so it's all ready for you."

Later, sitting in the living room before he went to bed, they talked about Willie, and Mrs. Lewis said he was one of the nicest boys she had ever met, so friendly and full of fun. "And he looks like a cherub with his dark, curly hair and wonderful smile. As soon as you see him, you want to mother him."

She also talked about her next-door neighbor, an elderly widow named Mrs. Anthony.

"She's a good woman in her way, but she is nosy. So, of course, she asked me about my overnight visitors."

She gave him an embarrassed smile. "I don't know why I felt guilty about having you boys in my house. Good Lord, I've got two sons older than either of you. But I did. So, I told her you were my cousin's son from Pittsburgh, and you and your friend stopped off to see me on your way to California.

"Anyway, I'm sure she'll ask me why you came back again so soon, so I'll have to ask you to please go along with my little deception in case we run into her."

Mike assured her he would, and remarked about how suspicious some people were, and how they misinterpreted even innocent acts. He said he felt sorry for people like her.

The next afternoon he went to visit Willie. The day after that was a Saturday and Mrs. Lewis went with him. They found Willie sitting up in bed, his plaster cast propped up on a pillow.

Before they left, Mrs. Lewis placed a hand on Willie's shoulder. "I'd feel much better if I knew you boys were going home when Willie leaves the hospital. Mike tells me you almost killed yourselves more than once."

Willie looked at Mike, "What do you say?"

"I'm ready to go back if you are, but someday I'd still like to see California."

"We will," Willie said. "We'll save our money and, next time, ride a bus."

Mike nodded. "I've had it with trains. When we start back to Philly, we'll hitchhike."

Willie seemed relieved to hear it. "Now you're talkin'."

That night, Mike and Mrs. Lewis sat in the living room listening to the radio. At nine thirty, Wayne King and His Orchestra came on. Across the room, her foot began to tap.

"I did so enjoy dancing the other night," she said. "It was the first time I'd danced in years."

The band was playing a slow, catchy tune, and Mike jumped to his feet.

"Would you like to take a chance with me and my two left feet?"

She stood up, smiling. "You're not so bad. Just relax and follow the music."

He box-stepped her around the room, even managing to embellish the simple pattern with an occasional pause. When the song ended, they stayed together waiting for the next one to begin and, again, he started off without a mishap.

The softness of her body brushing lightly against his created a wave of warmth coursing through his genitals, and he backed away, embarrassed. She reacted by pulling him close, and suddenly they found themselves pressing together and kissing. They moved toward the sofa and fell onto it, still clutching each other.

✦✦✦

When he awoke the next morning, he lay alone in the big bed, but through the open bedroom door wafted the aroma of bacon frying. He got up, pushed his arms into the flannel robe laid on a chair, and went downstairs into the kitchen. Mrs. Lewis stood by the stove, dressed in only a light-blue bed-shirt. Her nipples stood erect.

"Good morning," she said without looking at him. "Do you like salt pork?"

"Good morning. I've never eaten it before. But it smells great, and I'm sure I'll like it."

"How do you want your eggs?"

"Whichever way's the least..." He balked at her frown. "Sunny side up, please."

They ate breakfast in silence, then she removed the plates and poured each of them a fresh cup of coffee. He tried not to look, but her nipples still pushed through the thin fabric.

She placed her hands around her coffee cup and stared down at it. "I'm forty-three years old, and you're not quite eighteen, so I guess I should feel ashamed," she muttered. "But I didn't plan what happened, it just did, and I'm not sorry..." Her voice trailed off and she looked up. "Unless you are."

Mike shook his head. "I'm not sorry. I'm glad... unless you're not glad."

She didn't answer, so he added. "You said last night you can't get pregnant, and I know I don't have any diseases. So, what's the harm? Besides, being with you is a beautiful experience."

He walked around the table and pulled her to her feet, and she followed him like a child, upstairs, and through the bedroom door.

Afterwards, as they lay there, she ran a finger along his collarbone. "There's just one thing. I will feel ashamed unless I know you won't tell anybody about us, even people I don't know back in Philadelphia."

He made his voice solemn. "You have my absolute promise I will never, as long as I live, tell any living soul about what happened between us."

She reached over and patted his cheek. "I believe you. Now... come here."

✦✦✦

Every afternoon he visited Willie, and every night he slept with Constance Lewis, further discovering the marvelousness of a women's body. Her breasts were not large, but her nipples always stood erect. She had long, slim legs, as smooth as a young girl's, and when he told her how pretty they were, she acted absurdly pleased. When he entered her, he lost himself in a miracle of silken warmth and undulating movements, unlike anything he ever imagined.

Once, when Mike became so excited he ejaculated too soon, Constance surprised him by making a risqué joke about it. "One good thing about making love with a boy your age... if the first erection doesn't do the job, another one will come along any minute."

It was true.

✦✦✦

The hospital discharged Willie eight days after his accident and, when he returned to the house, clumping along nimbly on his walking cast, he didn't suspect a thing. Constance welcomed him back with a hug and a peck on the cheek. When he thanked her for taking care of his old friend Mike, she smiled and assured him that the pleasure of his company had more than compensated for any trouble.

After supper, Mrs. Lewis dug out some road maps and they plotted the trip home. If they followed U.S. Route 30, it would join up with the new Pennsylvania Turnpike, and...

The next morning, Mrs. Lewis cried softly when they said good-bye, and tears clouded Mike's and Willie's eyes as well.

"We'll write, that's a promise," Willie said in a shaky voice. "And thanks for everything."

Mike leaned over and brushed her cheek with his lips. "I'll write."

✦✦✦

They made it home in three days. As soon as they arrived in Ohio, they hitched a ride with a young couple in an old Hudson roadster with a rumble seat. Andy, the husband, was a skinny, medium-sized man with stringy blond hair, and glasses. His wife Anna had stringy, dark hair. Andy had lost his job in a shoe factory in Joplin, Missouri, and they were on their way to where Anna's family lived in New Jersey.

The Swansons dropped them off at the Harrisburg turn-off at eleven o'clock Saturday night. It took four more rides before they got over the Delaware River Bridge, and a streetcar home. At nine o'clock Sunday night Mike stood at the door of his house. He had been gone sixteen days.

The house stood dark, and he searched inside the basement window grate for the key, but it wasn't there. Rose's house looked dark, too, but she was probably home, so he walked up the street and rang her doorbell. Moments later, a light went on in the front bedroom. When Rose opened the door, a wrapper thrown over her nightgown, she let out a happy shriek and pulled him inside. In the hallway light, he saw his father standing at the top of the stairs in a bathrobe. He had always assumed his old man and Rose were sleeping together, but to catch them practically *in flagrante* embarrassed him, and he must have looked it. Rose clutched his arm.

"It's all right, Michael! You're father and I were married yesterday in the rectory."

Mike gave her a big grin. Old Rose hadn't waited a minute longer than necessary after Teresa's wedding.

Part III

Hawaii

Chapter Fourteen

Bang! Bang! Bang! Mike hated the sound, but felt, in some odd way, it would play a part in his destiny. Looking back later, he realized the noise drove him to join the Army.

He had worked for the Regal Belt and Suspender Company for two months, placing the rounded ends of belts into a metal die, and banging down on a pedal with his right foot to imprint the crease near the edges. Bang!

For this monstrously monotonous labor, they paid him twelve dollars a week. Or, as Karl Jennssen, one of the cutters trying to unionize the place, put it, "Thirty cents an hour, plus the privilege of buying evening dress suspenders at reduced prices."

Harry Aaronson had gotten him the job through a friend, and Mike gave Rose seven dollars a week for board. Rose spent most of the board money, though, buying him clothes, including a sharp, blue gabardine suit, and a snazzy raglan topcoat. Nowadays, when he went to the dances at the Moose Hall, or the Liederkranz, he looked almost as dapper as Dominic Angelo.

Rose still worked as a floor lady at Strawmaker's, and his father tended bar at Rafferty's, so money was coming into the house. He didn't know how much Rose made a week, but he figured it must be around forty dollars. Rose had enough to convert Teresa's room for him, including the installation of a new bookcase. Yet, still he joined the Army.

Things just hadn't seemed the same since he came back from bumming the trains in April. In only a little over two months, things had changed. Dutch Koenig finally went to work with Stash at Vogt's, and was engaged to Marie Drean. Sam was studying his balls off at the Philadelphia College of Pharmacy, and nobody saw him anymore. He didn't see Willie at all. Two months after they got home, Willie joined the Civilian Conservation Corps (CCC). He lived in a camp in a place called Pine Creek Furnace, and was having a ball.

He already had shacked up with one of the local girls, whom he described in a letter. "If she had as many peters sticking out of her as she had stuck in her, she'd look like a pincushion. But right now she's all mine..." Willie had finally lost his cherry.

Mike tried to join the CCCs with Willie, but Dooley said it wasn't fair. "Your old man's workin' part-time." The real reason had been his father's Democratic Party registration.

He still saw Doc Greene now that he was eighteen and working steady, and he and Doc grew closer than ever. A couple of times a month they paid Aunt Sadie a visit, usually early in the week when business was slow. Sometimes Angelo and Lynch would go along and Doc would call Sadie to tell her they were coming, and she'd close the place to other customers. She'd cook them a meal and, afterwards, they'd sit around drinking beer. Whenever they were ready, they'd go in to see one of the girls.

Mike wrote Mrs. Lewis every week, but after a couple of months the letters stopped. After all, how often could he write and tell her Willie was still in the CCCs.

He saw Mr. Goldman, Sylvia, and Naomi at least once a month. Naomi was going steady with Bernie Gottbaum and, now that they weren't rivals anymore, Bernie had turned out to be a nice guy. The last time he had been to Eugene Debs Hall, Bernie had brought along a friend of his who was trying to raise money for the Spanish Loyalists.

The man, Victor Kirsch, talked passionately about the rise of Fascism in Spain and the need to fight it. He said if the Fascists won there, they would go everywhere.

"Europe is full of Fascists," Victor explained, "real and incipient. Forget, for the moment, Hitler and Mussolini, and that bush-league Benito, Dr. Salazar. Look at the rest of Europe. In France, there's Colonel de la Rocque and his *Croix de Feu*, lusting to smash the Popular Front and its Jewish leader Leon Blum."

He paused to study each face. "In England, there's Sir Oswald Mosley and his Union of British Fascists. That bastard's a real turncoat. He used to be a member of the Labor Party. Incidentally, his wife Lady Curzon had a Jewish grandfather. Then..." he circled the table, "in Austria there is Prince von Starhemberg with a private army financed by Mussolini. Even Belgium has a boy Hitler, an idiot named Leon Degrelle. And others are full of Jew haters, which is the first step toward Fascism."

When he finished, he passed the hat and Mike threw in all he had—four dollars. Bernie threw in his signet ring and wristwatch. Mike thought that if Victor had been recruiting for the Abraham Lincoln Brigade, he and the others might have joined. But he wasn't, so that was the end of it. Instead Mike joined the Army.

◆◆◆

The impulse that led to his enlistment triggered during his lunch hour while walking on his way back to work. Just as he turned a corner, a touch of color caught his eye and he walked back to investigate. Halfway up the block, he saw a poster with the words "Travel and Adventure" in large type, and a picture of a young soldier in a light-colored uniform, against a background of waving palms. What a sharp-looking guy the young soldier on the poster was, and how inviting the warm breezes that ruffled the palm trees.

"Are you interested, son?" a voice behind him asked, and he looked around to see a middle-aged man in an Army uniform regarding him with a speculative eye.

"I sure am," he answered.

"How old are you?" the soldier asked.

"Eighteen."

"Can you get your father's permission to enlist?"

"Sure."

"Okay. Come up to the third floor of this building at two o'clock and I'll let you talk to the recruiting officer."

He started down Broad Street, and Mike ran after him.

"Hey, mister!" he shouted. "Is there any chance the Army won't take me? I got a job and if I'm not there at one o'clock, I'm liable to lose it."

"Sure, there's a chance. In times like these, we get more applicants than we can use."

"But I have a good chance, haven't I?"

The soldier looked Mike up and down.

"You got anything wrong with you?"

"No."

"How much education you got?"

"I've been to high school."

"You got a good chance, then. The Army can always use educated men."

He walked down the street, and Mike stood looking after him until he disappeared into a lunchroom. Doubts began to assail him. *I could be exchanging one form of bondage for another,* he thought. He checked the time. Ten minutes to one, still time to make it back to the job.

He looked again at the colorful poster. To hell with the Regal Belt and Suspender Company!

Rose threw her hands in the air and sat in a nook chair when he broke the news to her that evening. "Why, Michael?" her voice trembled. "You've got a job, and a nice home. Haven't I made a nice home for you?"

Mike put his arm around her and kissed her cheek.

"The nicest, Rose," he murmured. "The best I'm ever likely to have."

"Then, why?"

Visions of Herman Melville's *Typee: A Peep at Polynesian Life,* and *Omoo;* and the adventures in Nordhoff and Hall's *Mutiny on the Bounty* danced in his head.

"It's Hawaii, Rose," he answered. "It's in the middle of the Pacific Ocean, two thousand miles from California. I ought to be paying them but, instead, they're paying me."

Rose began to cry, so he pushed on. "I'll only be gone three years. I'm bound to have experiences I can write about. I might learn a trade, and get a better job when I get out."

"Maybe he's right, Rose," Paddy injected. "With a trade, he can find a good job."

Rose asked Paddy, "What trade do you think he will learn? Shooting? Marching?"

She turned to Mike. "If this will make you happy, I guess that's what you'll have to do. I only hope and pray you're doing the right thing."

"I know I am," he said, with a confident smile.

✦✦✦

Two days later he was sworn in, given a three-day pass, a bus ticket, and a set of orders directing him to "report to Fort Slocum, N.Y. not later than 2400 hours, 16 October 1936."

On the way home, he stopped at a telephone booth and called Mr. Goldman at his house. Goldman went silent when he heard the news.

"What in God's name made you do that?"

"You know I'm gonna be a writer, so I have to do some traveling, have some experiences."

"There's a taproom at 9th and Allegheny. Can you meet me there at eight?"

"Sure."

"Okay, I'll see you then."

✦✦✦

Lester Goldman sat at the bar drinking a beer as Mike walked in. He finished his beer and ordered two more, and they carried them to a booth and sat down.

"Well, Kane, when you quit school I told you you'd come to no good, didn't I?"

"Yes, you did."

"And I was right, wasn't I?"

Mike sipped his beer. "The jury's still out on that by a long sight."

"Yeah, right," Mr. Goldman snorted. "Why don't you also return to your church? That way all your problems will be solved."

Mike grinned in response.

Mr. Goldman leaned closer. "Have you ever read about Smedley Butler's Armistice Day speech?"

"Sure, he's that retired Marine General who compared his military service to racketeering for big business. How does this apply to me? He was a general, and I'm only an infantry private."

"So, he was a chief, but he used lots of Indians. That's you, one of those Indians."

"You've heard of Roosevelt's Good Neighbor Policy? Those bad, old days are gone now."

"But suppose Roosevelt loses the election next month?"

"Are you kidding? Roosevelt losing to Alf Landon?"

Mr. Goldman smiled faintly. "Yeah. One of the few certainties in this uncertain world is the stupidity of the Grand Old Party. In 1940, they'll probably nominate Charles Schwab."

"Seriously, Kane, there is another thing you can be certain of," he went on, "and that is the outbreak of war in Europe, followed inevitably by our involvement."

Mike held up his hand. "On that point I can absolutely reassure you. There will be no war until after October 16, 1939, which is when I get out. I got that straight from Mary McDevitt."

"Who is Mary McDevitt?"

"She's very religious and has always been looking out for me. She's doing two novenas, one to Saint Teresa of Avila, and another to Saint Teresa, the Little Flower."

Mr. Goldman shook his head. "You know, Kane, H.G. Wells once said something to the effect that nobody with an ounce of brains or sensitivity would willingly embrace the life of a soldier. But, in the case of idiots like you, Wells was wrong."

Chapter Fifteen

Mike finally boarded a ship bound for Hawaii after a six-week indoctrination at Fort Slocum, New York, an Army recruit depot located on an island in Long Island Sound. He had personal experience with the Army's ethos of "hurry-up, and wait" during those first weeks, but now he saw it in practice on a grander scale. Hundreds of soldiers left Fort Slocum at five o'clock on November 30th, but they didn't get under way to Hawaii until late afternoon.

They had crammed into an Army tug that took them down the East River to the Army Pier in Brooklyn. Though jam-packed, Mike and two of his new friends, Jeff and Reggie, managed to stay together. Despite their excitement about the seven-thousand-mile trip through the Panama Canal, and then northwest across the Pacific, they sat silently, listening to a prior-service soldier behind them telling everybody stories about the wahines, or Hawaiian beauties, he left behind.

When they got to the Brooklyn Army Pier, a large transport jutted out of one of the slips, with the name *Republic* painted on the port, left, side of the bow. Everybody began to cheer, and many shouts rang out.

"There she is!"

"That's the tub that's gonna take us over!"

They disembarked from the tug and marched to where the transport was tied up. Other units already lingered there, waiting for their turn to board. At the bottom of the gangplank, a sergeant with a shipping list called out last names. Soldiers answered with their first names, middle initials, and serial numbers.

When Mike was waved through, he staggered up the gangplank under the weight of his gear. When he got to the top, another sergeant directed him down a spiraling iron stairway. A sergeant at every landing sent him still lower until finally the stairs ended in a dimly lit cavern crowded with four-tiered rows of bunks.

The bunks consisted of strips of canvas, strung on metal frames. The space above each bunk measured around twenty-four inches, but it reduced when the bunk above you was occupied because the canvas sagged. The aisles between the endless tiers stretched about thirty inches wide, and Mike developed a queasy feeling in his stomach. Then and there, he made a vow to spend as little time as possible in this hellish sleeping compartment.

His friend Jeff followed right behind him and, together, they managed to snare two prized upper bunks across from each other. Jeff was fastidious about his appearance, but otherwise he was great fun. Mike left him stretched out on his bunk polishing his boots, and went to look for his other buddy Reggie. He found him and helped him stake his claim to another top bunk by throwing his bag on it. They then left to carry out a plan devised back at Slocum.

From talking to prior-service men, they knew every recruit must perform a function on the ship. Some were unpleasant, like guard, and kitchen cleaning. There were a few, more pleasant jobs, like helping the ship's baker, working in the crew's mess, and in the first-class library. They wanted that last job, and the man they went looking for was the Ship's Chaplain, who had the job at his disposal.

They found his office on A Deck, two decks above the Main Deck. It belonged to a world vastly more pleasant than the subaqueous depths of the troop compartments. When they knocked, a voice told them to enter. They removed their hats and went in.

The chaplain was a cheerful major who smiled at them warmly.

"You boys looking for jobs in my department?"

"Yes, sir," Reggie said. As a Harvard graduate, he did all the talking.

"Well, I need somebody to help me get the troop lounge ready for church services."

Reggie assumed a pained expression.

"No offense meant," the chaplain blurted.

"I also need somebody to run the ship's newspaper."

"I haven't had any experience in that field, sir," Reggie said.

"What kind of a job were you two looking for?" the chaplain asked.

"We were thinking of the first-class library, sir."

"Have you had any experience?"

"Yes, sir, I worked in Widener Library when I was a student at Harvard."

The chaplain's eyebrows rose, "You're a Harvard man?

Reggie smiled modestly. "Yes, sir."

"Well, you should be able to handle our little operation."

He turned to Mike. "What about you?"

"I'm a librarian, too, sir," Mike lied. "I worked in my high school library."

The chaplain nodded and reached into his desk to pull out two slips of paper and two green tags. He wrote their names on the slips of paper and the word "Library" on the green tags.

"Here," he said, handing them across the desk, "give these slips to the troop sergeant major and these tags will get you past the guards when you want to come up to the officer's deck."

When Mike got back to the troop compartment, Jeff still lay on his bunk polishing shoes. His extra shoes and toilet articles were stowed neatly between the pipes in the ceiling.

"Did you get the job?" he asked.

"I sure did," Mike answered.

"I got a good job, too."

"You did! What kind?"

"In the crew mess."

"How the hell did you get that?"

Jeff shrugged. "I was layin' here, dozin' off, and a seaman taps me on the shoulder and asks me where I'm from. After some chitchat, he offered me the job. He said it meant good chow and no dirty details. I said okay. He got my name, gave me this tag, and left."

◆◆◆

Mike thanked God he hadn't joined the Navy. They sailed in the late afternoon, and the ship was only rocking gently when he began to feel queasy. He wasn't really sick, but felt sickly, particularly when he went near the troop mess, or down to the troop compartment with its nausea-producing smell of combined latrine odors, sweaty clothes, stale vomit, and tobacco smoke. Mike could not eat anything, so Jeff smuggled six or eight pieces of dry toast out of the crew mess every day. The toast, combined with Hershey bars from the ship's canteen, was the only food that didn't nauseate him, and he never entered the troop mess hall during the voyage.

Claustrophobia might have been the reason, as Mike hated these confined spaces. He tried sneaking up on deck to sleep there, but the troop commander had issued strict orders against it, and the guard chased him back downstairs. After that, he just stayed topside until he couldn't keep his eyes open, then went down for a few hours of uneasy sleep.

The troop commander was a tall, gaunt, wild-eyed major, with gray, crew-cut hair, and horn-rimmed spectacles. He made the recruits stand inspection on deck every morning at eight o'clock. As Mike quickly discovered, all officers have particular items they concentrate on when making inspections, and this one's particular items were waist belts and campaign hats. If he found a frayed belt, or a dirty hat, he would fix the culprit with a baleful stare and, in the case of a belt, unbuckle it, jerk it from around the offender's waist, and throw it over the side. If a hat affronted him, he would whip it off and sail it out as far over the water as he could. Everybody watched as the hat glided over the waves and plunked gracefully into the ocean. Then the major would turn back to the despoiled soldier, a relieved smile on his face, and say, "Buy a new one."

The two hours he spent each morning, afternoon, and evening in the airy spaciousness of the officer's lounge—the location of the first-class library—made the trip bearable for Mike. In the salon atmosphere of the lounge, people were uniformly polite and, in Reggie's case, even something more than polite.

The word had gotten around Reggie was a Harvard man, so second lieutenants, fresh from West Point and the Infantry School at Fort Benning, arrived to reminisce about trips they had made to Cambridge to play hockey, or tennis, or baseball against the Crimson.

One lieutenant named Gaines told Reggie about his upcoming assignment. "It's a really good job, teaching at the West Point Prep School at Schofield Barracks. By the way, Royal, how's your math?"

"I was a math major," Reggie answered.

"And he graduated cum laude, sir," Mike added.

"Look me up when you get settled at Schofield," Lieutenant Gaines said.

As he walked away, Reggie winked at Mike. "Remember how I told you something good would turn up in Oahu?"

The library's best customer was an infantry captain named Ogden G. Anderson. The towering, muscular, fifty-year-old man, with immense sloping shoulders, walked with a stiff-legged, clumping stride that shook the deck. The absence of a West Point class ring on his finger may have been the reason he still remained a captain at his age. Whatever the faults in his education, he read faster that anyone Mike had ever seen. The library housed a small section on military history—Herodotus, Caesar, Napoleon, Ardant du Picq, Clausewitz—perhaps two dozen books in all, and Captain Anderson read every one of them in the twenty-one days they stayed at sea. However early they opened up in the morning, the captain already waited for them. As soon as the bookcases were unlocked, he would select a book and check it out. Next, he would settle in a chair he considered his own, light up a big-bowled pipe, and begin to read with fierce concentration.

"It certainly doesn't take you long to select a book, sir," Reggie told him one morning.

Captain Anderson frowned at him. "Makes no difference. I've read them all before."

Lieutenant Gaines told them the captain was a widower, and pointed out his daughter Myrna. She was about twenty and very pretty, with blonde hair, dark-blue eyes, and a figure that made every male on board fantasize about losing himself in its billowing curves. She never went below A-Deck, but sometimes she could be seen moving along the rail above. The mere sight of her made Mike's senses tingle, and he surely wasn't alone.

✦✦✦

It took six days to get to Cristobal on the Atlantic side of the Panama Canal, and most of a day to go through the locks and Gatun Lake. When they got to Balboa on the Pacific side, everybody was given a six-hour pass and five dollars partial pay.

Reggie, Jeff, and Mike headed for Panama City. As soon as he got ashore, Mike's appetite revived miraculously, and he ate a big dinner of hamburger steak, fried potatoes, sliced tomatoes, and Boston cream pie at the YMCA cafeteria.

They hailed a horse-drawn cab and told the driver to show them the sights. He drove them through town to a district known as the Cocoanut Grove, waved them out of the cab, and galloped back for another load of soldiers.

There, an army of prostitutes had set up lean-toes with beds inside.

Reggie looked around. "Compared to the Cocoanut Grove, Sodom and Gomorrah were Puritan communities."

Shouting with laughter, they ran up the street to the corner where a low, flat building, made of galvanized tin, bore the sign "Red Teatro—Stag Movies." They paused, and went in.

Inside the dingy theater, the wooden benches were filled with soldiers and a sprinkling of merchant seamen, so they stood at the back listening to the whistling and feet stamping of the impatient audience. When the lights extinguished and the first flickering images appeared on the screen, an instant quiet fell on the room. The film was an old, silent movie, with a plot involving the ruler of an unnamed Middle Eastern country who had lost his virility. When the picture opened, the ruler was shown lying naked on a couch, his penis flaccid, while members of his harem, also naked, danced around him. After a few minutes, he dismissed them with a languid wave of his hand, while in the background, a bearded man, evidently the ruler's chief counselor grimaced.

Mike whispered to Reggie, "How would an audience at Harvard act at a movie like this?"

"As raptly attentive as this audience," Reggie whispered back.

As the story developed, the audience discovered the country was going to pot because the king was too preoccupied with his personal problems to govern properly. Finally, the chief counselor hit on the idea of offering a reward to anyone who could concoct a potion to restore the king's virility. This led to a succession of scenes showing elderly men mixing steaming draughts, which the king drank, followed by nude dancing by the harem girls. They all failed. At last, one wise man mixed a potion, the king drank, the girls danced and, presto, the king was cured. The return of his potency was indicated by a close up shot of an erection that filled the screen, followed by an orgy that left no doubt that the cure was genuine.

On the way out, the ticket taker grinned. "You go get some tail now, hey?"

"Forget that!" Jeff said. "I'm worried I'll catch a disease just breathing around here."

✦✦✦

The fifteen-day passage from Panama to Hawaii passed slowly. After those rich hamburger steaks, Mike's stomach shrunk back to accommodate a diet of dry toast and Hershey bars. He became used to less sleep, and to the strange life, and even got some pleasure out of it.

The sky in the latitudes they traversed arced above, breathtakingly beautiful and crowded with a multitude of stars never seen in the heavens over Philadelphia. The water—a deep, midnight blue—lit up eerily with flecks of phosphorescent marine life.

In the evenings after they closed the library, Mike and Reggie would meet Jeff at the stern of the ship, and Reggie would sing songs like "The Sweetheart of Sigma Chi," "The Whiffenpoof Song," and "Do Ye Ken John Peel." An audience would gather, including A-Deck passengers looking down from above, and soon it would turn into a group sing.

Finally, Diamond Head hove into view, and the *Republic* steamed around it and slipped into Honolulu Harbor. A band playing "Song of the Islands," "Aloha 'Oe," and "The Cockeyed Mayor of Kaunakakai" met the ship. A group of pretty, native girls, dressed in grass skirts, stood on the dock with flower leis for the officer passengers.

The officers and their families got off the boat first, and an hour passed before the troops disembarked. The hour moved swiftly, while watching swarms of brown-skinned boys dive into the depths of the harbor to retrieve coins thrown overboard by the soldiers, and staring at the obelisk-shaped Aloha Tower, pointed like a gigantic finger into the brilliantly blue sky.

When the troops' turn came, they marched off the ship and were assembled in a large open space, and then divided into smaller spaces, each marked with a number.

Noncommissioned officers, or NCOs, called names and placed men into the numbered spaces. Mike and Jeff found themselves assigned to the 27th Infantry Regiment. Reggie went to headquarters.

Chapter Sixteen

They rode to Schofield Barracks in ungainly, two-and-a-half ton trucks, with canvas covers that made them look like prairie schooners. They paced a steady forty miles an hour down the macadam road past bright, green pineapple fields, and jungles of sugar cane. In the intolerably hot confines of those fields, tiny Filipino, Chinese, and Japanese women performed labor that would prostrate a two-hundred-pound white man. They rolled past dusty villages, and children came out to greet them. Their bright faces showed the blood of all the races of Asia and Polynesia, plus a more recent breed called half-Schofield. They drove down Waianae Avenue, the main thoroughfare of Schofield Barracks, and the truck bearing Mike and the other soldiers destined for the same regiment turned into the 27th Infantry Regiment's compound.

After unloading, the officers separated the prior-service men, and marched the recruits across the grassy quadrangle. They lined up on a street facing a row of concrete, three-story barracks where a short, middle-aged sergeant called the roll. His bright blue eyes looked out of a red, broken-veined face, and he sported a round paunch, and a pair of spindly legs neatly encased in shorts and leggings. When he finished the roll call, he cleared his throat and began to lecture them in a voice hoarsened by smoking and years of shouting.

"My name's Sergeant Buck and the two men behind me are Corporals Vance and Larsen. For the next two months, it's our job to make soldiers outta you twenty-three civilians.

Some of you don't look too promisin', and maybe we won't succeed. But, by God, we're gonna try!"

"We're gonna treat you like men, and we expect you to behave that way. If you do what you're told, you won't have any trouble. If you don't..." He stopped and looked at them threateningly. "Well, they got a stockade here where you can break some rocks."

The winter sun made sweat trickle down their woolen shirts. With only five days left till Christmas, sweating seemed an odd thing.

"This guy can talk," Jeff whispered to Mike.

Sergeant Buck gave Jeff a warning look and continued. "Anybody here with previous military service take one step forward."

Three men stepped out of ranks. Buck spoke to the first one, a strongly built man, with heavy, dark eyebrows, and a jutting chin.

"What's your name, soldier?"

"Private Groth, William B., Sergeant."

"Where'd you get your previous military service?"

"In the Marines," Groth answered, "and I was told I wouldn't have to take recruit training."

"It won't hurt you none," Buck said. "I can use you as an acting corporal."

He turned to the next soldier, who stood tall and looked athletic.

"What's your name?"

"Private Hughes, Terry M., Sergeant."

"Where'd you get your previous service?"

"In the New York National Guard," Hughes answered.

"Get back in ranks, you fuckin' recruit!" Buck roared, and a burst of laughter went up as Hughes stepped, red-faced, back into ranks.

He looked at the third man, a wiry medium-sized fellow who appeared to lean forward.

"What's your name?"

"Maxwell, Thomas B., Sergeant."

"Where did you get your previous service?"

"I spent two years at the Black Fox Military Academy in Los Angeles."

"I might be able to use you." He took two steps down the line and stopped. "Now that we are done with that, let's continue."

"Right behind me is the Recruit Company Barracks you people will live in for the next eight weeks." He gestured his thumb over his shoulder. "As soon as I dismiss you, move your barracks bags onto the grass and file into the mess hall. And no runnin'!"

He scanned them with a kind of tired truculence. "Dismissed!"

✦✦✦

The next morning at six o'clock, a violent shaking of his bunk awakened Mike, and he looked up to see Corporal Vance shouting for him, and the others, to get up. Scrambling out of bed, he grabbed his towel and raced for the washroom with the stampede of others. He had only thirty minutes to wash, shave, get dressed, and fall out for the six-thirty Reveille formation.

He made it with minutes to spare, and spent the next hour and a half performing an early morning routine he was to follow every day during his time in the 27th Infantry Regiment. It started with police call, or picking up trash in the company area, followed by breakfast, making his bed, and taking part in whatever cleanup detail his squad had for the week: squad room, latrines, or porches.

Drill call came at eight o'clock but, instead of drilling the first day, Sergeant Buck told them Corporals Vance and Larsen would march them to various depots to draw rifles, field equipment, and suntan uniforms—the khaki uniform Mike saw in the recruiting poster.

When they got back to the company, Vance and Larsen showed them how to stow their gear neatly in their wall and footlockers, and assigned each man a spot in the iron rifle rack.

It stood in the middle of the squad room and was opened every morning and locked every night.

After lunch, Sergeant Buck made them fall out on the grass, and told them he would take them on a tour of the post to acquaint them with their new home. "It's a short walk of about ten miles," Buck said, "but before we go, I'm gonna give you a little lecture on the Pineapple Army."

"To begin, this grass you're sittin' on is the regimental parade field, and it's been marched over by soldiers whose shoes you people ain't fit to shine. But, be that as it may, its bounded on four sides by regimental buildings, thus forming a square or, as we call it, a quadrangle. Each infantry regiment consists of three battalions of four companies each: three rifle companies and a machine gun company. The first battalion is made up of A, B, C, and D Companies; the second battalion, of E, F, G, and H Companies; and the third battalion, of I, K, L, and M Companies. D, H, and M are machine gun companies, and the regimental band, consistin' mostly of Filipino bandsmen, lives on the third floor of M Company."

He stopped and looked at the circle of recruits sitting around him. "Anybody notice anything wrong with the way the companies are lettered?"

Mike put his hand up, along with a number of others, and he called on Jeff.

"There's no J Company, Sergeant."

Buck nodded his head. "Anybody know why?"

This time nobody raised a hand. "I don't know, either. There're lots of possible explanations, includin' some that sound like plain horseshit. But, the only one I ever heard that makes any sense is the one that says a J was written too much like an I in the old days, so they left it out to avoid confusion.

"Okay. There're fourteen companies in a regiment, three battalions, plus a Service Company, and a Headquarters Company."

He wrinkled his face and twisted his head around. "What's a Service Company?"

Hughes raised his hand, but withdrew it when Buck's bright, blue eyes rested on his.

"You wanna answer the question, Hughes?"

"No, Sergeant, I'd rather listen."

"Okay. Service Company does just what it says—provides service and transportation. When you people get put on the regimental trash detail to haul the rags and used condoms away from the officer's quarters, Service Company will furnish the wagon, the mules, and the driver."

Buck waited for the expected laugh, and resumed.

"Okay, the regimental area forms a perfect square. The first battalion faces the second battalion, and the third battalion faces the wing made up of Service Company, Headquarters Company, and the guardhouse. Smack in the middle is an archway leading out into Waianae Avenue. We call it a sally port. Who knows why it's called that?"

He let his eyes drift around the circle, but nobody volunteered.

"It's called a sally port because the Romans used to build their forts in a square and they always left an open space so soldiers could make attacks, or sallies, against the enemy.

"Okay, that takes care of the 27th Infantry Regiment... the Wolfhounds. They earned that nickname when they fought in Siberia in 1919 against the Communist Russians. Now, let's go on to the Hawaiian Division, whose insignia is the poi leaf patch we all wear..."

"Now that we got that over with, let me say a few words about your pay in the Pineapple Army. Outta your twenty-one dollars, they'll take a buck fifty every month for laundry, two bits for the Old Soldier's Home, and two bits for the Regimental Athletic Fund. For those of you who can't count, that leaves nineteen. But that ain't all that's comin' outta your pay at the end of the month. The Army knows soldiers can't handle money, and that most of you will be broke by the tenth of the month, so on the tenth, and again on the twentieth, they'll let you draw credit checks from your company orderly rooms: two dollars' worth of canteen checks, two dollars' worth of restaurant checks, two dollars' worth of movie checks, and one dollar's worth of barber checks. That'll leave twelve dollars you draw across the pay table.

"Now there're guys in this regiment who will lend you money for twenty percent interest: you borrow five, you pay back six. So, say you borrow ten, and get twelve at the pay table. Now, you gotta hand over your twelve bucks to pay off the moneylender. That is if you ain't got any sense, which I can see right now most of you don't.

"Another thing you can do here is gamble. Every company's got a nickel-and-dime blackjack game, and most have five-dollar poker. The two biggest games on post are the twenty-dollar game up in the 13th Field Artillery, and the craps game in the 19th Infantry.

"All these games are cut by the guys runnin' them. In the blackjack games, they cut a nickel every time a blackjack comes up because the deal changes hands, and the edge is always with the dealer. In poker, they cut ten percent of every pot and, in craps, ten percent after the second pass."

"How do they get away with cutting games, Sergeant?" Hughes asked. "If the game goes on long enough, the cutter will end up with most of the money."

Buck shook his head. "They only cut ten percent. And nobody even notices it, what with new players comin' in all the time to replace the ones who get tapped out."

"But gambling is against regulations. How do they get away with doing it so open?"

"I'm glad you asked that question, Hughes, because what you mean is that somebody's bein' paid off. That isn't happening, I promise you."

"The commander of this regiment is Colonel John J. Maynard. If Colonel Maynard even suspected anyone was takin' money, he'd have his ass. If not, Commanding General Hugh A. Drum, would have Colonel Maynard's ass for good measure."

Buck shook his head. "Twenty-seven years I been in the Army and hearin' stories like that for every one of them.

They're all bullshit, them stories! One hundred percent bullshit! Good leaders see gambling as inevitable, so they let it happen, but always keep an eye on it."

He glared, waiting for somebody to disagree. When nobody did, he continued. "Okay, on your feet and line up in a column of twos in the company street."

When they lined up, Buck marched them down Waianae Avenue to Wheeler Field with its rows of blue and yellow P-12s and P-26s that looked like planes used in the World War. Then he marched them to the Post Chapel, the gymnasium, the Post Theater, and back past the regimental athletic field out toward Kolekole Pass to the Post Stockade.

"They kept John Dillinger in that stockade, and made him toe the line," Buck said. "So don't any of you punks get the idea you're tough!"

Chapter Seventeen

They started training the next day, and Mike and Jeff were assigned to the second squad, with Acting Corporal Groth as squad leader. Sergeant Buck also changed his mind about Hughes, and put him in charge of the first squad. Three squads were all Buck could muster with twenty-three men, and he turned the third squad over to Maxwell.

Sergeant Buck marched them at attention out of the quadrangle, with Corporal Larsen as platoon guide out front, and Corporal Vance behind counting cadence. When they got to Kolekole Road, which led to the regimental drill field, Buck gave them "Route Step" and they were allowed to walk less formally in ranks. When they arrived at the drill field, Buck began to initiate them into the mysteries of close-order drill. He knew every word in the Infantry Drill Regulations by heart, from the six-paragraph description of how to assume the position of Attention, to the page-long explanation of how to execute Squads Right, Front, and Into Line.

Mike quickly learned that most military learning came by repetition and memorization and, with his retentive memory, he sailed smoothly through the storms of recruit training.

The unnecessary routine made the days blur together. In the mornings they practiced close-order drill, extended-order drill, or bayonet drill. In the afternoons, on the porch of the recruit barracks, they assembled and disassembled the Browning automatic rifle; the water-cooled, .30-caliber machine gun; or the Springfield rifle, caliber .30, Model 1903.

Buck also gave them lectures on map reading, or interior guard duty, or chemical warfare. In the evenings, Buck expected them to memorize the Morse code, used for signaling with lights or flags; or the Twelve General Orders for Sentries; or to work on their rifle stocks with a bone and linseed oil; or to polish their bayonets.

"Don't you know if you ever hafta stab an enemy with this goddam thing, the poor bastard could get blood poisoning if it ain't properly cleaned," Buck said, straight-faced.

With Christmas falling on Friday, they had only Wednesday and Thursday left for training during their first week in Hawaii. Buck seemed to want to make up for lost time, and before Mike knew it he was demonstrating push-ups with Buck's boot on his back.

"Alright, son, let's see what you can do."

In response, Mike performed rapid push-ups, clapping his hands twice between each one.

"Okay, Kane," he pointed at the biggest recruit. "He's shot, pick him up like I showed ya." Mike ran over; checked for wounds, breathing, and heartbeat. He grabbed another recruit, threw him down, and did the same. Picking both up, he moved them thirty yards, as prescribed.

Mike wasn't done. On Thursday, he fired expertly with his rifle, with a score that set a new regimental record. Later, he challenged the bayonet trainer and beat him.

Mike had decided to be more than just the kid from Etting Street, and people caught on.

On Christmas Eve, they got off early to attend services, and Mike and Jeff went to Catholic Mass. Christmas day, they received a full breakfast, and a light sandwich lunch. At four o'clock, they sat down to a festive dinner, with all the trimmings. The band played the traditional songs, and everyone laughed and sang joyfully.

Mike, and others around him whom he knew were Christians, had tears in their eyes.

New Year's Eve and New Year's Day followed quickly the next week. Meals were not festive on New Year's Day, but the night before was special, even in the Army. At seven o'clock, Buck announced he wanted them to celebrate bringing in 1937, but alcohol was strictly forbidden in the barracks. His solution involved his squad leaders marching them to the beer garden at ten-thirty, where they would stay together, and have no more than three beers at their own expense. After the singing of "Auld Lang Syne," they would march back to the barracks.

Buck didn't mention that his career would be ruined if just one recruit made a scene that brought attention to Buck's decision. The Army made it clear that recruits couldn't drink. Not one man caused a problem. That was how Buck gambled, he bet on his troops every time.

◆◆◆

Every night on his way to the regimental restaurant to get his nightly cargo of beer, Buck stopped in the squad room, looking dapper in his serge shirt, tailor-made britches, fox leggings, and freshly blocked campaign hat. Ostensibly, he appeared to check on training, but his real purpose was to find an audience to listen to his stories. Back in the twenties, he had done a hitch with the 15th Infantry Regiment in Tientsin, China, and he loved to talk about it.

"They paid us in gold, and we traded it off, four to one, for a Chinese currency we called Mex," Buck said. "I was just a recruit myself in those days, with only fourteen years' service. But, I made corporal, and with three longevity fogies—or bonuses, for you civilians—that came to two hundred local dollars a month. On two hundred dollars, you could live like John D. Rockefeller. Better than him, in fact," Buck said, grinning, "because, all the poontang old John D. gets is what his Old Lady lets him have."

"Was there plenty of available women in China, Sergeant?" Jeff asked.

Buck looked at him wistfully. "In them days, Tientsin was fulla White Russians who had escaped the Russian Revolution. You ever fuck an aristocrat lady, boy?"

"Not in Jersey City," Jeff said, and received a round of applause and laughter.

Buck stared off into the distance like he was talking to himself. "Polina Suslova is her name and she had blonde hair down to her kiester. She had blonde hair under her armpits and between her legs." He wagged his head. "Man, them was the good, old days."

After he left, Groth murmured, "He forgot to mention the VD rate. I knew some Marines who were in Tientsin, and the corporals had to give their squads short-arm inspections every morning."

Hughes laughed. "Yeah, milk it down, boys, so we can see if the love bug bit you."

"If Buck's a cocksman," Jeff said, "then I'm John Barrymore. Buck has a pot gut!"

Mike laughed. Buck in the washroom, shaving, was a strange sight, standing in his underwear, his big paunch hanging over the washbowl, and his spindly legs white, and completely hairless from years of wearing wrap leggings. But Jeff had old Buck wrong. Buck wasn't a bullshitter, he was a teacher trying to give them the tools to survive in a world he knew well. He was a Mr. Chips, turned drunkard but, nonetheless, a Mr. Chips.

✦✦✦

During the last week of training, Sergeant Buck came into the squad room one night and made an announcement that turned into his usual lecture.

"Tomorrow afternoon you're all goin' over to the gymnasium for boxin' try outs. The regimental trainer, Punchy Adams, wants to see if there are any prospects amongst you for the regimental team. If you're any good with your dukes, it's a ticket to easy street. Jockstraps don't hafta soldier to get ahead and, of all the jockstraps, the punchies get the best deals."

He shook his head in disgust. "Take some of the noncoms in this regiment, who I won't mention. When they went through recruit trainin' they were barely acceptable and now, for Chrissakes, they're corporals and sergeants. But, orders are orders, so you're gonna pay Punchy a visit instead."

◆◆◆

They reported the next day to the regimental gymnasium, and Punchy paired them up according to weight and size. Mike found himself in the ring with a recruit named Williams whose idea of boxing was to swing wildly and hope to hit his opponent. Mike didn't want to hurt him, but he was forced to put him down by the third round. Punchy wanted to fight Mike next.

Punchy, a leathery redhead with a spade-shaped face, had passed his prime as a good lightweight about five years before. He fought flat-footed and crouched, in a style that had become classically American: first a left jab, then a left hook, followed by a right cross and a flurry of body blows. Whistling expulsions of air through his disfigured nose, accompanied his exertions.

Punchy's reactions had slowed considerably, and Mike managed to stay away from him during the first round. During the second round, Punchy tried to hit him just under the breastbone with a right, but Mike stepped left and smashed him in the face. Punchy hesitated and looked surprised, then Mike leveled him with an upper cut that put him down on his ass.

Punchy jumped up and yelled: "Good job, Kane. I want you on our roster!"

Mike smiled, but he had no interest in being part of this crazy bastard's boxing squad.

Punchy put Mike's name on the list of potential fighters he gave to the officer-in-charge, but Mike declined the offer in a personal interview with the officer.

Hemingway was a fighter and a writer, but I'm gonna use all my spare time to become a writer, Mike thought. *Why waste my time boxing? I already know how to fight.*

Chapter Eighteen

When Sergeant Buck completed training them and turned them to duty, Mike and Jeff were assigned to C Company, Captain Ogden G. Anderson, commanding.

When they reported to the C Company Orderly Room, Mike was excited by the prospect of joining a company of real infantry soldiers. Surely, there would be some small ceremony to mark their emergence from the chrysalis of recruit-hood.

When they knocked on the Orderly Room door and got permission to enter, though, the first sergeant merely glanced up at them and, without saying a word, waved them toward the company clerk. First Sergeant Miller Warren was a puffy-faced man in his early forties with almost colorless eyebrows and eyelashes, and washed-out blue eyes. The clerk was Albert Stanley, a tall, skinny Private First Class, or PFC, with dark-brown hair.

He handed each of them a typed bunk tag. "You're both in the sixth squad with Corporal Dillon. Go to the third floor, and you'll find two empty bunks. Hang your bunk tags on and move in."

When Mike and Jeff lugged their gear up to the third floor, it was eight o'clock in the morning and the squad room sat deserted. They stowed their clothing and equipment neatly, and made their beds with white collars just as Sergeant Buck had taught them. By nine-thirty they had everything ready for inspection.

"Let's go have some coffee," Jeff suggested. "I got some restaurant checks."

"Don't you think we oughta ask somebody if it's all right to leave?"

"Who? That miserable lookin' bastard they call the topkick? He can't talk."

"I'll bet he can talk, all right. Especially if he catches us in the restaurant."

They started out of the squad room, and almost bumped into a soldier coming through the door. The tough-looking PFC—about twenty with coarse, crinkly hair, a large bent nose, and bulging biceps and chest—smiled at them.

"You the new recruits?"

They said they were.

"I'm Rizo. Dan Rizo."

After they told him their names, Jeff cocked his head. "You got the day off?"

"No, I been on sick call," Rizo answered. "I hurt my hand punchin' the heavy bag."

"You a fighter?" Mike asked.

"Class Two middleweight," he answered, ducking into a crouch and taking a playful punch at Mike's stomach. "An' this year I'm gonna become Class One, that's at the top. You guys jockstraps?"

"I'm a pool player," Jeff said.

"I'm goin' out for track." Mike swung his elbows front and back. "I run the dashes and do some broad jumpin'."

"It won't do you any good in this company," Rizo said with a scowl. "Not any more." He pointed to the PFC stripe on his arm. "Look at me, a Class Two fighter, an' about to be Class One, an' this is as far as I'm gonna go."

"How come?" Jeff asked.

"It's Captain Anderson. He's the only company commander in the regiment who hates jockstraps. If I'm in any other company, I'm a cinch to make corporal."

Mike shook his head sympathetically: "We're goin' over for coffee, you wanna come along?"

"Can't do it, kid," Rizo said. "Gotta watch the weight. I'm up to a hunnert an' seventy."

He pulled a *Ring* magazine from under his pillow, lay down, and began reading.

They said their farewells and walked on over to the restaurant. Presently, a young Chinese man came by to wait on them.

"What you guys like to eat?"

They both ordered the western omelet and coffee.

After they finished, they walked back to the company. The squad room remained deserted, except for Rizo snoring in his bunk. They stretched out on their bunks and also soon fell asleep.

The clatter of shoes and the banging of rifles in the arms rack awakened them.

Mike sat up, and a corporal with black hair and a dark complexion walked over to him.

"I'm the squad leader," he said. "Corporal Dillon."

He opened the door to Mike's locker where he had hung up his clothes, the wool shirts on the left; then the suntans, all buttoned up, with the sleeves overlapping from left to right. He nodded, and opened Mike's footlocker, motioning for him to lift up the tray so he could see how the underwear, socks, and towels were folded. He looked at Mike's shoes, lined up on the bottom of his footlocker stand, and asked for his rifle.

Mike walked over to the arms rack and brought it back. Dillon took it and flipped it over expertly in his hands while he inspected its serviceability.

"The stock needs work if you ever wanna make orderly when you go on guard. There's a diddy box under my wall locker with some linseed oil and a bone. Help yourself. Get squared away, we've got fatigue detail at thirteen hundred."

Mike knew Dillon played third base on the regimental baseball team, and had made All-Schofield five times. He was half-Cherokee Indian and everybody called him Bama.

✦✦✦

When they fell out for fatigue detail, Mike and Jeff were selected for trash pick up along with a husky, blond-haired soldier named Rawles. A farmer from Maine, he spoke with an accent that made him pronounce corporal as "capral," cards as "cads," and hearts as "hats."

They walked over to Service Company where the driver, a PFC named Rupp, waited with a wagon drawn by two mules.

"You'll do better in the wagon," Rawles told Jeff.

Jeff bridled. "Why should I get in the wagon?"

"Cause you're not big enough to lift those cans up over your head all afternoon."

"I don't want shit all over my new shoes," Jeff said.

"It's the easiest job. All you gotta do is tip the cans over, we gotta lift them up to you."

Jeff climbed into the wagon and Mike and Rawles walked behind it. First they emptied the company trashcans around the quadrangle, then they went to the officer's quarters.

"If we move, we are done by three," Rawles said. "That's what I like about this job."

"It's kinda messy, ain't it?" Mike asked, thinking of Sergeant Buck's description.

"Ain't no worse than sloppin' pigs back home," Rawles answered.

All of the quarters had maids, most of them Japanese, and Mike could see them peeking through windows when they stopped. If he smiled and waved at them, though, the girls turned away.

When they started up the last row of quarters, a girl stood outside of one of the houses emptying trash into a can, and she waited until they came up to her. She was tiny, with delicate features, and shiny black hair, tied with a bright red ribbon.

"Hello, Harriet," Rawles said, a smile lighting up his face.

"Hello, Rawles," the girl answered in a flute-like Japanese accent.

She gave the big farmer a brilliant smile and went back into the house.

"Hey, how did an ugly joker like you get to know that pretty, little thing?" Jeff asked.

"She's Lieutenant Hanson's maid."

"You mean Lieutenant Hanson in our company?"

"Yep. I'm his orderly."

"You mean his 'dog robber.'" Rupp, the driver, smiled over his shoulder.

"You mean to say you dog rob for Lieutenant Hanson?" Jeff asked. "Ain't you ashamed?"

"Nope. He pays me five dollars a month."

"You just lost your job," Jeff said. "I'll do it for two fifty."

"I'm planning to marry Harriet," Rawles whispered.

Rupp nodded. "You can meet the maids at the Kaala Club on Saturday nights. They all go."

Jeff turned his head, "Where's the Kaala Club?"

"It's that building by the chapel. They hold dances every Saturday. All the maids go."

"I know where I'm goin Saturday night," Jeff said.

"I'll go with you," Mike added.

✦✦✦

Mike's first official contact with the two company officers occurred at Saturday morning inspection. First, the company stood inspection outside in ranks for Lieutenant Hanson. The skinny, black-haired officer reached about five feet-eight, and his crooked incisor teeth gave him a sad, wolfish look when he smiled, which was seldom. Al Stanley, the company clerk, later told Mike the West Pointer was only five years out of the academy, so was still a second lieutenant. Apparently, head over heels in debt, he suffered a skinny, sharp-featured wife who looked like the kind who didn't allow the lieutenant much intimate homework.

Mike was nervous when Lieutenant Hanson started down the ranks, but he turned out not as tough as Sergeant Buck. Besides, a soldier next to Mike dropped his rifle when he tried to throw it up to inspection arms, and this created so much stir that Hanson hardly looked at Mike's.

While they walked upstairs after the inspection, Mike asked Jeff how he did.

"What do you think?"

It was an academic question. Jeff was one of the neatest soldiers in the regiment. The first month in recruit training he had bought himself a pair of fox leggings, and the second, a Stetson hat. He had also gone into debt at the tailor shop for two serge shirts and two pairs of tailor-made britches. When Mike asked him how he would manage to pay those off, Jeff just laughed.

"Every dayroom has a pool table. This place must be loaded with suckers."

They stood by their bunks while Captain Anderson inspected them, and when he got to Mike's bunk he gave no indication that he remembered him from the ship's library. He pulled an undershirt out of the footlocker to see if it was properly marked, and replaced it neatly. He walked around to the side of the bunk, stooped down, and ran his finger along the inside of the bed rail. When he straightened up, dust smudged his finger with gray. He frowned, and Miller Warren screwed up his face and began to write on the pad. Mike's heart constricted, and he could already see himself on Sunday kitchen police duty, or K.P., cleaning the kitchen.

Captain Anderson shook his head. "He's a new man and everybody's entitled to one mistake."

When he walked away with his clumping stride he remembered why the troops nicknamed him Poppa Bear. They also nicknamed his daughter Myrna "Baby Bear," which spawned a standard company joke.

"Did you ever see Baby bare?"

"No, but I'd sure as hell like to."

That night after supper, Mike lay on his bunk reading his first letters from home.

Jeff came out of the washroom and saw Mike still lying on his bunk.

"For Chrissakes, Mike, the dance starts in thirty minutes and you ain't even started gettin' ready. What's more, you hafta go to the beer garden first to fuel up for dancing."

Mike grabbed a towel and his soap, and ran to the washroom. When he came back, Jeff waited impatiently as he pulled on his clothes. While he tied his tie, Mike felt his cap being jammed on his head. "You're the only dogface in the Army with your own dog robber."

The beer garden was almost deserted when they walked through the gate and up the path to the roofed-over bar. It was the twenty-fifth of the month, and payday was five days away. The Hawaiian bartender leaned on the bar, but came to life when they gave him their order.

"Six beers it is," he said, scooping up their money and flashing a gold-toothed smile.

They carried the bottles out to a table under a palm tree and sat down.

"Let's get this shit down fast and get goin'," Jeff said, gulping down one of the bottles.

They quickly finished the six beers, and when they got up Mike felt bloated and sluggish instead of exhilarated. By the time they walked to the Kaala Club, though, a faint glow appeared in the pit of his stomach and began to spread.

The barn-like club featured a raised bandstand at one end of the room and a scattering of chairs around the walls. The band was made up of musicians from one of the regimental bands, which took turns furnishing music for the weekly dances. They dressed in flowered shirts, but the rest of the club churned with an almost solid mass of suntan uniforms. Those in attendance included some two hundred soldiers and perhaps three-dozen girls.

Jeff surveyed the room. "Rupp said all the maids come here. Shit, there ain't thirty."

Over by the bandstand, they spied their platoon sergeant dressed in a cream-colored tropical suit. Everybody called Walter Paige "Flash" because he was the division and department middleweight champion, the man keeping Dan

Rizo away from a chance at the title. Not only was he in charge of the Kaala Club, a job that paid him fifty dollars a month extra, he also ran a five-dollar game in C Company that netted him a great deal more.

They went up to him, and Jeff asked, "Hey, Sarge, what happened to all the girls?"

"Nothing, kid. This is an average turnout."

"But there must be hundreds of maids on this post."

"Sure there are, and most of them think they're too good to associate with dogfaces."

"Look, kid. The ridin' academies in Honolulu got the best lookin' whores I ever seen. Then you have the cheap joints down River Street. You can also play the tourists, but you'll probably hafta settle for some old doll whose tits hit her knees. Take it easy, kid, you got options."

He laughed, and walked away.

✦✦✦

When they left the club, they saw Paige's Buick roadster parked around back of the building. A girl with long, blonde hair sat in the front seat.

Jeff gripped Mike's arm. "Ain't that Baby Bear?" he whispered.

Mike looked. "It sure as hell is. Boy, I hope Poppa Bear never finds out about this."

They heard the sound of footsteps, and a whispered voice sounded behind them. "Kane! Kincaid!"

They looked around and saw Flash Paige looking down at them.

"Did you guys see who was in my car?" he asked through bared teeth.

"Yeah, Sarge," Jeff said. "How lucky can you get?"

"Listen, you two, and listen good," Paige said, his voice hard and threatening. "If either of you tell a soul what you seen, I'm gonna beat the living shit outta ya."

"Jesus, Sarge," Mike said. "I'm not gonna tell anybody. I give you my promise."

"Me, neither," Jeff said. "You got my promise, too."

Their evident sincerity seemed to mollify Paige.

"Okay," he said. "You're both good kids. I know I can trust you. Go, get outta here."

Chapter Nineteen

Mike came away from the pay table with nine dollars, and Jeff walked out with two.

"Look," Jeff said, "I could take these two to a blackjack game and try to run it into a five-dollar takeout. But blackjack's a game of chance, and I'd rather play where I can use my talents. You gimme three dollars, I'll play in Paige's poker game, and we'll split whatever I win."

Mike handed him the three dollars and they headed for the game.

Six players sat around the circular, blanket-covered table with a cut-out near Paige, where he could slide chips into its slot. The game had just begun and action was slow so, while Jeff waited for a seat, Mike went to the mess hall for some chow.

By the time he came back, Jeff was in the game with about twelve dollars in chips in front of him. They were playing five-card stud with no jokers and nothing wild, and Jeff was playing tight. Mike watched him turn down six hands in a row, and then catch a pair of tens, wired, with the visible card matching the facedown card. The player across from him—a corporal from M Company—had an ace of hearts showing and bet two dollars. Jeff and one other player stayed, but Jeff didn't raise.

On the third card, Jeff caught an ace, too, and the corporal an eight of hearts. This made Jeff's the high hand showing— with his ace, and tens—and he bet three dollars. The corporal and the other player stayed, and on the fourth card Jeff drew a king, and the corporal the third heart up.

Mike didn't pay attention to the other player because he couldn't have had anything but a pair smaller than Jeff's tens, but the corporal either had aces or was going for a heart flush.

Jeff, still high man showing, counted his stack carefully and looked across the table at the corporal.

"If you wanna draw that heart flush it'll cost you seven clams," he said, pushing all chips he had into the pot. The other man dropped out, and the corporal eyed Jeff. "Are you sure I ain't got aces?"

"I hope you have," Jeff said, "cause then I got you high carded."

"Well," the corporal said, counting out seven dollars and pushing the chips into the pot, "there ain't but one way I'm gonna find out."

When the fifth card was dealt, the corporal drew an eight of spades, giving him a pair showing, and Mike's heart sank. Paige flipped over Jeff's fifth card and it was another ten.

"Three tens," Jeff said, turning up the ten in the hole and dragging in the twenty-nine dollar pot, minus the three dollars Paige snaked out.

"The lucky bastard drew out on me," the corporal said, turning over aces and eights. "I bet you wouldn't a stayed if ya had about fifty bucks in front of ya I could a bumped."

"Sometimes it pays to be poor," Jeff said, stacking his chips neatly.

Mike watched Jeff all afternoon and his luck fluctuated. Once he dwindled to ten dollars, and another time he stacked up as much as fifty. But, while Mike ate supper, Jeff's luck really kicked in. When Mike came back, almost ninety dollars lay in front of his friend.

Mike stared at the pile of chips, thinking what an immense sum it represented, and wishing Jeff would quit. Jeff read his mind, and he turned to him and smiled.

"I know what you're thinkin', and I ain't gonna do it. If you want, I'll give you half the dough and play it solo from here on out."

"I don't want it," Mike said. "Play as long as you feel lucky. I'm goin' to the show."

"When you come back, I'll have all the dough in this game."

"He ain't kiddin', neither," the corporal from M Company said. "If I had his luck, I'd be up in the artillery game hittin' a real lick."

"I might just do that," Jeff said.

When Mike got to the parking lot in front of the Post Theater, he saw the familiar blocky figure of Reggie Royal walking toward the box office. He shouted his name and, when Royal turned around, Mike saw buck sergeant's stripes on his sleeve.

"Hey, Reggie, I see you made it. I ran into a medic who told me you transferred to the Prep School and were gonna make sergeant."

They grinned at each other and Mike slapped him on the back. "How do you like it?"

"It's great. I get fifty bucks a month extra. With my pay, I make over a hundred a month."

Mike whistled. "I'll bet you're the first non-jockstrap in the history of the Pineapple Army that ever made sergeant on his first enlistment."

"That's right. Didn't I tell you something good was going to happen to me in Oahu?"

"You sure did. And you were right, too."

Reggie generously bought tickets for both of them, and they went into the theater. The program started with a Charley Chase comedy, and featured a newsreel. It covered a sit-in strike at General Motors, with shots of grinning workers making thumb-up signs at the camera. The following shot showed two union organizers named Richard Frankensteen and Walter Reuther, their faces bloody from a beating at the hands of what the announcer called "unknown assailants."

The story of the dull movie *Ladies Love Brutes,* acted by George Bancroft and Ann Dvorak, involved George building skyscrapers despite the machinations of villainous Stanley Fields.

As they walked out of the movie, Reggie turned. "It's been great, but I gotta run. I have to do bed check at ten o'clock."

"Are you going to the track meet Saturday?" Mike asked.

"Hey, that's an idea. It starts at two, right?"

"Yeah."

"See you there. Too bad you got here too late for track this year, or I could see you run."

"I don't know if I can make the team, but next year I'll be twenty and I'll have a better chance."

✦✦✦

When Mike got back to Paige's poker game, Jeff was gone.

"He cashed in a hundred and forty bucks and went to the artillery game," Paige told him.

Mike hurried up Waianae Avenue toward the 13th Field Artillery and into the supply room where they held the game.

The setup was bigger, and a green-shaded lamp lit the room dimly. Jeff sat at the table playing, and Mike's eyes bugged out when he saw the stacks of chips in front of him.

Jeff grinned at him. "What did I tell you, Mike, I got almost a thousand dollars here."

Mike bent down and put his lips to Jeff's ear. "Cash in, Jeff," he whispered.

Jeff shook his head. "This is my night to get rich. I ain't quittin' till I win everything."

"Or somebody gits all of yours," an ordnance, technical sergeant said, scowling at Jeff.

Jeff laughed. "Hey, Sarge, you're havin' pipe dreams."

He was still trying to play tight, but the fever had gripped him and he started to call on hands he should have turned over.

By midnight, his pile had dwindled by almost half, and his face was white and drawn with fatigue.

Finally, after three jacks folded up on a hand that cost him a hundred and twenty dollars, he turned around and grinned at Mike.

"My ass is draggin'," he said, shoving his chips toward the dealer. "Cash me in."

The dealer counted his chips and handed him three hundred and eighty-two dollars. Jeff stuffed the money carelessly into his pocket.

"Let's go, Mike," he said, settling his Stetson on his head and swaggering out of the room.

"A hundred and ninety-one apiece. Not a bad lick, is it?" He patted his pocket. "I'm gonna buy me some civilian duds, and you oughta do the same. We'll ask Paige where he buys his clothes."

◆◆◆

On his advice, they went to the Liberty House Department Store on Fort Street. Each bought a cream-colored sharkskin suit, and two extra pairs of slacks in different colors, an assortment of Aloha shirts, and a pair of brown and white shoes.

So, on Saturday afternoon, they donned their new civilian clothes and made their first girl-hunting run on Honolulu.

"Where we goin'?" Mike asked as they walked toward the gate where taxis parked.

"To Waikiki, to gladden the hearts of female tourists," Kincaid answered. "Lonely dames... school teachers and secretaries, who save their dough for years and blow it on one big bust in Hawaii. They're dreamin' of romance, and I aim to make their dreams come true."

"There must be plenty of dogfaces tryin' to pick them up."

"That's where you're wrong, Mike. The average dogface takes his few miserable dollars to town on payday and blows it on one drunk and a trip to a whorehouse. The rest of the month he spends beatin' his meat and sittin' on his dead ass in the day room waitin' for payday so he can do the same thing. Pretty soon, he can't talk to a woman who isn't a whore. Haven't you noticed these old soldiers... mosta them are afraid of women. Look at old Buck, for instance. The only way he knows to approach a woman is to hand her three bucks and take off his pants."

"How about Polina Suslova, Buck's White Russian girl friend in Tientsin?"

Jeff snorted. "Shit, she was probably some fat whore."

When they got to the gate, they found a taxi that only needed two more passengers to make a load, handed the driver fifty cents apiece, and hopped in. In thirty minutes, the driver let them off at the taxi stand near the Army-Navy YMCA.

"How far is it to Waikiki?" Jeff asked the driver.

"Three miles."

"How do we get there?"

"You could take a taxi," the driver said with a grin.

"Let's walk," Mike said. "It'll give us a chance to see some of the town."

"Don't you walk enough all week?" Jeff protested.

"Come on, it won't hurt you. It's the best way to see things."

"Okay, but if we're gonna walk, let's fuel up first."

He led Mike across the street to the Black Cat Cafe and they drank two quick sloe gin fizzes. When they left, they walked down Richards Street and turned onto King, and past Iolani Palace, the territorial capitol building. Across from the palace they stopped to see the statue of King Kamehameha, the First, arrayed in the feathered cape and headdress of a Hawaiian warrior.

"They say he tips his feather helmet every time a virgin walks past," Jeff said, "and he ain't tipped it once in all the years he's been standin' there."

Mike stood gazing at the majestic statue with the bas-reliefs on its base, depicting events in Kamehameha's life, until Jeff tugged on his arm. They continued down King Street and turned into Kalakaua Avenue, which took them to Waikiki.

The most popular part of Waikiki stretches for about a mile from the Halekulani Hotel, near Fort DeRussy, to the Natatorium War Memorial swimming arena. Within this stretch are the Royal Hawaiian and other large hotels, and fronting the hotels is the celebrated beach.

They rented a bathing locker and put on their new flowered trunks.

"Let's go surf-boarding first," Mike said.

Jeff shook his head. "I didn't come here to make a spectacle of myself."

"Well, I'm goin'."

"Okay, muscles, I'll case the beach for dames."

"Where'll I meet you, then?"

"On the beach."

"Suppose I can't find you?"

"How could you not find me? It's not a big beach."

Mike walked down to where a boy rented surfboards. Though made of heavy wood, turned gray by water and age, the boy assured Mike they would be easy to use.

"Look," he said, pointing to where a boy about twelve, poised on one of the boards, made a beautiful run toward the beach, framed against a background of sky and water.

Mike handed the boy fifty cents and carried the board toward the water.

"Surf over by the Outrigger Canoe Club!" the boy said. "Surf there easy for beginners."

Mike paddled the board out to where the breakers began their rush toward the beach, and watched the expert riders line their boards up with the waves, catch them at their peak, and ride them in. With a few quick strokes, their boards began the long, graceful, arc toward the beach.

However well he thought he gauged the breakers' approach, though, Mike was unable catch the forward rush of the water. Instead the waves treated him like a cotton ball and had their way with him. He tried for an hour, then made his way to the beach and returned the board.

"How you make out?" the boy asked.

"Lousy."

"You try again. Two-three times more, you just like beach boy," the kid said, grinning.

"Two-three hundred times is more like it."

He started along the beach looking for Jeff. He found him lying under a tree next to a girl in a beach robe and a huge, coconut hat. He was so engrossed with the girl, he didn't see Mike sneak up around the other side of the tree and lay down behind it to listen.

"Linda," Jeff cooed. "What a beautiful name."

"Have you ever been in Saint Paul?" the girl asked.

"No, I'm from Jersey City."

"I've never been to Jersey City."

"What does your Dad do in Saint Paul?"

"He's a lawyer. What does your Dad do?"

"He's a doctor."

"Are you going to follow in his footsteps?"

"Not me," Jeff said. "I couldn't stand that life."

"What are you going to do?"

"Well, when I'm twenty-one, I'll come into some money my mother left me, and I'm gonna open a nightclub. One of those small, intimate places with a small band and a fabulous girl singer."

He looked the girl over, an admiring smile on his face. "You can sing, can't you? In a year or so, I'll be looking for a girl singer. One who looks good in a tight evening gown."

"I can't even carry a tune," the girl said, laughing.

"Where are you staying?" Jeff asked.

"My aunt and I have taken an apartment here at Waikiki. Where are you staying?"

"My cousin Mike and I are at the Halekulani, just up the beach."

Behind the tree, Mike listened enviously to Jeff's glib lies, but enough was enough. He got carefully to his feet, backed off, and made a wide circle before approaching Jeff and the girl.

"This is my cousin and roommate at the Halekulani, Mike Kane," Jeff said without turning a hair. "His Dad's a doctor, too, just like mine. Mike, this is Linda Wayne."

The girl smiled up at Mike and she was very pretty, with dark red hair, and green eyes.

"Sit down," she said, but just as Mike did, she looked at her watch and uttered a shrill cry.

"It's six o'clock. I have to run. My aunt will think I'm lost."

"When am I going to see you again?" Jeff asked. "How about dinner tonight?"

"I'm sorry," Linda said. "My aunt and I are going to meet family on the inter-island steamer, but we get back tomorrow. I can meet you here tomorrow afternoon if you like."

"Is three o'clock all right?"

"That's fine, till tomorrow, then," Linda said as she walked away.

"I'll be waiting for you," Kincaid called after her.

Waiting until she was gone, Mike shook his head. "You're line of bullshit is outrageous."

Jeff laughed. "That's what you think. You oughta hear my old man."

"Oh, the doctor, you mean?"

"Well, he doctored enough whiskey during Prohibition."

"And your mother left you a pile of money, too."

"She left me a five-hundred dollar insurance policy that matures when I'm twenty-one."

"And you're gonna open a night club?"

"Sure. I'm openin' a pool hall. That's a poor man's night club."

Mike laughed. "Jeff, you're a bigger liar than Frank Harris, and he once told a girl 'going to bed with me is a noble and enriching experience, like visiting Chartres Cathedral.'"

"Who the fuck is Frank Harris?"

"A friend of Bernard Shaw."

"And who the fuck is Bernard Shaw?"

"A good Irish welterweight," Mike said. "He fought as Cash Byron."

"He never fought in Jersey City," Jeff said.

They put on their clothes, and Jeff looked at the deserted beach.

"It looks like the tourist season is closed for the day, and I ain't goin' back to Schofield without getting' my end wet. I don't wanna pay, but I'm too hard up to stand on principle."

"Me, too," Mike said. "Where shall we go?"

"They say the Congress has the best lookin' girls, and they all charge three bucks."

They walked to Fort DeRussy and ate supper at the snack bar. When they came out, they found a cab and Jeff told the driver to take them to the Congress.

They walked up to a heavy front door, with a smaller door built into it at eye level. Jeff pushed the buzzer and the smaller door opened. A tall Hawaiian woman looked down at them.

"We're dogfaces from Schofield," Jeff said, and the woman unbolted the door. She led them into a room with two long sofas against the walls, and some easy chairs. There were no other customers, but three girls sat on the sofas in abbreviated playsuits. All were attractive, and the most attractive of them was the girl Jeff met on the beach.

Jeff gasped in shock to see her sitting there. She turned red and tried to avoid his stare.

"How are things in St. Paul?" he asked.

"Not so good," she said. "Do you want to go into one of the rooms and talk it over?"

Jeff nodded. She stood up and led him by the hand through the door to the rooms.

Mike stood at the far end of the room, and one of the girls walked over to him.

"You're new at Schofield, I bet," she said smiling.

Mike nodded.

"Do you like me?"

Mike nodded again. She took his hand and led him to one of the rooms.

The room was furnished with a bed, a sink, a chair, and a small table, with a white, enamel basin and a bottle of deep-purple disinfectant liquid on it. A light-green bedspread covered the bed, and a small white towel hung from the foot of it.

She closed the door and put her hands on his shoulders, "My name's Pat. What's yours?"

He told her and she inclined her head toward him. "Are you nervous, Mike?"

"No."

"Will you give me the money, please?"

He handed her three dollars, and stepped out of his pants and shorts.

"How long is it since you were laid?"

Mike counted quickly in his head. "Seven, eight months."

"Then I better do this very carefully or you won't need my services."

She milked his penis gently, and then rolled the condom on. Reaching up behind her, she untied the strings that held her playsuit up and, stepping out of it, lay down on the bed.

"Okay, honey, I'm all yours."

It was over in seconds, and then she led him over to the washbasin full of purple liquid.

"We'll wash you up, then you take a pee, and there's no way you can catch anything."

When she finished, she patted him on his backside. That gesture vaguely irritated him. All girls treated him like they were his nurse, or his mother, or something like that.

While he dressed, Pat douched herself, and together they walked back to the waiting room. Jeff was still in the room with Linda.

When Jeff came out, they walked back down the wooden steps and out onto Hotel Street.

"What did you say to each other?" Mike asked.

"She started apologizin' for givin' me that snow job on the beach."

"And then you told her you were just as big a liar as she was."

"Wait, I'll tell you the story. Like I said, she's apologizin' while I'm undressin', and I'm tellin' her she should be ashamed of herself. I got her practically in tears, but when I get down to my shorts, she takes one look at my GI underwear and lets out a scream. 'Why you phony bastard,' she says, 'you're a dogface' and we both fell on the bed, laughin'."

"But the big romance you built up on the beach is out the window, right?"

"Hell, no. She's still meetin' me at Waikiki tomorrow. It's her day off. She has got an apartment at Waikiki, but the aunt she lives with ain't her aunt. It's Mrs. Ellsworth, the madam who runs the Congress."

"I think this is starting to get interesting," Mike said.

Chapter Twenty

One Wednesday, the regiment earned a training holiday through outstanding individual and unit performances. Mike had received the first place award for the inter-regimental bayonet combat competition, and second in marksmanship. Others in his company also received awards for various events. They did so well that the entire 27th Regiment was given the day off. The squad room resounded with snoozing soldiers, snoring off their heavy noon meal.

Jeff came in with his hair wet from the shower. "Okay, Mike, off your ass and get dressed. We are meeting Linda at two. Jablonski left me money to spend on her."

◆◆◆

The night before, Jeff beat Sergeant Jablonski out of thirty-five dollars at pool, and Mike won twelve dollars on a side bet. He also witnessed what a risk-taker Jeff had become.

Jablonski, supposedly the best pool player in the regiment, played Jeff in three games of fifty points each: the first for five dollars, the second for ten, and the third for twenty. Jablonski took his losses philosophically.

"Okay, kid, so you beat me outta thirty-five clams. But if you was a real hustler, you'd a let me win that last game, then beat me outta a big bet."

Later, Jeff told Mike that Jablonski was right. "But what he don't know is that all I had was three dollars when I walked in there, so I never had enough to pay off any of the bets."

◆◆◆

When they got to the Congress, an empty waiting room greeted them. The two girls on duty, Linda and Pat, shared some Crab Orchard wine with them, and talked until Pat's boyfriend came in.

"You might as well leave, Linda," Pat said. "The other girls will be in any minute, and we won't have any rush of customers this late in the month."

"Thanks, honey," Linda said. "I'll do as much for you sometime."

The apartment Linda shared with Mrs. Ellsworth on Kalia Road had a tiny kitchen, a slightly larger living room, and one bedroom, crowded by two single beds. Mrs. Ellsworth owned the two-story building, and there was another apartment, now vacant, on the second floor.

Linda started for the bedroom to dress, but stopped Jeff from following her.

"Mrs. Ellsworth is in there sleeping," she whispered. "We'll just have to wait until later."

She disappeared into the bedroom, and Jeff plopped on the sofa and looked at Mike.

"Do me a favor and take a walk. Better still, don't come back here at all. Meet us at Waikiki Tavern between six and seven for supper."

"It's only two-thirty," Mike protested. "What the hell am I gonna do till then?"

"You got money, ain't ya? Go have a beer someplace. Or case the beach for dames. If you pick one up, bring her to the Tavern with ya and I'll pay for her meal."

Mike walked outside and saw Mrs. Ellsworth's bicycle leaning against the building. Deciding to borrow it, he stuck his head inside the door to ask permission. Jeff already had his pants and shoes off and scowled when he saw Mike.

"Do you think Mrs. Ellsworth will mind if I borrow her bike?" he asked.

Jeff waved him away. "Take off, man. She won't mind. I'll tell her you took it."

Mike wheeled the bike out into Kalia Road and began pedaling northeast toward John Ena Road, which ran into Kalakaua Avenue. A vague idea of visiting the Bishop Museum, way over in the Kalihi District, meandered into his mind. Supposedly, it held a treasure trove of Hawaiian artifacts.

The fresh air cooled his face and his chest inside the loose-fitting Aloha shirt, and he admired the colorful flora along the route. Before he knew it, he passed city hall, and soon stopped in front of the museum.

The most spectacular displays in the museum were the feathered cloaks and helmets worn by ancient Hawaiian warriors. Made from the feathers of such exotic birds as the mamo, the oo, the iwii, and the amikiki—most now extinct—they provided brilliantly colored examples of man's conspicuous consumption. The display plaque told him it took a hundred years to gather enough mamo bird feathers to make the magnificent, yellow cloak worn by Kamehameha the First.

The replica grass shack made of pili grass and braided ukiuki leaves disappointed Mike the most. He entered it eagerly, sure he was about to witness the abode of romance and indolent living. Instead, he found a windowless, dark, damp-looking dwelling with a female mannequin pounding poi who didn't measure up to the truly pretty Hawaiian girls he knew.

Mike left the museum determined to meet a descendant of one of the lovely girls who had lived in a hale pili. According to Schofield lore, the prettiest girls on the island could be found on the campus of Punahou School. Mike looked at his pocket map and located it in the Lower Manoa Valley. He set out immediately and biked to the school on Punahou Street.

The striking campus showcased brilliantly green lawns surrounded by rock walls covered with night-blooming cereus. The white petals of the cereus flowers stayed closed against the sun, but the girls were in full blossom. They appeared as lovely mixtures of Polynesian and Asian blood, of Polynesian and Caucasian, Asian and Caucasian, and the polychromatic co-mingling of all three.

Mike walked purposely around the campus, hoping he would be taken for a student. After all, he told himself, I'm nicely dressed and I'm not much older than the seniors. I'm not carrying books, so maybe they'll think I'm a graduate, returning for a look at his alma mater, a former football star and president of the student council.

He sat on a bench and tried to look condescending and friendly at the same time, as befitted his status as a distinguished alumnus. Groups of pretty girls came by, and he was sure he looked the picture of casual composure.

Finally, one lovely, dark-haired girl, about seventeen, with skin the color of walnut ice cream, came up the path. She was searching for something in one of her books. When she came to Mike's bench, she plopped the books down and sat beside them.

In his mind's eye, Mike imagined her gliding with the undulant grace of a hula dancer from the entrance to her hale pili, and smiling at him, the white God Lono, with adoring eyes. He lost his composure completely.

The pile of books sat between them, and Mike stole a glance at the name printed in bold letters across the face of each paper-covered volume. Her name was Noelani Kreuger. Though she remained fully engrossed in her search, he smiled at her tentatively, half-hoping and half-afraid she would look up. She didn't, so he mustered the nerve to speak.

"Studying hard?"

She raised her dark, lustrous head and looked at him. His heart raced.

"No," she said, then closed her book, gathered up the pile, and walked away.

He stared after her as she went up the path, swaying and indifferent to his existence. If only he could talk to girls the way Jeff could. She was about to enter one of the buildings, and just before she went through the doorway, she looked back at Mike and smiled. Then she disappeared.

He jumped to his feet, grabbed the bike, and raced away down the path in tempo with the pounding of his heart. Noelani Kreuger... the name sang in his head. What a lovely name for a lovely girl. Red-lipped Noelani. Noelani of the long dark tresses and bright eyes. I'm in love, he whispered to himself, and her name is Noelani.

✦✦✦

When he got to the Waikiki Tavern, Mike walked through the bar area to get to the dining room where he saw Jeff and Linda seated. They hadn't noticed that they had drawn the attention of some men at the bar. As Mike passed, he overheard one of them comment. "Oh, she's nice. She must be a pro, or she wouldn't be with that weaselly-looking shithead."

"Excuse me," Mike said. "You're talking about my sister."

"I don't care whose sister she is, you want to go a round?" he asked, pushing close to Mike.

Mike knocked him out with a swift uppercut, and walked away rubbing his hand. There was hardly a fuss in the loud bar, but he saw the guy's friends dragging the poor bastard away. Mike straightened his clothes as he walked over to where Jeff and Linda sat. *It's amazing,* he thought, *how well the Rec prepares a guy to work his dukes.*

Jeff was drinking Asahi beer, and when the waiter came over Mike ordered the same. They had not seen the altercation, and he didn't mention it.

"So you struck out, huh?" Jeff said.

"Whadda ya mean?"

"Where's the tourist I told you to pick up?"

Mike had decided to keep the existence of Noelani a secret from Jeff. At least until he got to know her, a situation he was determined to bring about, though he had no idea how.

"I didn't even try. I went to the Bishop Museum."

"I've never been there," Linda said. "Is it interesting?"

"Yeah, it gives you a good idea of how the natives lived before Captain Cook got here."

"It's too bad Pat's mixed-up with Henson," Jeff said to Linda, "or maybe you coulda fixed Mike up with her." He looked at her hopefully. "Maybe you still can."

Mike spoke up before Linda could answer. "Never mind fixin' me up. Besides, how could I ever beat Henson's time? The guy's, what... six-one, and a hundred and ninety? And, he's an enlisted Marine pilot. Hell, he makes as much money as a second lieutenant."

"The money's got nothing to do with it," Linda said. "Pat makes maybe five times as much as Jimmy does. She's simply in love with the guy."

"What about one of the younger girls?" Jeff asked. "Lorayne, or Annette, or Jacky?"

"Annette and Jacky already have boyfriends—civilians who never come into the Congress. And I wouldn't stick a nice guy like Mike with Lorayne. She's a bitch. None of the other girls like her, and neither does Mrs. Ellsworth. When her six months are up, she'll be on the first Matson liner to the States."

"Is that how long the girls usually stay, six months?" Mike asked.

"That's how long Mrs. Ellsworth hires them for. You have to have variety in our business if you want the customers to keep coming. But, if you're not a troublemaker, and you're popular, like I am, or Pat, you can stay if you want to. There's a girl named Charlene at the Senator who's been there five years."

She took a sip of her gin fizz. "But that's too long. Poor Charlene will never get out of the business now."

"How long do you intend to stay in it?" Mike asked.

"I've been here a year now. Another year ought to do it. By then, I'll have enough money to go into business for myself."

"Your current business?" Mike asked.

Linda smiled faintly. "No, honey, a legitimate business. A shop of some kind, or maybe a beauty parlor. When I was a kid, I always wanted to go to beautician's school. Or maybe Jeff will give me a job racking balls in his nightclub. Or maybe I'll open a night club of my own and hire Jeff as a singer." She leaned over and kissed him on the cheek. "Wouldn't he look gorgeous in a tight-fitting tuxedo?"

"Maybe I'll do better than that. Sergeant Buck says hookers make the best wives."

"I'm not a hooker, Jeff," Linda whispered. "Lorayne's a hooker. I'm a working girl."

"I'm sorry, baby," Jeff said. He reached over and hugged her, a penitent look on his face.

Linda patted his hand. "That's okay, honey, I know you didn't mean it like it sounded."

"Unhand that lady, soldier, or I'll call the MPs!" They looked up to see Flash Paige grinning at them.

"Hey, Sarge," Jeff said. "Sit down and I'll buy you a drink."

Paige slid into the booth next to Mike. "I'll have a bourbon and water."

When the drink came, he took a sip and looked at Linda. "Don't you have any manners, Kincaid? Introduce me to the lady."

"Oh, yeah. Linda Wayne, this is Sergeant Paige, our platoon sergeant."

Paige took another sip of his drink and looked at Linda closely. "Linda. That name's familiar. Don't I know you from someplace?"

An awkward silence yawned before Paige nodded. "Sure, you're one of the new girls at the Congress. I've heard the guys talk about you."

"Not exactly new," Linda said while making direct eye contact. "I've been there a year."

"Well, I ain't been there in a while. How's my old friend, Annie Ellsworth?"

"Oh, she's fine. You're the first person I ever heard call her by her first name."

"Hell, I've known Annie since I first came here as a seventeen-year-old punk, ten years ago. She's a good skate, and she runs a good place: clean, no pimps allowed, and no rough stuff."

He finished off his drink and signaled the waiter to bring another round.

"She still got that place on Kalia Road?"

Linda nodded her head. "That's where we live."

"She still rent the apartment upstairs?"

"It's empty now. But she'd like to rent it."

Paige stared into his drink thoughtfully. "Look, tell Annie I'll be in to see her at the Congress some night this week, probably tomorrow night. Tell her I want to rent the place."

He stared at his drink again, a worried look on his face.

"Myrna's about to drive me outta my mind, the chances she takes. I have to find a safe place were we can meet. Can you imagine what the old man would do if he found out?"

"He'd bust your ass, for sure," Jeff said. "And ship you back to the States."

"We wanna get married," Flash said, his voice quieter. "As soon as we can work things out. Hell, Myrna's already got me takin' correspondence courses so I can qualify for a reserve commission. Everybody knows there's gonna be a war." He shrugged his shoulders and looked hopeful. "Who knows, maybe it will work out okay. In the meantime, I've got to protect myself in the clinches. Every old punchie knows that."

He finished his drink and stood up. "I gotta pick Myrna up at eight thirty at the university. She's takin' classes three nights a week." He grinned at them. "She wants me to enroll. Take English and Literature so I can talk like an officer."

"Why don't you do it, Sarge? I'll help you out, if you need any help," Mike blurted.

"You know anything about literature, Kane?"

"Jesus, Sarge, he wrote the book on it," Jeff gushed.

Paige shrugged and mumbled something about thinking about it. He stood up and said his goodbyes.

After he left, Linda's gaze moved between Mike and Jeff. "What was that all about? Who's Myrna?"

"Myrna is Baby Bear," Mike said. "Poppa Bear's daughter. And Poppa Bear is Captain Ogden G. Anderson, our company commander."

"And her father thinks she's too good to go out with enlisted men?"

"You can say that again," Jeff croaked. "Especially dogfaces who are jockstraps. Poppa Bear hates jockstraps like the devil hates holy water."

"And he loves Baby Bear like Saint Francis loved the poor," Mike said.

Chapter Twenty-One

Mike didn't see Noelani again until a year later, at the 1938 Island Track and Field Summer Championships. By then, he had consigned her to the part of his mind that harbors bittersweet memories. When he met her again, he was instantly smitten once more.

❖❖❖

Six months prior, on March 11th—the day before Hitler's "Anschluss" with Austria—Mike had taken part in the inter-regimental track meet and won the hundred-yard dash in 10.2 seconds, and the 220 in 22.4. His track coach, a lieutenant named Brandon Pardieu, almost hugged him.

"You're as full of faults as a hound dog is of fleas," Pardieu told him, "but when I get through teaching you the mechanics of speed running, you'll do 9.9, maybe 9.8."

Lieutenant Pardieu knew his stuff. He had been a fifteen-second high hurdler at West Point. During graduate work at California, the famous Brutus Hamilton coached him.

The secret, he told Mike, was not to try too hard.

"If you come off your marks and just dig as hard as you can, you'll actually run slower than if you drive straight down the track with controlled power, lengthening your stride until you create the lift that comes when your technical form is correct. Remember the hundred-meter dash at the 1936 Olympics?" he asked, almost out of breath with excitement.

"Owens won, but who was in second place at the seventy-meter mark?"

"Ralph Metcalfe won the silver medal," Mike said.

"I know!" Pardieu almost shouted. "But who was in second place for most of the race?"

Mike looked at him with a blank expression.

Pardieu rushed on. "Wykoff! Frank Wykoff! And Metcalfe asked Wykoff after the race, 'What happened, Frank? You were in front of me, then suddenly I went past you like you were standing still.' 'I know;' Wykoff told him, 'I lost my head and started trying too hard.' And not only Metcalfe passed him, but so did the Dutchman Osendarp. Wykoff finished in fourth place."

Mike never did learn the secret that makes great sprinters from runners who have nothing but natural speed. Three sprinters at Schofield Barracks could run the hundred in ten seconds or better. One, Jim Straub from his own regiment, held the division and department record of 9.7. Doggedly, Pardieu started Mike in every hundred-yard dash at every meet, hoping to play Pygmalion to his Galatea. Mike was a fast starter and, invariably, leapt out of the starting holes ahead of everybody else. Inevitably, though, around the halfway mark, Straub would breeze past him, along with one or two others.

❖❖❖

Only once did Mike get the "lift" Pardieu always talked about, and that had been an accident. It happened that specific day at the 1938 Island Track and Field Summer Championships where he ran start-off for the Army 880-yard relay team.

The meet was held at the University of Hawaii's stadium in Manoa Valley. Besides the Army team, teams represented the University of Hawaii, Saint Louis College, the Town Team Athletic Club, McKinley High School, Roosevelt High School, and the Punahou School.

The Army team, with 25,000 men to draw from, won the meet easily. But the outstanding individual performer turned out to be a half-Hawaiian, half-German student from Punahou; a tall, lithe, eighteen-year-old senior named Henry Kreuger.

Mike could not ignore Henry's presence, nor his sister Noelani. He heard her cheering when Henry won the 100 in 9.7, the 220 in 21.4, and the 440 in 48 seconds flat. Also, when he took a second in the broad jump, and another second in the javelin. He personified the nearest thing to a one-man track team since Jim Thorpe.

When they drew positions for the 880-yard relay, Punahou drew the pole position and Army the second lane. As they lined up for the start of the race, Henry Kreuger came jogging up with a baton in his hand, which meant he would run start-off for Punahou. It also meant he would run against Mike, since he was the Army's start-off man. Kreuger's positioning surprised Mike, because the fastest man on a relay team usually ran last.

They practiced a few warm-up starts, and while they were walking back from one of them, Kreuger held out his hand and introduced himself. Mike told him his name and congratulated him on his impressive one-man show so far that day.

The starter called them to their holes, and Mike crouched down, tensely awaiting the sound of the pistol. When it went off, he got his usual good start, and drove for the first turn. Halfway around, he increased the length of his stride and felt Pardieu's miraculous lift, which made him feel like he was floating. When he hit the homestretch, he had gained on the men in the outside lanes, and couldn't see Kreuger on his left. He slapped the baton in the back-stretched hand of the number two man, who took off like a greyhound.

Mike stayed in his lane until the track cleared, and walked onto the oval where his sweat clothes lay on the ground. Henry Kreuger came up behind him.

"Nice race," he said. "I don't think I gained a foot on you."

Mike started to thank him, but Noelani came running across the field shouting her brother's name. She carried his sweat suit under her arm.

Mike made an effort to watch both her and the race, as she approached her brother. "Put on your sweat clothes before you catch cold."

Henry waved her away impatiently until Jim Straub came into the homestretch about six yards ahead of the Punahou anchorman. At that point, he took the clothes from his sister's outstretched hand and started to pull them on.

Mike couldn't take his eyes from Noelani, so when Henry poked his bundle of black, curly hair through the sweatshirt and saw him still standing there, he could not avoid introducing them.

Noelani held out her hand, and graced him with a dazzling smile.

Lieutenant Pardieu came running across the oval with a stopwatch in his hand.

"We just set a new island record of 1:27.6!" he shouted, "And, you just ran a 21.9 two-twenty!"

Noelani and her brother congratulated him and walked away smiling, and Mike stared after them.

"Yes, sir," he said, only half-hearing Pardieu's words.

Across the field, in front of the stands, he saw Reggie Royal waving at him. A girl in a bright-green dress stood next to him, and Mike walked their way. Reggie had bought out of the Army, and now held a civilian job working for American Factors Limited.

Reggie pumped his hand. "Mike, you were really flying," he said, a beaming smile on his round face. He had grown a pencil moustache and, beneath it, his teeth gleamed.

He held the arm of the girl next to him. "Angie, this is Mike Kane, an old buddy of mine. Mike, this is Angela Nielsen, my fiancée. Her father's a major in the 13th Field Artillery."

Angela, a chubby girl with slightly protruding teeth, smiled at Mike primly.

"I'm pleased to meet you, Private Kane."

Mike shuddered. *She called me Private Kane? That'll end my future with old Reggie.*

"I'm pleased to meet you, Miss Nielsen," he said, standing stiffly.

Reggie patted his fiancée's hand on his arm. "People say Henry Kreuger's a cinch to make the 1940 Olympic team in some event."

"Four hundred meters, maybe," Mike said. "He's not fast enough for the dashes."

"I work with his father at American Factors," Reggie went on, "and we met Henry and his sister a couple of weeks ago at the Kawaiaha'o Congregational Church... the tourist literature calls it 'the Westminster Abbey of the Hawaiian Kingdom.'"

An idea flashed into Mike's head. "Is that where the Kreuger's go to church?"

"Yes. You should go, Mike. It's beautiful and the choir is really something to hear."

In the stands, Mike saw Flash Paige grinning at him, his hands raised above his head in a clasped boxer's salute.

Mike had already seen Baby Bear sitting in the officers' section with the boxing team officer Lieutenant Thompson, and the snotty bastard gave him a congratulatory wave. *If he only knew that Baby Bear was using him for a cover while she shacked up with Flash on Kalia Road.* Not that Mike could have sworn in a court of law that they actually cohabitated. They were extremely circumspect and he had never seen her there.

"I better go get dressed, Reggie," Mike said. "It was nice meeting you, Miss Nielsen."

As he walked away, Reggie called after him. "We'll have to get a beer sometime."

The idea registered, but Mike's thoughts focused on the Kawaiaha'o Congregational Church. They're about to get a new parishioner, if that's what Protestants call it.

◆◆◆

Mike couldn't meet Noelani at church right away because, after the end of track season, the company went to Waianae for a two-week, machine gun firing exercise. They were to leave on Saturday but, on Thursday, First Sergeant Miller Warren called him into the Orderly Room.

"I gotta job for you, Kane," he said. "You're gonna be orderly for the company officers at Waianae. You report to the officers' tent every morning after breakfast, make their beds, shine..."

Mike interrupted him. "I don't want to be a dog robber, Sergeant."

Warren had been looking down at some papers, but Mike's words brought his pale blue eyes up and into focus.

"I didn't ask you what you wanna do, Kane. I'm tellin' you what you're gonna do."

Mike looked over at the company clerk, but Stanley remained bent over his typewriter, banging away industriously.

He returned his gaze to Sergeant Warren. "I was told that dog robbing is voluntary, and I don't want to volunteer."

Warren's eyes narrowed. "You'll either do it, or you'll go to the stockade!"

Mike stood as straight as he could and clicked his heels. "I request permission to speak to the company commander."

"Okay, wise guy, you can see the old man for all the good it will do you. Now get your ass outa here."

That night, Mike spoke with some of the old soldiers in the company.

"They can't make you do it, kid." Bama Dillon clearly knew all about it. "According to Army Regulations, the duties of orderly are performed on a strictly volunteer basis."

Friday, just before noon, Al Stanley walked over to Mike's bunk.

"The old man will see you at thirteen-thirty."

Mike looked at him. "What do you think, Al?"

Stanley shook his head. "I don't know. I can tell you that Miller Warren is not the old man's favorite first sergeant. But, of course, he won't tell you that." He grinned. "Good luck."

At one-thirty sharp, Mike stood outside the Orderly Room door, his shoes shined and collar ornaments and belt buckle gleaming. Warren was shuffling papers, but Mike stood where he could see him. Warren looked at his watch, and then stuck his head inside Poppa Bear's office. Instantly, he pointed his index finger at Mike and jerked his thumb backwards.

Mike marched straight through the Orderly Room and into Captain Anderson's office. He saluted and began to recite the formula for reporting to officers.

"Sir, Private Kane has the first sergeant's permission to speak to the company commander."

Captain Anderson looked up at him, his massive frame making the sturdy chair appear miniature. *Jesus, he's big,* Mike thought. *He's bigger than Caz Nowicki.*

"Oh, yes, Kane," he said. "Sergeant Warren spoke to me about you." He leaned back in the chair and looked steadily at Mike while he spoke. "Kane, you have been in the Army long enough to know we all have to do things we don't like to do. Take me, for example. This afternoon, I will go to a Brigade meeting. Do you think I want to go? I have to go. Now, somebody has to take care of the officers who don't have time to do it themselves. The first sergeant has picked you for the job, and I can't for the life of me see why you object."

He stopped and looked at Mike. Mike took a deep breath and spoke his mind.

"Sir, can the first sergeant make me do it? If not, I don't choose to volunteer."

Captain Anderson hunched forward over his desk and smiled. "You're absolutely right, Kane. The first sergeant can't make you do it, and neither can I. You're dismissed."

✦✦✦

Mike was told later that Poppa Bear had called Warren into his office and asked him how a first sergeant could pick a man for orderly, when he should have known the man didn't want the job?

Mike grinned at Stanley. "I'll bet old Miller is out to get my ass now."

Stanley shrugged. "What can he do? He's got you marked down as a Bolshevik, and he knows if he puts you on K.P. or guard out of turn, you'll have somebody from the Inspector General's office looking at the duty roster. Just don't fuck up, that's all."

That was the last Mike heard of the matter, but he had to admit that what happened to Sergeant Warren at Waianae probably had something to do with the sergeant's restraint.

✦✦✦

Waianae is a small town on the east coast of the island about halfway between Pearl Harbor and Kaena Point, and it can be reached by walking over the mountains through a breach made by Kolekole Pass. The distance from the regimental barracks to the top of the pass is about seven miles, and the approach is comparatively easy. At the top of the pass, the terrain becomes steep and broken, making it difficult to maneuver down the other side. Even the mules find the going difficult.

In Waianae, they pitched tents about a hundred yards from the ocean in a sandy grove dotted with palm trees. The squad tents slept eight, but only three to five men were assigned to each tent, so the guys enjoyed plenty of room.

Mike occupied a tent with Jeff, and Dan Rizo. After they unloaded folding cots, Jeff set his bed up and collapsed on it.

"Piss on this life," he said. "If I ever get outa this goddam Army the highest thing I'm gonna climb is a Jersey City bar stool."

"You found a home in the Army, Jeff," Dan Rizo said. "You're a thirty-year man."

Jeff put his hand on his crotch. "I got your thirty-year man right here."

They hiked over there to practice how to fire machine guns accurately at waterborne targets that simulated invasion craft. According to Poppa Bear, because of the coral reefs that surround Oahu, only a few places existed where an enemy force could land. Permanent gun emplacements covered those places, and they trained units like Mike's as backups.

The guns were set up at intervals of twenty-five yards, and fired at targets pulled across in front of and toward them. They fired in the daytime and at night. Every tenth round was a tracer bullet and, in the darkness, it looked like Fourth of July as the guns blazed away.

When they fired during the day, they finished by noon and could take the rest of the day off. When they fired at night, they were done by eleven and took the whole next day off. There was no guard duty, and men who might spoil the company's firing record pulled K.P.

A little store not far from the camp sold California muscatel for a dollar a gallon. Even women were available. An abandoned sugar mill about a mile from Waianae had a railroad siding, and two girls set up shop in an empty boxcar. They charged two dollars, and did a roaring business the first few nights. Towards the end of the exercise, when money got scarce and lines dwindled, they took as little as fifty cents.

Mike didn't go to the boxcar. He preferred to lie on the beach, drink wine, and think of Noelani. That time, he reflected later, amounted to the most pleasant two weeks he spent in the Army.

From the first day, the two-week exercise took on the air of an extended picnic. Even Poppa Bear, working with his beloved machine guns, was in good humor. He lost his temper only once. The object of his wrath was Miller Warren, who almost ruined their shooting record.

Machine gun firing exercises were conducted with two men on each gun. The number-one man served as the gunner, and the number-two man fed the ammunition belt into the gun. Other men waiting their turn crouched down about ten feet behind the gun. When Poppa Bear shouted, "Change!" the number one man scrambled out from behind the gun, the number two man replaced him, and the first man in line behind them ran forward to take the number-two's place.

One night, it became Miller Warren's turn to take his place as gunner. The man he replaced grabbed the elevating knob when he was getting to his feet, and accidentally raised the elevation about five clicks. When First Sergeant Warren fired his first burst, it sailed ten feet over the target. Poppa Bear shouted at Warren to lower the elevation. In his excitement, Warren turned the knob the wrong way, and his next burst sailed even higher. Poppa Bear erupted like a volcano. "Jesus suffering Christ!" he bellowed. He charged the gun, grabbed Warren under the armpits, and threw him aside. Plopping down, he made the necessary adjustment, and fired a stream of lead accurately into the target.

That started the beginning of the end for Miller Warren. It took Poppa Bear a while to make the arrangements, but six months later Warren boarded a boat to the mainland, on his way to take over a supply unit at Fort Lee, Virginia. Mike might have rejoiced over Warren's ruin, but Flash Paige boarded the same ship, another victim of Poppa Bear's wrath.

Chapter Twenty-Two

The Sunday after he returned from Waianae, Mike put on a freshly cleaned suit, carefully knotted a brown linen tie, and caught a taxi to Honolulu. He was standing in front of the Kawaiaha'o Church at nine thirty in the morning, but a passer-by told him the services began at ten thirty, so he went to a restaurant for a cup of coffee. He returned just after ten in case Noelani arrived early.

He turned from watching the congregation members filing into the church and saw Noelani and her brother walking up the street. She was dressed in a light-colored dress, with a small, light-colored hat perched on top of her shining, black hair. Mike's heart skipped a beat as she walked toward him. He threw his cigarette away and moved toward them, timing his footsteps so they arrived in front of the church simultaneously.

"Why, hello," he said, with what he hoped was well-simulated surprise.

Henry looked at him for a moment, and his face broke into a quick smile.

"Oh, yes. You're the Army start-off man. I didn't recognize you without your track suit."

Mike nodded, and Henry began to introduce Noelani. He stopped and grinned. "We've been through this before. You met Noelani at the meet."

Noelani repositioned her hat. "You're the boy Henry couldn't catch in the first leg of the relay. Are you going to church?"

"Yes," Mike said. "You, too?"

They both nodded, and Henry placed a guiding hand on his sister's back. "We better go in before the services start."

A Hawaiian usher welcomed them at the door. He shook hands with Mike and Henry, winked at Noelani, and gave each of them a program printed in Hawaiian and English.

The service was overwhelmingly different from anything Mike had experienced. The primarily Hawaiian congregation sang and prayed with all their hearts, creating in their hymns a magical, otherworldly sound. "E Nana Oluolu Iesu E," they intoned in the liquid accents of their native tongue. They followed in English, "Oh Jesus, grant me thy gracious smile."

The soft splendor of Noelani's profile as she bent over the hymnbook they shared, overcame Mike even more than the waves of melodic sound.

When the service ended, they walked out into the bright sunlight and stood in front of the church. For the first time in his life, Mike regretted the end of a church service.

"I got my jalopy parked up the street," Henry said. "Can I drop you someplace?"

"Which way you going?" Mike asked.

Henry pointed in a vague easterly direction. "We live out in Maikiki."

"No, thanks, I'll probably just take a bus to Waikiki."

"Hey, that's where we're going," Henry said, "after we stop by the house to pick up our swimming suits. Why don't you come along with us?"

Mike glanced at Noelani, and her friendly smile matched her brother's.

"Gee, then, okay."

They walked a block to his 1934 Model A Ford, and climbed into the front seat.

"You know," Mike said "I'm gonna have a little trouble swimming without my trunks."

"That's all right," Henry said. "I've got an old pair I can lend you."

When they got to the house, Henry jumped out of the car. "Come on. We change in the house and ride to the beach in our trunks."

Mike held the door for Noelani and followed her into the house. "My dad isn't home," she said as they walked into the living room.

Henry waved Mike into his bedroom. "Yeah, he's gone to visit friends in Hauula and won't be back till tomorrow. Saves us the trouble of introductions."

The track star threw him a pair of trunks, a sweatshirt, and a pair of battered sandals. When they finished changing, Henry banged on Noelani's door.

"Wikiwiki," he shouted, "or we'll leave without you."

A faint protest sounded from behind the door, and Henry returned to the living room.

"May as well settle in," he said. "She won't hurry. You got any sisters?"

"Nope."

"Then you don't know what a pain they are. Where you from in the States?"

"Philadelphia."

"Boy, you're a long way from home."

Mike nodded his head in agreement. "You ever been to the States?"

"No, but I'm going to the University of Southern California this September. Noelani wants to go, too. She's a senior like me, even though she's a year younger. But, my dad says he can't afford to send both of us. He wants her to settle for the University of Hawaii."

"Man, you're lucky. Southern Cal's a good school. They always have great track teams."

"That's why I'm going there. My dad keeps saying I'm going to hit the books, but I tell him it won't do any harm to earn a couple of varsity letters if I can."

"You'll earn them all right," Mike said. "Next year you'll be running the quarter in forty-seven seconds and, by the time you're a sophomore, you'll be matching Archie Williams' time."

"I don't know. I'm half-Hawaiian, and we islanders sometimes develop faster than you mainlanders. Maybe I'm at my peak now. Maybe I'll never get any better."

"Don't worry," Mike said. "One day I'll be reading your name in the record books."

Henry shook his head. "I don't know about that."

In the course of their discussion, he revealed that his mother had passed, and his father had been born in Germany but immigrated to the States when he was a small child.

"They lived in upper New York State, near Albany, and after Dad graduated from college he came here to work for American Factors. He's still with them. He's in accounting."

"Hey, that's an important job." He wondered what he would say about his own father if Henry asked. So he blurted out a small lie. "My dad only finished high school, like me. He wanted to send me to college but, with the depression, he couldn't afford it."

"Gee, that's too bad."

"Yeah, when times get bad, people stop buying insurance policies."

"Is your father in the insurance business?"

Before he could answer, Noelani flounced into the living room. She wore a short, beach jacket and a light-yellow bathing suit that emphasized her slim voluptuousness.

"If Dorothy Lamour is ready now, maybe... hopefully... we can go," Henry growled.

Noelani made a face at him, and they went outside to the Model A.

"Don't spoil her," Henry said as Mike held the car door. "She'll expect it again."

"Not from you, King Lunalilo" Noelani said. "But some boys are gentlemen."

When they arrived at Waikiki, Henry parked just off Kalakua Avenue and they walked to the beach. They picked a spot near the Outrigger Canoe Club and spread out their towels. Before they sat down, Henry ran toward the beach shouting, "Last one in's a wahine."

Thus began a day that glowed in Mike's memory with a bright radiance. They swam, and rode the surf, this time with Henry riding the board to steady it, while Mike stood shakily in front as they moved swiftly down the waves.

They lay on the beach and talked, and Mike was alone with Noelani for almost an hour while Henry walked up to Kalakua Avenue to see a friend who worked in a gift shop.

Mike told her he had talked to her on the Punahou campus, and she said she remembered. This emboldened him to tell her he had gone to church that morning for the sole purpose of meeting her. She looked pleased. He also admitted he had looked up the meaning of her name. *Noelani: beautiful one from heaven.*

"Your name describes you perfectly," Mike said.

She blushed.

He asked if he could call her sometime, and she said yes, but suggested he call in the daytime when her father wasn't home. "My father is pretty strict, and it would be better that way."

When Henry came back, they went home to the house in Maikiki, and Noelani made sandwiches. Afterward, Mike helped her with the dishes. At nine o'clock in the evening, he walked to the taxi stand across the street from the Black Cat Café. The sidewalks beneath his feet provided a soft and billowy path, as if feathers shod his feet.

Chapter Twenty-Three

Mike called Noelani every week during the next month, and they often met on a corner near the Punahou School. Each time, they drank soda and talked, and walked to her home holding hands. They talked about their plans and dreams, and noted how they had both lost their mothers early in life. They promised their love to one another on their third date. On their fourth, Mike brought a gift.

"My mother would have loved you as much as I do, Noelani. She was pretty, and strong-willed, but gentle, and always smiling. She would know you are the right girl for me. You are smart and caring, and someone who others gravitate to. And, you are beautiful. I want to give you this, my four-forty race gold medal. My name is inscribed on it so you won't ever forget me."

She blushed and smiled, and tears filled her eyes. "I love you, Mike."

Another time, they stopped under a blossoming shower tree, three blocks from her house, and she gave Mike a fleeting goodnight kiss.

Kissing was as far as they ever went. With perky breasts needing support as much as those on the statue of Venus de Milo, she wore an armored under-garment against his stealthy brushes. She upheld the morals of a girl determined to go to her marriage bed a virgin, and with her private parts un-fondled as well. Mike loved her even more for her convictions, and discipline.

Though they found the sexual frustration difficult, an even more challenging obstacle loomed... facing up to her father.

"I know what he thinks. Dogfaces are social outcasts who couldn't make it in civilian life."

"But you're different, Michael," Noelani said.

"But will he be able to see that?"

Noelani breathed deeply, "He is very hardheaded about things, so there is no telling."

They continued to meet outside the house until Henry found out and delivered an ultimatum. "Mike, if you want to date Noelani, you will have to come to the house to meet her."

"But, if I do that, your father will run me off the first time I come around," he protested.

"That's a chance you'll have to take. Besides, maybe he won't. You don't look or act like most of the soldiers I see running around Honolulu. Maybe he'll see that, too."

Most dogfaces went to town in un-pressed slacks, sloppy shirts and, likelier than not, wearing their high-topped garrison shoes and Army socks.

I don't look like a dogface, Mike thought, thanks to Jeff's taste in clothes and skill at pool and poker. Anybody can see I am different.

◆◆◆

When Mike finally met Mr. Kreuger for the first time, he made a good impression. It happened one Sunday after Henry laid down the law. He met Noelani and Henry at church, and, afterward, went back to the house with them to change and go to the beach.

When they arrived at the house, Henry introduced Mike to his father. Mr. Kreuger was a tall, thin man, with brown hair just beginning to turn gray, and a sober Germanic face.

"I'm pleased to meet you," he said, giving Mike a firm handshake.

Mike grasped his hand with equal firmness. "Pleased to meet you, sir."

"Well, let's get dressed," Noelani said, starting for her room.

Henry and Mike went into Henry's room and, when they came out, Noelani was already waiting.

"Hurry up, you slowpokes," she said, jumping to her feet and starting for the front door.

Her father called her back. "I think you should have something to eat before you go."

"We're not hungry, Dad," Noelani protested. "We just ate breakfast."

"That was three hours ago. And how do you know our guest isn't hungry?"

"I'm not hungry, sir," Mike said, smiling. "I ate a big breakfast. But thanks anyway."

"Well, it's still a good idea to have something. You won't be back for hours."

"But, Dad," Noelani pleaded, "we want to get to the beach before the crowd."

"Now, honey, don't argue." Her father took her gently by the arm. "It won't take long. I've got a fresh pot of coffee and the sandwiches are already made. Don't want to waste them."

He led the way to a breakfast nook just off the kitchen, which looked out on a spacious lanai. Beyond the lanai, stretched a green lawn and a Poinciana tree decked with scarlet blossoms. Under the tree sat a green wicker table and four chairs.

He compared it to the tiny yard behind his rented house on Etting Street, with its sagging, wooden fence, drooping clothesline, and malodorous outhouse. *The kind of home dogfaces come from*, he thought to himself. *No wonder Mr. Kreuger's got a hard-on for us.*

Henry plopped into a chair, but Mike helped Noelani with hers. Mr. Kreuger smiled.

"It might be a good idea if you performed gentlemanly acts like that for your sister once in a while, Henry," he suggested with a wink.

"Oh, come on, Dad," Henry protested. "Don't you think she's spoiled enough already?"

"If I am, it's certainly not by you," Noelani retorted, and Mr. Kreuger held up his hand.

"Please, no arguments at the table."

They ate the sandwiches and left without Mr. Kreuger asking Mike about who he was or where he came from. Mike guessed that Mr. Kreuger assumed he was one of Henry's classmates.

When they got outside, Noelani turned to her brother, "What now, King Lunalilo?"

"As long as you meet at the house, dad can find out for himself. I'll stay out of it."

"I'm sorry," he said to Mike. "I haven't got anything against you. But if you two are getting serious about one another, Dad's got a right to know about it."

◆◆◆

They got away with it for almost two months because, even though Mike lived up to the letter of his agreement with Henry, he managed to avoid Noelani's father. Mr. Kreuger prided himself as a joiner who belonged to the Lions, the Rotarians, the Chamber of Commerce, and God knows what else. He was away from home two or three nights a week to attend meetings, and on these nights Mike visited Noelani.

One night, the axe fell. He came to meet with Noelani and her father was home. Her glum face when she answered the door should have warned him. When Mike closed the door behind him, he was surprised to see her father sitting in an armchair with an even glummer face.

"Oh, good evening, sir," Mike said as calmly as he could, attempting to mask the shock.

"Are you surprised to see me?" Mr. Kreuger asked.

"No, sir. I'm glad to see you. You're not home very often."

"How do you know that?" Mr. Kreuger asked quickly.

"Well, I've been here a couple of times to see Henry, and you weren't home."

"Sit down. I want to talk to you."

He motioned Mike to a chair and Mike sat, smiling. He watched as Mr. Kreuger pressed the tips of his fingers together, looking alternately at Mike and his hands.

"I've known for some time something was bothering Noelani," he began, "and tonight I found out what it is. She told me about you. When I asked her who you are, she said you are in the Army, but she doesn't know your rank or position. Suppose you tell me."

"Do you mind if I smoke?" Mike asked, instantly regretting he did so.

"Not at all. Noelani, bring an ashtray, please."

Mike lit a cigarette and inhaled deeply.

"I am a soldier, sir," he said, almost relieved to come clean. "A private in the infantry at Schofield Barracks."

"And what are your intentions toward my daughter?"

"Someday I'd like to marry her, sir."

"And when is the wedding to take place?"

"When I get out of the Army and get a decent job."

"What kind of a job?" Mr. Kreuger asked, his voice rising for the first time. "Driving a Schofield taxi? Where will you live? In one of those shacks on River Street like the rest of the ex-soldiers married to native girls? Or do you expect me to support you?"

Mike started to answer, but Noelani broke in. "It's not his fault he's in the Army. When he finished high school, his Dad wanted to send him to college, but he had business troubles."

"What kind of business is his father in?"

"The insurance business."

Mike's heart sank at the lie he had told Henry. He looked down at his knees and heard the air pour out of his nose. Then he clenched a fist.

"Your father may as well know the truth, Noelani. I didn't graduate from high school. And my father's not in the insurance business. He's an Irishman who quit school in the sixth grade and worked all his life as a laborer, when he wasn't unemployed."

Mike's voice shook with pent-up anger and he stopped and pointed dramatically at Mr. Kreuger. "But your father doesn't have any right to look down on me, or on my father, either, just because he happened to be born with two strikes against him!"

"And so were you, boy!" Mr. Kreuger shouted, jumping to his feet. "And so were you!"

He walked across the room toward Mike. "Get out of my house!" he shouted threateningly. "And don't ever come back!"

"I'm going, don't worry," Mike said. He looked over at Noelani, but she was staring at the floor. He felt the adrenalin retreating from his system, and he walked slowly toward the front door.

He put his hand on the knob and pulled the door open. He paused and looked back at Noelani again, but she continued to stare at the floor, crying softly. He felt hopeless and exhausted as he stepped outside and let the door close gently behind him.

◆◆◆

Mike moped around for a week until his confidence revived sufficiently to call Noelani. When her voice answered the phone, he said, "Noelani, it's me, Mike."

"I'm going to school in California next month, and I promised I'd never see you or talk to you again," she said, her voice unnaturally flat. A soft click sounded and the line went dead.

Chapter Twenty-Four

The sound of heavy footsteps approaching his bunk made Mike open his eyes to Dan Rizo standing over him, a broad smile on his face.

"Hey, Mike, I'm the new middleweight champ!" he said.

"That's great, Dan. How did that happen? Is Paige gonna retire?"

"We just had a meetin', and Punchy's gonna make a welterweight outa Paige. That way we can win two division titles."

Mike and Dan saw Bama Dillon walking along the porch, and Dan ran after him.

"Hey, Bama, wait'll I tell ya the news!"

Mike watched him waving his arms while Bama looked on impassively. He closed his eyes again. Dan is really happy, but I bet Flash Paige is not. He'd have to take off a lot of weight and Flash hates to train.

So, why would he agree to undergo this ordeal? After all, Punchy, at the same rank, couldn't make him do it.

Later he got the full story from Paige, himself.

It turned out that the idea came from Lieutenant Thompson. He had come up with it when the 35th Regiment announced their great welterweight Timmy Blaine was coming back.

Timmy was a legend at Schofield Barracks because a West Coast fight manager once offered to buy him out of the Army and make him welterweight champion of the world, and

Timmy said no. Nobody thought he was crazy, though. As a staff sergeant, he ran a poker game in the howitzer weapons shack. A famous fighter should have had it so good.

Paige had protested at changing weight classes. "I'm twenty-eight years old, and takin' that extra weight off will weaken me."

"I'll worry about that," Punchy had answered. "He's thirty-two and over the hill. You can take him."

"He didn't look over the hill when I saw him slaughter some gob three months ago."

Punchy just grunted and considered the discussion closed.

✦✦✦

The night Timmy and Paige were scheduled to fight, an enthusiastic crowd crammed the bowl. Mike sat with Jeff Kincaid and Al Stanley. Each had brought two blankets, one to cushion the hard and cold concrete seats, and the other to ward off the damp, chilly air. March marks the end of the rainy season in Oahu, but it had been raining fitfully all day.

Up ahead of him, in the ringside seats reserved for officers, Baby Bear and Lieutenant Thompson sat together. He pointed them out to Jeff, but he just grunted. He was feeling down because Linda had left that day on a Matson liner for San Francisco, and it would be six months before he would be discharged and going back to join her.

Dan Rizo climbed into the ring for his middleweight title fight against a Class I fighter from the 35th, and Jeff perked up a little. He had ten dollars bet on Dan and the dopesters had picked Rizo to win. They hunched forward expectantly in their seats as Dan made prophets out of the forecasters by knocking out his opponent in the first round.

The same dopesters had picked Timmy to win. They figured that, despite a two-year layoff, he could still beat anybody else, even Paige.

As one Honolulu sportswriter put it, "Timmy may be over the hill, but the hill in question is such a gigantic eminence that nobody else has been able to climb it."

Timmy was the first man through the ropes, and a tremendous roar of excited cheering rose when he entered the ring. The normal excitement that grips a fight crowd was heightened in this case because most of the spectators had a bet on the outcome. With Timmy at eight-to-five to win, most of the money was on him, including a rumored five hundred dollars belonging to halfback Reilly, the biggest moneylender in the regiment. Loyalists, like Mike and Jeff, could cover the Timmy money. Mike had five dollars on Paige and Jeff had twenty.

A more subdued roar greeted Flash when he slid through the ropes parted by Punchy Adams. When the referee called both to the center of the ring for instructions, you could see Paige was two inches taller and looked ten pounds heavier than Timmy.

During the first round, both fighters tested each other's reflexes and abilities. Timmy fought from a semi-crouch, throwing punches in a series of lightning combinations. Paige fought in the stand-up position, always moving in a circle away from his opponent's right hand. Timmy hit Paige a couple of good punches to the body, but Flash's midriff was harder than rock. On his part, Flash piled up points with his marvelous left hand.

In the second round, Timmy moved in with the supremely confident air that marked all his actions in the ring, and hit Paige with even more solid combinations to the body. But Flash seemed to weather them well, and he kept punching out a left hand that seemed to have eyes of its own. Near the end of the round, he stepped inside when Timmy was coming in, and hit him with a sharp, right uppercut that knocked his opponent down. But Timmy was more surprised than hurt, and jumped to his feet before the referee could start counting. The bell rang, ending the round.

Mike glanced at Reilly sitting in front of him, to see if his behavior would confirm the rumor he had bet against his regiment. He simply sat there, impassive, staring at the ring.

In the third round, Paige boxed as beautifully as ever, and a mouse appeared under Timmy's left eye. About halfway through the round, though, he hit Paige with a left hook. Flash fell to the floor. The halfback in front of Mike got up and walked toward the exit.

"Where the hell you goin', Reilly?" Mike yelled at him, "It ain't over yet."

"The hell it ain't," he said without looking back. He was right. Paige got up at the count of eight, but Timmy hit him with a left to the body that made Flash sag. He followed with a whistling right that dropped him to the floor in an inert heap. Punchy pulled him out before the referee could count.

Next, and even more shocking than the sudden knockout, Baby Bear jumped to her feet and climbed into the ring. Paige was slumped on his stool, his legs spread out in front of him and his head hanging with Punchy dousing him with water from a sponge. Brushing Punchy aside, Baby Bear took Paige's head tenderly between her hands and kissed him on the lips. She climbed out of the ring and ran up the aisle toward the exit, tears streaming down her face, followed by an obviously worried Lieutenant Thompson.

✦✦✦

The next day, everyone at Schofield Barracks had heard the story, and that afternoon the regimental commander held a meeting in his office with Poppa Bear, the executive officer, the first battalion commander, and the chaplain. They kept Paige waiting in the anteroom with the regimental sergeant major while they discussed his fate. The upshot of the meeting involved Paige's temporary transfer to Headquarters Company, pending his departure on the next boat, which left in April.

First Sergeant Miller Warren was on the boat with him that month.

According to regimental scuttlebutt, Colonel Maynard also told Poppa Bear he, too, would be on the next boat if he couldn't control his daughter. This was all bad news to the company, but its ill wind blew some good Bama Dillon's way.

Bama got Paige's vacancy, as well as his fifty-dollars-a-month-extra job at the Kaala Club. The added money really helped his family.

That night, Mike read Doc Greene's letter. Doc only wrote about twice a year, like Mr. Goldman. Good old Rose was the only one who wrote regularly: once a week rain or shine.

Doc's latest letter was an answer to one Mike had written shortly after his break-up with Noelani. He had felt in sore need to tell somebody his troubles, and when it came to making a choice, he chose Doc.

His friend's literary style tended to be slightly florid, a combination of 18th Century rhetoric and neighborhood slang, and Mike enjoyed his letters tremendously. He unfolded the pages.

"Dear Mike,

I should have answered your letter sooner—when you were more in need of any solace an answer might have brought, than you are, I trust, at the moment. But, Lord Chesterfield I am not, and neither am I a Horace Walpole, as a lifetime of large telephone bills will attest.

Still it wasn't entirely epistolary indolence that stayed my laggard pen. It was, as well, awareness that a man who chuckled when he read your heart-rending message was not the man to comfort your distress. And I did chuckle. The reason I chuckled is, at 42, I am in possession of certain knowledge, which you, too, may now be able to dimly perceive. I know that nobody ever died of a broken heart. I know that time heals all wounds, especially romantic ones. I know that Noelani is not unique. However splendid she is in mind, body, and spirit, there are thousands of girls just like her in the world, even some here in Brewerytown. Have you forgotten Patricia Ann Galvan?

(Apropos of Patricia, she just married a guy who played second string halfback at Villanova last year, and who is the son of a man I know well: Judge of the Quarter Sessions Court, Aloysius O'Leary. I say I know him well, though I never met the thieving son-of-a-bitch personally. Every time I got pinched for bootlegging, his bagman arranged to have my case put on Judge O'Leary's calendar, and it cost me five hundred bucks to have the charges dismissed for lack of evidence.)

Anyhow, Mike, I forbore (is there such a word?) from answering until time, as I knew it would, made you more receptive to the essential reality of unromantic truth. I might add another reason I chuckled is that there is nothing easier to be philosophical about than another man's troubles.

You wrote your letter in September, the month Chamberlain made his pilgrimage to Germany to appease Hitler's romantic appetites, at least temporarily, by allowing him to swallow Czechoslovakia. (One can only hope he discovers he has swallowed a nation of Good Soldier Schweiks.) Adolph's next move, obviously, will be against the Polish Corridor and Danzig. The British and French will have to quit kissing his ass sometime. And when they do... Bingo! World War II. Yet, there was no mention of these things in your letter. Didn't it occur to you that the paperhanger is a bigger threat to your well-being than rejection by Aloma of the South Seas? *Probably not, since it's not in the nature of twenty-year-olds to worry about the future..."*

And so it went on, lovingly spiritual and fatherly.

Mike folded the letter and closed his eyes. Old Doc was really something. But he was wrong about Noelani. She was special and he really did love her. She was the one.

Chapter Twenty-Five

Near the end of August 1939, Mike and Jeff got the pieces of paper they had been yearning after for almost three years—orders sending them back to New York for discharge.

"You'll be back," Steiner, the new company clerk, said. "You found a home."

"Yeah," Jeff said.

"You never had it so good, Jeff," the clerk said. He had replaced Al Stanley.

"Yes, I did. I once did a stretch on the Georgia Chain Gang."

They walked into the Day Room and read the orders carefully—they were to sail on the USS U. S. Grant on the ninth of September.

Jeff folded his copy carefully and put it in his shirt pocket.

"You know," he said, "when I get to Frisco, I'm gonna go to an Army-Navy store and buy me a surplus Springfield rifle. Then I'll throw it in the back yard and watch it rust away to nothin'. And if it don't rain often enough, I may piss on it once in a while to help it along."

"You ain't kidding me, Jeff," Mike said. "You'll probably buy a pup tent and sleep in the back yard every time you get homesick for C Company."

"You're right," Jeff said, "and Papa Bear's gonna marry Mae West and open a bar."

They both remained quiet for moment.

Jeff looked at Mike. "You think we're gonna make it?"

"We got the orders, don't we?"

"But suppose a war breaks out in Europe? Today. Or tomorrow. We still got ten days."

"A war is gonna break out, and soon. But we're not involved. Roosevelt says so."

"Jesus, I hope so. Linda's doin' good with the diner and she needs me back there to help."

✦✦✦

Two days later, Hitler invaded Poland. Mike heard the news at Reveille from the new first sergeant Ward Clements, who announced it off-handedly before he dismissed them.

While they policed the company area, Mike worked his way over to where Sergeant Clements, a tall, rangy man in his late thirties, was smoking a cigarette.

"Sergeant Clements, that fighting in Europe? How's it gonna affect us over here?"

Clements grunted. "It ain't any skin off my ass, Kane. Let them fight."

"I mean me and Jeff. We got orders to go back to the States for discharge."

Clements shrugged. "You got me, kid. I don't know any more about it than you do. But if you got any sense, you'll stay here. We're seven thousand miles from Europe."

He turned away and walked toward the mess hall, and Mike stared after him. "Then I'm going home," he muttered to himself. "If there's gonna be a war, I'm gonna be in it."

✦✦✦

It was late morning when Mike ran to the Day Room, where he found a gathering of quiet soldiers clustered around the radio. Steiner put his finger to his lips.

"You're just in time to hear Hitler."

Mike slipped into a chair and hunched forward. A reporter's voice, quietly urgent, filled the silent room.

"It's Friday evening here in Berlin, and we are in the Kroll Opera House where Chancellor Adolph Hitler is just about to address the German Reichstag. The Chancellor is dressed in a field-gray uniform and there is little doubt that the subject of his speech will be Poland, which German armies invaded at dawn today along a wide front..." The reporter's voice lifted with excitement. "Here is the German leader."

Hitler's speech was short, the voice curiously flat, and Mike couldn't understand a word of it. Occasionally, the sotto voce sounds of the translator intruded on his consciousness. "I am wrongly judged if my love of peace and my patience are mistaken for weakness or cowardice. I can no longer find any willingness on the part of the Polish government to conduct serious negotiations with us... I have therefore resolved to speak to Poland in the same language that Poland, for months past, has used toward us. This night, for the first time, Polish regular soldiers fired on our territory. Since five forty-five a.m. we have been returning the fire, and from now on bombs will be met with bombs..."

Only once did Hitler's voice take on the dramatic quality familiar to Mike from American movie newsreels. Listening, half to the translator and half to Hitler, he made out many of the words.

"I am asking of no German man more than I was ready, throughout four years, to do. I am, from now on, the first soldier of the German Reich. I have once more put on that coat which is most sacred and dear to me. I will not take it off again until victory is secured..."

The reporter resumed his commentary. "The German Fuehrer is leaving the Kroll Opera House and you can hear the cheers. But their reception to his speech was restrained when compared with the wild enthusiasm after other Hitler speeches in this historic hall..."

Steiner burst out. "He's already got Austria and the Czechs! What more does he want?"

"I don't know. But the Brits and Frogs are not putting up with his bullshit any longer."

"Hope so, Mike, but others say they'll fiddle around until it's too late, like before."

As everyone left, Steiner looked around and caught Mike's gaze. "Wait, Mike, I just remembered there's a new man in the 27th and he also wants to write. Hey, Jones, come over here."

When the soldier came over, Steiner said, "Jim, this is Mike Kane."

"Hi, Mike, I'm James Jones. Steiner says you're also interested in writing?"

"Yes, I am, but I'm still looking for experiences to develop into a good story."

"Me, too. I figure there have to be some stories here where you have Hawaii, the Army, and a possible war brewing. I think I'll find what I need right here," he said.

"I hope you're on the right trail. Those experiences eluded me, and I say good luck to you. As for me, I'm being discharged and heading home on the next boat."

"What a shame. I would have enjoyed getting to know you. Oh well, man. Whatever happens to us in the months and years ahead, please know you can reach me anytime at James Ramon Jones, General Delivery, Robinson, Illinois. Here, I'll write it down for you."

"Thanks, James. I'll surely be in touch."

Jones gave him the paper with his address, and shook Mike's hand before leaving.

"Who the hell was that?" Jeff asked.

"Oh, just a guy who still has a dream."

✦✦✦

Two days later, England and France declared war on Germany and, that afternoon, Captain Anderson called Mike and Kincaid into his office. Mike went in first, and Poppa Bear was smoking a curved, briar pipe, and held a pleasant look on his face when he took the pipe out of his mouth to return Mike's salute.

"At ease," he said.

He put the pipe back in his mouth and puffed out clouds of smoke while he talked.

"Are you goin' to reenlist when you get back to the States, Kane?"

Mike shook his head. "No, sir."

"It's not too late to reenlist here, you know. I can still get you off shipping orders. I could even promote you to PFC, and you could make corporal before your next enlistment's up."

Mike was flattered by the old man's kindly and interested tone, and the prospect of two butterflies on his sleeve attracted him powerfully, so he answered quickly.

"No, sir, I couldn't stay here. I wrote home and I couldn't disappoint them now."

"Well, it's your decision," Poppa Bear said.

He pushed back his chair and, standing half erect, extended a huge hand over the desk.

Mike put out his hand, and he shook it vigorously.

"Good luck, Kane. I'm sorry to see you go."

"Thank you, sir," Mike said. There was a warm feeling inside him as he walked out.

Later, Jeff told Mike the old man had said the same things to him.

"You know what I told the old bastard?"

"What?"

"I told him the only things with two stripes were corporals and skunks."

"You did like hell!"

Jeff grinned. "You're right, I didn't."

For the next week, they were members of the regimental elite, the shortest short-timers, and the men making the next boat. Every time they walked into the beer garden or the regimental restaurant, somebody would spot them and shout, "Short-timers, sound off!"

Mike and Jeff would bellow back, "Seven and a butt," or whatever number of days and fraction of a day remained.

On the morning of the ninth, the sound of the regimental band playing the traditional short-timers' song awakened them and, while the rest of the company stood Reveille, Mike and Jeff folded up their blankets, sheets, and mosquito netting, and turned them in.

After breakfast, they carried their barracks bags out to the waiting trucks and threw them in the back. The band was formed up on the street in front of headquarters, and they lined up behind it with the other men going home.

When the bandmaster gave the musicians a downbeat, they all stepped off smartly. They made one circuit of the quadrangle, waving at the dogfaces leaning over the porch rails watching them. When they got to the spot where the trucks were parked, they broke formation and climbed into them. The drivers started the engines and they drove slowly out of the quadrangle.

A private named Reuben Case, who looked like he had worked a farm in his prior life, stared out the back of the truck. "Well, we done it, boys. We've done our hitch in hell."

He recognized the phrase "Hitch in Hell" as the title of a sentimental poem about Schofield Barracks.

Mike smiled, but he thought of Noelani.

Chapter Twenty-Six

Mike was out of the Army and home. But, now what? It took nearly three weeks for the ship to get him back to New York for his discharge. With all that time to think, Mike still had no idea what to do next. On impulse, he bought some clothes so he would fit in back home. He dipped into the eighty-seven dollars he had saved and bought a double-breasted, gray suit, with white pin stripes, and a gray, felt hat.

On the morning of his discharge, arrayed in his new clothes, he took the subway to Manhattan and boarded a bus for Philadelphia. When he stepped off the Philly streetcar, the first person he saw was Caz Nowicki.

Caz pumped his hand. "You look good, Mike. I think you grew a little and gained some weight." His eyes traveled up and down Mike's frame, and stopped at his hat.

"That's a sharp suit and I like your shoes. But that hat must go. Nobody wears wide brims anymore. You look like you just stepped off the boat from Poland."

Mike took the hat off, and crammed it in his suitcase. "How's Stash?"

"He's fine. Him and Teresa have a nice, little apartment on Columbia Avenue. Dutch and Marie Koenig live right across the hall from them. Hey, you never saw their little boy Stanley, did you? He's two years old now and, thank God, he looks like Teresa instead of Stash."

"How about Sophie, Caz? That girl you were goin' with when I left. You still seein' her?"

"Old Soph? Nah, we broke up over two years ago. But she's doin' good. She married some Polack from Bridesburg. He owns a big hardware store, and they live in Mayfair."

"Boy, she was beautiful!" Mike said.

Caz grinned at him. "Yeah, but there are more fish in the sea than ever came out of it."

Mike looked at his watch. "I gotta go, Caz. I ain't been home yet and they're waitin'."

"Then you better get goin'. Your old man and Rose are dying to see you. Rose hasn't talked about anything else in weeks. Before you go, though, I'm makin' a date. Tomorrow night at Rafferty's... a welcome home party on me and Doc. We'll have everybody there—Stash, Dutch, Willie, Dominic, Nat Brennan will tickle the eighty-eights—the whole gang."

"Hey, thanks, Caz, that sounds great. What about Sam Schwarz? You seen him lately?"

"Sam? Jesus, I haven't seen him in months. I know he's still goin' to Pharmacy School. I see his old man once in a while when I go by the store and steal an apple."

"How about Esther and Abe Brodsky?"

"Ain't you heard? Him and Jake Mandel had a big argument, and Jake threw him outa the apartment. Last I heard, him and Esther were living somewhere around Fourth and Girard."

"Okay, Caz, I'll see you tomorrow night, if I don't see you before then."

He walked down the street and threw his hat in the first trashcan he found. The better part of five dollars shot in the ass, but if Caz thought it looked funny, it wasn't worth five cents.

When he got to the house, the door flew open as he walked up the steps, and a beaming Rose pulled him inside. Behind her, in the narrow vestibule, his father stood, grinning broadly. Rose led him to the dining room and hugged him, then pushed him back to arm's length.

"Let me look at you, Michael!"

She inspected him, her eyes bright with tears.

"You look wonderful. You've grown some, but you lost weight."

Mike turned to his moist-eyed father and hugged him, his eyes tearing up as well.

"I just saw Caz Nowicki, and he says I gained weight."

His father thumped his shoulders and upper arms.

"He's right, Rose. Jeez, Mike, I bet you weigh more than I do."

"A hundred and fifty, Pop. I gained quite a bit in Oahu, but I lost some on the boat comin' back. The food was lousy."

"See! I knew you lost weight," Rose said. "But I'll take care of that."

Rose pointed to the dining room table, laden with a white linen tablecloth, and all her best dishes.

"I've got all the things you like best, Michael. Picnic ham, and cabbage, and turnips, and potatoes, all cooked in the same pot. And Gulden's mustard. And Boston cream pie."

Mike hugged her again.

"Knowing you, Rose, I coulda guessed you'd do this for me."

"Your room's waiting for you. Go and wash up. But hurry, the food will be ready soon."

His father grabbed his suitcase and walked up the stairs ahead of him. When they got to the bedroom, Paddy put the suitcase inside and stepped back.

"You still workin' weekends at Rafferty's, Pop?"

"Sure, I'm still workin'. I work every weekend." Paddy answered, a note of pride in his voice. "And I'm doin' good, too. Times are pickin' up."

"Can you get off tomorrow night? Caz and Doc are throwin' a welcome home party at Rafferty's for me and everybody's invited."

"Sure I can get off. Charlie Hubbell will fill in for me. Okay, wash up now!"

When Paddy went back downstairs, Mike looked around his room. Rose had put a new brown-and-white bedspread on the bed, and light-brown curtains on the windows, and the bookcase was polished. He walked over and ran his hand over the backs of the books, all still there, like soldiers ready to do battle against the dragons of ignorance and superstition—with Hemingway, Shaw and Wells in the vanguard. Shaw and Wells, the two writers who had started him on the way to being a truly educated man. And Ernest Hemingway, who didn't offer much in the way of instruction, except how to fish and hunt and fight, and how to write. Old Ernie could write like an angel. He took down *A Farewell to Arms* and read the opening sentences describing a house overlooking a stream, and the stones and water. He felt he was being pulled into the story immediately.

God, they were beautiful sentences. He closed the book and put it back on the shelf. Smiling happily, he went into the bathroom to wash up. He was home again.

❖❖❖

The welcome home party was a ball, and he made a maudlin speech, ending with a pretentious flourish that nobody understood, except Doc Greene.

"Thomas Wolfe was wrong," he had declaimed drunkenly. "You *can* go home again."

Willie was the first one he saw when he walked into Rafferty's. At first he didn't know who he was until he turned around and Mike was looking at a tall body below Willie's head.

"Jesus, Willie, you grew up while I was gone."

"I told ya, Mike, I could eat soup off James Cagney's head," Willie said with a laugh.

At that point, Jake Hoyt reached down and pulled up Willie's pant hems.

"Adler shoes, guaranteed to make you three inches taller."

"Unhand the haberdashery, Hoyt, or you'll pull back a stump," Willie growled.

Rose had already told him Willie had a job at Budd's Manufacturing, and was going steady with a girl named Angela he met at a cousin's wedding.

"Wait'll you see Angie." Willie dragged him into the back room to meet her.

She turned out to be a thin, nervous girl, with long, lustrous hair, and beautiful teeth, and a chip on her shoulder.

She originated the conversation. "So you're the famous Mike Kane."

"I'm famous?"

"Willie says you're going to be some day. What were you in the Army? A general?"

"General Nuisance," he quipped, trying to make light of her obvious hostility. *What kind of a threat do I represent to this girl?*

She wasted no time telling him.

"Willie told me about your trip to California. Well, I can tell you right now he's not going on any more trips. He's staying right here."

Mike grinned at her. "Me, too, Angie."

Willie and Mike found some time that night to talk and drink like the old days. After they caught up with the details of the last three years, Willie paused. "Mike, I never thanked you for bringing me home from our train trip. I wasn't up to it, but you got me through it. And, it turned out to be the best experience of my life. I learned a lot."

"Na, you're makin' a big deal out of nothin'. It was a learning experience for me, too."

"No, I mean when you stood up to those seven sick bastards on the train to protect me. You and I both know it wasn't over when I kicked that pervert in the nuts. They would've come back in the night. But you confronted them and kicked the living shit outa their biggest guy, then threatened them with instant death if they even looked at one of us... and for fucking *ever*."

"Nothing you wouldn't do for me, Willie. I love you like a brother, maybe closer. You're my best friend in life, and that's forever. Book it."

"Same here, Mike. I gotta say the way you were that night, though... well, I never saw you like that. You're usually so easygoin', where did that Superman shit come from?"

"I have no idea, but I hate bullies and I protect my family, and you're my family. Something comes over me, and I can't explain it, because I don't think about it. I'm good with my fists. So good, they wanted me on the boxing squad in Hawaii, but that wasn't for me. I won first prize in bayonet proficiency in the regiment two years runnin', and I think it's related to my hand-eye coordination. I think like a nice guy, but I act with my fists."

"Wow, Mike, I'll never forget that, and our adventure. Love you, man!" Willie hugged Mike. "You know I don't like to write, but you always know I'm thinking of you all the time."

"Love you too, brother!" Mike's eyes grew moist. "Don't worry about letters. I'm always there for you, no matter what." They hugged again, and Willie left to find Angie.

✦✦✦

He had been out with Sam Schwarz exactly once since coming home, when he took Sam and Natalie Mandel to Lew Tendler's on South Broad Street for a steak dinner. Natalie was as pretty as a picture—a sweet, quiet girl who didn't say fifty words all night long. Sam looked like he had spent the last three years wandering in a desert. He had grown six inches and gained nary a pound. No wonder, going to school and working full-time at a Walgreens.

Yep, wedding bells, engagements, and going steady had already broken up that old gang of his. Except for the born bachelors like Doc Greene and Caz Nowicki, who changed girlfriends every three months, or so.

"They still around, Jumbo Case, and Walleye, and the rest?" he had asked when Charlie Hubbell told him about Georgie joining the bottle gang.

"Still around, but not for much longer. They all look like warmed-over corpses."

"They still sleepin' at Sol Rudnick's?"

"Still there, them and the rats."

♦♦♦

Most of the guys were tied down to some girl, but didn't seem much happier than he. At Teresa and Stash's apartment, when different couples visited and the guys got to belting down the booze and getting raucous, the mouths of the girls tightened up. Twice, Marie Koenig walked out and left Dutch looking foolish. Another time, Dom's wife Jennie really acted up. She crammed Dom's new Stetson down on his head, threw his topcoat at him, and practically dragged him out of the apartment. Old Dom, whom Mike could still see at the corner rolling a crooked de Nobili cigar in his mouth.

Only Stash seemed content. If there ever lived a man born to be married, Stash was it. Just like Rose had said, he spoiled Teresa rotten and seemed to revel in it. Also, in their case, there was little Stash, a real charmer.

"Thank God," Teresa said, "he's got Stanley's disposition instead of mine."

Little Stash was a plus all right, especially when he crawled into your lap and called you Uncle Mike.

Yet, Mike decided he would not end up in a two-room love nest.

The only guy who stayed mostly the same was Doc Greene, except for his hollow cheeks were leaner; and his sparse, brown hair, sparser, and graying at the temples. After Aunt Sadie retired, Doc also acquired a part-time mistress he slept with once a week.

Annie Phillips, a divorcee with no kids, lived on Corlies Street. She was as old as Doc, but better preserved, even though not considered a beauty. Still, she was friendly, and Mike always enjoyed himself whenever he went out with them.

Doc had also acquired a 1938 Studebaker, and often drove them to their favorite spot: Jimbo's on Erie Avenue. The restaurant and bar's namesake and owner – a guy Doc knew from back in his bootlegging days—once ran a speakeasy.

Thank God Mike found a decent job at the Frankford Arsenal, which allowed him to pay his share when they went out together. Three days after he came home, Mary McDevitt told Rose about the job opening. He took their test and they hired him two weeks later. The job paid twenty-eight dollars and twenty cents a week after deductions, but Rose only took ten bucks a week for board.

Jesus, though, the job bored him. Small-Arms Ammunition Inspector they called him, and all day long he went from one to the other of six machines that spewed out .30 caliber shell cases, inspecting them for cracks, and calipering them to make sure they measured to the right size. Women ran all of the machines and, one of them, an old grouch named Mrs. Babcock fell apart every time he found a defect in her work. Christ, you'd think she was paid on piecework the way she cried when he closed down her machine for adjustment. He really couldn't get mad, though, she was an old woman who worried management would think she couldn't do her job.

Besides, Mrs. Babcock was responsible for one good thing. She inspired the first thing he had written in a long time.

◆◆◆

Mike had called Lester's house four times without getting an answer. When he finally called Sylvia Weiss' apartment, Lester answered the phone. Obviously, Lester had moved in the minute Naomi and Bernie got married and left for New York City. They made a date to meet the following night at Sylvia's and, when Lester answered the door, Mike worked to keep his jaw from dropping. Lester's hair now sported almost as much gray as black, even though he barely just turned thirty-seven. Sylvia, even at three years older, appeared more attractive than ever.

"It's too bad you didn't have Naomi and Bernie's address when you passed through New York, Michael," she said. "They'd have loved to have seen you."

"How does Bernie like his job at Gimbel's?"

"Oh, he likes it well enough. And they love New York City. They live in Morningside Heights, and Naomi's taking some courses at Columbia."

"Do you ever hear from Andy and Harriet Lane?"

"Yes, they write now and then. They like it in James, Iowa. Iowa State's there, so they're not without intellectual stimulation."

"How about Harry Aaronson? He's retired now, isn't he?"

"Yeah, Harry's sixty-five now and on Social Security," Lester said. "His health hasn't been too good; some kind of prostate trouble. He gave up the apartment around the corner, and moved in with his sister and her husband in West Philly."

"Does he still come to the meetings?"

Lester grimaced, "What meetings? The New Deal, and the onset of prosperity have just about sunk the Socialist movement in Philadelphia."

His face took on a gloomy look. "This is the age of Fascism, Mike. The Fascists have taken over Spain, and now it looks like the British and French are going to sit on their cans behind the Maginot Line until Hitler gets ready to take over the rest of Europe."

"He'll never do that," Mike purported. "The British and French aren't the Poles."

"No, they aren't," he said. "The Poles were willing to fight."

Lester rose to his feet, a tense look on his face. "I'll get us some beer."

While he was in the kitchen, Sylvia said: "I'm worried, Michael. He's obsessed with this war, and full of guilt feelings because he isn't involved personally."

Lester came back with three bottles of beer and some glasses and handed them around.

"Let's change the subject. How's the great American novel coming, Mike?"

Mike grinned. "I haven't started it yet."

"When are you going to start?"

"One of these days."

"When are you going to write anything?"

Mike said. "I have written something."

"Aha! A short story!"

"It's not a short story. It's a poem. A short poem."

"Did you bring it with you?"

Mike reached into his inside jacket pocket and pulled out a folded sheet of paper.

"There's this lady who works at the arsenal. Mrs. Babcock's her name, and she must be seventy. Anyhow, every time I find something wrong with her shell casings, she cries. She's just frightened, and without much hope, like lots of old people. Anyhow, she inspired this poem."

He unfolded the paper, and Lester took it and looked it over silently. He began to read it aloud, his strong voice, muted.

Young Men At Their Orison

Existence is an act of faith,
A never-ending prayer.
The primal virtue's name is hope,
The primal curse, despair.
We shall risk a kind of loving,
Such as old men never dare.

Mike's chest swelled with pride. The way Lester read it, it really sounded good.

"It's beautiful, Michael," Sylvia said.

"Do you really like it?"

"Oh, I do. It's a lovely poem. You must give me a copy."

Mike looked anxiously at Lester. "What do you think? Is it any good?"

"Well, Mike, it's got a catchy title. And it rhymes and scans. As for its literary quality, I'd place it somewhere between John Milton and Edgar A. Guest."

Mike's face fell, and Lester laughed heartily.

"No, I'm only kidding. It is good. Try it on the *Atlantic,* or, *Harper's*, or the *New Republic*. Maybe, even on *The New Yorker*."

◆◆◆

Mike tried the poem first on the *Atlantic,* making sure to include a self-addressed, stamped envelope. In two weeks, he got it back with a form rejection slip. Then he sent it to *Harper's* with the same result. In succession, he tried it on *The New Yorker*, *New Republic*, *The Nation,* and *The New York Times*, and they, too, sent it back. Finally, he sold it to *The Christian Science Monitor*, which paid him five dollars, and sent him a tear sheet of the published poem with his name in bold print as the author. He must have read it twenty times with a kind of dazed wonder when it first arrived. It was a far cry from the five thousand dollars Ernest Hemingway got from *Cosmopolitan* for a short story but, at least, he was a published writer who had been paid for his work.

◆◆◆

Mike also acquired a part-time mistress. One night, as he sat in Jimbo's with Doc and Annie Phillips, a friend of hers walked in. Catherine Quinlan and Annie greeted each other with cries of surprise at their fortuitous meeting. Doc invited her to sit down, and Mike let her slide into the booth next to him. In her late thirties, and fairly attractive, she lived with her widowed mother just four blocks from Jimbo's.

She smiled at Mike. "I was getting my mother's prescription filled, and stopped in for one drink before I went home." She looked around. "I've never been here before. It's nice."

"How is your mother, Cassie?" Annie asked.

"Not good. Not good at all. She hardly gets out of bed anymore."

Cassie had one drink, a whiskey sour, and left to deliver the medicine and put her mother to bed. She came back in a half hour, and when they got ready to leave at eleven o'clock Annie suggested Mike see her home safely.

Cassie smiled at him, the promise of a reward in her eyes.

Mike smiled back at her. "With pleasure, Cassie."

Though fair-skinned and freckle-faced with big teeth and a wide mouth, Cassie had ample breasts and a plump backside, and Mike was so hard up he would have settled for a lot worse. She came with gasping sobs when they made love on the parlor sofa.

In the months they were together, Mike never once saw Cassie's mother, and never once did Cassie put a light on in the house while he was there.

"Decent people," she told him primly, "do it in the dark."

Aside from that, she made an enthusiastic partner.

They established their routine on their first meeting. Once inside the house, Cassie stole upstairs and came down moments later dressed in a robe and carrying two bath towels. Mike was already undressed and in an aroused state, and while she spread the bath towels on the sofa, he cupped her breasts in his hand, lifted up her robe and came at her from behind.

"Not without protection! Good God, suppose I got pregnant."

"Just for a second," he pleaded. "I promise I'll pull out before anything happens."

"No," she demanded. "If you do, neither of us will want to stop."

"You're a strong woman, Cassie," he grumbled, reaching for his jacket to get a rubber.

"It's a good thing one of us is strong," she whispered, and pulled him down on top of her.

In between lovemaking, they smoked and talked in the dark. She had two sisters and three brothers, all older and married. As the only single sibling, it fell to her to care for her mother.

"They treat me like an old maid who couldn't get a man. They think if they invite me to family events, and take Mom for two weeks in the summer, they've done their part."

She reached over and fondled him, and when he started to stiffen, she giggled. "If they only knew."

When her fondling had no effect, she was content to cuddle and whisper in the dark.

"Four times, Cassie," he said, "And John Thomas needs a rest."

"Let him rest," she breathed in his ear. "That way he'll be ready for next week."

At times her mood was less playful.

"I feel like I'm robbing the cradle. You're twenty-two and I'm thirty-six. I could be your mother."

"You're not my mother and we're both adults, and that's all that matters."

"Oh, well," she said, "it can't last forever. Sooner or later you'll find a girl your own age."

"You're all the girl I need, and then some."

"You're just saying that."

"No, I'm not."

"Yes, you are."

"I tell you, I'm not just saying that. I mean it."

"I wish I could believe you."

"You can believe me," Mike argued. "Because it's true."

Other times she worried about the sinfulness of her behavior. "How can I go to confession Saturday afternoon and do this with you on Saturday night?"

"Any time you go to confession, you just tell me and I'll stay away that night."

"But you'll be back again the next week and we'll start all over. I'm doomed."

He reached for his clothes and began dressing. "Maybe we better call it quits for tonight."

"Will I see you next week?"

"Will you be at Jimbo's?"

She shrugged. "I don't know."

"Well, if you are, you'll see me."

More than once, Mike wanted to call it quits. He wasn't in love with her, and he was keeping her from finding someone else. Plus, her irksome behavior wore away his interest in her.

Yet, come Saturday he would be as horny as ever, and go to Jimbo's hoping Cassie would show up. She always did.

✦✦✦

It finally ended in June 1940, when Mike went to Canada in the wake of Lester Goldman. The breakup happened suddenly after Sylvia Weiss telephoned him with the news that Lester had joined the Royal Canadian Air Force.

"He left the day after school ended," Sylvia said. "He told me he wanted to visit his cousin in Buffalo, but today he called from Ontario. Dunkirk upset him, and I should have expected this."

The news excited Mike, but he kept his voice grave. "After the Germans overran Denmark, Norway, and Holland, I guess Dunkirk was the last straw for him."

"He said he's training as an intelligence officer, and I'm not to worry because he couldn't have a safer job. Is it a safe job, Michael? You were in the Army."

"Gee, I don't know, Sylvia. It sounds like it is."

As soon as he hung up, Mike began to make plans to follow Lester to Canada.

✦✦✦

Mike did not succeed in his attempt to join the Canadian Air Force, or even to find Lester Goldman. He spent three frustrating weeks in Canada working through Canadian military requirements. The most time-consuming activities involved finding his birth certificate, which Doc accomplished within days, and taking high-school equivalency exams. Then, with great optimism, he addressed the final hurdle—a battery of physical exams. He got his results from a doctor named Morris.

"I'll come to the point. You've been turned down. They say you have bronchiectasis."

Mike's face fell. "Bronchiectasis?"

"Chronic infection of the air tubes." Morris spread his fingers out on the desk. "I know something about the disease. I have it myself. See, my fingertips are clubbed. Let me see yours."

Mike spread his fingers out on the desk and Morris looked at them.

"Yours aren't, and I don't think you have the disease. But, the sods at the examiner's office have the last word."

"Does that mean you won't take me?"

Morris looked at Mike. "I'm afraid so."

"What should I do about it? The disease, I mean."

"Well, if you had the disease, I'd tell you to quit smoking and drinking."

He smiled and held out his smoking cigarette. "I'd quit smoking myself if I could quit drinking. But that's when I enjoy smoking the most. And I enjoy drinking too much to quit."

"When I get back to the States, should I see a doctor?"

"It wouldn't hurt. But, you can stay in Canada if you like. I'll give you a medical rejection slip and you can get a job in a defense factory. There's good money to be made."

Mike shook his head.

"No. I'm going home. Sooner or later we're bound to get in this war, and I'll try again."

Man, I even screwed this up. Will I ever amount to anything? Mike wondered.

✦✦✦

He waited seventeen months for U.S. involvement as a result of the Japanese attack on Pearl Harbor on December 7, 1941. Though following the news, the Japanese attack shocked him. The Japanese attacked without a prior declaration of war, which violated the commonly accepted conventions of war. The papers reported it as a "sneak attack," and it enraged the general population of the U.S.

While reading papers and watching newsreels at the movies, Mike tried to recognize details of what he had experienced and knew of Pearl Harbor and the rest of Hawaii. The most vivid memories he evoked, though, involved haunting images of beautiful Noelani.

What had happened to her? His heart sank thinking of the Japanese bombs and machine gun fire raining down on the entire area around Pearl Harbor and Waikiki. He thought to write her, but he knew her father would destroy his letter before she saw it. Besides, he'd shown her who he really was, and would not want to hear from him again, especially under the guise of a concern for her welfare. It would be judged a cheap trick, typical of a person with strikes against him, as her father so clearly pointed out on Mike's final visit. His heart ached, but he would just have to shut down those feelings and move on. Noelani would always be his one true love, but he knew he must live without her.

His next thoughts focused on his buddies in the 27th Regiment. He could at least write to Steiner and find out how they were getting on. He realized, though, it had been more than two years since his discharge, and a lot of the people he knew would have moved on by now. The sudden feeling of being on the sidelines of life depressed him. How did he end up circling back to zero, to nowhere? He needed to change that right away. He decided at that moment he would go back into the Army the next morning, and get into the war. No more sidelines. No more bullshit.

Mike Kane decided to dive into the center of the world's swirl in January 1942.

Part IV

India and Burma

Chapter Twenty-Seven

The Japanese exploded across South Asia by May 1942, six months after their attack on Pearl Harbor, and the new U.S. Army camp at Malir, India, was still a collection of wooden-floored, British squad tents, scattered in rows around an airfield. The camp remained barren of other structures except for a huge, ramshackle hangar, and a tiny control tower. A motley collection of airplanes parked alongside the runway: British Hurricane fighters, U.S. P-40s, British Blenheim and Wellington bombers, several taped-together U.S. B-24s, and one active U.S. B-17, all unprotected from the sun and the dry, swirling dusty winds that blew across the Sind desert.

The 24s and the one 17 belonged to the 15th U.S. Bombardment Group, which pitched its row of squad tents closest to the hangar. Mike laid in one of those tents, sweating heavily on an Indian rope bed. Except for him, the tent remained empty, but the two other beds held red mattresses. They belonged, Mike already knew, to the two men who made up the Gun Turret and Gun Sight Section of the 15th Bombardment Group: Technical Sergeant Hennessey and Staff Sergeant Oakes. The squadron clerk had told him their names when he directed Mike to his tent.

"They won't be back till suppertime," the clerk said. "May as well sack out till then."

He shifted uncomfortably on his bed. He had stripped down to his shorts, and the ropes cut into his bare back and legs. Finally he rolled over and sat on the edge of the cot.

Jesus Christ, it was hot. It must be a hundred and twenty degrees. Well, it was better than that goddam boat. When the boat pulled alongside the quay this morning, he had never been so glad to see anything in his life as Karachi's big, busy, strange-smelling harbor.

He read in one of Negley Farson's books something about how the best sight in India was viewing it from the stern of an outgoing steamer. But old Negley had never spent fifty-nine days on a troop transport, loaded with thousands of smelly, hungry, pissed-off troops. Any land—even the Danakil Desert or the far side of the moon—would have looked good after two months travel on the worst means of transportation ever devised.

◆◆◆

The trip had been a horror show on the so-called, converted luxury liner *Brazil*.

Converted, my ass!

One-quarter converted—half converted, maybe—with no showers at all for the first two weeks at sea and, after that, a few skinny streams of salt water rigged up on the port side of the after deck. They had even run out of food and, on the last leg of the trip—the run up the Indian Ocean from Cape Town to Karachi—they had eaten nothing but hard-boiled eggs twice a day. It surely ranked as the most fucked-up trip in the annals of the Military Sea Transport Service.

Even the civilian crew had been pissed off, and those guys had eaten and slept pretty well on that boat. No, pissed off wasn't the phrase to describe the crew. To say they were pissed off was like saying the crew of *HMS Bounty* was disgruntled. Our crew came near to mutiny, too.

The screw-ups for the crew began when they had checked onto the boat back in Charleston, South Carolina, expecting to go back home to get their clothes and say goodbye to their families. They hadn't been allowed to leave the boat, and had gone to sea in the clothes on their backs. Some had even left their cars parked on the dock.

One crewman Mike befriended served as a waiter in the officer's mess. Milt Friedman hailed from New York City, and used to sneak food out of the mess to feed the hungry troops. Old Milt talked disparagingly about the officers, a lot of them doctors and nurses on their way to set up a field hospital somewhere in India.

"They're pigs," Milt told him. "They're up there stuffin' their fuckin' faces full of roast beef and turkey while you guys are eatin' garbage." Milt's voice grew shrill with rage. "No, they're worse than pigs. They're degenerates. You know what I caught one of the nurses doin' today? Jerkin' her boyfriend off under the table. I swear it! She was givin' him a hand job under a napkin. It's like Rome, up there, just before the barbarians took over."

He didn't know whether Milt was a Communist, but he knew, for sure, if the capitalist system collapsed tomorrow, Milt wouldn't lose any sleep.

✦✦✦

Mike got up, dug two towels out of his bag, and walked to a hanging Lyster Bag full of chlorinated drinking water. Soaking the towels, he carried them back to the tent, spread them out on the bed and lay down again. That felt so good he let out a loud groan.

He closed his eyes and remembered how excited he had been when he first boarded back in Charleston, two months to the day after re-enlisting. After hearing about Pearl Harbor, he had stood in line for hours to get back into the Army, and was ordered to report in on January 17th. They embarked on March 17th, Saint Patrick's Day—the most appropriate of days, since rumors pegged their destination as Ireland.

Even when they headed due south, hugging the coast, the rumor persisted. We're just going a roundabout way to confuse the enemy, a lot of the guys said. When they stopped briefly in

San Juan harbor, headed due south and east across the Atlantic, and spent three days in the harbor at Freetown, the rumor finally became ridiculous.

His first sight of Africa—Conrad's heart of darkness—and Freetown's huge harbor, took away his breath. He counted more than a hundred ships, many of them British troop transports, headed for the Middle East. Dakar lay just up the coast, and everybody said what a bunch of sitting ducks they would be if the Germans decided to send a squadron of Stukas after them. By then, though, they knew they were on their way to the China-Burma-India Theater.

The two days in Cape Town with their eight-hour passes, served as the only bright spot on the trip. Mavis and Audrey, their names were... Three drinks after they picked them up in a pub, Mavis leaned over and whispered in his ear. "Me knickers are wet, love." When he stared at her, wondering if he had heard right, Mavis removed all doubt. "We'll go back to me flat and you can take them off before I catch me death of cold."

Lying in bed in her shabby flat, he could see the picture of the soldier staring at him from the dresser. Mavis had seen him looking at it and had gotten out of bed and laid it face down.

"It's me husband, George. He's in Tobruk," she said. "But don't you worry about George, love. George is getting his little bit of crumpet wherever he is. Bet on that."

He had felt guilty about poor George, off fighting in the desert while another guy was in bed with his wife. Guilty feelings or not, he had gone back the next day for another session. Well, Doc always said, a stiff cock has no conscience, and neither does a pair of wet knickers.

Either feast or famine dictated the way a guy's sex life went if he wasn't married. First, there had been Naomi, then Constance Lewis, followed by Cassie Quinlan, and blue-eyed Mavis, with one blue eye slightly askew. Not much of a score for a man who would be twenty-four in less than two weeks.

He had sure fouled up with Cassie. Doc had introduced her to Charlie Hubbell, and they had hit it off. That put Mike Kane out in the cold after he came back from Canada.

He had quit his job at the arsenal, but the job he ended up with in the carpet mill after his time in Canada, only paid twenty-two bucks a week. Well, pushing rugs around on a truck had required no mental effort, and there hadn't been any Mrs. Babcocks around to make life miserable. Life had been dull, though.

Willie married his skinny-assed Angie, Sam married Natalie Mandel, Doc still saw Annie Phillips, and Lester Goldman was east of London flying missions in a bomber.

Mike hadn't written anything, either. But what the hell could you write about if you lived in Brewerytown and worked in a carpet mill? Well, the war would solve the problem of a lack of interesting experiences. If he ever got to see any fighting, that is.

That recruiting sonofabitch at Jefferson Barracks had really fucked him up when he sent him off to Lowry Field for training as a turret gunner.

"We just got in a quota for a new course," he had announced at a formation one day, "training gun turret operators for B-17s and B-24s."

Mike's hand shot up. Shortly afterward, he took the train to Denver, Colorado, only to discover it was a course in the maintenance of Martin Upper Turrets, Bendix Tail Turrets, Sperry Ball Turrets, and the Sperry Automatic Computing Gun Sight. So, now he was a maintenance man instead of a gunner, and one without much mechanical aptitude.

They had fouled him up at the recruiting office, too. He had walked in there ten days after Pearl Harbor intending to join the infantry, and they had given him a simple intelligence test. Mike scored a hundred on the test and ended up in the Army Air Corps. Those who didn't, had been sent to tote rifles, no questions asked.

Well, the Japanese had taken Singapore and Rangoon, and then Mandalay, and supposedly now headed for India. Maybe things would get interesting for him after all.

He had started a writer's diary. So far, Milt Friedman was in it, and Mavis, and Barney Welch, the good old boy from Georgia he met on the boat. He'd probably never see Barney again. Barney was in the Air Transport Command, and Christ knows where they had sent those guys.

He began to feel drowsy, closed his eyes and, moments later, fell asleep.

✦✦✦

Mike already lay awake again when both tall, husky men in their late twenties came into the tent, dressed in rumpled khaki shorts, short-sleeved shirts, sun helmets, and sandals. He thought they were British soldiers, until he saw the American stripes on their sleeves.

He rolled over and sat up.

"So, you're Mike Kane. I'm Al Hennessey, and this is Cliff Oakes. Where ya from, Mike?"

"Philadelphia."

"I'm from Seattle. Cliff's from Salt Lake. He's a Jack Mormon, so don't worry."

Al grinned. A tooth missing in front gave his plain face an engaging look.

Oakes laughed. "Yeah, I learned about girls early on."

He could have passed for Hennessey's brother, except for his intact teeth; and black hair, sweat-plastered against his skull. Hennessey's light-red hair was thinner and lay in dank streaks across the crown of his head. They both exuded the same kind of calm and good humor, and Mike breathed easier.

"How are things in the States?" Oakes asked.

"I don't know. I left there two months ago."

Hennessey shook his head. "We left in November, so you're more current than we are."

"November 1941? That was before the war started."

"That's right. We were headed for the Philippines, but halfway between there and Hawaii the Japs bombed Pearl Harbor. So, we headed for Fiji, then Australia."

"Were you flyin' or on a boat?"

"On a boat. The planes went in the other direction. Across the Atlantic and Africa. They went through here on Christmas Day on their way to Java." He pointed in the direction of the airstrip. "Them B-24s and that old B-17 are the only planes that got outa Java, and only two of them still fly. We used them to haul women and kids outa Rangoon just before the Japs took over."

Oakes sat on his bunk. "Me and Al got in enough combat time for an Air Medal—one hundred and twelve hours."

Mike looked at them enviously. "You guys been flyin' combat?"

Hennessey grinned his engaging grin. "You could call it that. We had to use guns to keep mobs from overrunning the plane."

"Since then, we ain't done a fuckin' thing except fly anti-submarine patrols," Oakes said. "And that's mainly to let the pilots get their flyin' time in."

"You think I could do some flyin'?" Mike asked eagerly.

"That's what we had in mind," Hennessey said. "It's the best way to learn, Mike."

Al stood up. "I'm gonna take a shower before I eat."

Mike went with them to the showers, made from rigged up gas tanks from cannibalized B-24s. As quickly as the water tanks emptied, natives filled them by negotiating ladders with five-gallon cans perched precariously on their heads. They were skinny men with white teeth flashing, and Hennessey called them shower "wallahs."

"Everybody in this country's a wallah of some kind," Hennessey said.

Oakes laughed. "There's a little wog runs a whorehouse on the outskirts of Karachi and Al calls him the pussywallah."

They walked back to the tent, Hennessey and Oakes dressed in loose-weave, British shorts and shirts, and Mike, already sweating heavily, in his stiff American suntans.

"Where'd you guys get them clothes?"

"Bought 'em from the Brits," Hennessey answered. "You got any money?"

"Seven bucks."

"That's about twenty rupees. That won't be enough. I'll lend you some.

"Are there a lot of British here?"

"The place is loaded with limeys, the ones who got outa Singapore and Rangoon. And the Dutch who got outa Java. And what's left of the Flyin Tigers—that's the nickname for the American Volunteer Group... the AVGs. And there are the guys who bombed Tokyo last month. Some of them are here, too."

"Is Colonel Doolittle here?"

"Shit, no!" Oakes said. "He's back in Washington getting a medal. Some of the guys would like to be back there with him getting some grateful pussy handin' out to heroes."

"Some of the Flyin Tigers ain't too happy, either," Hennessey said. "I was talkin' to one of them named Boyington, who was a first lieutenant in the Marines. He'd be a major now if he hadn't fucked up and joined the Flying Tigers. Now, he says Chennault wants to make him a second lieutenant in the 23rd Pursuit Group. He says Chennault can shit in his hat, he's goin' to rejoin the Marines."

"Wait'll you see some of the poker games in this camp," Oakes said. "Them AVGs are loaded with dough, and so are some of the British."

"Yeah," Hennessey said, "the British emptied the banks in Rangoon and burned the money so the Japs wouldn't get it. Except that all of it didn't get burned. I've seen ten thousand rupee notes floatin' around this camp."

"How long do you think we're gonna be in Malir, Al?" Mike asked.

Hennessey shrugged. "Till we get some airplanes and crews. Then we'll move east to Assam, and begin to operate. If the Japs ain't taken over by then, that is."

He stood up. "Let's go see what they did to the C rations this time."

Chapter Twenty-Eight

Mike couldn't place it on a civilian map, but he found himself and his squadron in an abandoned Indian Army camp in Assam, ten miles from a place called Banda, in early August 1942. It was somewhere north and east of Calcutta, lying on flat land that shimmered in the heat of the great Ganges plain. To find it, he bought a book in Karachi by an Indian journalist named Frank Moraes, which listed 700,000 villages in India. Banda, as small as it was, wasn't one of them. The train stopped there, mail was delivered, it had a store and, occasionally, one could see English people walking about, but it only appeared on military maps.

A real village, called Chota Banda, lay halfway between the airstrip and the camp, though. It looked like all the other villages he had seen. It had a well, and a cluster of huts with matting walls, straw-thatch roofs, and dirt floors smeared with cow dung, surrounded by the village fields. The cow, he had learned, was sacred to the Hindu, so they used its excrement as fertilizer and, watered-down, ascribed disinfectant properties to it. After a few weeks in India, his nostrils became accustomed to rural India's universal smell: the odor of burning cow dung.

The squadron lived in huts, or bashas, made of thatch roofs and corrugated tin sides. They slept on the ubiquitous charpoys, with wooden T-bars for hanging mosquito-net tents. Ammunition boxes nailed together made shelves for their belongings, but they learned that anything edible—including soap, toothpaste, and shaving cream—needed to hang from strings tied to the rafters to keep rats from eating it. Because of poisonous snakes, and a wide variety of crawling insects, they learned to shake out their shoes and clothing before putting them on.

The rats were incredibly brazen, sometimes leaping at the dangling tidbits from the rafters, trying to execute a bite in mid-air. Once Mike made a threatening gesture at one on the rafter above Hennessey's bed, causing the rat to run along the rafter and disappear into the eaves. Mike laid back down and continued with his reading, but kept one eye on the rafters.

Moraes' book brimmed with facts about India, including its religions. The country included Hindus, Muslims, Buddhists, Jains, Parsees, and Sikhs, just to name the major religious groups.

Gandhi tried desperately to unify the country politically with his Indian National Congress Party, whose president was Dr. Azad, a distinguished Muslim theologian. Most of the politically conscious Muslims, though, supported Mohamed Ali Jinnah's Muslim League, and Jinnah was talking about a separate Muslim state called Pakistan, "The Land of the Pure." To add heat to the cauldron, a fanatically pro-Hindu party, called Mahasaba, flew a party flag decorated with that ancient Aryan symbol, the swastika.

Most of India's four-hundred millions, though, belonged to no party—inarticulate, apathetic, and more concerned with the problem of staying alive than with politics. Countless thousands of beggars wandered homeless across the land, lying down to sleep where night found them. Many of the beggars were children, and they filled the streets of the cities with cries of "Baksheesh, sahib. No momma, no poppa." And, since the Americans had come, the chant lengthened to include, "No Uncle Sam." Most of the poor were peasants, tilling the land as tenant farmers, and eternally in debt to the landlord or moneylender. They made up ninety percent of the population and these, Mike knew, he would never understand.

The way to the airstrip led past Chota Banda, and he often saw the farmers plowing the paddies with wooden plows hooked behind the humps of their bullocks: dark, reed-thin men, dressed in clout-like "dhotis," and loose, cotton shirts, with a rag, wrapped turban-like, around their heads. He saw the women sometimes, too, cotton saris gathered around the waist, then flung over one shoulder, occasionally exposing a withered, or a plump young breast.

Some of the young women were attractive, certainly more so than the girls in pussywallah's establishment near Karachi. Jesus, he had been so afraid of catching something the only time he went there, he had worn two rubbers, one on top of the other. The village girls' habit of carrying jugs of water on the head seemed to do something for the carriage and the lift of the bosom. Their bathing frequently at the village well didn't hurt, either.

The peasants in Bengal seemed poorer even than the ones in Sind, though in Sind he witnessed a sight he would carry to his grave if he lived to be a thousand. A new friend named Dick Haines had been with him, and it shook Dick just as much.

They had gone for a walk down the dusty road leading away from camp into the desert. They had traveled miles, enjoying the end of the hot season, and the heat rash that had plagued them both. At one point, Dick pointed to the vultures wheeling in the light-blue sky.

"Obscene bastards. You know how they eat? They start by shoving their beaks up the ass and pulling the guts out. And they don't always wait until the breath of life is out of the banquet."

One of the vultures peeled off and swooped to a landing about a hundred yards from them. It crouched over something lying in the still sand, pecking at it with its beak.

"Must be a dead dog," Dick said. He picked up a stone and threw it, and the vulture flapped away. Dick walked over toward the bird's meal. Halfway there, he stopped.

"It's a child," he said in a cracked voice. "A girl, I think."

269

He began to run and Mike ran after him. Together they stood staring at the remains of a girl about eight or ten. What was left of her was well preserved: her young face, ineffably peaceful; her upper body, hollowed out, and consisting of flaps of desiccated skin hanging over her ribs.

They stared for long seconds, then turned and walked back to the road. While making their way over the miles back to camp, they were too shaken to speak. Dick kept saying "sonofabitch" over and over again, but he spoke to himself.

Thinking about it, Mike shivered on his bunk. No way would he ever understand people whose religion, or culture— or Christ knows what—made them apathetic enough to put up with things like that. No way he would ever be able to communicate with them, except on the level that Cliff Oakes used with the little man who made their beds and swept out the basha.

Chotawallah, Cliff called him, and blamed his skinniness on excessive copulation. "You chota bit you got burra cock." Here Cliff would make signs to show that Chotawallah was hung like a stud buffalo.

Chotawallah would laugh. "No, sahib, me got chota..." And he would wiggle his little finger.

I thanked God all Indians weren't like poor Chotawallah, who became richer than ever before in his life on the fifty rupees a month they paid him.

A young student they met in Karachi was passionately convinced the British would never voluntarily grant India its independence. The student quoted Churchill, "I did not become His Majesty's first minister to preside over the dismemberment of the British Empire."

Dick had tried to explain that the Atlantic Charter guaranteed freedom to all people, and that, by God, Franklin D. Roosevelt would see to it that the charter was enforced.

The student had laughed at Dick. "You Americans, how fond you are of making noble speeches. At least Churchill's a truthful rogue."

✦✦✦

Thank goodness Dick had been assigned to the 16th, too. They could just as easily have ended up in one of the other three squadrons. Dick's pilot, the new squadron commander, Major Kirke, knew how slipshod and hasty their training had been, and he ordered Hennessey to set up a training program for the new crews.

"Some of these maintenance guys don't even know how to get out of the gun turrets in case the power fails," he had told Hennessey. "Even show them how to work that useless computing gun sight, in case they need to show a gunner."

Mike agreed with Major Kirke about the gun sight. You had to track a target long enough to load information into the sight before it became effective. By that time, an enemy fighter could shoot you full of holes. Not that he had ever shot at anything except the waves in the Indian Ocean on the anti-submarine patrols. At least, he had swiveled the turrets around under power, and manually. If the hydraulic system failed, he knew from his training with Hennessey how to crank them back by hand so he could get the doors open and get out. At least they had taught them that much.

Dick had flown three combat missions as a rear-turret gunner: one on Moulmein, and two on Rangoon to bomb the docks.

"I didn't see hide nor hair of the old Moulmein Pagoda," Dick said after the first raid. After the second, he just shook his head. "All we did was churn up water. We must have missed the docks by a good half mile."

Mike wondered if he would be as nonchalant as Dick, if he ever went into combat.

He remembered meeting Dick for the first time in the hangar where Hennessey and Oakes had rigged up a turret to train the crews. It was in September just after the monsoon rains ended. The rains had made everything wet, and green with mildew including, Cliff Oakes said, his testicles. Shortly after, it turned hotter than hell, and Dick—with his floppy blond hair and fair skin—suffered heat rash from his scalp to his toes. His nose was so sore he couldn't wear glasses.

"How the fuck did you ever get to be a gunner, Dick?" Hennessey had asked him. "You can't even see."

Dick had put his glasses on gingerly. "The fuck I can't, man. I hit .350 on my high school baseball team back in Baldwin, Missouri. I got the sharpest eyes in baseball."

Mike captured them all in his diary. Hennessey and Oakes, two guys he thanked God for, made it into the record. As far as he could tell, neither of them had ever read a book, but they could fix anything mechanical, hydraulic, or electrical, while he—who had read everything—couldn't fix a thing.

Chotawallah made it in there, too, and so was the Karachi student who hated Churchill. Most entries, though, detailed his new best friend. Dick Haines, from the University of Chicago, which he talked about constantly, and made sound like the intellectually, artistically, and materially exalted Periclean Athens.

"You have to go back with me after the war, Mike," he kept saying. "We'll have us a rare old time."

"How will I get in without a high school diploma?" he asked, and Dick dismissed his academic deficiencies with an airy wave of the hand.

"They don't care if you never saw the inside of a school," Dick said. "As bright and well-read as you are, I guarantee they'll take you. I tell you, Robert Maynard Hutchins has created a revolution in American education. All you have to do is pass the entrance exam, which is nothing but an intelligence test. If you pass it, you're in. If you don't, you're out."

"How will I pay for it?"

"The government," Dick said. "They gotta give us our forty acres and a mule."

Thank God for Dick. Now he knew what he would do with his life when the war ended. He would attend the University of Chicago and become a truly educated man. He would find a girl there for him, too. A mid-western Natasha Rostova, as pretty as Noelani Kreuger and as smart as Naomi Weiss. He'd marry her and write the great American novel.

After that, he, Natasha, and Dick would devote themselves to the making of a world in which children didn't starve to death and get eaten by vultures.

No, it wouldn't be Natasha. It would be Noelani, or nobody.

✦✦✦

Shortly after his arrival, Al and Cliff took Mike aside to talk about their responsibilities and what was expected of the three of them. They didn't make it formal, they made it more like three friends sitting around a table discussing the next football game at high school. Al and Cliff wanted to be sure Mike became oriented with their expanding organization and responsibilities, and their area of operation, or AO, so he could operate as a full teammate in their combat support missions. They took turns going through details about their unit, its equipment, munitions, maintenance issues, and trends.

Mike learned that his bombardment group consisted of less than one hundred men at the moment, but that it would swell to over two thousand men in the next months, and that his group was part of the Tenth Air Force that would eventually have hundreds of organizations like his. For the moment, however, the little band he joined would have to put up a good show until the throngs arrived.

Cliff also talked about the AO in a way that painted a visual picture in Mike's mind. "Our AO is primarily Burma, which is on India's border to our east. If you don't have a map, think of our AO like this: Burma looks like a man standing on his left leg, visible as he faces you now." Cliff drew a pencil character on a note pad as he talked. "Mandalay is his heart, Rangoon his penis, Victoria Point is his only leg's big toe, Ledo and Imphal are his right ear and throat, and Akyab is in his right armpit.

"You will hear some other location names you should take note of, like Meiktila and Prome, both on the Irrawaddy River south of Mandalay. These are both important Japanese supply points, and our targets. If you are grounded north of Mandalay, walk northwest for two or three weeks to cross into India, and safety. Going west of Prome you'll walk two weeks and find yourself on a beach. Not a good thing since you'll certainly become a prisoner. If you're down around Rangoon, forget about walking west. Nothin' but sharks, saltwater crocs, and sea snakes out there. Your only way out is to follow the Irrawaddy north until it meets the Chindwin River and take that northwest like you would outta Mandalay."

Cliff paused to check Mike's understanding. "This is only for your visual perspective, since you work with the air crews. It'll help you follow what they're talking about. Oh, and you've heard of the plans for constructing a 'Burma Road' to send supplies over to China? Well that road would cut the man's head off. Hope that helps the visual. What are your questions, Mike?'

"Are there tigers and snakes in the jungle?"

"There are tigers, and cobras, and about six other snakes that will kill you in a snap. There are also wild elephants, pigs, and bears, leaches, and other bad bugs, and a lot of scary viruses. Try not to visit down there anytime soon."

"Can I have your sketch?"

"Sure, buddy. If you want, we can do this again on something you want to know about. Who knows, if the Japs keep pushing, we may soon find our AO where we sit right now, bombing their asses while they sleep in our beds."

"Thanks, this was good," Mike said, at once thankful, and yet a bit woozy from it all.

Chapter Twenty-Nine

Looking out of the window of the parked B-24, Mike saw the jeep barrel down the runway and come to a screeching stop. Dick jumped out and ran to the plane.

"Hey, Mike!" he shouted up. "Have I got a deal for you!"

"Yeah? What kind of a deal?"

Dick grinned up at him. "The old man sent me to Banda, and I met two Anglo-Indian girls. They live in a village between here and Banda, and they said if we drop in tonight about eight, they'll give us a graphic demonstration of the interaction between a lingam and a yoni."

"They musta been bullshittin' you, Dick. Anglo-Indian girls don't live in villages."

"These two do. And so does their father. He's a Canadian. His name's Barker."

Mike said. "The British wouldn't allow a white man to go native."

Dick looked at him indignantly. "Listen, I gave them a ride back to their village and I met their old man. He's from British Columbia. Shit, man, I even know the family history. He was invalided out of the British Navy, and he decided to settle here. He married a lady in Calcutta, and here they are. Also, the guy's a drunk."

Mike smiled down at him. "Okay, Dick, so they weren't bullshittin' you."

Dick was instantly mollified. "How soon you gonna be done up there?"

"Ten minutes. I just have to check the hydraulic fluid in the rear turret."

"Okay, I'll wait for you."

On the ride back to camp, Mike turned to his friend. "How old are these girls?"

"Old enough to diddle. The younger one's about 18, the older one, maybe 20."

"What do they look like?"

Dick's face took on a rapt look. "Remember Fletcher Christian's girlfriend, the beautiful Tehani, in *Mutiny on the Bounty*. Well, these girls make her look like the south end of a north-bound skunk."

✦✦✦

After supper, they drove to Banda and bought a bottle of Tiger Brandy. Returning to Barker's village, they parked the jeep at the end of the lane that wandered through it. They walked down the lane and found Barker sitting outside his hut, dressed in an old topi, and faded khaki shorts and shirt.

Mike eyed him distastefully. Not only was he fat, he looked like he suffered from liver, heart, lung, kidney, and circulatory disorders. His face was mottled and broken veined, and he spoke with a panting, asthmatic wheeze. Dick handed him the bottle of Tiger Brandy and he chuckled convulsively.

"Good boy. You came back to see me like you promised you would."

He struggled to stand on his swollen legs, and shuffled into the hut. Dick and Mike followed him into a room with an English bed, a table, some chairs, and a wooden chest.

Barker let out a gasping shout and his wife came out of an inner room with a water glass. She handed it to her husband and went back into the inner room.

"I hear you're from Canada, Mr. Barker?" Mike asked, as Barker poured himself a drink.

He took a long swallow before answering. "Vancouver," he wheezed.

"You're a long way from home."

"I am that." Barker refilled his glass. "I never regretted a day of it. God's country, British Columbia is, but cold, and I was always delicate, even as a lad."

He took another long swallow and waddled over to the chest to extract a photograph. "Rose and Jane, my two sisters, and me," he said, handing the photo to Mike.

The picture showed two girls and a teen-aged Barker, looking porcine even in his youth.

Barker took a drink and smiled expansively at Mike. His wheeze was noticeably better.

"I'm happy I settled here." He winked at Mike. "One thing you have to say for the British—they know how to run things. Here a man can live by the virtue of the color of his skin. And, I haven't done too badly. That grand bed used to belong to a British brigadier."

"How are your two girls, Mr. Barker?" Dick asked, and Barker uttered another shout.

Two girls came out of the inner room, both were dressed in green cotton saris, and Mike was bedazzled by the masses of shiny, black hair, and flashing white teeth.

"We'll see you later, Mr. Barker," Dick said, and Barker waved them off. Outside, he introduced Mike to the girls. Mike was shocked at their beauty.

"Victoria," he said to the older of the two girls, "this is my friend, Michael. He's nice." He turned and smiled at the younger girl. "Mike, this is Enid, Victoria's sister."

Dick took Enid's hand and started up the lane to the jeep. Mike and Victoria followed.

"Where are we going?" Victoria whispered to Mike.

Mike whispered back, smiling. "We passed a banyan grove on the way here that looked very romantic. It's a nice night and we have blankets with us."

He took out a twenty-rupee note, and held it out to her. "Here, this is for you."

She hesitated a moment, then took the folded note and tied it in a corner of her sari.

Dick and Enid already sat in the front seat of the jeep and Dick turned back to watch them climb in. "The banyan grove is all right with Enid."

"It's all right with Vicky, too," Mike said.

When they arrived at the banyan grove, Dick jumped out of the jeep clutching two blankets. He and Enid walked briskly toward a clump of trees about fifty yards away.

"We'll see you two in a couple of hours," he called over his shoulder.

Mike put his blankets under his arm and walked Victoria toward another clump of trees in the opposite direction. He spread the blankets out, lay down on them, and pulled Vicky down beside him. He began to unbutton his coveralls, and smiled at her. "This is my jump suit."

She looked embarrassed. When he tried to pull her close to him, she resisted.

"What's the matter?"

"I need to tell you," she said, her voice low. "It's my... you know... time of the month."

Mike took a deep breath. "So what do we do now?"

"We wanted to earn the money, and Enid said she could take care of both of you."

He shook his head. "Old Dick wouldn't appreciate me interrupting him."

She sighed deeply. "Here is your money back. I'll be okay next time."

She began to untie the knot in her sari and Mike put his hand on hers. "It's okay, Vicky, keep it."

She kissed him. "I'm sorry. I didn't know it until just before you arrived. It came on suddenly."

"It's okay, but I'm in a bad way." He gestured at the bulge in the crotch of his overalls.

She lay back on the blanket and cooed. "If you want... I could... you know... play with it."

"Would you?" he asked, his voice more eager than intended. "I really would like that."

✦✦✦

Afterward, they huddled together under the blanket and talked.

"How old are you, Vicky?"

"Nineteen. Enid is eighteen."

"How is it living in the village?"

She frowned. "It isn't good. Daddy's pension would keep us if he didn't drink it up."

"How do you get along with the other villagers?"

Her frown deepened. "We don't get along. Mummy's brother lives there and even he doesn't speak to us. He doesn't approve of the way we earn money."

"But you can't make much money doing this sort of thing. There weren't many white men around here before we came. Surely, you don't..." Despite himself, Mike couldn't keep the note of disapproval out of his voice. He felt awful.

"Of course, I don't," she said. "They're black and I'm white, or, whiter than they are."

"We're all God's children," he murmured.

"I wish that were so. But the British look down on us, too. They call us Jammies."

Mike laughed. "Jammies. What does that mean?"

"I don't know. But it's not a nice word."

He pulled her closer. "Let's look at the bright side. There could be independence soon."

"I hope the British never leave India!" The intensity in her voice surprised him. "While they're here, there's a chance a white British soldier will marry me."

They lay silently for a moment, until Vicky turned in his arms and looked toward the treetops. "There was a British unit at Chota Banda before you Americans came. And there was a sergeant, a boy named Wilson, from Dover. He might have married me. But they sent him to Burma and he's probably dead now."

Mike turned to her impulsively. "Vicky, if I give you some money every month, say a hundred rupees? Could you live on it and not see any other man but me?"

She looked at him, her eyes wide. "Oh, Michael, I'd love that."

"Okay, it's a deal then."

She kissed him, and the warmth of her body pressed against his.

After a while he whispered. "Would you do it again for me, Vicky?"

Wordlessly, she slid her hand down his pants, and he asked, "Shall I play with you, too?"

She answered breathlessly. "You don't have to. It's... messy. But, I'm in a bad way, too."

✦✦✦

Driving back, Mike told Dick about his deal with Vicky. Dick burst into laughter.

"That is a coincidence. Except I suggested a hundred and twenty-five rupees."

"Okay," Mike said. "I'll make mine the same. Hell, as staff sergeants, we can afford it."

"But we oughta use rubbers every time. We don't want to leave any bastards behind."

"Sure, Dick. It would be a shame to knock them up. We're not gonna marry them."

"That's right. We're just gonna do a little light housekeeping while we're here."

He grinned at Mike. "Did I tell you I had a deal for us, or didn't I?"

"You sure did," Mike said.

But he was thinking of Nicole Bouchere, Doc Greene's French girlfriend from the last war, who was the spitting image of Simone Simon, and how Doc had left her behind.

Chapter Thirty

Mike flew on his first combat mission three months after he and Dick made their arrangements with Victoria and Enid. It wasn't planned, it just sorta happened.

On the way to Barker's, Dick glanced over at Mike. "There's gonna be a vacancy on our crew. Joe Schmidt, our left waist gunner has malaria. The job's yours if you want it."

Mike kept his voice calm. "Of course, I want it. If Major Kirke will accept me, that is."

"I know he will. I already talked to him. He wants to see you in the morning." Dick laughed. "Let's celebrate. We'll buy an extra bottle of Tiger brandy and drink it up ourselves. Get us a coupla whiskey hard-ons and diddle all night."

"The way you and Enid argue, she's liable to get pissed off and not let you have any."

Dick grinned at him. "No way, man. No way. She's devoted to me."

They each had a couple of stiff drinks of brandy on the way, and when they arrived, Enid stood outside the hut, a sulky look on her face.

"I expected you last night, or the night before! You don't really want me," she screamed at Dick.

Dick took a swig of the brandy and winked at her.

"The jeep, you know, the jeep. I told you before I can't get it just any time I want it."

"You could walk, couldn't you?"

"Hey, kiddo, it's eight-miles round trip."

"If you wanted to see me badly enough, you'd walk!"

Dick laughed. "If I walked, I wouldn't have the strength to do anything when I got here."

He put his arm around her, but she ran. Dick handed Mike the bottle and went after her.

Mike saw Vicky standing in the doorway and he smiled at her. "Hiya, Queen Victoria."

She smiled back. "Hello, King Michael."

They walked into the hut. Vicky's father slept stertorously on his garish bed. Her mother stood silently by the table staring at him. He put the brandy on the table and bowed to her, his hands, palms together, in front of his face.

"Salam alai-kum, Memsahib."

She bowed back, "Wa alai-kum Salam."

"Ap kaisa hain?"

"Acha," she answered, and turned and went into the inner room.

"Your mother's not exactly a chatterbox, is she?" he quipped. "And a good thing, too. I just exhausted my store of Hindustani: 'hello,' and 'how are you.'" He gestured at the brandy bottles on the table. "Will you get us some glasses, please? Dick and I are gonna have a drink."

"You're already tipsy, Michael. Are you celebrating something?"

"No, we just feel like having a drink."

She returned with glasses. Mike sipped his slowly, and Dick and Enid came into the hut.

"Aha!" Dick shouted. "We're just in time for the party." He saw Barker sleeping on the bed, and he walked over and shook him. "Get up, George! The brandy's here."

Barker opened his eyes and looked at Dick uncertainly. When he recognized him, a smile lit up his plum-colored face. He struggled from the bed and shuffled clumsily to the table.

Dick poured Barker's glass half full, and poured a smaller amount into the other glasses. Barker lifted the drink carefully to his lips and downed it in two gulps. He shuddered, and Dick poured him another drink.

"You're a good boy, Dick. Of all the suitors Enid's had, you're my favorite." He finished off the second drink, and put a fat hand on Dick's shoulder. "I'm happy my little girl will have somebody to look after her when I'm gone."

"You old coot, you'll outlive us all. And what a bonfire you'll make when you do go."

Enid glared at him and ran out of the hut. Dick stared after her.

"Uh-oh, I've done it again," he said, and ran after her.

Barker chuckled. "True love never runs smooth, as my missus can tell you on occasion."

A moment later Dick came back. "Let's go, me and Enid got some heavy making up to do."

Mike pulled Vicky away and waved at Barker. When they got outside, Enid already sat in the back of the jeep. Vicky climbed in beside her, Mike got into the front seat, and they drove silently to the banyan grove. Enid jumped out and stalked off in the darkness.

Dick followed her, and Mike and Vicky walked to their clump of trees. He spread out the blankets and they lay down together. Across the banyan grove, they could hear Enid shouting.

"What a filthy thing to say to my father! You look down on him. And, on me, too. You think you're better than I am?"

"Me?" Dick roared. "Me, Dick Haines? Member of the working class and defender of the common man? I don't think I'm better than anybody!"

"Then why did you say it?"

"Because I'll probably burn up before he does!"

"Don't say that, Dick! If you die, I'll die, too!" Enid sounded instantly contrite.

"Enid, honey, I was only fooling. Hell, I'll die in my bed."

After that silence fell, and Mike raised his eyebrows at Victoria. "Now they're making up."

"For tonight, yes. But they'll argue again tomorrow," Vicky said, and they both laughed.

"You're right. But Dick shouldn't have said bonfire."

Vicky turned to him. "You really don't understand, do you, Michael? It wasn't Dick's stupid remark that made Enid angry. She's angry because she wants Dick to marry her." She moved closer to him. "Don't worry, Michael, you don't have to marry me. You're generous and you treat me decently, and I'm happier than I have been for a very long time."

Mike whispered. "But how do you know I don't want to marry you?"

She put her hand over his mouth. "Hush, Michael. Don't say things you don't mean."

✦✦✦

The next day, after he came back from talking to Major Kirke, Mike wrote Doc Greene a letter. He wanted to do the right thing by Victoria, and he asked Doc to make it happen. He explained that he couldn't ask Paddy, because Rose would find out and worry herself sick. She last knew he was in a nice safe maintenance job, not a waist gunner. He gave Victoria's address to Doc and swore him to secrecy. He sealed the letter in an envelope addressed to Arnold Greene, Doc's real name. He had already decided that if Lieutenant Kosko, the squadron censor, wouldn't pass it unread, he would have Vicky send it through the Indian post.

When he finished, he did feel better for having written the letter. Maybe he would marry Vicky. He sure as hell couldn't just walk off and leave her as Doc did Nicole. For Vicky, it would be much worse, simply because India wasn't France. If he did take her back to the States, nobody would know she had slept with other guys for money, except Dick, and he would never tell anybody. Old Dick was one of those guys you could trust. Besides, Vicky wasn't a real whore, anymore than Linda and Pat from the Congress in Honolulu were real whores.

What if she did look down on people darker than herself? She had accepted the white man's values. That shining example, drunken George Barker, had enunciated a universal truth when he said a white man could live in India by virtue of the color of his skin.

✦✦✦

He took the letter to Lieutenant Kosko, a short, heavy-set first lieutenant from Scranton, Pennsylvania, who served as Major Kirke's co-pilot.

"Sir," he said, "this letter contains some highly personal family business in it, which I wouldn't want anybody to read."

Kosko laughed. "Don't bullshit me, Kane, it's a hot letter to your little tootsie back in the States."

"No, sir, I swear it's not. It's family business."

"You're sure you're not bullshittin' me?"

"Yes, sir, I'm sure."

Kosko took the letter and stamped it "Passed by the censor."

Chapter Thirty-One

Two days later Mike's name appeared on the operations bulletin board with the rest of Major Kirke's crew. The order instructed them to report to the squadron operations office at nineteen hundred hours for a briefing. There was only one crew listed and Mike breathed easier when he read it. If only one crew was going, it couldn't be a bombing raid.

A bomb-site technician asked Mike, "Hey, Kane, where the hell you guys goin'?"

"Whadda ya mean?"

"Well, you're goin' in that old B-17. You know, the one that's glued and wired together?"

"Yeah, so?"

His smile broadened. "They also told me not to put a bombsight in it."

Mike shrugged. "So, we're probably goin' on a recon of some kind."

He laughed. "Shit no, you ain't! They're puttin' bombs in. Two-thousand pounders!"

Mike shrugged again. "Then I guess I'll find out when we get briefed tonight."

✦✦✦

When the crew assembled for the briefing, the intelligence officer stood up front with Major Kirke. The elderly major, a veteran of the last war, still wore his outdated pilot's wings. He began the briefing by aiming his pointer at a large map on the wall.

"The target is a bridge over the river at Myitnge," he said, resting his pointer on the map. "The Japanese have built a railroad between Rangoon and Bangkok, and from Rangoon they transport supplies to their troops in North Burma. The bridge is the sole connection to the north, so you can appreciate its importance."

Mike smiled nervously at Dick, but he was watching the map, an intent look on his face. Despite his efforts to concentrate on the intelligence officer's words, Mike's attention wandered. Everybody knew about the bridge at Myitnge. Every squadron in India had taken a crack at it in recent months. The 16th had tried low- and high-level attacks. Even the P-51s had tried to dive-bomb it. The bomb ordnance men joked that the only way to solve the problem was to parachute men in and dismantle it with wrenches.

Major Kirke took over the briefing, using his cigar as a pointer.

"We're gonna skip-bomb the bridge. That's why we don't need a bombsight. We're going down the river as low as we can get and skip the bombs into the bridge foundations. That's why we're taking the B-17; it's more agile. And don't worry about the old seventeen. It's only seven or eight hours to Myitnge and back, and it'll fly that long."

He puffed out a cloud of smoke and smiled at Lieutenant Kosko. "Old Kosciusko and I are gonna fly that sonofabitch like a P-51." He turned to Captain Jessup, the bombardier. "Jess, you and Kos get together with the ordnance people and figure out how soon to release the bombs at our planned air speed. I'll see you later on. The rest of you guys, outside with me."

They followed him out, and he gathered them into a circle around him.

"This is my idea and I think it will work," he said, looking at Mike while he talked. "But I want anybody who has any reservations about going along to speak up. I assure you that neither I nor anybody else will hold it against you." His lips curled in a smile around the clenched cigar. "Though, where I'm gonna get a replacement for any of you this late in the game, I have no idea."

His eyes traveled around the circle: from Wagner, the engineer and top turret; to Sylvestri, the tiny assistant engineer who rode the ball turret in the belly; past McCullough, the radio operator; Connors, the other waist gunner; on past Dick Haines; and rested on Mike.

When nobody spoke, he nodded once. "Okay, then, that's it."

◆◆◆

That night Mike didn't sleep very well, and got up to go to the latrine. Hunched over the urinal, he looked at his watch and saw it was two o'clock. Jesus, he wasn't going to get much sleep before his first mission. He shook his head wondering how he would hold up tomorrow.

The other guys had sure acted calm enough. Back in the basha earlier, someone passed a quart of Tiger around and then they went to bed.

As Sylvestri had pulled up his bed covers, he asked the group, "If we knock out that bridge, do we get medals?"

McCullough laughed. "At least a Distinguished Flying Cross."

I'll settle for being alive this time tomorrow, Mike had thought.

He walked back from the latrine, slipped back into bed, and fell asleep immediately. When he was awakened at six o'clock, he felt sure he had just closed his eyes.

◆◆◆

They took off at o-eight thirty, headed southeast. Myitnge lay just beyond Mandalay and about 700 miles from the airstrip at Chota Banda. They flew across the northern tip of the Bay of Bengal, turned south past Chittagong and Cox's Basar, and hit the Burmese coast at Akyab. They turned east and flew over mountains, then dropped down to two hundred feet altitude.

Standing at the waist window, Mike watched the ground below rush by, but he saw only fluttering patches of green and brown countryside, and the glint of water. The wind rushing in his face warmed his skin, but he felt cool and alert, and almost giddily happy that fear didn't grip him. He looked back at the tail turret and breathed a silent prayer of thanks that Dick sat in it instead of him. He knew from flying the submarine search missions how cramped it was in there, and how it rattled in the wind. And, Sylvestri in the ball turret... he didn't even want to think about him. They ought to give the little sonofabitch a medal just for getting in it.

He could hear the frequent chatter of the other waist gun firing and he knew Connors was firing at anything that moved. He'd never do that. There could be innocent women and children down there. Besides, it was a waste of ammunition he might need later.

They crossed the Irrawaddy River north of Pagan, and hit another river Mike thought must be the one that led to Myitnge, then turned due north. Flying right down next to the water, the river below flashed by so fast it became little more than a sparkling blur.

The navigator came up on coms. " Target should be coming up soon."

"Hey, they're shootin' at us! See the tracers?" Connors yelled angrily.

A moment later, the navigator came up on coms again. "There she is!"

"Are you sure it's the right bridge?" Major Kirke asked, but the answer was garbled. Suddenly, Mike felt a swift lift and a sharp bank to the left. He grabbed his window for balance.

As they swept past the bridge Mike got a quick glimpse of a section lying in the river. *"My God, we hit it!"*

The thought registered a half second before Major Kirke said, "It's the wrong bridge." His voice sounded calm, but disappointed.

Somebody asked, "Are you sure?"

"Yes, I'm sure, damn it."

They stayed low, heading for the mountains they had already crossed on their way to the target. When they got over the mountains, the plane nosed down to treetop level.

The squadron commander's laughter filled the headset. "I always wanted to be a fighter pilot..."

Kirke's co-pilot, Kosko, interrupted. "Something's wrong with number four engine. Oil pressure's near zero."

"Better shut it down and feather the prop," Major Kirke said.

"I can't. The mechanism won't work! Hey, Wagner, get your ass down outa that turret!"

After a long minute of silence, Wagner's voice came through. "It's bad! The prop's startin' to windmill!"

"Hold onto your hats, boys, and hope we don't shake the rivets loose." How the squadron commander could keep his sense of humor in such a situation baffled Mike.

The plane began to vibrate violently, and Mike knew he was going to be sick.

When the need to vomit became urgent, he lifted his headset, snatched his cap off, and threw up into it. Immediately he felt better, and tossed the cap out of the waist window, hard and straight down. He looked around to see if Connors had seen him throw up, but the other waist gunner had his back to Mike, his legs spread for balance, while he chewed on a sandwich from his lunch bag. Mike began to feel dizzy again, but he willed himself not to throw up anymore.

Over the Bay of Bengal, Major Kirke finally spoke again. "Relax, boys, we got it made. This old sonofabitch flies like a bird on three engines." His voice sounded like gargling in time with the plane's vibration, but they kept going.

When they landed at Chota Banda, Mike staggered from the plane like a drunk.

Major Kirke grinned at him. "Feeling a little airsick, Kane?"

"Yes, sir," Mike managed to croak.

Kirke patted his shoulder. "Well, don't let it worry you. It happens to the best of us on rides like that. I felt a little woozy myself."

Chapter Thirty-Two

In the next week, they flew two missions. The first to bomb the railroad yards in Mandalay, and the second to hit a supply depot in Prome. Both succeeded, and they encountered only some gray puffs of inaccurate anti-aircraft fire.

"The B-24 was known to drive like a truck," Major Kirke had explained. But their B-24, *Jackie Sue,* droned along so smoothly that Mike no longer got airsick. He even napped a little.

The squadron's morale got a boost when Colonel Eddie Rickenbacker visited on his way to China. Rickenbacker gathered them all around him and gave an extraordinary pep talk.

The stooped and skinny old man with his lined face, dressed in loose-fitting suntans and wore a sweat-stained topi. As he spoke he peered into his audience, seeking every face.

"I just came in from the States," his rasping voice began, "and it's enough to make a man vomit to see all the phonies and wheeler-dealers running around." His face wrinkled with disgust. "You know the kind, the guys you couldn't get in a uniform without roping them and tying them down? You boys are doing the only thing a man with any self-respect would want to be doing. I'd give my right arm to be in this outfit. But I'm too old and stove up, and nobody will take me."

Jesus, he did look like an old bronc buster who had broken most of his bones, Mike thought.

The sweat ran down his face while he spoke, so he took off his topi, and wiped his face and balding head with a big handkerchief.

"Some of you fellas may know I used to be a racecar driver, and I remember one race I was leading with only a couple of laps to go, when I lost the nuts on my left front wheel. The guys in the pit tried to flag me in, but I willed the wheel to stay on, and it did, and I won."

Mike listened to him pop-eyed. At face value, the stories were ridiculous. But he found himself believing every word of them.

"I remember another time, back in the thirties when we started Eastern Airlines. I was on an inspection trip when the plane crashed. I was all busted up and pinned to my seat, and the plane started to burn. The flames moved closer but, again, I willed those flames away."

He wiped his face and head again, and grinned.

"But that's enough stories about me. Let me tell you a joke I heard in Washington. When I was getting ready for this trip, I met a pretty little WAAC, and asked her if she had a story I could take with me to the boys in the CBI. She told me to ask you guys if you heard the story about the girl who got lost on the Burma Road. She was looking for a Mandalay."

They all roared with laughter.

Afterward, Major Kirke took him around the circle to shake hands and, when they got to *Jackie Sue's* crew, Kirke introduced each of them by name.

Rickenbacker shook Mike's hand. "Good boy, Kane," he said, causing a chill to run down Mike's spine. This skinny old man was a genuine hero, in company with Richtofen, Guynemer, and Frank Luke, and here he stood treating Mike Kane from Etting Street like an equal.

Mike could only grin idiotically, unable to speak.

On the way back to the basha, Dick shot Mike a dubious glance. "You know, politically, Rickenbacker is about six inches to the left of Ivan the Terrible."

"Yeah, I know. But he has earned the right to think anything he damn well pleases."

✦✦✦

That night, Mike got a brilliant idea for his novel. It leaped into his mind as he relaxed in bed, pleasantly drowsy after drinking his entire monthly beer ration.

The idea went like this... After the war, the University of Chicago would enroll hundreds of veterans from every theater of the war, and he'd let the novel tell the story of those guys.

He could already hear the fascinating bull sessions in the smoky taverns Dick had told him about along Cottage Grove Avenue. Not to mention the conversations over coffee in Hutchinson Commons—modeled, Dick said, after the hallowed commons at Oxford. He'd write it all down.

There would be fierce arguments between articulate Rickenbackers, and the eloquently passionate proponents of a more just social order. But they would be friendly arguments, for hadn't they all been brothers fighting Fascism? His eyes closed. He would sketch out the plan for the novel tomorrow.

✦✦✦

The next mission's orders, for another solo mission, were nothing like Mike's first. While the other eleven planes in the squadron distracted the Japs by bombing Rangoon, Kirke's plane was to sneak in low and lay mines in the Irrawaddy River north of Rangoon.

The mines were British so, in preparation, they flew to Dum Dum Airport, near Calcutta, where RAF ordnance men could load them up.

Takeoff wasn't scheduled until twenty-one thirty in the evening, so they spent the waiting hours talking to the British servicemen at the edge of the runway. In the course of the conversation, Mike discovered that a private here was paid about four dollars a week, or about seventeen dollars a month, while the American private received more than twenty.

"That's your bloody Winston for you," one of the Brits told Mike.

Another added, "What do you expect? Churchill's half-Yank you know."

Mike took offense. "Listen, bud', I'm a Yank, and I'm here in the same place as you. I don't run you down for getting your ass run outa Burma and needing our help, do I?"

The second Brit went insane, lunging at Mike like a madman. Mike stood his ground and, at the exactly timed split second, stepped aside and let him fall over himself. Mike felt sorry for the Brit and wanted to find a way to make it right. Still, he couldn't abide anyone running his country down. The enraged Brit got up and approached Mike more tactically, rotating his fists.

Mike backed away. "I don't want to hurt you. Let's call it a day."

The Brit's response included a missed swing at his face and a very near-miss kick to his groin. Mike stayed alert for what he knew would come next. The man felt embarrassed and insulted, and the only way out of his situation was to take it out on Mike.

This time, he took his time and circled Mike while calling him every insulting name imaginable, with saliva flying from his sneering mouth. He came in low and slow, his right arm held back, his left arm cocked. Mike repeated that he didn't want to hurt him, but that only made the man crazier. The Brit attacked, jabbing at Mike with his left. Mike parried and took the thrust from the right arm in both hands, twisted, and swung the man up, then down over his turning back. The motion slammed the man into a pile of ammo cases. The Brit didn't move after that.

"Don't mind him, mate," the first Brit said. "He's bitter because his missus is back in Blighty fucking one of you bloody rich Yanks."

"Hey, that's what I'm talking about. Cut that bloody rich Yank shit! Why can't we respect one another?"

They responded only with shrugs and mumbles, as they went to pick their friend up from the crates.

"What the fuck is this? Aren't we allies?" Mike yelled after them, but got no answer.

"Give Winston his due," an elderly corporal protested, talking to his beer. "He's the bloke who held England together after Dunkirk."

"I'll give him his due," the first Brit said. "A great wartime leader he is, right enough. But he's not the man to lead England through the changes we'll bloody well demand when this bloody war's over."

✦✦✦

They got to their target about o-two thirty in the morning, dropped down to about fifty feet, and started plopping mines into the river at intervals carefully marked on a chart. That would help the British find them after the war. A couple of miles away, explosions flashed from the rest of the squadron's Rangoon bombing diversion.

Everything went smoothly, so they laid their last mine and started home. When they got over the mountains, Mike opened his lunch bag and stood at the waist window, looking out while eating his sandwich. They were well away from danger now, and the steady hum of the engines droned a hypnotically comforting sound. Staring down at the tranquil moonlit jungle, and up at the star-filled sky, a feeling of happiness flooded him so strongly he could have shouted aloud.

He pulled out the epigraph for his novel. The notion of writing an epigraph for his book had come to him while reading *Main Street*. It was a long epigraph, he recalled, and said something about *Main Street* being the climax of Western Civilization.

He'd hate to have to tell Sinclair Lewis the next time he saw him that his epigraph stunk. Smiling happily, he unfolded the sheet of paper to read by the light of the bright Burma moon.

Unexpectedly, Mike heard the urgent, loud rattle of the top turret's twin machine guns. Wagner was shooting at something, Mike thought, only vaguely remembering Kirke's warning that a Jap Zero squadron might be stationed near Rangoon. Connors opened up next, behind Mike. Then, Dick started firing his twin .50s. Instantly, *Jackie Sue* filled with a deafening cacophony of shooting, explosions, and metallic-ringing sounds.

Mike dropped his sandwich and notes, gripped his gun, and began searching for a target in the moonlight. Nothing. All hell was breaking loose, and he was left out of the fight. He spread his legs, took another deep breath, and glared at the night sky. His focus was so intense that he became only dimly aware of a new noise, like those heard back at the belt and suspender plant.

A flickering movement registered in the corner of his right eye, and he looked just in time to drop below a line of thumb-size holes stitching through the fuselage above him. When they passed, he bounced back up onto his feet and fired a steady stream into the black shape hurtling past his front.

There was another sound amongst the overload of noise: a deep thumping, felt more than heard. *The Zeros must be firing their 20 millimeter cannon up at the plane's belly from below*, Mike thought. These hits were entering *Jackie Sue's* vital organs from a place only the ball turret gunner could defend. *Poor little Sylvestri*, Mike thought.

Mike leaned into the gun, and forced his vision out into the night. If they came his way, they were meat, he declared to himself. The plane groaned and shook from the cannon fire, and the wide holes created in its structure. Men shouted, metal twisted, machine guns fired, and explosions deafened him, even through his headphones. His emotions balanced on the sharp-edged border of panic.

He smelled smoke... a very thick and suffocating black smoke, and a very bright light silhouetted his image from behind. He turned to check on Connors, and flames licking at the gun portal blinded him. The two right engines blazed with fire. Connors lay motionless on the floor, face down, his arms under his body.

Mike looked to his right and saw Dick's tail gun position... only a gaping hole remained. Dick, his best buddy, had disappeared into the night without Mike knowing it.

Had he been looking at me and screaming for help in his last minutes? Mike silently asked the smoke billowing around him. His heart sank, and he began to blame himself for not being bigger, better, more, faster, smarter. If he had been any of those things, he might have saved Dick, and Connors, too.

At that point something clicked in his brain, and caused Mike to shake off the rising depression. *No time for that! Snap out of it! Get that gun and fight!* He spun around and leaned into his gun with an intense determination.

Just then, *Jackie Sue* began to roll over to her right, where both engines on Connors' side still burned. Those two flaming engines, serving only as dead weight to the plane, pulled the B-24 over. Mike held on, remembering from training drills that Major Kirke and Lieutenant Kosko would be fighting the plane's balance, and the engine fires.

The plane pitched erratically as the strong muscles of the two officers manually horsed the ship back into trim. Soon after, they extinguished the fires. Amazingly, the B-24 still remained in the air.

A Zero suddenly appeared and sprayed the left side—Mike's side—of the plane, from the rear forward. This time, Mike was ready. He led the Zero in his gun sights, pouring rounds into it as it cruised by. Fire leapt out of its cockpit before it went down. Another Zero followed close behind, and Mike just shifted over to that one until it exploded. Another Zero came right behind, and he killed it, too, but not before it took out *Jackie Sue's* remaining two engines. They both caught fire, and the fire-extinguishing process began anew.

Major Kirke's clear and steady voice came up on coms. "Sorry, fellas, but we better prepare to crash. We radioed in our location so they can send out the posse to find us. See you on the ground. Good luck. Out."

As if on cue, another stitching of machine gun fire ran down the right side of the plane, but no return fire came from *Jackie Sue*. Mike didn't care anymore. The ground was coming up faster than any Zero he had seen tonight. Standing and holding on to his gun for support, Mike prepared for impact. The mountain ahead quickly became much larger, and the nose of the plane turned inexorably down. Nothing good could come from this: if Major Kirke gained more altitude, they would go smack into the mountain's side. If he nosed steeper, they would drill straight into the ground. Their only hope would be sliding to a stop in the foothills. That appeared to be Major Kirke's intention.

Mike's thoughts moved much more slowly than the events occurring in front of him. The ground came up fast and, even in the moonlight, he saw trees and boulders. Suddenly, a scraping of tree branches sounded on the belly, then the wings. Mike held onto his gun for support and closed his eyes in prayer. The plane's nose burrowed into the trees, and hit something hard. Some huge force caused the crashing plane to swing urgently to the left, splitting the fuselage apart in the middle. Mike sensed being catapulted, colliding with things, and the eerie sounds of metal twisting and groaning around him. Mercifully, he lost all consciousness at that point.

When he opened his eyes, he found himself slumped over the exposed roots of a large and ancient jungle tree. The severe heat had awakened him. The plane burned not thirty feet away, directly in front of him. The intense flames caused the brush near him to begin to smoke and ignite. He jumped up, and thrashed through vines and branches to position himself a safe distance from the flames. He hunkered down while his mind pieced together what had happened to him.

Mike realized that, if he got out, maybe others did, too. On impulse, he set out to search for his friends. He used his natural sprinting ability to easily dodge around trees, run through brush, and jump over boulders, yelling names. "Dick! Major Kirke! Anyone! Yell! Wave! Move so I'll find you."

He started his search by circling the plane as close as the heat would allow. He made two circles, calling names, hoping someone had also been thrown out away from the plane. He found no one. He began to accept that he might very well be alone, but he had to be sure.

After a third pass, he stopped to catch his breath, only to realize how much his chest hurt. A sharp pain struck him with every breath. Mike dismissed it as altitude sickness, and began to circle the plane for the fourth time, only slower. "Kosko! Wagner! Somebody say something or wave! Sylvestri!"

Mike was sobbing when he yelled for Sylvestri. He knew the little man was blown away when the Jap cannons made those thumping noises from below. The shots tore right through his ball turret position where, alone, he hung upside down firing his guns to defend the plane.

Though he had chosen to put that knowledge aside in the heat of battle, he could no longer. Why was he calling for Connors, whom he knew died on the floor behind him. Or, for Dick, who disappeared into the night along with the entire tail gun position. He wondered, *am I dead? Am I now a ghost?* He felt stupid and hopeless. He wanted to find a hole and roll up in it.

Instead, he decided he needed to try to find the one or two others who survived. *I know they're out there*, Mike thought. *I must try!*

"Come on, damn it! Wave! Yell! Roll over! Help me see you! McCullough! Connors!" Mike's voice choked again, but he fought it off. "Connors, you goof-off sonofabitch, get up and help me find the others! Dick! Major Kirke! Kosko!"

No one responded.

The flames reached higher into the night sky, once they found a new source of fuel within the fuselage. The bright fingers turned the night into high noon. Black smoke billowed so thickly it blocked out the moon and stars. At the ground level, the acrid stench of burning rubber, fuel, ammunition, and flesh, made him gag. His face felt sunburned. The heat surge forced Mike to move back away another hundred feet up the mountain.

Mike finally reasoned that no one else had survived. He found no trace of anyone thrown from the plane, and certainly no one still on the plane could have survived the inferno.

He must have been running around like a crazy person. How long had he searched and yelled, when any sensible person would have made a reasonable search then run like hell? He started to panic when he realized how much time had gone by while every Japanese shit-head who could see these flames would want to investigate, and bag an easy kill.

Running uphill into the thickest jungle he could find served as his best course of action. By doing this, he hoped the impenetrable jungle thorn bush would dissuade any Japanese pursuers. After an hour, exhausted and with every breath painful, Mike sat down on a root of a huge oak-like tree to take serious stock of his situation. First, he checked his watch. It showed three minutes after four in the morning. Surprisingly, he had still been in the air only forty-five minutes ago, but dismay hit when he realized he had only two hours before sunrise. By then, he must be far away.

Next, he searched his pocket. Besides his dog tags, which required the Japs to treat him like a POW—and that was a laugh—there was nothing. He realized then, he would die. He'd ignored his training and left his bag behind. He wore boots, khaki pants with a belt, and only a tan uniform shirt. With the chill, he wished he had grabbed that bag.

He also assessed his physical status, at least he remembered to do that much from training. He touched the painful parts of his body, starting with his chest. Strange that the breathing pain had become sharper now that he rested. He felt his ribs, and found the pain source in the upper left portion of his rib cage. If he pushed in a little, the pain lessened when he breathed. It also felt wet, though. Mike brought his hand up and saw glistening black liquid, the color of blood in moonlight. *Oh God,* he thought. He ran his hand along the flow and found a six-inch gash on the side of his upper left arm. It musta been caught on a jagged piece of metal. He found a similar wound on his left thigh. Alarmingly, both wounds still bled, and his clothes were soaked with blood. He immediately tore off his shirt and pulled off his left sleeve to make bandages. He wrapped both wounds as tightly as he could, and applied pressure until his breathing became less torturous.

Mike leaned back onto the tree and summed up his situation. He was breathing, but maybe he already bled to death, and just didn't know it. He knew he was thirsty, so thirsty he could drink his own piss. He dismissed that idea since he had no urge to pee.

Mike felt fuzzyheaded, so he tried again to fix his status in his mind. He was injured and had lost a lot of blood. He had a watch, but no weapon, no compass, and no map. His thirst raged, but he had no water, and didn't know where to get it. He reasoned he would find water if he moved west toward India... and help. Hell, Burma was full of rivers.

Okay, okay, I don't have a chance in hell but, when the end comes, I'll make my buddies proud. I'll find an honorable way to die, and avoid capture. Everyone knew about how the Japs treated prisoners. He had seen pictures of them using prisoners for bayonet practice, and Mike Kane would pass on becoming part of the Jap's training program. He knew that Dick, Major Kirke, and the others, were watching him, and expecting him to make some smart decisions.

Chapter Thirty-Three

M ike saw all their faces: Major Kirke and the rest, and they were all smiles. Dick walked over and started talking, reminding him of his pledge to take care of Vicky. Mike started to answer when he heard a radio, no not a radio but a foreign voice speaking to him. He suddenly realized he had dozed off, so he girded himself for Japanese imprisonment and opened his eyes. Asian eyes, fierce-looking Asian eyes, stared close into his.

"Get up," the voice behind the eyes whispered in English. "I am friend. We must go."

Mike tried to jump to his feet, but fell down. His first sensation was shame for being a U.S. Army soldier who couldn't stand up. He struggled and willed himself to sit up, his eyes never leaving the level gaze of those eyes. He sensed the movement of others around him. He couldn't get a good look at them in the moonlight, but they didn't look like Japs. They appeared thin and dark, and wore turbans.

Two of them hauled Mike to his feet, and the man with the fierce eyes spoke to him. "Mister, I am La Raw. We were sent by America to get you. We must go far away quick, or we die. If you can't walk fast, we will carry you."

"I can walk," Mike whispered, "but do you have a medical person with you?"

"I am medic, and leader. I was trained by America. What hurts?" La Raw asked, his eyes less fierce.

"Two bleeding cuts, a bump on my head, and it hurts when I breathe. I'm very thirsty."

La Raw started his examination in the dark. "Where hurt to breathe?"

"Here," Mike whispered, pointing to the spot on his left rib cage.

La Raw pressed his hand forcibly on that spot. "Breathe now."

Mike breathed deep and felt much less discomfort.

"Better?" La Raw whispered.

"Yes, much."

The man fastened a leather strap tightly around Mike's chest. It amazed him how he could breathe again without as much sharp pain.

"Where are cuts?" La Raw asked, and then rattled off some strange words to the others in his band. Immediately, a hand poked out of the darkness holding a canteen of water.

"Left arm and left leg," Mike pointed, while swigging half the water in three choking gulps.

While La Raw tended Mike's cuts, another hand gave him a pasty ball and tapped his mouth, signaling he should eat it. In the short time it took for his two wounds to be wrapped, he downed a fist-size rice ball and almost all the water. Without warning, they hoisted him to his feet, and held him on each side for support. They completed the work in less than five minutes.

La Raw looked at Mike. "Now we go fast. We talk more later," he whispered.

✦✦✦

They walked briskly for more than two hours up the dark mountain, through whipping branches and slippery mud, and stopped to rest just as the sun came up behind them. Mike got his first clear look at his rescuers: twenty dark-skinned men, standing about five to five-and-a-half feet tall, and wearing variously colored open shirts and loin cloths. Each went barefoot and wore a light-colored turban, with a top-not. Lean and athletic, they looked well muscled, but not like weightlifters. These were jungle people, born and raised to be as nimble as cats. Each carried a U.S. .30 caliber carbine and a thick sword slung diagonally across the chest.

The men fanned out a safe distance from one another to prevent one enemy grenade or mortar round from hitting more than one of them at a time. He learned this same precaution back in his Army infantry days in Hawaii.

He sat down at a distance from the others and ate the rice ball he was given. It was understood there would be no noise, not even the sound of a branch breaking, and only whispered conversations when absolutely necessary.

A man approached Mike. He smiled and offered water and another pasty rice ball. "I am Maji Tu," he whispered, bowing with his hands together. "If you need something, tell me first."

Mike bowed and whispered, "Okay, Maji Tu. I thank you for saving my life."

"I pray we save your life, but you not saved yet. Are you Christian like me, Mister?"

Mike smiled and reached out his hand to another Christian in the form of a barefoot native in the jungle hills of Burma. "Yes, and I'm happy to meet you as a brother. Please call me Mike."

Maji Tu's whispered voice spoke evenly, but his eyes lit up with his devotion to Jesus. "All's well, brother. Today is blessing from our Lord. We must be happy for His gift."

"Amen," Mike whispered, truly smiling for the first time in years, maybe since birth. He clasped the man's hand in fellowship. "Amen, brother," Mike repeated, with a wide smile.

Maji Tu tended Mike's wounds, and left silently with only a nod. Mike settled back to rest like the others, but La Raw came over.

"Mister," he, too, whispered, "my boss, Mister Quinn, said we should find survivors. He from America, like you. We are Kachin Jingpaw Rangers," he said proudly, "from our homes in the north. This place is not our land, but we at home in this forest. We are trained by America, and Japs are enemy to us for all the bad things to our wives and families. I am in charge of this patrol. We mostly kill Japanese, but sometimes we help friends. We searched your burned plane and you are alone. We very sorry."

Mike leaned forward and listened intently, seeking to hear every word often masked by dialect and the low whisper. He remembered hearing about the Kachin Rangers during his escape and evasion training. Wow, they actually exist, and here they were, trying to save him from the Japs in this vast jungle. As his memory became clearer, he recalled they were part of the American OSS, a clandestine organization based in the Burmese state of Kachin, and operating throughout Burma behind Japanese lines.

La Raw continued to deliver his message. "My English is not good. I will practice and get better. We all learned English at church, but don't use it much. So, please listen carefully. We find you quick because we already on alert and close. Lucky we knew the Jap Zeros near and waiting, I think. We see your trail at crash and we walk over yours to cover your tracks. In daylight, Japs see our trail and follow us. Not safe here, but must wait for night. No choice."

In short order, Mike learned a lot about this patrol of twenty Kachin Rangers. La Raw and Maji Tu were American-trained combat medics. All Christians, they learned English thanks to the tireless English missionaries who had persevered in this British colony over the years. The Kachin ancestral home lies on either side of Burma's border with China. They are not fond of the Burmese, or Chinese, who look down on them, but hate the Japs even more for their atrocities.

La Raw handed Mike a U.S. .30 caliber carbine, saying they were sure to encounter Japs. He tied a rope on it to replace the leather sling they had used to wrap around Mike's chest.

La Raw leaned closer, his eyes intense. "Listen, Mister. Today we close to Homalin, a Jap camp on Chindwin River. This camp sent soldiers to your crash. We watch them pass us hours ago. Japs go east, we go west to here. This bad spot. We between those Japs and their home camp. When Japs see your boot prints at crash, they radio home camp, I think. We wait and pray Japs dumb, maybe they not look very good. We must cross river in the dark and before they radio. Then we get safe into India. Your friends be there in two weeks," La Raw held out two fingers for emphasis. "So, Mister, you help us move quick and stay ahead of Japs?"

"Yes! I'll march fast, no matter what. And, please call me Mike, not mister. That goes for everyone. If we live or die, we do it together. You are now my brothers, my crewmates."

La Raw smiled and handed him a cloth bag containing carbine magazines. "Okay, Mike," he whispered, smiling. "Carry bag over shoulder like we do. Rest and be ready at dark."

Mike laid back and allowed himself to nod off, occasionally waking and watching how the Kachins worked together. He saw La Raw moving among his men, whispering to each one. He had three subordinate leaders under him, and communicated with each using a combination of dirt-drawings, whispers, and hand signals. At his direction, scouts went out, and guards were posted. The camp resembled a beehive. Their location, in thick pine trees with undergrowth that concealed them at ground level, positioned them on the western side of a mountain. The sun was bright, but they secluded themselves in a very heavily shaded location.

Maji Tu tended Mike's wounds and found two leeches on his groin.

"Mike, check for leeches always. They carry bugs that maybe kill you sure as bullet."

"Okay, I will, but what about my head? Is it okay?"

"Oh yes, Mike, for sure. If not, you be dead now." Maji Tu beamed.

Mike slept and dozed the day away. He was given food and water periodically by smiling men, who often sat with him for a time without whispering a word. He clearly felt he was in good hands. La Raw kept everyone positive, and communicated the operations plan without a lot of hoopla.

Hemingway was all about communicating honestly, truthfully, and clearly, Mike thought. It provided a lesson he needed as a writer: the fewer words the better. *If I survive, I will write about this experience with honesty and clarity as well, only better than Hemingway.*

They waited until dusk to quietly move down the western slope toward the river in the valley far below. Three hours later, they arrived at the Chindwin River, about ten kilometers south of the Japanese stronghold at Homalin. La Raw led them to a cable the locals used to cross the thirty meters of swift, cold water. They waited, listening and watching for anything out of the ordinary. Mike smelled the sweet and sour aroma of wet plants and damp earth, and heard the vibrating insect sounds all around him. The night birds made their sounds and some wild pigs started grunting a short distance away. Clearly, nothing ominous lurked nearby.

A finger click by La Raw sent two scouts across like otters. They scouted the other side and soon signaled all clear. The rest—including Mike—crossed two at a time, low in the water, all but invisible in the moonlight. The last three held back as the rear guard until La Raw signaled them to cross, and they swept away all evidence of the patrol and followed the main body.

The Kachins moved like ghosts, Mike thought. *I have found myself among some very remarkable people.*

Once together again, they moved swiftly into the tree line and made their way up into the mountains, taking care to avoid trails. As before, the rear guard used short branches to sweep away all footprints. They straightened bent vegetation with their fingers, and often paused to listen. After an hour of climbing up a steep rock cliff, they paused to rest. While Mike caught his breath, two scouts searched the way ahead. They returned quickly and led them to the edge of a well-used trail. La Raw made everyone crawl into the thick brush along the trail to observe. They didn't have to wait long. Within ten minutes, a fifteen-man Japanese patrol walked by talking and laughing, using torches to light their way. These were the first Japanese Mike had ever seen, and they did not at all resemble the wily jungle experts of military lore.

They waited until the Japanese torches moved beyond some trees before following. They didn't step into the tracks of the Japanese, as Mike had thought they might, but carefully walked along both sides of the trail on the pebbles and grasses, while the rear guard busily tidied up as they went. Mike realized they did this so, in daylight, the only visible prints on the trail would be those of the Japanese. In the meantime, the trail afforded an opportunity to gain some distance before dawn. The tactic offered a slim chance, but La Raw decided to take the risk. Through his experience matching wits with the Japanese, La Raw knew specially trained trackers in the Japanese units would search relentlessly until they found the trail. The key was to move faster than they, and reach safety before they found you.

They didn't go far before they had to stop and hide, as the noisy mob ahead of them replaced a like number already in an ambush position along the trail. Mike saw it was two in the morning, an odd time to make a change like that. Ambush positions in any Army usually stayed put, quietly, all night. The Japanese must feel very much in control of this area, Mike guessed. While they made their changeover, the Kachins moved quietly around them, like dust in the wind. Scouts went out in advance to ensure there were no other Japanese traps, and they moved fast the rest of the night. At dawn, they rested in deep vegetation, high in the mountains in a spot far from any trails. They spent the daylight hours like before: napping, eating, scouts coming and going.

Maji Tu wrinkled his nose as he unwrapped Mike's wounds. "Not good, Mike. Not healing. Maybe river water gave you bad bugs. Both cuts have bad color and too much bad smell and pus. Soon you be swelling, I think," Maji Tu said, his eyes studying the wounds.

Then Maji Tu changed his delivery. "All okay, brother, don't worry. I'll clean you up and put ointment on these spots more often as we travel. I got some medicine from my family that will help, too. This infection is deeper than I can get to... maybe some metal pieces in there. We must get you out as fast as we can... No problem, we will out run the bugs, and the Japanese," he whispered. He shot a dramatic fist in the air, and grinned impishly.

Mike tried to stifle a laugh, noise discipline as it was. No doubt Maji Tu would see to it that he got out.

✦✦✦

Outrunning the Japanese might be harder than they thought. The next day was the third day since the crash. While resting as usual, two scouts ran back into camp and directly to La Raw. The leader listened intently, then motioned his three assistant leaders to him: Maran Ja, Jang Kham, and Zaw Min. Mike knew who they were, although they hadn't had the opportunity for introductions.

He sensed something unpleasant pending, so he held the St. Christopher medal on his dog tag chain. As he prayed, he realized he should probably, instead, hold a St. Jude medal, the patron saint of desperate cases and lost causes.

The leaders broke up and a flurry of activity began. Mike noted the lack of panic, and no urgent or somber expressions. Only a calm, positive flow directed the leaders' movements as the patrol split up into four squads, led by the three leaders and La Raw. All communications were virtually soundless: dirt drawings with sticks, clicking tongues, faint finger snaps, pointing, and hand gestures.

La Raw motioned for Mike to stay with him, and they set out through the thick brush. Mike kept up with the others, and thirty minutes later they converged with two of the other squads at the bottom of a high rock escarpment. An animal trail there ran from right to left along the bottom to reach a gap ascending steeply to the top. On signal, all sixteen of them crawled into the brush on the downhill side of the trail.

Everyone froze in place and listened. Birds sang and small mammals scampered through the brush, unconcerned by their presence. When La Raw was satisfied, he began assigning firing positions along the trail, placing the two leaders where they could control a specific sector. On the far right edge of the firing line, he placed his three highly skilled rear guard rangers facing backward, to guard against a Japanese attack from their rear. Finally, on the far left, La Raw and Mike took a blocking position where the trail bent to their left toward the gap at the top.

From there, Mike could see straight down the trail to where it disappeared to the right. The Kachins lurked along the trail on his right, and the escarpment and gap stood to his left. Carefully camouflaged and silent, everyone settled in to wait. The view of the ambush site from a low-flying aircraft might be that of a Z in a mirror.

Mike realized La Raw had changed his tactics. Instead of running, he meant to try to bloody the Japs in an ambush and blunt their enthusiasm for pursuit. Normally, the Japs would eagerly chase a foe and gain an easy kill, like a fox chasing a rabbit. But, La Raw had learned about three thousand Chindits, British, and Indian soldiers under General Wingate, who were making long-range penetrations into Jap-held Burma north of where they were. He was betting the Japs would not waste more soldiers to capture one airman. If this ambush did the job, they stood an even chance of shaking off the Jap pursuit.

All choices have consequences, Mike thought, *and we'll soon find out what we get from this one.*

He looked at his watch. Only fifteen minutes had passed and he had to pee. But he knew he couldn't roll sideways to relieve himself because the Japanese would smell it and be alerted. La Raw said everyone must control his body out in the jungle, especially at times like this. "We don't eat what Japs eat, so we smell differently and must stay downwind of them,"

La Raw had said. Mike's replay of the jungle warfare lessons he had learned so far kept his mind off his need to pee, but it didn't mask the sound of feet running urgently up the trail.

La Raw laid his hand on Mike's carbine as a signal to relax. Zaw Min and the fourth squad, five men making the noise and footprints of twenty, ran up the trail directly at Mike. The rabbits luring the fox. Just before reaching him, they turned to Mike's left and began climbing up the gap. Zaw Min passed within an arm's reach of Mike, but didn't make so much as a nod in his direction. After the sound of running feet faded away, the forest around them became very still. No birds sang and no small mammals moved... the only noise came from the breeze in the trees, and the crazy thoughts in Mike's head.

No telling how long they waited before the first Japanese soldier materialized at the far end of the trail. Mike simply blinked and there he was. He was obviously the point man for his unit, and responsible for ensuring his buddies didn't walk into a trap. Suddenly, Mike realized he could smell the soldier, just like La Raw had said. The breezes came toward Mike carrying a distinctly tart fishy smell, new to his senses. The Jap wore a brownish uniform with boots and wrapped leggings almost to his knees. His soft cap was brown-colored, with a visor and a gold star in front. He carried a rifle, with a bayonet attached, ammo pouches, water canteens, and a low-riding backpack. He stopped and looked around. His eyes searched the ground, then the ridge above him, obviously considering that would be the origin point for any threat.

It's instinctive, Mike thought, *for people to think danger will come from above... and La Raw had planned for that.* From the moment the Jap looked to his right and up, he never looked back to his left again, even though that was where all the Kachin guns waited.

Mike could imagine now how this drama might play out, but he focused on his assigned mission. La Raw had whispered to him while the fourth squad ran by, "Shoot the radio man first, that's the one with the antenna. Shoot the officer next, the one with the sword."

They waited.

Just like poker, back in Hawaii, Mike thought, *the first man who blinks, loses.*

Long minutes passed while the Jap crouched down, seeming in no hurry, and appeared to enjoy the day. American infantry soldiers referred to the numbing wait at times like this as the *little death*. It meant their lives were not yet over, but could be very soon. More minutes passed. It became so still Mike thought his heartbeats might tip the Jap off.

It occurred to him that the Jap soldier currently in view was more like what he expected: a mysterious and disciplined character, radiating coiled energy from an undersized body, in too-large clothes, and carrying a too-long rifle.

Finally, the Jap stood up and waved for those hidden behind him to move up. He then trotted up the trail directly at Mike, apparently not seeing him, and sprinted up the gap toward the top of the ridge. Mike feared, but at the same time felt relief, from what he knew must come next.

Suddenly, a unit of Jap soldiers advanced swiftly, two abreast, up the trail and into the ambush killing-zone. They, too, glanced up toward the ridge top, and rarely toward the thick vegetation down to their left. Like their point man, they were short, bandy-legged, and wore the same uniform and gear. Mike saw an antenna poking up from one man half way down the trail, and he pushed the carbine's safety switch to off. Otherwise, he did not move a muscle or blink. No one did, everyone waited like monoliths until La Raw's signal. Mike swallowed hard, staring straight at the face of an advancing Japanese soldier only ten feet away.

When La Raw shot the soldier Mike had been staring at, all hell broke loose. Mike fired two shots into the chest of an enemy directly in front of him. He swiveled, using his waist gunner skills, and looked for another target. He needn't have... another enemy was looking for him. Out of the shadow of his first kill came his second, who died before he hit the ground.

Mike raised his sights to find yet another, which took four rounds to topple. He quickly picked another, then another. The din from the more than fifty guns blazing away at once intensified until the loud roar blocked out all but two of Mike's senses: seeing a target and touching a trigger.

Bloodlust grew so strong in Mike he only vaguely realized he was out of bullets when his carbine didn't bring down the bayonet-wielding Japanese soldier a few feet away. With no time to reload, Mike rose up to meet the attack head on. Law Raw shot the charging Japanese three times, toppling him backward, and preventing him from lunging the bayonet forward toward Mike as he died.

Mike frantically began reloading his carbine when he saw yet another Japanese thundering through the brush at him. He immediately swung around, pushed the Japanese bayonet aside with the butt of his carbine, stepped to the left, and chopped down with his own bayonet across the enemy's neck. The Japanese fell to the ground like a bag of rocks. Mike's bayonet drill back in Hawaii had finally paid off.

He pivoted to take on any next enemy, but realized his friends were all standing up and moving out onto the trail. All the Japs were down. Three Kachins ran up the gap, and soon returned, dragging the dead body of the Jap point man. They counted forty-two Japanese dead.

Zaw Min and the fourth squad came up the trail behind the Japanese and confirmed none had escaped. The best they could tell, there were no radio transmissions once the shooting started since Maran Ja had immediately killed the radioman. Certainly, a recent location report would have been transmitted... La Raw guessed it would be sent on the hour and half hour. It was now one fifteen in the afternoon, and no one knew the exact time the ambush launched, or how long it took. Though exhausted, thirsty as hell, and with some wounded, they could not exalt in this huge victory. They needed to push on before the next report was due, probably in fifteen minutes, when the Japanese would send a search party. They quickly picked over the dead Japanese, looking for documents, unit identity, signal codes, anything useful to the head office. They then moved into the trees like ghosts in the wind.

How unbelievable that twenty Kachins could kill forty-two Japanese, and in only a few minutes. None of them had time to dwell on it, however. They had to move fast and far while they could, and without leaving a trail. He looked at their faces and saw pride glowing in their expressions, but knew each also felt great relief for having survived. Only two Kachins had been shot, and six received bayonet wounds, but everyone could walk and continue the mission.

Mike was very glad these small soldiers were on his side. La Raw and Maji Tu had furiously tended to the wounded before they left, and now they moved swiftly westward through the formidable mountains. The rear guard swept up their tracks, as always, and made it look like the ambushers escaped up the gap and disappeared into the thick brush toward the southwest. Having daylight to work in, it was possible for them to practice their craft cleverly enough to delay their pursuers a day or more, if any Japs chose to follow.

♦♦♦

The rest of the day and all night they pushed on, using the ancient and secret mountain trails of the opium smugglers. The main opium trail to India lay only a few miles north of them, but it was too dangerous to use now with the Japanese certainly alerted. They used the clandestine spider web of less efficient, but more secure, smaller trails that took them in the same direction. It rained steadily through the night, so they trudged through mud up and down the steep trails and dense forests of the Naga Hills. That's when Mike learned to worry about more than just the Japs. His heart sank to his feet when they told him about the Nagas.

"These are the Naga Hills," La Raw explained. "The Nagas are headhunters, and they are unfriendly to all outsiders, even other Nagas. We must be cautious all the way to India, and even beyond, because their ranging territory is large on both sides of the border."

Mike had no words to say in response to this news. He merely nodded stoically, trying to grasp the presence of yet another, even more bazaar threat. *Headhunters! Jesus Christ! I thought the worst would be to fall into Japanese hands but, oh no, we have fucking headhunters.*

Hadn't he been through enough already? He ached all over, suffered from debilitating diarrhea, and the smell of his own wounds ashamed him. Weakness dragged at him, and he had the thought that a walk across a street in Philly would even be too much for him. He slumped over for three uncomfortable breaths, then forced himself out of the self-pitying hole he was digging for himself, and re-entered the real world.

"Snap out of it, asshole!" he whispered to himself. "Let's get this done! Let my living or dying be someone else's worry."

From that point on, La Raw allowed only brief rests, and moved them night and day. They ate while they walked, always a little rice and a stick of dried meat. Every second day, Maji Tu collected special jungle leaves to add to their diet.

Mike had two Jap water bottles, so he didn't need to ask for water anymore. He filled up at the streams like everyone else. This, and his performance at the ambush, allowed him to feel more like a member of the team.

He knew the only reason the Kachins were laying their butts on the line was to get him back to a bomber, where he would kill more Japs than they could. If he had died with his buddies, they would all be back with their families and friends, defending their villages.

He felt embarrassed. Shit, he wasn't worth this. *And, here comes the depression again*, he thought.

On top of his weakening emotional state, he was quickly deteriorating physically, and he recognized the Kachins might have to carry him soon. Until then, though, he knew he had to earn his way by soldiering-up and facing all obstacles with courage. He would fight off that black dog of despair that seemed to follow him everywhere. Perhaps it had always been there, all his life, but now it had found him weak, and circled in for the kill.

◆◆◆

It was more of the same the next day, March 8, 1943. Mike had scraped a mark on his rifle for each dawn he stayed alive. He was energized by surviving his fifth day in the jungle of Burma, thanks to the Kachin Jingpaw Rangers, especially Maji Tu.

At dawn the next day, they found the trail wet and slippery, and the air humid and hot, until they worked over to the shadier side of the mountain. There, it suddenly turned cold. Wet from sweat and rain, the rapid change in temperature shocked the body.

At dusk, they descended a steep slope and, in the fading light, saw a cloudbank below them. The sight was at once both awe-inspiring and disheartening. Mike's nagging sense of self-pitying hopelessness began to take over his emotions when he thought of how far down they would have to go to find bottom, only to climb back up yet another steep mountain like the one he was on, and maybe many more mountains beyond that. The realization of how high they would have to climb after they reached the valley floor made the trip down under the clouds like a trip into hell.

◆◆◆

Their first meeting with the Nagas could have happened the next afternoon, on March 10th, the seventh day of Mike's journey. While descending a steep slope, they smelled smoke, and immediately moved around the area at a safe distance. La Raw had told Mike the Nagas supported the British and hated the Japanese. Unfortunately, they were also unpredictably hostile to any outsider. They needed to be avoided at all costs.

Up until now, Mike had fought his emotional depression to a draw, but he suddenly felt like he should finally throw in the towel. Every movement or exertion pained him. His infected wounds oozed with pus and smelled outrageously. Every muscle burned stiff and sore, and fatigue often obscured vision in front of him. Beyond the threat of the Japanese, tigers, leeches, germs, and bugs of all kinds... add fucking headhunters likely to stick his head on a pole as a decoration. He was a beaten man, he decided, and now he had to do the right thing.

He had twenty Kachin friends on this journey and they would give their lives to get him out, yet they could do nothing to save him from his throbbing pain, his lack of energy, his painful breathing, the cold, the heat, the rain, the mud, and the humiliating smell of his own wounds. He felt like an insect, caught in a sewer with no escape. He decided then that he would end it by simply falling off one of the many cliffs along their way. The Kachins could then go home, take care of their families, and not be put on a Naga spike.

That decided, the thought suddenly struck that when the current rest break was over they would start climbing another fucking mountain. All he needed to do was get high enough to fall off a cliff and die. Mike closed his eyes and drifted off in deep despair.

Chapter Thirty-Four

"**H**ullo there, American," someone shouted from beyond the trees, addressing the camp in the loud voice common to a British drill sergeant.

Everyone took cover and peered out over their weapons. Mike sensed the movement but, in his self-pitying delirium, only heard the commanding British voice, so odd under the circumstances. Like an apparition, out stepped a strange-looking man carrying a small branch even Mike could see was not menacing, and probably a symbol of peace. He was short, maybe shorter than the Kachins, and thin, but heavily muscled and bare from the waist up. A dark loincloth hung between his legs from a thick belt of ropes. On his head, he wore a brown-colored conical cap—adorned by several bore tusks and a Mohawk-style sprout of hair—and sticking up from it was a large white feather colored with a black tip. He had the looks of a deranged killer forcing a smile. He wore large solid-white earrings and, around his neck, lay a riot of color forming a bead necklace. Below that, he sported a very large black V-shaped tattoo, which started at his navel and spread to touch each shoulder. He also wore large white armbands on each arm above the elbow, and numerous red bracelets on each wrist. He was barefoot with a black wrapper around each leg between the ankle and knee. He was the most fascinating person Mike had ever seen.

"Hullo there, American, and his friends. I am Sesha," he said raising the branch of friendship and his free hand together, as if in triumphant salute. "I am Chief of all the Nagas in this region. You all are now my guests and under my protection."

La Raw, previously silent and inert, upon hearing Sesha's words laid his carbine down and approached the newcomer. He marched forward in the exaggerated British style, halted smartly, and bowed slightly, while pressing his hands together in greeting.

Sesha returned the bow slowly, and quickly motioned for his hidden warriors to come out of the trees. The Nagas numbered more than twice the Kachins, and they came together smartly behind Sesha. Each dressed like their leader, but less colorfully. Each carried both a meat-cleaver-shaped sword and a long spear with black fur tied around the entire shaft.

La Raw lined his men up in a kind of formation and gestured for Sesha to bring his men forward. Sesha complied eagerly and Mike witnessed right then, in a flicker of gestures and style, La Raw taking control of the situation.

He saluted Sesha and the Nagas in the British fashion, and signaled that they should close ranks and mingle. In seconds, hands were being shaken, English was being spoken, and introductions made informally, as if at an old warrior's regimental reunion. Too weary to stand any longer, Mike plopped down and watched the activity. It was clear those indefatigable British missionaries had reached even the Nagas, and now everyone present rejoiced in Christian brotherhood and the English language. Soon, they shared food, and happy conversations about homes and families turned into occasional laughter. It resembled a church camp for wayward boys.

Sesha drew La Raw aside to talk seriously. "You have come a long way, brother, and your brave men must be weary—especially the American, who looks very sick. If you will allow me, I will send my scouts out and secure our camp so all of your men can rest safely for a few hours. When it gets dark, we will guide you into India, maybe two, three, days from here. We were told your friends await you there."

"Thank you, sir," La Raw responded. "Your kind offer is a great gift from Heaven."

La Raw and Sesha called to everyone to end the social time, and promised there would be more opportunities in the days ahead. They each said some nice things about team and comrades in arms against the hated Japanese, and how they would prevail. Then they went to work.

Sesha organized his security patrols, and La Raw gathered in his scouts and huddled the Kachin team together to eat and sleep. In wonderment, Mike considered how the very monsters he feared the most, the Naga headhunters, had suddenly brought him hope. He could feel his strength returning. The dullness of his senses had been replaced by a tingling of eagerness to move on. He was now more assured than ever in his life that his God had blessed him, and he felt renewed.

Mike needed a good sleep and he finally got it. They set out at dark, and were guided up and over a mountain, and down a steep ridge to the bottom of a deep ravine. After a short rest, they climbed a steeper mountain along a rocky trail and rested at the top. Mike was at the edge of collapse from the exertion, and each labored breath failed to provide enough oxygen. After they rested, down the slope they went into the blackness. Two Nagas, as sure-footed as goats, held Mike upright.

By dawn, Mike could go no farther. His muscles suddenly gave out and his body went limp. He knew he could no longer pretend to walk even with two strong Nagas holding him up. He lay on the side of the trail where he collapsed, his senses numb, watching the sunlight's fingers sliding through the gaps between and over the saw-blade edges of the mountaintops.

Mike closed his eyes for a few minutes. When he opened them, he saw La Raw and Maji Tu hovering over him, holding a makeshift stretcher built out of two sturdy saplings and several shirts and loin clothes donated from both groups. La Raw, Maji Tu, and the other Kachins, hoisted Mike's inert body onto the stretcher. Four Nagas carefully lifted the stretcher and, with a nod from La Raw, Sesha got everyone moving down the trail.

It took four hours to descend the steep slope to the bottom of the gorge where they rested beside a fast, cold stream. The spot seemed to hold some significance for the Nagas, and Sesha smiled at Mike and La Raw. "We are now in India. We have left the Naga Hills of Burma and entered the Nagaland of India. We are also close to your American and British friends. They are just over the next few mountains."

He puffed out his bare chest, his hands on his hips, and surveyed the mountains above them. Sesha's face became fierce looking, with clenched teeth and flint black eyes. "The Japs are watching us from up there, but they don't dare attack us now, because they are too far from help. They know we are the feared Nagas, and they are too afraid to show themselves." He paused and spat. "I think we are safe now."

+ + +

Mike noted by the notches on his carbine's stock that it took them almost three days to march over those last three mountains into the interior of Nagaland. They rested at a Naga village, named Omphin, where he saw no human heads on display. Only a tiger's skull hung from a tree, for what reason he had no idea. The village sat on a hilltop overlooking an alpine setting suitable for a holiday postcard from Pennsylvania. He smelled the rich pine smell of the forests around them, and the cold temperature compelled him to imagine things back home.

They ate with the Nagas, but Mike thought it strange they kept the women and children out of sight the entire time. The Nagas lived in smoky and cramped bamboo huts, built off the ground on pillars. This would allow enough room underneath for pigs, dogs, and children to run freely under them without ducking.

Mike and the Kachins were given gourds of rice beer, which they sipped through bamboo straws. Mike, just strong enough to sit up, sipped the beer eagerly and soon wooziness spun his head. He learned quickly that it didn't taste strong, but carried a violent punch, especially for a run-down kid from Philly at five thousand feet in altitude.

The Nagas seemed very happy to have Mike and the Kachins as guests, and they smiled and laughed, and promised that no Japs would survive long if they came near. The village chief welcomed them and said he took personal responsibility for their safety. He dispatched a strong runner to alert the nearest British camp of their impending arrival.

Then they ate. Men served them, with the food delivered to each person balanced on a large leaf. It consisted of grilled beef-like meat and fresh vegetables. The meal was tasty and filling. They stayed up awhile talking and drinking until they fell asleep where they sat. Maji Tu woke Mike right after he dozed off and insisted he force down large amounts of water.

In the middle of the night, Mike had to pee urgently but, unlike lying on the jungle floor where he could just roll over to urinate, he lay four feet off the ground, and was without the strength to stand, walk, or maneuver the ladder to the ground. While desperately looking for a knothole or crack in the floor, Maji Tu pulled him to his feet and walked him to the open door. No one was down below, so he let fly, moaning with relief. Maji Tu left him by the door, and he slept there until first light.

✦✦✦

The next day, March 15th, they reached Ukhrul and spent the night. Mike had gained enough strength to walk slowly around the village. He remained very weak from fighting the infection eating his ugly, disgusting-smelling wounds, and from the lack of oxygen at the mile-high altitude. The constant pain also compounded his every function, from simple breathing to moving his limbs. He pressed on, believing the next morning would magically bring more strength and more relief from pain.

That evening they shared more rice beer, dinner served on leaves and, best of all, talking and laughing in a cramped smoky hut. This was truly a legitimate men's club, Mike realized. A member's background was not important, but the price of admission was steep because a member had to have killed a Jap. Mike, even in his feeble state, had earned his way into this very exclusive club. It exalted him. In a flash of epiphany, he realized he was no longer living out of books, he was actually living a life. He was alive, and truly somebody valued by others for his deeds. Mike actually meant something to someone else on this Earth.

One of the Nagas, an intense and athletic-looking young man named Takshaka, asked Mike about the "sweep-chop" he heard Mike had used with his gun-spear to kill his sixth Japanese. Mike quickly recognized what the man was calling a "sweep-chop" was his modification of the bayonet drill learned back in Hawaii. Mike stood up abruptly. "What were you told about this "sweep-chop?"

"Only that it was hard to describe and different from what we do," he said.

"Okay, bring your spear." The room hushed. Takshaka returned with the weapon, his flint-black eyes wide with eagerness to learn.

Mike took it, inspected it, and gave it back. "Stab at me."

Takshaka balked. "I cannot hurt you, you are my brother!"

"Okay, then stab at me slower than you would at a Jap," Mike responded. In this instance, he knew he needed to appear strong but, more importantly, Takshaka needed to save face.

The Naga nodded and immediately thrust the spear at Mike's chest. He stepped left while swiftly pushing the thrusting shaft past him with his hands, then he stepped forward and chopped with both fists at Takshaka's neck, stopping short of contact. The movement was so fluid it transfixed his opponent. Mike smiled and patted the Naga's arm, then thanked him. Takshaka withdrew his spear, shook Mike's extended hand, bowed, and sat down smiling.

Mike said: "As Takshaka very cleverly showed you, once the thrust starts, your enemy is committed, but you are not. You can be agile and do what we showed here. It works well with a rifle, spear, sword, or a fist. The idea is to chop down quickly while your enemy is still off balance. A powerful chop with a blade and the man will die instantly, like the Jap I killed."

The entire crowed sat in shocked silence. Then, as one, they rose and clapped, cheered, and banged things together in applause. Mike immediately shoved his hand over to Takshaka and they clasped one another as comrades. "Thank you, brother, for helping me demonstrate this move so well."

Takshaka beamed with pride, and the crowd roared approval. When they settled down and began drinking rice beer again, Sesha rose and said they should all practice this new move so they could kill more Japs. He appointed Takshaka to lead the training in the region, starting with the men in Sesha's own home village. The Nagas bowed to each other; Takshaka had just been promoted.

The *men's club* settled back to the easy conversations and laughter Mike found so appealing. The Nagas and Kachins conversed *together* in small gatherings, without segregation. He watched everyone's faces as they talked, and saw that the Kachins really enjoying themselves among the Nagas. Somehow the lives of both the Kachins and the Nagas would be changed in a positive way from this experience, and maybe that would be the good that came of all this.

If so, that would be enough.

◆◆◆

Two days later, Mike awoke to the heat of intense sunlight on his face after a night march in pounding rain. They had moved hard since they left Ukhrul, and stopped to rest around four o'clock in the morning near a muddy dirt road. Mike had collapsed during the night and had to be carried much of the way. He lay wondering if the sunlight was a dream. It could have been any morning, since they had mostly traveled at night and slept through the day, but this time frantic activity sounded around him.

Alarmed that the Japanese were about to attack, he tried to rise to defend himself, but fell back. When his eyes finally focused through the lethargy, he sighed with relief at the sight of La Raw and Maji Tu. They smiled widely at him, but their eyes kept glancing behind him. Mike rolled over and, to his surprise, gazed up at two American faces smiling back at him. The Army medics asked his name, checked his dog tags, and began to make detailed observations and notes about his condition.

An officer arrived to ask Mike about his experience. He asked about the crash, if any others might be left behind, and any Japanese units, installations, he may have seen. Mike told him everything he could think of, and noticed others questioning the Kachins and Nagas. When the medics thought Mike could be moved, they abruptly interrupted the officer and carried him into a tent hastily erected for Mike's more detailed medical processing.

After he was cleaned up and medicated, they loaded him onto an ambulance truck for the bouncy forty-mile trip to Imphal, the capital city of Manipur, in northeast India. From there, they would fly him to the general hospital in Calcutta.

As soon as the truck lurched forward, he regretted not saying goodbye or thank you to the men who saved his life.

Chapter Thirty-Five

When Mike reached the hospital in Calcutta, they immediately rushed him to an operating room. There, the doctor and his two assistants dug out of his wounds pieces of metal, cloth, and dead tissue. He also suffered two broken left ribs, but they would heal with time. The doctor explained that open wounds like his in the jungle of Burma normally would have been fatal within a week. It was a credit to Maji Tu that he had been kept alive twice that long. Mike remembered Maji Tu using some family medicine on him, and he was sure that salve had enfeebled the jungle's bad bugs during their travels. Mike said a prayer that night asking for a special blessing on Maji Tu, La Raw, and all of his rescuers.

After surgery, Mike settled into the hospital routine. In general, they insisted he rest, and forbade him from walking around the hospital. Each day's routine consisted of a doctor's prodding as a wake-up call, followed by a nurse with medicine, breakfast, followed by two extremely boring periods punctuated by meals, more medicine, a doctor's visit and more prodding, followed by sleep. They augmented this schedule during his second week with short exercise periods in the mornings and afternoons.

White colored almost everything around him: the walls, doors, tables, towels, bedding, mosquito nets, doctors, nurses, and even his clothing. The main exceptions to the rule of white included the reddish highly polished floors, and two gray-metal chairs. Mike lay alone in a room containing four bunks, with room for more bunks if needed. That became the case in mid-April, during Mike's fifth week in the hospital, when the remains of the British-led Chindits began to filter back out of Burma.

During one evening visit by his physician, Dr. Carl Rea, Mike asked how long he would be kept at the hospital.

"Hard to say, son," Dr. Rea had answered. "Your leg and arm wounds became very infected and gangrenous, which means some muscle tissue was destroyed, so your body has some major repair work to do to get you back in the game. Your ribs will take a few weeks to set, or longer if you keep getting up on your own. You need to find ways to stay put and get your strength back."

"Thank you, sir. But all I ask is for your guess, given the gangrene and all."

"An additional six weeks, maybe more, depending on your behavior and cooperation."

"Thank you, sir. That amount of time will give me a good start on my novel," Mike said.

After Dr. Rea left, Mike gazed up at the ceiling and began to reconstruct in his mind the epigraph he had lost in the crash. When he remembered a part, he repeated it over and over until he memorized it, and he continued this process long after lights out. Just before sleep overtook him, he promised himself he would find some paper and pencils in the morning.

Mike was awakened early the next morning by Dr. Rea's prodding, given his medicine, and sat waiting for breakfast when Al Hennessey and Cliff Oakes walked in, chased after by a very irate and verbal nurse.

Dr. Rea intervened and gave the two visitors permission to stay and have breakfast with Mike. "Remember our deal, Mike, stay in bed until supervised exercise time, and no roughhousing!"

"Yes, sir."

Al and Cliff dropped their duffel bags, and sat on the empty bunk next to Mike's. Al wore his habitual shit-eating grin. "Who the hell does that nurse think she is? She came outa nowhere, swooping down on us like a witch."

"She's the head nurse around here, and we refer to her as Broomhilda," Mike said.

"I would keep an eye open after dark if I were you," Al said, rolling his eyes. "Anyway, Cliff and I are real glad to see your young ass back among the living. We got no word about *Jackie Sue* for two weeks, then we heard about you making it out. Of course, we immediately got drunk in your honor."

"Thanks, guys. I could almost taste the *Tiger* from where I was at the time," Mike laughed. He paused and lowered his eyes. "I remember you both tried to talk me outta this, and you were both right to warn me. It turned out to be a very difficult experience. Now that I've survived, though, I am glad I did it, and experienced what I did. It will take me awhile to think through all that happened and make it a positive thing in my life, but I will."

"Well, when you get outta here, rest assured you've got a nice safe job with us back at the 15th Bombardment Group. You've had your thrill, now you can sit out the rest of the fucking war with us." Al nodded in agreement with himself.

"Thanks guys, that sounds great right now."

"Hey, Mike," Cliff cut in, "did any others get out of the plane?"

"Not that I could tell. I ran around that plane a couple of times yelling my head off, and I couldn't find anybody. The Kachin Rangers, who tracked me down, also looked around and didn't find anyone either. I hope others got out, but I think I was the lucky one."

"We'll pass that along when we get back," Cliff said. "It's tough stuff losing all your buddies like that. But, I'm real glad you made it out."

"Your new Squadron Commander will be here tomorrow to visit you," Al said. "He would have come today, but he is flying a mission. He seems like a good guy, just like Major Kirke was... hands-on and close to his people. He is from the east coast, but we can't hold that shit against him. His name is Lieutenant Colonel Bill Brown, so be alert."

Cliff leaned forward, hands on his knees. "How did you make it out?"

"I didn't," Mike confessed. "The Kachin Rangers, with help from the Nagas, carried me out. I was in pain, but functioning until the sixth day when I physically fell apart. After that, I was so tired and sick I gave out several times, but those Kachins were relentless. They kept me moving and, when I couldn't move, they carried me on a stretcher made from their own clothes."

He met Cliff's gaze with a tight smile. "When the Japs found us, we ambushed them and killed forty-two without losing a man. One of the Kachins, named Maji Tu, was a trained medic and his efforts alone kept me alive for over two weeks. My doctor here said I shouldn't have lived a week."

"Boy, there's a story I wanna hear sometime. You were in some real shit! Next, you'll tell us you ran into some headhunters or cannibals, maybe some Amazons..."

An orderly interrupted, to bring in breakfast. They each got a metal tray containing scrambled eggs, two pieces of toast, three pieces of crisp bacon, a cup of coffee, and hot sauce. They became quiet for a time while they wolfed down a part of the food, coffee mugs balanced precariously on the wiggly mattresses.

Cliff wiped his mouth and studied Mike. "You still wanna write?"

Mike swallowed hard. "Hell yes. I've got this story running through my head, and I've got to get some paper to write it down. It's going to be along the lines of Hemingway's *A Farewell to Arms,* but a real soldier's story. This time I've got Hemingway by the balls. I wasn't some fucking ambulance driver like him, I actually fought and killed enemy soldiers, in hand-to-hand combat. If I had some paper and a pencil, I'd start writing this very second."

"Well, good news, Mike, because I brought you seven tablets of paper, a pen and ink, and six pencils." Cliff pulled them from his duffel bag. "I'll leave the bag because there's a bottle of *Tiger* in there, should you want a sniff. And, Mike, I'm not a literary type but, I'd sure like to read your book when it's done."

"Thanks, Cliff. You musta read my mind to bring paper and pencils."

Al piped up as he reached for the bag he'd dropped on the floor. "Hey, Mike. We also have a shit-load of mail for you in this other bag. Your new commander asked us to bring it today, knowing you would want it as soon as possible. And, there's another sniff of *Tiger* in there from me."

Mike looked at them blankly. "You mean letters from home, or some get well notes from the guys in the squadron?"

"Postal mail," Al answered.

"Shit, Al, there must be some mistake. Maybe another Mike Kane in the unit? I only get a couple of letters a year."

"These are for you, buckaroo," Al said as he held up a bundle of fourteen letters, wrapped together by two rubber bands. Your commander said all our mail got held up at some central postal unit, somewhere, and then the logjam broke. We all got mail about the time you took off."

Mike took the letters eagerly, but fought the urge to look at them. Putting the stack under his pillow, he picked up a piece of bacon. "So, what's the latest?"

Cliff started by telling Mike about the Germans pushing the U.S. Army around North Africa, and Al added the latest news on the British-led Chindits marauding around Japanese-held Burma. They finished the rest of their eggs, bacon, and coffee like wolves of the same pack, talking, and laughing, with their discussions meandering around disparate subjects. It was mid-morning when Al and Cliff reluctantly said their good-byes, promising to visit in a day or two. Duty called.

As soon as they left, Mike started opening his mail in no particular order. The news in the first letter shocked Mike at first, and it slowly led him to the numbness of despair. Doc Greene wrote that both Caz and Willie had died in North Africa in the last four months: Caz in Morocco in November, fighting the Vichy French; and Willie at the Kasserine Pass in February, fighting the Germans. Mike put the letter aside, closed his eyes, and pulled the sheet over his face until lunch. He looked at the food without interest, his body lifeless.

Mike knew the black dog of depression was biting deeply into him again, and he needed to fight to save himself from it.

Well, the game is over and life is taking on a new reality in a big hurry, he lectured himself. *I can either take on life standing up, or hide out in a safe place, but I have no control over if I live or die, either way. I can, though, choose to control my choices and behavior while I'm alive. My reputation and how my buddies remember me is all I really have, alive or dead. The guys from* Jackie Sue *are watching over me, and now so are Willie and Caz. I've got to snap out of this mood and get back to living, and do my part fighting this war.*

Mike picked up the spoon and sipped some pea soup, and then took a bite out of a peanut butter sandwich. Picking up the letter, he began to read where he left off. Doc went on in his loquacious style to tell Mike the gossip and comment on world events, ending by stating that Rose and Paddy were well. Mike then read Rose's three letters, which were full of positive news about each day, Teresa's little boy, and how well Paddy was doing. She ended each by telling him how much he was loved, missed, and prayed for back home.

The next letter in the pile hailed from California... from Noelani. His heart raced and his hands shook as he tore the letter open and read it carefully. She wrote that her father died in the Japanese bombing during the Pearl Harbor attack, and that her brother Henry left Southern Cal to join the Army, but was killed in a training accident in Texas in early January. Before he died, Henry obtained Mike's address for her from a Hawaiian friend who worked in personnel. She was still a student at USC and wanted to complete her degree in Literature.

"Please write me," her closing lines said. "I pray you are still alive and can read this. I want you to know that I've always loved you, Mike. I want to be with you. Please write and tell me you feel the same. Always yours, I love you, Noelani."

Mike tingled all over as if electricity sparked under his skin. He got up, seeking any mindless task to give him time to recover from this stunning news: the love of his life, the most perfect woman who ever lived, said she loved him. He worked himself into such a giddy state, the nurse and an orderly put him back in bed and gave him a sedative.

Mike dozed off until mid-afternoon, then reread Noelani's letter. He decided to answer her immediately, and used one of Cliff's tablets to write down his feelings for her. He got an envelope from an orderly and put the letter in the afternoon mailbag. He thought he'd lay back and look up at the white ceiling until evening meal but, instead, dug out another letter to read.

The letter came from Mr. Goldman. He said he was in England, and described his life and experiences in the war. He mentioned he had heard from Doc that Mike was flying as a waist gunner, and wished him safe returns and a long life so they could meet back in Philadelphia and compare their experiences when the war ended. Mike sensed a change in Mr. Goldman. A bitter and sad man wrote that letter. Perhaps Mr. Goldman had seen too much, and finally realized his idealism couldn't cut it anymore, or maybe never had.

In hindsight, Mike understood they had shared an idealistic view of the world, which brought them together, and they also likely shared the same underlying depression lurking in the shadows.

This moment brought Mike to think about his life, and about what lay before him. With all the discouraging embarrassments and failures, he had turned the corner when he found himself lying against the tree watching *Jackie Sue* burn. He understood that everything he wanted stood before him: the experiences he needed to write with emotion, and the possibility of a future with the girl of his dreams. If he was idealistic, then so be it. It had taken him this far, and he was not about to avoid the future it promised.

Mike Kane felt his role in the world stronger and better than ever. He would commit his life to Noelani, fight this war to its end, and write the book he always dreamed he would.

Mike sat up in his bunk and wrote. He rewrote the epigraph from memory, fine tuned it, and sat back to read it aloud.

"They came from places with odd-sounding names, like Myitnge and Tulagi, and Attu and Buna, and Bizerte and Medjez el Bab. They were young-old men, as fretful as porcupine quills and as patient as Job. They had lived lives of dreadful monotony, filled with sights that harrow the flesh and freeze the blood. They had killed and raped and pillaged, and their charities had been chronicled in a hundred tongues. And now, they descended on the centers of civilization and culture to claim the bounty of a grateful government. And the centers of civilization and culture were sore afraid…"

Mike loved it. "Sinclair Lewis, you are going to die when you read this!"

Mike wrote until Cliff's pencils grew too short to use. Time and the daily hospital schedule passed by in another dimension, and when the hour came for "lights out" he talked the orderly into turning the lights back on, and hanging a blackout sheet in his doorway so the sleepy nurses wouldn't notice. That same orderly would also bring more pencils and paper when Mike ran out. He could obviously see Mike was on fire and couldn't stop writing, and probably justified his actions in the interest of supporting a patient's healing process. Besides, that patient no longer skulked around the halls all night listlessly defying the doctor's instructions to the contrary.

✦✦✦

Just before lunch the next day, Lieutenant Colonel Bill Brown, Mike's new squadron commander arrived, escorted by a smiling nurse. Mike slowly recognized the woman as the same snarling bitch who snapped after Cliff and Al yesterday for violating visitor hours.

Colonel Brown stood tall and slender, and gazed at him with the friendliest eyes Mike had ever seen. He stooped to keep his brown hair from hitting the overhead beams. Mike thought he looked like a modern-day Abe Lincoln, without the creases on his face. He walked straight at Mike, radiating a big smile, and Mike couldn't help but look back at him in the same way.

"Mike Kane, welcome back!" Colonel Brown said with enthusiasm as he shook Mike's right hand and flopped on the bunk next to him, just like Al and Cliff. "You made it out, buddy. Good job! I'm proud of you. I'm also proud of your crewmates, and Major Kirke, because you all got the job done, and you went down fighting. I'm sad you may be the only survivor, but I'm glad you made it."

He pursed his lips and leaned forward slightly. "Sergeants Hennessey and Oakes gave me your report, but I still have to ask you if there is any chance someone might still be alive?"

"Yes, there is always that hope," Mike said, "but I searched the immediate area around the plane as it burned, and circled it several times. I found no one, and no one responded to my yelling. The Kachins who found and rescued me also searched for survivors and found only my footprints. I believe I am the only survivor."

"Why do you think that is, Mike?"

"Because everybody but me was probably already dead, or nearly so, at the time of the crash. Major Kirke told us to prepare to crash, and wished us good luck just before... maybe thirty seconds prior. Besides him, no one seemed alive during those last seconds. The other waist gunner, Connors, was down and immobile early on. The tail gun position had been blown out of the fuselage, leaving a gaping hole where Dick Haines had been; and then eventually I only heard silence. None of our guns firing, and no chatter on the intercom, just the Japanese Zeros circling and firing. During those last few seconds, I could feel someone at the controls was fighting against a nosedive, trying to crash the plane in a flat area at the base of the mountain. Whoever that was, probably Major Kirke, gave me my chance to live. Lieutenant Kosko, who usually spoke on the intercom more than anyone, had been silent for some time before the crash. Having said all that, I pray we find some other survivors."

Answering Colonel Brown, sharing the story in concise detail like that, lifted an unforeseen heaviness in Mike's heart and mind.

"May God bless you, son. With your wounds, you must have searched on pure adrenaline. Anyone else would have been no more than a basket case. We now have aerial photos of the crash and they show the left side of the plane, your side, had opened up on impact. That would have thrown you out into the trees before the fuel erupted and incinerated any survivors. The search will continue, and I will let you know if anyone else is found."

Mike appreciated the leadership of his new commander, his direct manner of speaking, and how much he cared about his people. So, he opened up and told Colonel Brown about the gross injustice burning a hole in his soul ever since the Army medics took him away from his rescuers without allowing him to say good-bye, or thank you.

He described La Raw and his crafty jungle leadership during the ambush of the Japanese. He talked about working with the Nagas, and praised Maji Tu, who kept him alive for more than two weeks. He also shared how some Kachins and Nagas had given up their personal clothing in the cold mountains to make a stretcher to carry him for six days when he became too weak to walk. He spoke on and on, faster than he could believe, until he realized he'd begun sobbing like a child. Mike hung his head and wiped at the wetness on his cheeks, embarrassed about losing his composure.

After a long moment, Colonel Brown's reassuring words persuaded him to continue his story. Mike felt it was okay to spill it all, as if he was talking to a priest.

When he finished, Colonel Brown took out a pad and asked for as many names of Kachins and Nagas as Mike could remember, spelling was not important. Mike gave him all he could remember, hoping word would get back to them that the American they saved was very appreciative and had not forgotten them. Perhaps their lives would be made a little better because of his report.

"Mike, this is a big deal. Your story makes me realize we had better pay more attention to our relationships with native rescuers, or they might not be so willing in the future. As far as your Kachins and Nagas are concerned, I will find out who we need to talk to, and we will both pursue this until everyone of these guys gets a personal note from you and recognition for his sacrifice while saving you. What do you think?"

"Sir, I feel like a large weight is off my shoulders. That's wonderful. They more than deserve it. I'd give them everything I have, and I *would* like to write my notes personally."

"Okay, I'll get on it today, and let you know soon how I'm doing. I've got to move out and get back to the squadron, but I also wanted you to know there were ground observers watching the last minutes of *Jackie Sue's* fight with the Zeros. They reported eight Zeros shot down, four of them from the left waist gunner. That is a remarkable record for a lone B-24 shooting it out with a dozen Zeros, and a remarkable record for one waist gunner."

"Thank you, sir. I'm glad we did well, and that I got my share of those bastards."

✦✦✦

It took four more weeks for the medical staff to bring the infections in Mike's wounds down to a manageable level, and clean out the last of the dead tissue so healing could begin. Soon after, he noted healing in the both wounds, and his breathing no longer caused discomfort.

Mike used every minute of those weeks to write, even ignoring meals, and he limited his liquid intake to cut down on bathroom runs. A surprising relationship also began to develop during this time. He couldn't remember how it got started but, nevertheless, every evening a young nurse would come by just before "lights out" to listen to what Mike wrote that day.

Doris, from Minneapolis, became a good editor and critic who challenged Mike to describe the smell, touch, sight, and action in each of his paragraphs. She would bring coffee and sit patiently while Mike read. These reading sessions helped keep Mike on track. She was cute and sweet, but Mike kept Noelani's smiling face in his mind to shut out any temptation.

The only other interruption to his writing commitment was the daily mail call. Noelani wrote every three days, and Mike dropped everything to respond, often taking hours to express his love for her. Noelani wrote just as fervently in her letters. The correspondence between them made Mike happy beyond measure, but he ached because he wasn't with her. One of his major hopes for their future included the novel, and he drove ahead writing it despite everything. He knew his magic window of writing time would close someday soon. He decided he wouldn't reply to any letters but Noelani's until the book was done.

In the wee hours one morning, Mike's mind ran wild. Something must be amiss, because he really didn't deserve the wonderful things coming his way. He wondered if, perhaps, in his delirium during the last days of his trek, he had made a Faustian bargain. What was the price of these gifts, he wondered? The Mike Kanes of the world don't live happily ever after.

He might do better to guard himself against being too optimistic. After all, the disappointment would be less painful if he had lower, more realistic expectations. He would surely get hurt beyond recovery if he allowed himself to enjoy his thoughts about Noelani, the girl of his most fantastic dreams, or to ponder the reason he alone survived the most incredible, and dreaded situation an airman could imagine. He shouldn't feel truly happy, giddy happy, about being given this opportunity to write the novel of his dreams, should he? When opportunity's door slams shut, as everyone knows it will, Mike Kane will again find himself as the subject of one of the world's most cruel and wicked jokes.

"Bullshit," Mike yelled, fully awakening himself. He looked around, but no one stirred. He laid back on his pillow and spoke to himself quietly in the darkness. "Bullshit, Mike. Snap out of this crazy thinking. You are agreeing with all the smothering shit you've heard since you were born: that you are not good enough to be in good company, you don't deserve to get the prettiest girl, to have the greatest job, or have hopes for a successful future. You've been hearing this shit from your parents, your friends, even Mr. Goldman and Noelani's father, and you fumbled around until you made them correct. But now, it's different, damn it! You aren't on Etting Street anymore."

He lifted his hands above his head and stared at them, grounding himself in his current reality, and continued his quietly verbal personal rant.

"You now have the prettiest girl you can imagine, if you don't give her up out of fear. You survived a horrendous experience, and no one can take it away from you. And, now you have a story inside you that needs to be written, unless you also throw that away as not good enough. No one gave you these wonderful things, you fucking earned them. Let someone else worry about not being good enough. You've already proven you are beyond that crap. Snap your ass out of it!"

◆◆◆

Three days later, four Chindits moved into Mike's room. During the first few days, they slept a lot and stayed mostly quiet, but Mike knew that would change. So, he called on Doris to help him find a quiet place to write. She found an empty doctor's office Mike could move into except to sleep, eat, and get his medicine. It was a perfect set up, and Mike found it easier to write sitting up. The bonus was a typewriter and paper available there for him to use to his heart's content.

✦✦✦

Mike's eighth week in the hospital, the week of May 10, 1943, brought a tipping point. That week, he received two medals, a promotion, and he mailed off his completed manuscript to Charles Scribner's Sons, a publishing house in New York City. He chose Scribner's because they published Hemingway's *A Farewell to Arms,* and he knew his book would get their attention.

The medals and promotion came during Colonel Brown's visit on Wednesday. He arrived at lunch and stood slightly stooped under the beams, smiling at Mike like his long-lost brother.

"Mike Kane, how the hell are you?" Colonel Brown said in a loud voice. This time Broomhilda left him at the door with a condescending smirk on her face.

"Just fine, sir. I'm ready to get back to work before I'm too fat to get in the plane."

"Good, but the medical types told me they need to practice on you a little longer to make you handsome enough to rejoin the squadron."

Mike burst out laughing. "Okay, sir. I wouldn't want to set a bad example."

Colonel Brown laughed, too. "Yeah, we do have our standards. So, are you getting your mail and the extra pads of paper?"

"Yes, sir."

"Good. Are you getting enough to eat?" he asked.

"Yes, sir," Mike answered, but he was aware that the room's other occupants were quietly observing them. "Uh, Colonel, let me introduce my four new roommates. Next to me is Ian, with the Royal Scots. Over there is Tony from the 13th Regiment, The Liverpools. Next to him is Michael from the Burma Rifles; then Peter from Manchester, serving in the

Royal Birkshires. They were all with General Wingate's Chindits, and just exfiltrated out of Burma."

"I'm very proud to meet you men, very proud indeed. We've all heard a lot about your exploits, and we think the Japanese were very surprised to find you out there amongst them. We are sorry you had such a rough trek out and hope you are back to full form very soon. May God bless you all."

As spokesman, Michael, the Irishman from the Burma Rifles, thanked him for his concern and promised they would be back on their feet quickly.

The sudden arrival of lunch allowed Mike and Colonel Brown to continue their discussion.

"Your visitors kept me up-to-date on your progress, along with the medical staff, and said you are well on your way to recovery. Good job. I'm also very proud of your actions under fire, and during the walk out. Your mates back at the squadron also know of your record and share my enthusiasm for having you back on our team. We now have third-party verification of your shooting down four Zeros, surviving a crash as its only survivor, and killing six Japanese soldiers, one in hand-to-hand combat while you were wounded."

He fished two boxes from his pocket, and laid them on the bed. "For those actions, you are awarded the Silver Star medal for valor under fire." He opened one box and showed Mike, while the Brits applauded.

"You are also awarded the Purple Heart medal for suffering serious wounds in combat." He opened the second box for Mike to see.

"And finally, because of your exemplary conduct and leadership in the face of the enemy, you are promoted to Sergeant First Class, effective on the date of the crash. Congratulations, Sergeant First Class Kane."

Mike couldn't think of one word to say. Wild applause by his roommates brought his verbal skills back into action, but he could only muster a, "Thank you, sir."

Colonel Brown shook Mike's hand, pinned the two medals on his pillow, and gave him the official citations. He handed Mike two embroidered Sergeant First Class chevrons, with three stripes on top and two stripes on the bottom.

"You really did us proud, Mike. You really did. I would be pleased, very pleased, to have you back in the squadron when the doctors release you. Be aware, though, the higher-ups have alerted me you might be selected for a six-month temporary assignment back in the states for publicity and war bond tours. Also, Sergeants Hennessey and Oakes have told me they requested your transfer back to their organization after you're released from here. So, you've got choices to make, and I will support your decisions no matter what they are. As for your squadron, you will always be welcome home with us regardless of your choices."

"Thank you, sir. I'm bowled over by all of this." Mike paused. "My only intention, sir, is to return to the squadron. But a visit back to the states, where I could visit my girl, and buddies, and father, would be too hard to pass up. I also submitted my novel to a publisher yesterday, so I might be able to check in with them at the same time. If I could rejoin the squadron and also go on temporary assignment to the states—if selected, that is—it would mean the world to me. Al and Cliff are great guys and I appreciate they want me back, but I don't want to do that work. I want to get back in the air and be part of seeing this war through to the end."

"Okay, son. That's clear enough for me, and I'll do everything in my power to make the stateside trip happen for you. In the meantime, I won't let you paint yourself in a corner. Think over your options with Al and Cliff, and all that I told you. While you are here, you have a chance to think through your choices. Most of us don't get that chance; we are assigned by the Army and that's it. You, on the other hand, earned the right to choose. Just know, if you want to change your mind about returning to the squadron, I'll be here to support you, no matter what."

"Thank you, sir. That means a lot."

"Don't thank me! Hell, I'm proud to be in your company. And, by the way, so were those Kachins and Nagas you walked out with. Their leaders have responded that you made a very big impression on both of their groups. They also confirmed everything in your report. I'm still working out how we can pass on your thanks and reward them in some way that will be meaningful to them."

He held out his hand to Mike again. "Okay then, Sergeant First Class Kane. Heal up. Keep smiling. And above all, don't let these Brits warp your sense of humor!"

With that, the listening Brits busted their bandages roaring with laughter, and gave *Leftenant Colonel* Brown every assurance they would keep Mike on the straight and narrow until he returned to the squadron. Amidst the deafening good-humored uproar, Colonel Brown left with a wink and a smile.

Just as Colonel Brown ducked his head to pass through the doorway, Broomhilda came running in as if to subdue a rebellion. Doris stood behind her, and shared a huge secret grin with Mike. The orderly friend, playing his part in the comic drama, came forth holding a mop like a spear. Broomhilda finally gave up trying to impose order, and left shaking her head.

Doris stepped forward and took command of the situation. She merely raised her arms, and shook her ample boobs under her shirt. Quiet was instantly achieved. Broomhilda didn't look back.

The four Brits didn't let Mike off easy. They made him tell his story, which Mike did reluctantly. Afterward, he turned the tables and required each of them to tell his Burma story. As the afternoon wore on, their shared experiences created a strong sense of camaraderie. Mike surreptitiously passed around a bottle of *Tiger,* and learned a lot about Tony's family in Liverpool, and Peter's in Manchester, but Ian held back about his origins in Edinburgh. Though he liked them all, Mike found he gravitated more to Michael from Kilkenny, Ireland—two Mikes with Irish backgrounds sharing their past, their hopes, and their dreams.

✦✦✦

After the evening meal, Mike put his head on his pillow and thought about all his opportunities and choices. He let it all sink in. Though a high school dropout, he had now written a book, and earned two awards, a promotion, and a solid belief in a wonderful future ahead with Noelani. Most valuable of all, he had earned respect for himself and confidence in what he could achieve, and a true understanding of honorable behavior and dignity. *Beau Geste* came to mind, but he wasn't living out of books anymore, he was making books. These achievements came not from birthright, he earned them.

The next morning he focused on an object of unfinished business gnawing at him ever since he received Noelani's letter... how to end his relationship with Vicky Barker in a respectful way? He and Vicky had shared plans for a future and, although this could no longer be, Mike felt an obligation to do the right thing by her. Before the crash, he had told Doc that half his death benefit should go to her. He decided he would not change that. In the last few weeks, there had been a major shift in his life and he was unlikely to die. So, the question remained... if a death benefit was unlikely, then how could he give her a way out of India?

He imagined that Vicky and Enid had already heard about the crash and she would believe both Mike and Dick dead. He reasoned, if she got one thousand rupees in an "in-case-I-die" letter—left with and mailed by a friend—she would have her way out, without them having to meet again. Mike had two months of back pay coming as a sergeant first class, and that would help cover the three hundred and fifty dollars' worth of rupees he could send to Vicky. Later, if he did die in combat after this, she also would receive the five thousand dollars, as he had directed. Mike didn't feel good about pretending to be dead, but he felt he should not meet her again. Noelani was his only focus now, and no other women could exist to him.

After mail call the next day, Mike read that Mr. Goldman was killed on a bombing mission over Germany on April 7th. He crumbled up the letter, closed his eyes, and allowed the fond memories of all the good times he had shared with Mr.

Goldman to flow freely and merge with his dreams. Philly would never be the same for him now that Lester Goldman was gone.

✦✦✦

Two weeks later, on Saturday, May 29th, Mike prepared to leave the hospital and rejoin his squadron. He walked down the hospital hallway with a cane. His left arm was weak, but his ribs had healed. It was also his twenty-fifth birthday. Mike shuffled along proudly with a determined expression, wearing his medals and sergeant first class stripes.

Doris, the orderly, and his new British friends saw him off. Even Broomhilda came out and waved good-bye. This time she wore an uncharacteristic smile... lukewarm, but a smile nonetheless. Mike felt oddly sad leaving this motley gang, but he was eager to get back into the war and fight until it was won, so he could go home and live with Noelani, happily ever after.

Chapter Thirty-Six

Mike clenched his teeth and furrowed his brow when he heard he couldn't join a crew and get back in the air right away. He felt well enough, and told Colonel Brown he was ready. Yet, he was assigned to administrative duties at the squadron to give him time to grow stronger and continue to heal. His work allowed him the opportunity to take long walks and use training weights every day, so he channeled his anger into rehabilitation.

His wounded leg and arm had lost a lot of muscle volume from the infections but, with time, he knew he would regain all his strength. Mike pushed himself hard and, at the end of his second week with the squadron, was hard-marching six miles a day. He began jogging in the middle of week three, and never saw the cane again. His diminutive left arm also grew stronger every day, but it worried Mike. He was also worried about his dreams. Almost every night since leaving the hospital, he dreamed about the air battle and the crash, and sometimes he awoke shaking.

During the last week of June, Mike received a letter from Charles Scribner's Sons accepting his new novel *Hurray for Fairytales*. Mike had to sit down and let it sink in.

His life-long dream was about to come true; he was going to be a published author of a novel, a piece of American literature. He picked a private spot to reread the materials more closely without interruption. He read that Charles Scribner's Sons would send him a check for three thousand dollars upon receiving his signed agreement and release. He would also receive ten percent of book sales proceeds. Apparently, all he needed to do was sign forms and indicate beneficiaries in case of his demise. Mike signed and, when he came to the beneficiaries form, he wrote Noelani Kreuger. He knew it would never come to anything, but later, when they were together, she would know how committed he had been to her.

He read that when Scribner's received the forms, their editorial staff would make some changes as necessary to prepare the manuscript for publication. Mike had to sign that he also agreed to that. Scribner's assured him they would send their final manuscript to him as a courtesy. Mike signed everything and sent it out in the afternoon mailbag.

He sat back in the chair and placed his hands behind his head. He had become a truly satisfied and complete man, and he let the wonderful buzz in his body vibrate gently around him.

This book is done, he thought, *now I'll start the next one: a story about growing up during the depression and becoming stronger because of all the setbacks and broken dreams.*

Hemingway, in *A Farewell to Arms*, said something to the affect that when the world breaks you—which happens at some time to everyone—many get stronger at the broken parts. Some, whether brave or gentle or good, don't break, but die. It eventually kills everyone, no matter who they are, but maybe not immediately.

Mike loved the idea of that quote.

That evening he wrote to Noelani about his good fortune, but he woke up the next morning still clasping the pencil, with a wad of paper covered with illegible scrawl.

✦✦✦

The following day Mike requested an audience with Colonel Brown and, to his surprise, was rushed right in. The colonel rose from his chair and walked around his desk.

"Sergeant First Class Mike Kane, how the heck are you?

"I am very well, sir. I am walking without a cane now, as you can see."

"Yes, I can. You are recovering fast. Good job, Mike. Well, sit and tell me what's up."

"Well, sir, I feel fit for duty now, and want to get back to flying as soon as possible. I've been walking six miles each day this week without a cane, and I've been jogging three miles every day the last three days. I'd like to rejoin the squadron as a full duty soldier."

"Outstanding! I am very happy to hear about your fast recovery, Mike. You are the kind of fighter we need to go nose-to-nose with the Japanese. I'd take you with me on tomorrow's mission if it were up to me, but I've got to get the Flight Surgeon's okay first before I say it's a go. However, it will happen soon, and your reactivation will send an important signal to all of our people, especially our new guys."

He paused for a second, and then met Mike's gaze levelly. "Thanks for coming back to us, Mike. No second thoughts about working with Al and Cliff?"

"No, sir. No change from what I said before. I play cards with them, and drink with them, and they already know my decision. They still think I'm crazy," Mike said with a laugh.

"Great, Mike." He smiled broadly. "On another note, I have not heard anything new on your bond tour in the states, but it may help when they hear you're healed and back in active service. I'm guessing they wouldn't want someone who looked feeble to try to go around and motivate people to buy War Bonds. They want inspirational types who are winners. And you are."

He clenched his fists and punched the air. "So, I'll stir the pot a bit more intensely. If it works out, I've been told you will be gone for six months: five months on tour, and one month on leave to visit family and loved ones. It's a good way to reward our best people, and you would be one of the first selected from the China-Burma-India Theater." He grabbed a pad of paper and scribbled a note. "I'll set up a medical review with the Flight Surgeon as soon as possible."

"Thank you, sir. I want to get back to work as soon as I can."

"Good man, Kane." He smiled and bobbed his head up and down. Then his eyes got big and he pointed a finger in the air. "Oh, and I wanted to tell you the OSS communicated that your personal thank you letters had been delivered to each of La Raw's rangers. They also received the agreed-to monetary awards, and the special unit medals inscribed with "Kachin Jingpaw Rangers, March 1943." Each sent a note back to you, and their notes are all in this envelope for you to read later. We are still working through the Brits to contact the Nagas, and we will," Colonel Brown added, nodding his head and narrowing his eyes.

◆◆◆

The Flight Surgeon did not approve Mike, and it took him two more weeks of therapy before he passed the basic flight test. The biggest concern was his arm strength, needed to flip up and into the aircraft. After two weeks of strength and agility training, he could get in and out as well as anyone. He was cleared to fly in mid-July and joined the B-24 crew of *Sweet Pea,* Colonel Brown's flagship.

His first missions were non-eventful, but standing for hours as a waist gunner caused him leg pain. He toughed it out and, after a few missions, and became used to it. He still couldn't stop the continued trembling, though.

He quickly got back into the rhythm of a B-24 flight crew, specifically the unique culture of *Sweet Pea's* crew. His crewmates had all heard of Mike's experiences, and acted welcoming enough. He sensed, though, more politeness than real embracing.

Mike came to the crew with some issues. He was a veteran, and they were all new. He outranked everyone except the officers, and he was only twenty-five years old, barely older than the others. The squadron commander normally piloted *Sweet Pea,* and everyone knew Mike had a special relationship with the colonel.

Mike was sensitive to all of this, but knew he could not change the facts. He acted like he was unaware, and let the team process play itself out. He focused on merely doing his job and letting the chips fall as they may. He was also aware that he had changed since the crash. He became agitated and nervous from takeoff to landing, causing his body to shake, and he worried that he'd gone psycho.

Many of Mike's first missions involved laying mines in the waters south of Rangoon or in the Irrawaddy River north of the region. The Japanese were building up for something, and that area would be the nexus between their supplies and field soldiers.

As before, Mike took the left waist gun position. Jack Whitmore took the right. He was the first to step up and approach Mike in friendship. It happened after one of their offshore Rangoon mine-laying missions when they were jumped by five Zeros. Franko got one from the top turret and Jack got the second from his right waist position. The others high-tailed it.

After their debriefing at operations, Jack approached him. "Wanna get a beer, Mike?"

"Sure, Jack. Nice shooting, by the way. You belong in the movies," Mike grinned.

"Yeah, coming from a guy that got four in one fight..."

"True, but I needed to get at least one more, to change the outcome of that fight, didn't I? Your one could have made the difference."

"Wow, you're good. I'm springing for the beers."

They laughed, and Mike clapped him on the back. "Where you from, Jack?"

"Dillon, Colorado. How about you?" Jack handed Mike a beer out of an ice bucket. They sat in a makeshift crew club where one signed for the beers on the honor system.

"Philadelphia, PA," Mike answered.

Gary Mueller, the belly gunner, came over. "Hey, am I late for the four amigos' staff meeting? Oops, I guess I'm early because Ray isn't here yet. He was always dragging his ass. Ha, ha."

Jack grinned at Mike and rolled his eyes at the lame joke about the tail gunner.

Mike knew the four amigos referred to the four gunners isolated behind the bomb bay: the belly gunner, two waist gunners, and the tail gunner. The slender Gary Mueller stood five feet and three inches tall, which made it possible for him to get into that cramped bubble under the plane. Ray Brooks, the tail gunner, occupied a bubble looking out the rear.

Ray came in, grabbed a beer, and headed to the table. The four amigos clinked their beers and began their "staff meeting." Mike smiled broadly. The warmth of true camaraderie abounded among these young-old men. Their earnest congratulations poured forth to Jack for downing the Zero, and Mike felt like he had found a home.

He learned that Gary was also the assistant engineer, and twenty-three years old. He was the same age as Jack, the right waist gunner. Ray, the "dragging ass" tail gunner, was the youngster at twenty. Mike discovered, also, that they covered a wide range of the USA: Ray Brooks came from New York City, while Gary Mueller hailed from a farm in Iowa. Jack was born and raised in Colorado; and Mike, the Philly guy, rounded out a well-balanced west and east team. Two beers later, all background history had been covered. That's when Jack asked Mike to tell his story.

Mike was reluctant. "It will cost you a beer."

They all laughed, and Gary collected another round.

Mike didn't want that crash to be his defining feature. It was also a complex story, with many sidebars, the telling of which would exhaust him. Yet, these rookies had a right to hear about some things that might save their lives.

"Well, as far as the actual combat is concerned, I can't tell you much. I remember that I ducked down to avoid getting hit, and got back up in time to get my first kill. After that, it was chaos and sensory overload, at times so loud it blocked out everything except what I could see. When I knew we were gonna crash I didn't do the smart thing. I didn't grab the bag containing my knife, pistol, compass, map, first aid kit, and canteen of water... You know, that bag we talk about all the time? I survived the crash, but that mistake almost killed me. I screwed up in the confusion of the fight, but for me it turned out okay in the end because we all have help down below. Let me tell you, down in that dark forbidding jungle are the most remarkable people you'll ever meet: the Kachin Jingpaw Rangers and their friends the Naga headhunters. All you need to do is grab that bag and survive the crash, and they will find you."

"Gentlemen, a toast to the Kachins and Nagas," Jack said, and four bottles clinked in salute.

✦✦✦

Colonel Brown pulled Mike aside before they climbed into *Sweet Pea* for their fifteenth mission together: "Hey, Mike, I just read a message from Washington, and you've been selected for their next bond drive. Congratulations, you are one of the first from our theater of operations. I am proud you'll represent us back in the States, but you have to leave tomorrow morning. You need to hurry to get packed and ready, so I have a back-up who will take your place today."

The news stunned Mike, along with the timing. How incomprehensible to be geared up to go on a mission, then hear you can't because one of your biggest hopes just came true.

"But, sir, I can't leave my post on such short notice. I haven't yet fired a shot at the Japs after my recovery, and the new guy won't know the team..."

"It's okay, Mike. He had the job before you. You need every minute merely to complete the wagonload of paperwork required by tomorrow morning. We've got you covered."

"Yes, sir, but we'll be back in six hours and, with help, I can do the forms in time. Packing my stuff takes fifteen minutes. Let me make this one more mission before I go."

"Mike, this is nuts. Are you sure?"

"Yes, sir. One more before I go. Besides, it will look good in the publicity."

"Okay then. I wouldn't agree to this if we didn't have heavy fighter cover the whole way. This should be a cakewalk. If you're sure, let's go get 'em, Mike!"

"Yes, sir. Let's go get the bastards."

◆◆◆

Mike enjoyed the uncommon daylight mission. The view was better than the movies: rich green mountains and valleys, with their sparkling rivers, rose majestically, framed by the snow-capped mountains to the north. He knew what the ground looked like close up, and he much preferred to see it from up here. He could see the British fighters flying above and behind them, and he began to feel relaxed.

The shaking continued, though.

The truth was that Mike was on a mission of his own: he had to know that he could defeat the trembling that had crippled him ever since the crash. Functioning normally on a plane would forever be out of the question unless he beat this thing here and now. He hid it from his crewmates because they rarely looked at one another while on a mission. If he went on the bond-tour trip to the USA in his condition, he would be in a straightjacket before he got to the States. He needed to face this thing and confirm he could do this one more time. He needed this mission to settle himself, and, so far, he felt fine.

Mike glanced over at Jack, who was calmly enjoying the view. Jack differed greatly from Connors, who had always seemed agitated. He began to see the faces of Connors, and Dick, and then the faces of little Sylvestri, Major Kirke, Kosko, Wagner, McCullough, and then Dick again... but this time he yelled for his friend to get down.

Mike realized he had dozed off and, when he came to, Jack was yelling at him and grabbing at him from across the passageway.

"Mike, we got bogies coming right to left! The Brits are engaging, but some may get past them. Sharp eyes! Sharp eyes!"

"Okay, Jack. I'm on it."

Colonel Brown's calm voice came up on the intercom: "Okay, boys. We are two minutes from target, so hang on!"

Mike saw a Zero bowl over *Sweet Pea* and turn to dive right at his position. Mike responded quickly. In a flash, he made mental adjustments for windage, speed, and angle of dive, then fired. His first shots hit dead on, and he kept adding lead to the target until the Zero disintegrated in a series of explosions. Mike suddenly felt very tranquil—aware he was in combat, but settled and calm. He realized this feeling was not unlike the pain medicine he received at the hospital.

I get it, I'm not afraid of flying like I thought. I need the combat. Without it, I'm like a shivering hound dog before a hunt. Shit, I've become a combat junky!

The clarity brought him peace.

Another Zero came up from Mike's left and he poured rounds into it. The enemy fired back at the same rate as Mike, and it became a duel to see who blinked first. Bullet holes began stitching the wall toward Mike but, this time, he didn't duck. He kept firing, and yelling. "You're going down there this time, not me, you Jap sonofabitch! You try walking out of there! Ha! There are some boys down there that will be happy to see you. Here you go, special delivery! Say hello to La Raw and the gang, you sorry sack of shit!"

Mike could see the pilot was all but dead, obviously trying to fly into *Sweet Pea* as a kamikaze. Mike shot the Zero into pieces of flaming wreckage that fell behind him.

"Two down. Bring 'em on," Mike whispered while calmly watching through the portal. He liked the feeling he was experiencing. He wasn't giddy-happy about it exactly, but confident. He liked the person he had become. He had found his place as a man. Mike Kane had become the big man on the block, the man those Jap bastards had to beat. And best of all, he wasn't a bit ashamed to say so. Not anymore he wasn't. "Come get me you assholes!" he shouted.

"Hey, Jack. I got two. How are you doing?" Mike yelled over his shoulder. No answer came back, but it was noisy and windy so he yelled again. Still no answer, so he glanced behind him. He saw Jack slumped against the wall below his machine gun.

"Oh, shit! Jack, roll over, and get up! Show me you're okay!"

Mike saw Jack move. He was still alive and trying to get back on his feet. Mike turned and took the two steps needed to help him up. Jack took up his machine gun and started firing immediately.

"That's the way, Jack, give 'em hell!" Mike was back at his gun in a flash.

Colonel Brown's voice came up over the intercom. "Okay, boys. Keep it up! We're going in. Hold them off for just thirty seconds more."

Suddenly, Mike heard a fresh roar of machine gun fire erupt from Franko's top and Gary's belly turrets. Jack blasted away and Ray began firing from his tail gun. Three of the four amigos, fully engaged... I had better get my ass in gear! As he peered out of his firing window, a Zero dove down right in front of him. Mike fired instantly, and on target, but the first rounds were already inbound from the Zero. Those bullets missed Mike, and he poured it on as thick and accurately as he could. He felt truly alive for the first time in his life. He was calm, and enjoying the challenge of shooting it out with this Zero. He knew he would win, this was his day, and he wasn't going down. Not this time, not ever!

✦✦✦

Major Kirke's voice came up on the intercom "We are well away from danger now. I'll see you soon on the other side. Out."

"Major Kirke? What the hell? What's going on?" Mike asked the wind.

For a fraction of an instant Mike felt the monstrous force of the blow that hurled him to the floor. He tried to get up, but couldn't move. His eyes remained open, but he couldn't see. The vision from within his head was a brilliant flash of light that illuminated the center of his brain. It faded to nothing. Black.

For a time, he lay under his machine gun unnoticed by the others still actively engaged against the Zeros. At first, it had been peaceful, but slowly he began to make out faint noises that seemed to come from far away. His first thought was that he was back on the ground reliving his first crash. What if this is a new crash? Am I dreaming this? I hope so, because I couldn't go through that shit again. Maybe I'm heading for heaven and Major Kirke and the guys from *Jackie Sue* are taking me home. Yes, that's it; they've come back for me, and now I'll find peace."

Sudden bright lights and loud noises stunned his senses. He couldn't see who shook him, but he recognized the voice.

"Hey, Mike, wake up!" Jack said. "You're okay man, just a glancing head wound that put you out for a few seconds. Mission complete, man, and you got three Zeros. Congratulations, man. We'll get you cleaned up and then we'll get you squared away and outta here tomorrow. Don't worry, you're gonna' make that plane to the States..."

Jack finally came into focus, and Mike never felt so glad to see someone's face than at that moment. "Tell me Jack, are we alive, or are we headin' for heaven?"

Jack laughed, "Buddy, I can't speak for myself, but for sure you are alive and headin' to state-side girl heaven. Now, lay back and relax, your friends will take care of everything."

Mike grinned. There is only one girl I wanna see, and her name is Noelani.

With the recognition that he was safe among friends, he passed out.

The End